INTERNATIONAL PRAISE FOR *THE SHADOW WOMAN*

BY ÅKE EDWARDSON

"An extremely accomplished cross between crime fiction and psychological thriller . . . on par with P. D. James."

—*Helsingborgs Dagblad* (Sweden)

"Masterful . . . While Åke Edwardson possesses an undertone of humor, his work is full of darkness . . . With *The Shadow Woman* [he] establishes himself among the most exciting crime thriller writers in the country."

—*Motala & Vadstena Tidning* (Sweden)

"Erik Winter could be related to Elizabeth George's Sir Thomas Lynley, and the almost clinical descriptions might evoke pathologist Kay Scarpetta in Patricia Cornwell's books, while the social ambience could well be inspired by both P. D. James and Minette Walters."

—*Smålänningen* (Sweden)

"A dramatic crime chase in Gothenburg, intelligently and excitingly told."

—*Der Spiegel* (Germany)

"[Here is] the opportunity to discover a Swede well removed from the 'Swedish model' and enter into the world of Åke Edwardson. Try this voyage, and you will return to it."

—*Marianne* (France)

ABOUT THE AUTHOR

Åke Edwardson has won the Swedish Crime Writers' Academy award three times. His eleven Erik Winter novels have been published in twenty-one countries. He lives in Gothenburg, Sweden.

THE SHADOW WOMAN

AN
INSPECTOR ERIK WINTER
NOVEL

ÅKE EDWARDSON

TRANSLATED FROM THE SWEDISH BY
PER CARLSSON

 PENGUIN BOOKS

PENGUIN BOOKS

Published by the Penguin Group

Penguin Group (USA) Inc., 375 Hudson Street, New York, New York 10014, U.S.A. • Penguin Group
(Canada), 90 Eglinton Avenue East, Suite 700, Toronto, Ontario, Canada M4P 2Y3 (a division of Pearson
Penguin Canada Inc.) • Penguin Books Ltd, 80 Strand, London WC2R 0RL, England • Penguin Ireland,
25 St Stephen's Green, Dublin 2, Ireland (a division of Penguin Books Ltd) • Penguin Group (Australia),
250 Camberwell Road, Camberwell, Victoria 3124, Australia (a division of Pearson Australia Group Pty
Ltd) • Penguin Books India Pvt Ltd, 11 Community Centre, Panchsheel Park, New Delhi - 110 017, India
• Penguin Group (NZ), 67 Apollo Drive, Rosedale, North Shore 0632, New Zealand (a division of Pearson
New Zealand Ltd) • Penguin Books (South Africa) (Pty) Ltd, 24 Sturdee Avenue, Rosebank, Johannesburg
2196, South Africa

Penguin Books Ltd, Registered Offices:
80 Strand, London WC2R 0RL, England

First published in Penguin Books 2010

3   5   7   9   10   8   6   4

Originally published as *Rop fran langt avstand* by Norstedts Forlag, Stockholm.

Publisher's Note
This is a work of fiction. Names, characters, places, and incidents either are the product of the author's
imagination or are used fictitiously, and any resemblance to actual persons, living or dead, business
establishments, events, or locales is entirely coincidental.

CIP data available
978-0-14-311794-0

Printed in the United States of America
Set in Dante MT with Eras
Designed by Daniel Lagin

For three years a massive drug war between the Hells Angels and the Bandidos has ripped through Scandinavia. Antitank rockets swiped from the Swedish military have been launched at clubhouses, gunfights have erupted in airports, car bombs have been planted and bystanders killed. A well-publicized truce will soon bring the Great Nordic Biker War to a close, but not before dozens of lives are claimed by the violence, many of them innocent.

THE SHADOW WOMAN

PART 1

SHE SAT WITH MOMMY A LONG TIME. SHE SLEPT FOR A WHILE in the backseat and then crawled up front. It was cold there and Mommy started the car and let it run for a while and then turned it off again. Mommy hadn't answered when she'd asked, so she asked again and Mommy's voice was hard. So she went quiet. "Why isn't he coming?" Mommy said, but straight out and not to her. "Where in God's name is he?"

Someone was supposed to come there and pick her up and then drive her home, but nobody came. She wanted to be with Mommy, but she also wanted to sleep in her own bed. It was darker now and it was raining. She couldn't see out because the windows were fogged up. She crawled closer and wiped the window with her sleeve. Cars drove past and the headlights twirled around inside the car where they were sitting. "Why can't we go?" she had asked. Mommy hadn't answered, so she asked again. "Quiet now," Mommy said this time. Then she didn't say anything after that, didn't dare when the voice from the front seat was so stern. Mommy said a few bad words. She had heard them so many times that it didn't matter. She had said words like that herself and nothing had happened to her. But she knew it was wrong somehow anyway. The rain pattered against the roof. *Pitter-patter, pitter-patter.* She thought about the rain like that for a long while, drummed her fingers on the seat next to her: *pitter-patter, pitter-patter.*

"Oh God," Mommy said, and said it a few times more. "Stay here." Mommy opened the door up front. "You have to stay here while I go over there and make a phone call."

It wasn't quite evening yet, but it was dark out anyway.

"I can barely see you," Mommy said. "You have to answer me."

"Where are you going?"

"I'm just going over to the telephone booth on the corner to make a call. It won't take long."

"Where is it? Can't I go with you?"

"I told you to stay here!" Mommy said in her stern voice, and she said yes and Mommy slammed the door and she got rain spattered on her in the backseat. She gave a start from the drops of rain hitting her.

Then she sat quietly and listened for footsteps outside and thought she heard Mommy's shoes against the pavement, like a *clickety clickety clack*. It might have been somebody else, but she couldn't see. It was foggy outside.

She gave a start when Mommy came back. "Nobody there!" Mommy said, or more like shouted it. "Jesus Christ. They've left."

Mommy started the car and they drove off. "Are we going home now?"

"Soon," Mommy said. "There's just something we have to do first."

"But you said I was gonna go home."

"We are going home." Mommy stopped the car again, and then she got out and came and sat in the backseat with her.

"Are you sad, Mommy?"

"No. It's just the rain. Now listen to me. First we're going to go to this other place to pick up some men. You hear what I'm saying?"

"We're going to pick up some men."

"Yes. Now, these men are going to run to us when we drive up—it's this game we're going to play with them. And when they come, they're going to jump into the car before it's stopped. Do you understand?"

"They're going to jump into the car?"

"We're gonna slow down, and then they're going to jump into the car, and then we're gonna drive off again."

"Then are we gonna go home?"

"After a little while we will."

"I wanna go home now."

"We're going to go home. But first we're just going to play this little game."

"It's a stupid game."

"It's very important that you lie down on the floor when we play the game. You have to lie down on the floor when I tell you to. Do you understand?"

"But why?"

Mommy looked at her, and she looked at her watch many times too. It was sort of all blurry in here now, but Mommy could see her watch.

"Because they're going to run really fast and there may be other people who aren't in the game who might try to jump into the car too. And they might bump into you or something. That's why you have to lie down on the floor behind my chair."

She nodded.

"I want you to try doing it now."

"But you said that they—"

"Lie down!"

Mommy grabbed hold of her and it felt hard, smarting around her neck. She lay down on the floor and it smelled bad and wet and it was difficult to breathe. She coughed and lay against the coldness. Her arm hurt.

Mommy went back up front and started the car, and she sat up again. Mommy told her to get back down on the floor.

"Is it starting now?"

"Yes. Are you lying down?"

"I've crawled on the floor now."

"You mustn't get up," Mommy said. "It can be very dangerous."

And Mommy said more stuff about how dangerous it was. "And you have to be quiet too."

She thought it was stupid for a game to be dangerous, but she didn't dare say that now.

"Be quiet!" Mommy said in a stern voice even though she hadn't said anything.

She lay still and listened to the sounds from underneath—it was almost like lying on the road, *shakety shakety shake*, *bumpety bumpety bump*— and suddenly she heard a scream and then another, and then Mommy shouted something. The door above her was yanked open. She felt something hard on top of her, and heavy, and she wanted to cry out but she couldn't. Or maybe she didn't want to. The doors opened and slammed shut, and opened again and slammed once more, and she heard a bang when one of the doors up front slammed against the car; it sounded like fireworks and as if the rain was hitting the car much harder. Diagonally above her she saw that the window had cracked but held together anyway, so no pieces of glass fell down on her or onto the backseat.

Everyone was shouting and screaming, and she couldn't hear what they were saying. She listened for Mommy but couldn't hear her. The car swerved back and forth, and now they were driving again. There was something like a scream from underneath the car; she heard it because she was lying so close to it. And now she heard one of the men sitting in the backseat and it sounded as if he was crying. It was strange to hear a man making that kind of sound. This was a game she didn't like.

1

ERIK WINTER WOKE UP LATE. HE'D GOTTEN WRAPPED UP IN HIS sheets and had to wriggle around to disentangle his body from the bedclothes. The sun was hanging in place off the balcony. The apartment was already hot.

He sat on the edge of the bed and ran his hand over the stubble on his face, his head heavy from something between sleeping and waking. Then he walked across the wooden floor to the shower and stood there, waiting for the water to warm. Wuss, he thought to himself.

He lathered up, feeling his testicles tighten. Two nights before, Angela had come home from a double shift at the hospital. In the morning hours they'd played the beast with two backs, and he'd felt young again and strong; the orgasm had surged through him for so long that he'd cried out.

But when he moved afterward, it was with the relaxed motion of an old man. She lay on her side and looked at him. Yet again he gazed in awe at the contours of her hips, at her hair, which partially concealed her face. The ends were wet, of a darker hue.

"You think you're using me, but it's the other way around," she said, and twirled her finger slowly in the thick hair on his chest.

"Surely nobody here's using anyone."

"But I've come to the conclusion that we need something more than just sex."

"What kind of nonsense is that?"

"The fact that we need more than just sex?"

"The suggestion that all we do is have sex."

"Well, what else do we do, then?" She took her finger away from his chest.

"Well, right now, for example, we're having a conversation. A conversation about our relationship."

"It might be the first time ever." She sat up in bed. "One conversation for ten couplings."

"You're kidding me now."

"Maybe, but just a little. I want something . . ."

"Like what?"

"Erik."

"Maturity?"

"Yes."

"That I should take responsibility for the family I haven't got yet?"

"This just isn't enough for me anymore."

"Not even when you get to use me?"

"Not even then."

He was thirty-seven and an inspector at the district CID, in homicide. He'd made inspector at the age of thirty-five, a record in Gothenburg and the whole of Sweden, but it meant nothing to him other than that he didn't have to take orders as often as he used to.

Now he sat alone at the kitchen table, with two slices of toast and a cup of tea, the sweat returning to his hairline as the heat seeped in through the blinds. The thermometer on the shady side of the balcony read eighty-five degrees and it was just eleven o'clock. He had four days left of his second round of vacation. He was going to continue relaxing.

The telephone rang on the hall table, so he left the kitchen and said his name into the receiver.

"This is Steve, if you remember." The voice was Scottish.

"How could anyone forget the knight from Croydon?"

Steve Macdonald was a detective chief inspector in South London, and they had worked together on a difficult case earlier in the year. They had become friends—at least Winter saw it that way.

"If anyone's a knight here, it's you," Macdonald said. "Shining armor and all that."

"I think that's history now."

"What?"

"I'm unshaven. And I haven't had a haircut for months."

"Did I make such a powerful impression on you? As for me, I've been over on Jermyn Street, looking for a Baldessarini suit. Thought it might command more respect. If you'd stayed at the station much longer, they would have started taking orders from you."

"How'd it work out?"

"What?"

"Did you find a suit?"

"No. Mere mortals can't afford the stuff you wear. I have to ask you again, by the way—is it true that you don't pine for your monthly pay-check like the rest of us?"

"Where did you get that idea?"

"Something you said last spring."

"Clearly, I didn't listen carefully enough to what I was saying."

"So you do depend on your paycheck?"

"What do you think? I've got a little money in the bank, but no great sum."

"Glad to hear it."

"What difference does it make?"

"I don't know. I just wondered."

"So that's why you called?"

"Actually, I called to hear how you're doing. It was tough going last spring."

"Yes."

"Well?"

"What?"

"How's it going?"

"It's hot. Summer's supposed to be over. I'm still on vacation."

Winter heard the static breaking up the signal as it crossed the heated waters, then Macdonald clearing his throat softly.

"Give us a call sometime."

"I might come over before Christmas to do a bit of shopping," Winter said.

"Cigarettes? Shirts?"

"Jeans, I was thinking."

"Careful that you don't end up like me."

"I could say the same."

They said good-bye, and Winter hung up. Suddenly he felt dizzy and grabbed hold of the tabletop. After a few seconds everything around him settled down, and he went back to the kitchen and took a sip of his tea, which had gone cold. He considered brewing a fresh pot but instead took the cup and saucer to the sink.

He put on a pair of shorts and a cotton shirt and slipped his feet into a pair of sandals. Just when he grabbed the door handle, he heard the post-man's trudge outside and the mail crashed down onto his feet.

Included in the pile, along with the latest issue of *Police* and a couple of envelopes from the bank, was a notice for a heavy envelope, weighing over a kilo, which could be picked up at the post office on the Avenyn.

The heat was so thick that the square at Vasaplatsen rippled before him like the dazzle of glass filament. A handful of people were standing in the shade of the streetcar shelter, their bodies black silhouettes from across the park.

He fetched his bicycle from the basement and rode along Vasagatan, up past Skanstorget. His shirt was wet before he reached Linnéplatsen, and that was a nice feeling. He decided to keep heading south instead of biking to Långedrag and pedaled in the stark light all the way out to the beach at Askimsbadet. There he took a break and drank a can of soda water and after that continued past the golf course at Hovås and down past Järkholmen, parking among the other bicycles along the path. Then he climbed down to the little beach and plunged into the water as quickly as he could.

He lay in the sun and read, and when it got to be too hot, he went back into the water. It was his vacation.

2

ANETA DJANALI HAD HER JAW SMASHED IN THE MINUTES JUST
after midnight. She'd been walking southward on Östra Hamngatan,
and there were people all around her. She wasn't on duty, but even if she
had been it wouldn't have made any difference, since homicide detectives didn't wear a uniform on the job.

She'd been accompanied by a girlfriend, and the two women had
caught sight of an assault in progress a ways down on the darker Kyrkoga-
tan: three men punching and kicking someone lying on the ground. The
men looked up when Djanali called out and took a few steps into the
side street. Seconds later one of them hit her in the face as he passed, a
single blow; she felt no pain at first and then suddenly it filled her entire
head and spread down toward her chest. The men persisted as she lay
on the ground, the one who first hit her shouting something about the
color of her skin. This was the first time she'd been subjected to violence
because of it.

She never lost consciousness. She tried to say something to her friend
but nothing came out. Lis looks paler than I've ever seen her before, she
thought to herself. Maybe it's a bigger shock for her than for me.

The Gothenburg Party continued around them, people wandering back and forth between the various beer tents and stages. The hot
evening was thick with the smell of charcoal grills and people—the
streets stinking of booze, and bodies of sweat. The voices were loud,
all mixed together, and somewhere in the cacophony of cries Lis had
disappeared. This was the third time they'd strolled past that spot this
evening. Third time lucky, Djanali thought, aware of the rough asphalt
against her cheek. Her head didn't hurt so much anymore. She saw
many bare legs and sandals and boating shoes, and then she was lifted
up and carried into a vehicle, which she understood to be an ambulance.
She felt someone touch her gently, and then she passed out.

Fredrik Halders received the news when he arrived at the police station at seven thirty the following morning. He was a buzz-cut police detective who busted chops whenever he got the chance, preferably with Aneta Djanali and preferably about her skin color and background. He sometimes came across as unintelligent and was called a racist and a sexist, but he let it run off his scalp.

Alone following a divorce three years before, he was forty-four and always pissed off—a violent man with a hell of a lot of festering, unresolved issues, though he'd rather jerk off in public than see a shrink. The nervous energy surging through his body could lead him into a very dark place—he knew that already—and this only intensified when he heard what had happened to Djanali.

"No witnesses?" he shouted.

"Yeah, they—," Lars Bergenhem said.

"Where are they?"

"The girlfr—"

"Let me at 'em! Nah, fuck it." He made for the door.

"Where are you going?"

"Where the hell do you think?"

"She's sedated. Or at least she was when they were setting her jaw."

"How do you know that?"

"I just got off the phone with Sahlgrenska Hospital."

"Why didn't they call *me*? When have you ever been on assignment with her?"

"They don't know that," Bergenhem said quietly.

"What about the witnesses?"

"I've been trying to tell you that Aneta's girlfriend should be coming up here in," he checked his watch, "about fifteen minutes."

"Was she there?"

"Yes."

"Nobody else?"

"You know there's a party going on there. There were masses of people, which, of course, means nobody saw a thing."

"Christ al-fucking-mighty."

Bergenhem didn't answer.

"You like this city?" Halders asked. He'd sat down, stood up, and sat down again.

"It's a modern city. Entering a new, more nuanced age."

"More nuan— What the hell does that mean?"

"There are good things and bad things," Bergenhem said, instantly aware that he'd let a worn-out phrase slip from his tongue. "You can't tell a whole city to go to hell."

"Two people go for a walk along Hamngatan. Some bastard comes up and smashes one of their heads in. There's your nuanced city for you."

Bergenhem said nothing. How many violent provocations had they had over the past month? Fifteen? It was like gearing up for war. A guerrilla war between all the tribes of Gothenburg. And yesterday there was a melee.

"Who's gonna talk to the girl?" Halders's voice sounded far away. "The girlfriend?"

"I am and you can too, if you want."

"You do it," Halders said. "I'll get over to the hospital. How'd it go for that other poor bastard, by the way?"

"He's alive."

Halders drove impatiently, didn't even notice that the air coming through the AC vent was hotter than the air in the car.

Aneta Djanali was sitting up in bed when he came in, or rather she was propped up with pillows. Her face was covered in bandages.

She's just woken up and I shouldn't be here, he thought, pulling a chair to the bed and sitting. "We're gonna get them," he said.

She didn't move. Then she closed her eyes, and Halders wasn't sure if she had fallen asleep.

"By the time you wake up we'll have cuffed those bastards," he said. "Even the black citizens of this city deserve to be able to walk the streets safely after dark."

She didn't respond to that either. The mountain of pillows behind her looked uncomfortable.

"In a situation like this you gotta think it would have been better if you'd stayed back in Ouagadougou." It was an old joke between them. Djanali was born at Östra Hospital in Gothenburg. "Ouagadougou."

As if the word would calm her nerves.

"This is actually a unique opportunity," he said after a few minutes of silence. "For once, I can say important things without you butting in and getting all superior. I can voice my opinions. I can explain to you what it's all about."

Djanali opened her eyes and peered at Halders with a look he recognized. She's injured all right, but that injury is limited to the lower part of her skull, he thought. This is the only chance I'll ever have to get a word in.

"It's all about keeping your cool," he said. "When we catch those bastards, we're going to keep our cool for as long as we can, and then we're going to make one or two mistakes that prove we're human too. I mean, cops are also human beings." Halders paused for a moment before continuing. "They say Winter went a little loopy after last spring. He's been walking around all summer in a pair of cutoff jeans and a T-shirt that says 'London Calling' on it. Rumor has it he's been up to the department to pick up some papers and has a beard and long hair."

Aneta Djanali closed her eyes again.

"I miss you," he said.

Winter broke off his vacation almost the moment Bertil Ringmar called with the quick rundown. It wasn't out of duty, more the opposite. It was a selfish act, maybe therapeutic.

"You're not needed here yet," Ringmar said.

"I've gotten enough dirt between my toes," Winter answered.

In the afternoon he stepped into his office and angled the blinds upward. It smelled of dust and work, though the surface of the desk was clear. An ideal state, he thought. Maybe I can be like the chief—keep investigations off my desk by shoving them in drawers.

Sture Birgersson was the head of the homicide department, and he had the good sense to hand over all real responsibility to his deputy. That meant Winter was in command of thirty homicide detectives who worked to control the violence in society.

"Close the door," Winter said to Ringmar, who had just stepped across the threshold. "What's going on?"

"We're going through all the known troublemakers, but they could have come from out of town," Ringmar said.

"You think so?"

"That's what we're hearing," Ringmar said. "But the situation out there is pretty confused right now. I don't know how much you know, but I guess you watched the news."

"The demonstrations?"

"Yeah, but it doesn't stop there. The city is in a state of unrest, or whatever you wanna call it. Over the last few weeks we've had about a dozen gang showdowns, or close to that. Yeah, and a lot of brawls too. Who knows how many ethnicities have been involved, Scandinavians included. It's really nasty, Erik. Maybe there are some bastards trying to fan the flames from on high. Steering it, in certain areas anyway. There's something . . . I don't know what it is. Hate? Something that's causing people to get violent or, so far, mostly to threaten violence. But still. We're trying to do what we can."

Ringmar was the homicide department's third inspector and head of the department's surveillance unit: ten officers, with tentacles reaching down into the criminal underworld, assigned the task of keeping tabs on the city's worst troublemakers and professional criminals.

"Aneta isn't exactly unknown in this town," Ringmar said. "I think they'd think twice about hurting one of ours unless it's a case of extreme self-defense."

"Maybe that's just what it was," Winter said.

"What?"

"Since we think they know that we know that they know that we think they would never do anything like that, maybe that's just what happened," Winter said.

Ringmar didn't answer.

"What do you say?"

"Well, that's a classic dilemma, isn't it? If I've understood you correctly."

"It takes you back to square one in that case, doesn't it?"

"Appreciate the insight."

Winter stared down at his desktop. It had been polished till it shone, as if the office cleaner had made an emergency visit when it was clear he was coming back early. His hair looked, in the veneer, like a thick circle of thorns around his face. He grasped at the packet of cigarillos in his breast pocket and lit up a Corps; then he dropped the match and it singed him on the thigh. Ringmar had noticed his shorts but not said anything.

"If they're from around here, we'll find them," Ringmar continued.

"You believe in the good guys? Our informants?"

"I believe that the good guys among the bad guys are going to lead us to the bad guys."

"The worse guys," Winter said, "to the worst guys."

"Aneta's friend thinks she would recognize one of those three scumbags," Ringmar said.

"Did they brandish any Nazi symbols or other fascist crap?"

"Nope. Just good ol' regular guys."

Winter tapped his cigarillo into the palm of his hand. The ashtray had apparently been stolen while he was away.

"Other witnesses?"

"A thousand or more, but only a few of them have gotten in touch since we issued our request for information. And they're not sure what the guys looked like."

"Somebody will call, just when you least expect it," Winter said, and then the telephone rang. He lifted the receiver from its usual spot on the right side of the desk and mumbled his name to the desk sergeant.

Ringmar saw how he listened, brow furrowed and shoulders hunched forward, as he said a few short words and hung up.

"A guy who followed them is on his way over," Winter said.

"No shit. Why hasn't he been in touch before?"

"Something about having to take his kid to the ER in the middle of the night."

"Where is he?"

"Like I said, on his way. Speaking of which, I was up at Sahlgrenska Hospital to look in on Aneta. I met Fredrik on his way out of her room. His eyes were all red."

"Good," Ringmar said.

3

THE BACK OF THE CHAIR HAD LEFT A DAMP IMPRESSION ON Winter's back, and he gave a shiver as he stood beneath the air conditioner at the window. The patches of cold inside made the summer look cold and gray through the windows that couldn't be opened. Since the sky seemed undecided, the grass at Old Ullevi Stadium was under fire from water cannons.

He thought about Aneta Djanali and clenched his right hand. Whenever he considered what had happened to her, he felt . . . violent. The violence became part of him, a sudden sensation. A primitive urge for revenge, perhaps, and a little beyond that. He had returned to his violent world abruptly.

Ringmar was still seated, looking at him without speaking. He's fifteen years older than I am, and he's started waiting for a better world, Winter thought. When his last day here is finished, he may take the boat out to his cabin on Vrångö, never to return.

"What's that supposed to mean, the thing on your shirt?" Ringmar asked. "'London Calling.'"

"It's the name of a record by a rock band. Macdonald sent it to me."

"Rock? You don't know anything about rock, do you?"

"I've listened to one rock band. The Clash. Macdonald sent me the album together with the T-shirt."

"The Clash? What is that?"

"It's an English word meaning violent confrontation."

"I mean the band. Can you tell the difference between hard rock and pop?"

"No. But I like this."

"I don't think so. Coltrane is your man."

"I like it," Winter repeated. "It was recorded back when I was nineteen or something, and yet it's timeless."

"Hard rock, you mean," Ringmar said.

The witness arrived.

The man gave his account. The skin of his face was taut and looked brittle after a night without sleep. His little girl had suffered a severe allergic reaction that had nearly ended tragically.

Winter said something.

"I'm sorry, I didn't hear you. My mind blanked out there for a second."

"You said that you were walking behind the men."

"Yes."

"How many were there?"

"Three, like I said."

"Are you sure they were together?"

"Two of them waited while the third—the guy who hit her—they waited for him before moving on together." The witness ran his hand across his eyes. "I remember that the guy doing the hitting was smaller."

"He was shorter?"

"It looked that way."

"And you followed them?"

"As far as I could. Everything happened so damn fast—afterward. I sort of went into shock, couldn't move. Then I thought, 'This is heinous.' And I followed after them to see where they went, but there were so many people on the square, and then my cell phone rang and my wife started screaming that Astrid couldn't breathe. That's our little girl."

"Yes," Winter said, and looked at Ringmar, who had children. Winter didn't have children, but he had a woman who said she didn't want to wait any longer for him to become mature enough to take responsibility for a child. Angela said that yesterday, before going home to her mother's to fine-tune her biological clock. When she gets back, Winter had mused as she was leaving, I guess she'll tell me what time it is.

"It all turned out all right," the man said, mostly to himself. "Astrid's going to be okay."

Winter and Ringmar waited. The air in the room flowed back and forth, past a man dressed in the same shorts and tennis shirt he'd worn the night before. His chin had a thin shading of stubble and his eyes were craters sunken into his skull.

"We appreciate you coming by right after the accident," Winter said. "From the hospital."

The witness shrugged his shoulders. "There are so many people who do nothing," he said. "Going around beating people up. It really makes me angry."

Winter and Ringmar waited for him to continue.

"It's like at work, with all that damn talk about immigrants, as if it's become politically correct to talk about how there are too many immigrants and refugees and blacks in the country."

"Where exactly did you lose sight of these three men?" Ringmar asked.

"What?"

"The ones who assaulted our colleague. Where exactly did they disappear?"

"When we reached the indoor market, the one sort of facing Kungsportsplatsen. Before you enter the square."

"Did you hear them say anything?"

"Not a word."

"You didn't get any sense of where they were from?"

"Somewhere south of hell as far as I'm concerned."

"Nothing more precise."

"No. But they were Swedes, real Swedes you might say."

They asked him to describe the men's appearance, which he did.

Once the witness left the office, Winter lit up another cigarillo and dropped ash onto his naked thighs. "Did you notice that Aneta was a refugee in this guy's eyes?" he said.

"How do you mean?" asked Ringmar.

"People are always going to be looked upon differently for one reason or another, generation after generation. Regardless of where they were born."

"Yeah."

"Space refugees."

"What?"

"There's an expression for those who journey from country to country without ever being allowed into any of the paradises. They're known as space refugees."

"That's a nice expression," Ringmar said. "Sort of romantic. But that's not true of Aneta."

"No, but once you've made it into paradise? What happens then?" He killed his cigarillo in the ashtray he'd suddenly spied behind the curtain.

The sun was high, the blaze heavy out on the square in front of the district police headquarters. Winter had misread the shade from the trees, and the heat in the front seat was nearly unbearable. He adjusted the air-conditioning.

He drove eastward past New Ullevi Stadium and pulled over next to a big house in Lunden. A dog barked like crazy from next door, rattling its running chain.

The entrance to the house was in the shade. Winter rang the doorbell and waited, then pressed it again. But no one opened the door. He headed back down the front steps and turned left and started walking along the stucco wall.

Round the back of the house, the sun glittered in a swimming pool. Winter took in the smell of chlorine and tanning oil. At the pool's edge was a deck chair with a naked man sitting in it. His body was heavy and evenly tanned, a vivid color that shimmered mutedly against the Turkish towel protecting the chair from sweat and oil. Winter coughed gently, and the naked man opened his eyes.

"I thought I heard something," he said.

"Then why didn't you come to the door?" Winter asked.

"You came in anyway."

"I could have been somebody else."

"That would've been nice." The man remained lying there in the same position.

His penis lay shriveled up against a muscular thigh.

"Get dressed and offer me something to drink, Benny."

"In that order? Have you become homophobic, Erik?"

"It's a question of aesthetics." Winter looked around for a chair.

The man, whose name was Benny Vennerhag, got up and grabbed a white robe from the footstool and gestured at the water.

"Why don't you take a dip while you're waiting?" He sauntered off toward the house and turned around on the veranda. "I'll bring out a couple of beers. You'll find swimming trunks in the drawer of the footstool. Nice T-shirt. But who wants to go to London?"

Winter took off his shirt and shorts and dove into the water. It felt cool against his skin, and he swam along the bottom of the pool until he reached the other end. He got out, dove in again, and turned over on the bottom and looked up at the sky, the surface of the water like a ceiling of floating glass. There was a crackling down there from the tiled walls, unless the sound was coming from his eardrums. He stayed under the water for a long time before gliding back up to the surface. He saw a face flicker into view above him.

"Trying to break some kind of record?" Vennerhag asked, and held a beer out over the water.

Winter stroked his hair back over the top of his head and took the bottle. It was cool in his hand. "You live a comfortable life," he said, and drank.

"I deserve to."

"Like hell you do."

"No need to be bitter, Inspector."

Winter heaved himself up and sat down on the edge of the pool.

"Swimming in your underwear. What happened to your sense of style and taste?"

Winter didn't answer. He drank down the last of his beer and set the bottle on the paving stones, then took off his wet boxers and pulled on his shorts.

"Who was it that beat up my Aneta?" Winter asked, and turned toward Vennerhag.

"What are you talking about?" Vennerhag sat up again.

"A woman on my tea—from my department was assaulted and badly beaten last night, and if you find out who did it, I want to know," Winter said. "Now or in due course."

"That's not your style either."

"I'm a different man now."

"Well, you can sa—"

"This is serious, Benny." Winter had stood up. He walked over to the deck chair and crouched down, bringing his face close to his host's. He smelled alcohol and coconut oil. "I tolerate you as long as you're honest with me. As soon as you stop being honest with me, I won't tolerate you anymore."

"Oh yeah? And what's that supposed to mean?"

"Then all this is over," Winter said, stone faced.

Vennerhag gazed around at his property.

"What kind of a threat is that? And how am I supposed to know what happened to your fellow officer, Erik?"

"You know more lowlifes than I do. You're a criminal. You're a racist. If you've heard anything, I want to know."

"I'm also your ex-brother-in-law," Vennerhag said, and smiled. "Don't come here and start acting all cocky."

Winter suddenly grabbed hold of the man's jaw and squeezed hard.

"They smashed off this part of her face," he said, and leaned in closer and pressed harder. "You feel that, Benny? You feel that, when I squeeze here?"

Vennerhag jerked his head to the side, and Winter let go.

"You're out of your mind, you fucking bastard," Vennerhag said, and massaged his chin and cheeks. "You should get help."

Winter felt dizzy. He closed his eyes and heard the rasping sound as the other guy ran his hand over his chin again.

"Jesus Christ," Vennerhag said. "You shouldn't be free to roam the streets, you fucking maniac."

Winter opened his eyes again and looked at his hands. Were they his? It had felt good clenching his fingers around Vennerhag's jaw.

"That's how I oughta talk to Lotta," Vennerhag said.

"You don't go anywhere near her," Winter said.

"She's damn near as crazy as her brother anyway."

Winter stood. "I'll call you in a few days," he said. "Meanwhile ask around."

"Thanks for the visit," Vennerhag said. "Jesus Christ."

Winter stuffed his wet boxers into his pocket and pulled on his T-shirt. He left the same way he came in, climbed into his car, and drove toward town. He drove past the police station and continued to Korsvägen and drove across Guldheden to Sahlgrenska Hospital. The city looked cold again through the windows.

The street services had planted three palm trees at the entrance to the hospital, but through the tinted windows of Winter's Mercedes the trees looked frozen in their pots.

Aneta Djanali seemed to stiffen as she reached for something on the wheeled table by her bed. He saw the surprise in her eyes as he entered her room and went quickly to her bedside, smiling and handing her the newspaper.

"I'll just sit here for a spell," he said. "Until the worst of the heat has settled."

4

MOMMY WASN'T THERE ANYMORE. SHE HAD CALLED OUT FOR her, but the man said that Mommy would be coming soon, and so she waited and stayed quiet. It was dark and no one turned on the light. She had to go wee-wee, but she was too scared to say anything, so she held it in, and that made it feel even colder as she sat on the chair by the window.

She could see through the gap at the bottom of the shade that the forest was just outside the window. The wind blew through the trees. It smelled bad in here. Mommy's gotta be coming soon.

The man said something to another man who had entered the house. She crept closer to the wall. She was hungry but more scared than hungry. Why hadn't they gone home after that awful thing happened? When they drove away from there? There had been a man driving the car, and they had driven back and forth between the houses, and then another man had carried her with him when he jumped out of the car. Then they had jumped into another car, and that one had taken them away. She had looked around when she finally felt brave enough, but then Mommy wasn't there.

"Mommy!" she had cried out, and the man had said that Mommy would be coming soon. She had cried out again and the man had become really angry and squeezed her shoulder hard. He was mean.

They were all mean, and they shouted and smelled bad.

"What do we do with the kid?" one of them said, but she couldn't hear what the other man answered. He mumbled as though he didn't want her to hear.

"We have to decide tonight."

"Don't talk so damn loud."

"Let's go into the kitchen."

"What about the kid?"

"What do you mean? Where's she gonna go?"

———

She stayed sitting in the chair by the window after they left. She heard an owl hoot out in the forest and pulled back the shade a little so she could see better. There was a bush growing just outside. She saw a car. It was lighter above the trees now. She looked in at the room and kept her hand on the shade. A faint beam of light came in from the window. It was like a band reaching across the floor, and there was something lying in the middle of that band. When she let go of the shade, the light disappeared and she couldn't see the thing anymore. When she pulled back the shade again, the band came back and she saw that the thing on the floor looked like a piece of paper.

The men were talking somewhere. It sounded like they were far away. She kneeled down and felt along the floor with her hand and picked up the thing that was lying there. It was a piece of paper, and she stuffed it into the secret pocket on the inside of her pants. She had wanted to wear just those pants today, and they had a secret pocket inside the regular one.

She went back to the chair by the wall and climbed up onto it again.

She had a secret in her pocket. Stuff like that was usually fun and exciting, only not this time. What if the man who dropped the piece of paper starts looking for it and finds out that I'm the one who took it? I'll put it back, she thought, but then the men came into the room again and both looked at her. Then they came closer, and one of them lifted her up while the other looked out through the window.

They drove away from the house, and she tried to stay awake but her eyelids closed. When she woke up, it had become light all around. She thought about it and then asked about her mommy.

"We'll find your mommy," said the driver up front.

Why did he say that? Don't they know where Mommy is?

She started crying, but the man next to her didn't look at her. She had nothing to hold on to because she'd lost her dolly back when they'd jumped out of the car.

5

THE WITNESS'S NAME WAS JÖRAN QVIST, AND HE WAS ACCOMPA-nied through Kungstorget by Halders and Bergenhem. It was eleven o'clock at night and difficult to make headway because of all the people. A dance band was playing on the stage, and Halders thought the music was crap. He said so to Bergenhem, but his younger colleague pretended not to hear.

The homicide detectives and their witness slowly made their way down toward the water. Rock music was throbbing from one of the restaurant stands. A sightseeing boat passed by on the canal. The clamor of voices sounded louder down here than up on the square. A hundred skewers sizzled on big grills next to the wall. People thronged together, holding beer in plastic cups and balancing paper plates of *lángos* spread with black fish roe and sour cream. Most looked happy.

"Some fucking party," Halders said. "Junk food and overpriced beer in plastic cups. And so crowded."

"Some people enjoy this kind of thing," Bergenhem said. "Nothing wrong with that."

"It's garbage."

"Not everyone has your sophistication."

"What did you say?"

"Not every—"

"There they are," Jöran Qvist said.

Bergenhem fell silent. He looked at Qvist, who gave a slight nod at a table near the edge of the canal. One of the spotlights above the bar was directed right at the benches where the three men were sitting, with beer glasses in front of them and an umbrella above. The harsh lighting illuminated them as if on a stage. What arrogant bastards, Bergenhem thought.

Halders was strangely silent. He turned toward Qvist.

"Are you sure?"

"Definitely."

"Specifically those three? You don't just recognize one or two of them?"

"No. They're even wearing the same clothes. And the little one's got the same baseball cap."

"Let's call in the uniforms," Bergenhem said.

"Fuck that."

"Fredrik."

But Halders didn't hear. He was already on his way through the teeming crowd, sort of languidly, as if out on an aimless stroll.

Like an assassin, Bergenhem thought. "Wait here," he told Qvist, and started to walk toward the table where the men were sitting. They were maybe ten yards away, and Halders was already halfway there. One of the three suspects stood up to get more beer. He pitched suddenly and sat back down; the others laughed.

Bergenhem was sweating. He was hot before, but now the sweat was streaming down his forehead and stinging his eyes. He rubbed his eyes, and when his focus returned, he saw Halders sit down on the bench next to one of the three.

Halders sat there motionless. He seemed sealed within himself even when Bergenhem reached the table and sat down next to him.

There was no more room on the bench, so Qvist took a seat two tables away. Bergenhem saw how Halders was hovering as if primed for battle.

When Bergenhem touched his colleague's left arm, Halders peered at him with eyes that seemed to have no focus.

They sat there silently. Bergenhem didn't know if Halders was listening, but he heard the men speaking to one another.

"Do you get drunker when it's hot?"

"Nah."

"Sure you do, and you get uglier too."

"There's no more beer."

"Where's the vodka?"

"It's all gone."

"No it isn't."

"I'm telling you, it's all gone."

"I gotta have a beer."

The man who said this got up, and Halders rose at the same time, took his wallet from his breast pocket, and held up his ID.

"Police," he said.

"What?"

Bergenhem had also stood up.

"Police," Halders repeated. "We'd like you guys to come with us so we can talk to you about something that happened last night."

"What?"

"We're looking for information—"

The man standing in front of Halders kicked him in the shin and went dashing off to the left while Halders cried out and bent forward. The two others tried to run off but got tangled up among the guests sitting next to them. One of them turned to Bergenhem and threw a punch, but Bergenhem ducked and stood his ground. He cast a quick glance to the side and saw Qvist bend down over something that lay on the ground. Damn it, Bergenhem thought.

The man who'd botched the punch remained standing there, as if paralyzed or mesmerized by Bergenhem's gaze. I won't blink, thought Bergenhem.

The commotion had caught the attention of others, and a circle formed around the two police officers and the two suspects at the table. The rock music had cut out. The dance band had stopped playing right in the middle of a barre chord. The Gothenburg Party was holding its collective breath.

One of the suspects broke the stillness, throwing himself backward through the thin line of onlookers and plunging into the water. The splashing down below sounded like swimming strokes. The man in front of Bergenhem sat down again and started to throw up with his head propped between his legs. Halders rushed to the edge of the canal and saw the fugitive paddling awkwardly toward the brightly lit Storan Theatre on the other side. The spotlight from the bar had caught him. He stopped swimming and splashed around in confusion, with his arms above the surface, before he started to sink.

"He's drowning," Bergenhem shouted, but Halders had already dived in.

Halders—once those fucking scumbags were apprehended—changed into dry underwear. He didn't bother to pull anything over his torso but sat on a park bench outside the police station with Bergenhem, who was more tired than he could ever remember being.

"When the temperature stays above seventy over a twenty-four-hour period, the climate is tropical," Halders said, after a drawn-out silence.

"How do you know that?"

"Aneta told me. She oughta know," Halders said.

Bergenhem turned toward him, but he couldn't see if Halders was smiling.

Bergenhem looked up at the sky. It was getting lighter now, and the sun slid very slowly down the facade of the Social Insurance Agency on the other side of Smålandsgatan. A taxi drove past. A patrol car pulled up in front of the main entrance and sat there with its headlights pointed toward the front doors and the engine switched off.

"Why the hell don't they turn their lights off?" Halders said, and audibly drew in air through his nostrils.

The patrol car started up again and sat with the engine idling. After two minutes Halders rose and walked over to the forecourt in front of the darkened police station. Bergenhem could hear him speaking, loud and clear in the stillness of morning: "What the hell are you doing, fucking cops?"

Bergenhem heard a mumbled reply and then Halders's voice again: "Say that again!"

Bergenhem ran over and grabbed Halders from behind just as he was about to bury his fist in the head of the police officer who'd stepped out of his car.

"For Christ's sake, Fredrik."

"Want us to take him in?" the officer asked. "Is he drunk?" The officer was close to fifty, a self-assured man. He did a salute of sorts when Bergenhem declined, and then climbed back into the car. All along his colleague remained quiet in the passenger seat, as if he were asleep.

"There's a one-minute idling limit in Gothenburg," Halders shouted when the patrol car turned around and started back toward the street. The driver waved.

Three minutes later the call came in to dispatch and was immediately passed on to homicide, twenty-five yards from where Halders and Bergenhem were still standing.

The murdered woman lay on the edge of the Delsjö Forest. The summer was over. The season was beginning. The phone on Winter's bedside table rang. It was exactly four o'clock in the morning on Thursday, August 18. He picked up the receiver and said his name.

6

WINTER COULD SEE THE BLUE LIGHTS EVEN BEFORE HE DROVE up the hill toward the Delsjö junction. They rotated above the eastern wilderness. The only thing missing is a helicopter, he thought.

He drove under the viaduct and passed the café and the parking lot at the Kallebäck recreation area and continued on J A Fagerbergs Väg until he saw the tunnel beneath the Boråsleden highway. He pulled over in front of the parking lot, to the side of the entrance, as far away as possible from where the body had been found. Far too many of his fellow police officers were gathered. There were two technicians and the deputy head of forensics, which was good, and the medical examiner, which maybe was a good thing too. But it was enough to have the crime scene unit and at most one curious uniformed officer. God knows how many of them had trampled around the victim.

A uniformed officer was waiting at the police cordon. He was young and pale.

Winter flashed his ID. "Were you the first one on the scene?"

"Yes. We got the call and came straight over."

"The guy who called. Is he here?"

"He's sitting over there." The uniformed officer nodded toward the darkness.

Winter could see the silhouette of a head in the dawn light.

"Is everything cordoned off?" Winter asked.

"Yes."

"Good. What about the cars?"

There were five cars in the parking lot, in addition to the two radio cars and the two cars that the forensic team and its boss had arrived in. Next to the entrance was a road sign prohibiting the parking of mobile homes.

"What?"

"Did you take down the plates?"

"Take dow—"

"Have you written down the license plate numbers and started running a check on the owners and put a cordon around the cars?" Winter asked, as gently as he could.

"Not yet."

"Well, get to it," Winter said. "Our fellow officers over there seem to need something to do." He looked over toward the witness's silhouette. "Were there any other people here when you arrived?"

"Just that guy over there."

"Nobody driving off when you got here?"

"No."

Winter felt a sudden chill in his body, as if it had only just occurred to him what he was here for and what lay ahead of him. He needed a cup of coffee.

"Where can I walk?"

"What?"

"Where's the path in?"

The young officer didn't understand. Winter looked around. All the activity was taking place about fifty yards away, maybe seventy. He raised a hand and someone broke away from the group and walked toward the spot where Winter was standing.

"I just arrived," Detective Inspector Göran Beier said. "She's lying over here."

They walked between two cars and across the parking lot, carefully picking their way along the wide path, up to a ditch that was partially hidden by a pine tree and a few birches.

Winter heard the sound of a vehicle and looked around. He saw headlights whose usefulness was fast diminishing as daylight returned to the sky. Ringmar's car.

Winter turned back toward the ditch. A woman was lying there, on her back, behind the pine tree. She might have been twenty-five or thirty or thirty-five years old. Her hair seemed fair, but it was hard to tell since it was damp from the morning dew. She was wearing a short skirt and blouse and a cardigan or a sweater, and her clothes didn't seem to be in disarray. She was staring up at the pale sky. Winter leaned in even closer and thought he could see the red pinpoints on her ears and the hemorrhaging in her open eyes. He guessed that she'd been strangled, but he was no expert. It was light enough now that he could see that her face was discolored and probably swollen. Her teeth were exposed, as if she were about to say something.

The forensic technicians had immediately called for the medical examiner. Winter thought that was good, but he knew Ringmar wouldn't like it. Ringmar felt that visiting the body dump site created preconceived notions, and that the medical examiner ought to meet a body for the first time on a steel table at the pathologist's.

He nodded to Pia Erikson Fröberg, down in the ditch. She was studying a thermometer. It looked as if the corpse were waiting to be notified of the result, shifting its gaze from the sky to Pia's accomplished movements. She's in good hands, thought Winter. Her body is in good hands.

It was the most important moment of the investigation. The woman's body lay close to a sign that warned of high voltage. Immediately to the right of the ditch was the four-and-a-half-mile circuit around Big Delsjö Lake, part of the Bohusleden hiking trail. On the other side of the jogging path lay the water's edge. The lake glowed between the birch branches.

Winter heard a voice.

"What?"

"Eight or ten hours," Fröberg said. "Wasn't that your first question?"

"I haven't asked it yet."

"Well, there's your answer anyway. It's still a little uncertain, of course, since the heat causes rigor mortis to set in more quickly."

"Right."

"But I'm trying to factor that in."

Winter looked at the dead woman's face once again. It had an oval shape, rounded off. The eyes were set wide apart; the mouth was large. Her long hair looked unkempt, but Winter wasn't sure. That sort of thing could have to do with the victim's age, maybe with her style.

"She's got nothing on her," Beier said, standing next to Winter. "There's nothing there. No papers or ID, nothing."

Winter blinked at the technicians' flashbulbs. They were almost finished with the crime scene photographs. Photography of the naked body would begin at the autopsy. Then the professionals in the lab would take over, meticulously photographing each piece of clothing, each finger.

Another flash went off down in the ditch, and Winter was surprised that the flashbulbs were so intense in the daylight.

"I think she was moved here," Fröberg said. "The body hasn't been lying here for very long."

Winter nodded. It was pointless to ask any more questions right now. For the moment, they would assume that the woman died somewhere else and was brought to this place. Someone had been moving around here.

She was unidentified. It was no accident that she didn't have any ID. Winter knew that, felt it. There was a reason why she had no name—that, by itself, was a ghastly message. They would have to spend a long time searching for a name. He felt cold again, a chill through his head.

"What's that marking over there on the pine tree?" he asked Beier.

"I don't know."

"Is it from the forestry service?"

"I don't know, but somebody's painted something on the bark there."

"Is it red paint?"

"It looks like it. But the light—"

"There's something written there. What does it say?" Winter asked, but the question was really directed to himself.

"We'll take a sample," Beier said.

"I'll check with the timber company or the municipality or whoever it is that manages the forests around here," Winter said. "Can I continue along the path?"

Beier looked at one of his technicians. "Walk in the middle of it," he said.

Winter continued along the water's edge. The ditch on the left came to an end a few yards farther on. He passed several pine trees, but none of them had any markings, so far as he could tell. There's a meaning behind it, he thought.

I don't like murderers that paint on walls, or trees.

Winter looked out over the water. He saw no movement and couldn't hear seabirds anymore. Weren't there sports fishermen operating around here at all hours of the day and night? Someone who rowed past? Had the murderer come here by boat, disposed of his victim, and slipped away again?

"Check the entire length of the shoreline," he said when he got back to the dump site. "She might have come by boat."

Beier nodded. "You could be right."

Winter continued back to the parking lot. Attached to the far fence was a sign from the Sportfishing Association of Gothenburg and Bohuslän, stating that fishing in Big Delsjö Lake required a yellow fishing license. They would have to check everyone with that license.

After two hours the officers from the crime scene unit were finished with the preliminary processing. It was still early in the morning. The technicians covered all the surfaces of the body with clear tape and waited for the undertakers, who laid the body in a plastic bag on a gurney and drove it to the pathologist at Östra Hospital.

The woman's body now lay on a stainless steel slab. The lights in the autopsy room replaced the morning light that had shone in Winter's eyes as he drove behind the hearse.

In here, under the spotlight, death was definitive; the woman died a second time. She still belonged to the world while she was lying out there in that damn ditch, thought Winter, but now it's over. Her face was glowing with an obscene light and her skin looked taut and translucent.

Pia Erikson Fröberg and the two technicians, Jonas Wall and Bengt Sundlöf, began undressing the body. The tape was in place, securing any trace evidence of a possible murderer: hair, fibers from close contact, skin, dust, rocks.

When the body was naked, Fröberg began the autopsy, the external examination. The technicians took photographs while Fröberg spoke into a tape recorder, detailing all the visible injuries. Winter heard her describe the defensive wounds he could see on the body's forearms. He could see the petechial hemorrhaging that occurred when the woman's blood pressure shot up and the airways from her head were constricted and the hyoid bone fractured as she was strangled to death. If that was the cause of death. Fröberg spoke about the injuries sustained around the neck. The woman had worn a turtleneck sweater. Underneath it, around her throat, there were clear signs of bruising.

She had white spots on her stomach and chest and on the front of her thighs. She had been lying on her back when she was found. That confirmed that she had been moved after she was killed. Winter didn't believe this to be a case of suicide, with someone else moving the body afterward. But why not? It was a possibility.

What was certain was that she had died and then lain facedown for at least an hour, and as her circulation ceased, her blood gravitated to the lowest point in her body, and the blood vessels collapsed, and the body surfaces in contact with the ground turned white and still remained so, there beneath the lights.

The technicians took the victim's fingerprints.

Fröberg continued with the extended medical examination—the expensive one—ordered by Göran Beier. Winter had hoped for some clear distinguishing marks that might help them with the identification: tattoos, burn scars or marks from operations, piercings. But there was nothing other than smooth bluish purple skin, with patches of white. He hadn't noticed any smells.

"She's never colored her hair," Fröberg said.

"How old is she?" he asked.

"Around thirty is all I can say right now. For closer than that, you'll have to wait. She could be older or younger, a few years either side. She's got pretty nice skin. Smooth around the mouth and eyes."

"No smile lines."

"Maybe she didn't have much to be happy about."

Winter wondered briefly why Fröberg would make a comment like that.

"But now the sadness is over. Are you still going to be here when I start the medical assessment?"

"I'll stay a little longer," Winter said.

"I'm leaving now," Beier said, glancing at Winter. "I'll call you."

Winter nodded. He turned his gaze back to the woman's face. She looked older now with her eyes closed.

Pia Erikson Fröberg had examined the internal organs, saved the contents of the stomach, and taken a urine sample and a blood sample from the thigh vein when Winter stepped out of the autopsy room for a moment to call Ringmar.

"What are you still hanging around there for?" Ringmar asked.

"I thought we might get some help with the identification."

"Yeah, maybe. People tattoo themselves in the most bizarre places. So, you find anything?"

"No. Just a naked face. She wasn't wearing any makeup."

"What?"

"She didn't use makeup."

"Is that unusual these days?"

"It depends on your social scene. In more refined circles it may well be, but I don't think she belonged to any like that."

"What do you mean?"

"She seems poor. Cheap no-name clothes. Stuff like that. Or else that's not the case at all."

"What does Beier say?"

"He hasn't said anything yet."

"I have someone who's got a bit more to say."

Winter thought about the silhouette in the parking lot. He had spoken briefly to the man before handing over the rest of the questioning to Ringmar and joining the funeral procession to the hospital. "Yeah. So, what's he say?"

"He owns one of the cars in the parking lot."

"What was he doing there at four in the morning? Could he explain that?"

"He claims that he'd been to a party down in Helenevik and might have had one beer too many, and that he didn't dare drive farther into town, so he decided to pull into the parking lot at Delsjö Lake and sleep it off in the car."

"That's one hell of a tall tale. He tried to pull that one on me too, or parts of it anyway."

"He claims it's true."

"Did you give him a Breathalyzer?"

"As soon as we could. But he wasn't unfit to drive. He had been drinking but not enough."

"Okay, okay. So, what's he saying? What did he see?"

"After being in the car for a while, he had to go take a pee and wandered off a ways from the parking lot, and that's when he saw her."

"What did he say?"

"Before he had a chance to pee, he saw something lying a bit farther on, in the ditch, so he went over and found the body. He had his cell phone in his breast pocket and called us straightaway."

"We'd better check up on that call."

"Of course."

"What time was it?"

"When he called? Quarter to four, give or take. Dispatch has the exact time."

"So, what did he see? Anything else?"

"Nothing, he says. Nobody coming or going."

"Find anything on the other cars?"

"We're working on it."

"Morning prayer has been pushed back half an hour."

"You want everyone there?"

"Without exception."

Back in the autopsy room, the woman on the steel slab remained a dead body with no name. Usually when somebody was murdered, there was at least a name that could be laid to rest and, the terrible ordeal over, be handed back to the family.

"Decent teeth," Fröberg said. "Some discoloration but in good condition."

"That'll only help us if she's been reported missing," Winter said. "I want the autopsy report just as soon as you can get it to me. Thanks."

"As always."

"You're doing a good job, Pia."

"That kind of talk makes me suspicious."

Winter said nothing more. He walked toward the door. The dry air had made him feel thirsty and tired.

"What are you doing tonight, Erik?" Fröberg asked when he was halfway out the swinging door.

He stopped and looked at her. She was clearing off the autopsy table.

"I thought you were remarried or whatever you call it."

"It didn't work out. Again."

"I don't think it's a—"

"No. You're absolutely right. And the main reason I asked was to tell you not to push yourself too hard right at the start of the case."

"Tonight I'm going to sleep with Angela and maybe talk about the future." He was answering a question that was no longer being asked. "And think about this one lying over here."

"One last thing, just to give you something more to think about. This woman has given birth."

"She's got a child?" Winter repeated.

"I don't know if she does now, but she has had at least one child, maybe more."

"How long ago?"

"I can't say, at least not yet. But she shows signs of—"

"You don't have to give me all the details," Winter said, "not right now anyway." He felt a shiver spread across his head.

There could be some family out there. It could help in the investigation, or be a source of frustration, or maybe something worse.

7

THE WATCH COMMANDER WAS FANNING HIMSELF WITH A double-folded form, possibly "Lines of Inquiry in Felony Cases."

The corridor smelled of sweat and sun, and the waiting room off to the right smelled of stale booze. Some joker had hung a poster of a beach with a palm tree next to a recruitment ad for the homicide department. Winter stepped into the elevator and rode up to his office on the third floor.

He had perked up again on the drive down from Östra Hospital. Adrenaline was pumping through his body while sweat ran down his back. This was no ordinary murder investigation. He knew that much without knowing it. He felt the tension in his body. A tension that might not leave him for months.

He poured himself a mug in the coffee room and lingered there for a few seconds, gazing at the morning outside. The thermometer in the window showed eighty degrees, and it was only twenty past eight in the morning, but Winter knew that for him the swimming season was over.

The situation room filled up with people. The ones who'd been at it since the start looked tired; the others waited impatiently, their bottoms literally on the edges of their seats. On the whiteboard Ringmar had written, "Visualization relating to the murder."

Well, here we are again, after the summer's rest, Winter thought to himself.

He drew an X on the board.

"We've got an unidentified woman, approximately thirty years of age, probably strangled, discovered between three thirty and quarter to four this morning by a man whom we're going to question further over the course of the day. For the moment, this man is not a suspect, but as you're all aware, you never know."

Winter fell silent and stared at his X, then began sketching out a rough map as he spoke. "She was found here." He drew a circle at the spot where the body was dumped. "We'll take a closer look at the map later, but I just want to mark out the relative positions. If you continue underneath the highway on Old Boråsvägen, you come to a junction that leads toward Helenevik and Gunnebo, but we'll wait on that. So here's where she was found," he repeated, and pointed at his circle.

"That's where the lodge is," Halders said.

"That's right. As most of you know, the police department's recreation lodge is located a bit farther down the road."

"That's where I had my fortieth birthday party," Halders said. "Wasn't there something going on there yesterday?"

"Our colleagues over at the investigations department had a little do there in the early evening," Ringmar said.

"How early?" Janne Möllerström asked.

"The last man walked out of there at around four," Ringmar said. "Or rather hopped a cab."

"What the fu—," Halders began, but was interrupted by Ringmar.

"Naturally we're going to question our esteemed colleagues on the subject."

"That lodge can't be more than a few hundred yards away from the ditch where the body was found," Bergenhem said.

"Isn't there a dog kennel just before it?" Halders asked.

"Yes. Right after the intersection. We're going to question them too."

"What, you mean the dogs?" Halders asked, putting on an innocent expression.

"If necessary," Winter said. "There are a lot of houses along that road. The Örgryte shooting range is a few hundred yards farther up and then the Delsjö Golf Club and the GAIS football club's training facility. There are a number of houses at the intersection of Old Boråsvägen and Frans Perssonsväg. Here." He drew a few small squares on the board.

"And then we've got a bunch of drunken cops," Halders said.

Winter didn't answer. He finished sketching on the board and turned back toward his team sitting in the room.

"The site where the body was discovered is not where the murder was committed. She was moved postmortem to the ditch where she was found at least one hour after she was killed. She had been dead for eight to ten hours when we arrived on the scene. That's where we are now. I'm waiting for the autopsy report."

"Sexual violence?" Halders asked. He felt rested despite the late night.

"We don't know yet. But her clothes seemed undisturbed and Pia Erikson Fröberg saw no immediate indication of sexual violence."

"Any other witnesses?" asked Möllerström. He was Winter's database expert, a meticulous detective who saw to it that all materials were entered into the preliminary investigation database.

"So far no one's gotten in touch voluntarily, except for the guy sitting downstairs."

"We're looking at four cars," Ringmar said. "Two of them were reported stolen."

"That's good," Bergenhem said.

Everyone knew a stolen car could lead straight from a murder scene to a dump site.

"We're scouring the vehicles today," Ringmar said.

"What do the owners say about it?" Sara Helander asked.

Winter studied her. She had become part of his core group during the last investigation—an agonizing one—and he wanted to hold on to her permanently and not just have her on loan from surveillance. "Two of the owners were very happy that we'd found their cars—at least that's what they're saying—and the other two will just have to make the best of it."

"Why had they parked there in the first place?" Halders asked.

"Yeah," Veine Carlberg filled in, "why leave your car in that godforsaken parking lot overnight?"

"That's what we have to find out."

"Did she have any defensive wounds?" Helander asked, eyeing the two photos in her hands. "It's hard to tell from these."

"She appears to have fought for her life," Winter said. "There were injuries to her forearms, but we'll have to wait for the report to know when they were inflicted. Here are the photos from the autopsy," he said, and handed her a thin pile. "You can see there."

"So she's unidentified, huh," Halders mumbled.

"She's also had at least one child," Winter said. "That could be of help to us."

No one commented on this last statement. Winter studied the faces in front of him and started to hand out the day's assignments. The work they did that day could prove to be the most important of the entire investigation.

He already had people sifting through the lists of persons reported missing.

DNA samples were being analyzed, of course.

They would go through the criminal-records database in hope that the woman had previously been arrested and charged, maybe even sentenced, and that her fingerprints would help them find the murderer. But the chances of that were slim.

The photograph on the desk in front of Winter didn't reveal much of death. The woman looked like she was still part of the world, like she was resting.

They would hope that some fellow human being missed her, but they weren't going to sit around waiting for that fellow human being to get in touch.

Winter thought about the woman as a mother.

They would knock on the door of everyone who lived in the vicinity of the dump site. They would track down newspaper deliverymen and others who might have been moving around there during the night.

They would check the taxi companies. Halders was assigned that job, and he grimaced despite his interest in cars. It's pointless, he thought, but he didn't say it.

"I know you think it's pointless, but it's gotta be done," Winter said.

"This time it could be different," Halders said. "There must have been a few fares from the recreation lodge. But fuck, man, cabbies never get in touch and they never see anything. It was better back in the old days."

It was better back in the old days, thought Winter. Back in the day when he could have picked up the phone and dialed 17 30 00, and the central dispatcher would have made an announcement to all cars, "Anyone working last night call Winter," and the job of an investigator would sometimes be made a little bit easier.

The Migration Board needed to be notified. The woman could be a foreign national. Interpol. Easy does it, Winter.

He looked at the arrows and numbers on the whiteboard—almost nothing there. Just a point of departure.

"Well, welcome back for real now," Ringmar said. It was eleven o'clock, and they were sitting in Winter's office.

"I was starting to get bored anyway. Summer vacation."

"It's better to have a hobby," Ringmar said. "Then you make better use of your free time."

"I went biking and swimming," Winter said. "And listened to rock. You know, rock could become a hobby for me. Jazz is work but rock is like a hobby. It takes time to learn how to listen to it."

"Yeah, you said it," Ringmar said.

Winter heard the sound of engines outside and the jeering shrieks of the seagulls that followed the comings and goings of the radio cars.

"No one reported missing," Winter said. "That could be good or bad."

"What's good about it?"

"She was somewhere less than twenty-four hours ago, was moving around somewhere. Somebody saw her, maybe even spoke to her. And I don't mean the person who killed her. Just maybe."

"One might come in over the course of the day. Or tomorrow."

"Until then, her teeth are of no use to us."

"We need a dentist," Ringmar said.

"We need a name and a home address and leads," Winter said. "It feels like—as if it's indecent to speak about her. Do you feel that way?"

"No."

"I always feel that way when we have a murder victim with no identity. Well, you know. No peace."

Ringmar nodded.

"I'd like to hold off on the newspapers and posters for twenty-four hours," Winter said.

"Posters? We're gonna start putting up posters?"

"Yes. Our counterparts in London have started working with them, and I want to test it out here."

"Is it producing any results in London?"

"I don't really know."

"I see."

"I'll write up a draft tonight."

"What are you going to use?"

"I don't really know that either. Can't we use this?" Winter held up the image of the dead woman's face.

"Let me see," Ringmar said, and reached for the photo. He studied the portrait and handed it back.

"Doesn't really sit well. But I guess we'll have to if nothing happens soon. Freshly deceased and a reasonably good picture. It'll probably be the first time it's been done in Gothenburg."

Ringmar stood up and stretched his back, then raised his arms above his head and groaned. "It's evening for me," he said.

"Pull yourself together," Winter said.

"And then there's the press conference," Ringmar said, and sat back down again with one leg crossed over the other. His khaki pants and short-sleeved gabardine shirt were infinitely more elegant than Winter's shorts and washed-out hockey shirt.

"Press conference? Who ordered that? Birgersson?"

"No. They tried to get hold of you when you were on your way in from Östra. Wellman."

Henrik Wellman was district chief of CID. He was the one homicide inspectors had to turn to for money for any trips they had to make. Or new cars.

Above Wellman there was District Police Commissioner Judith Söderberg. After that, God.

"Is Henrik going to be there himself?" Winter asked with a smile.

"You have to understand him," Ringmar said. "Young woman murdered, unidentified. Parliament isn't back in session yet. The hockey season hasn't gotten started. The press is all over this. A summer murder."

"A summer murder," Winter repeated. "We're taking part in a classic summer murder. A tabloid's wet dream."

"It's the fault of this goddamn weather," Ringmar said. "If it hadn't been for this unrelenting heat, it would have been a different thing. For the press, that is."

"A fall murder," Winter said. "If it is murder. It is murder, of course, but it's not official yet. Well. Maybe it's a good idea to have a conference with our friends from the press. I assume I'll be the only one representing us."

"At two o'clock. See you later."

Ringmar stood up and walked out.

They needed a room now, a house or an apartment. If they couldn't get a name, they needed a space to start in. The possibilities would fade quickly if they didn't get an address to work from.

He took an envelope from the top left-hand drawer and opened it. Inside were more photographs from the dump site. He tried to imagine what had happened in the minutes leading up to the woman being deposited there. She could have been carried through the forest, across the bog. That was possible for a strong man. She didn't weigh more than 120 pounds.

She had been carried. So far they hadn't found any drag marks in the parking lot or on the path or in the grass. The parking lot. Had she been driven to the parking lot and hauled out of the car and carried over to the ditch? That was a possibility. The two stolen cars? Why not one of them? He would soon know. Somebody kills someone and walks down the street and steals a car and carries out the body and drives off? Would you do that if you had murdered somebody, Winter? Would you drive to Delsjö Lake?

He thought about the lake. Perhaps she'd come in a boat. He had people combing the entire lakefront. Almost seven miles of shoreline. How did one go about concealing a boat?

Could there have been some jogger out running around the lake at that hour? You never know with joggers.

There's always a meaning behind the choice of disposal site, even if the murderer himself isn't always aware of it. There's a clue hidden somewhere in his choice. Something made him drive there of all places. Something in his past.

The dump site. We'll start from there. I'll start from there again. I'll drive back there.

He put the envelope back in the desk drawer, closed it, and stood up so quickly that he felt dizzy for a split second.

Winter felt hungry earlier but the feeling was gone now. Still, he needed to eat something. He drove his car the short distance to the Chinese restaurant on Folkungagatan and ate a quick lunch and drank a quart of water.

3

WINTER LISTENED TO THE LOCAL NEWS AS HE PASSED LISEBERG
Amusement Park. "The police have no leads yet in the . . ." It was true,
no matter who it was that told Radio Gothenburg. This afternoon he
would clarify what they didn't know.

Various wheels were spinning around in the amusement park. It
struck him that he hadn't been in there in many years.

The asphalt was soft beneath his tires. Car and road melted into each
other, as if both were disintegrating. He passed a sign that measured the
temperature of the air and road surface: 93°F in the air, 120°F on the
road. Jesus Christ.

After the Kallebäck junction he saw a police sobriety checkpoint
on the other side of the road up the hill. A uniformed officer cordially
waved drivers over to the curb. Another officer, with a video camera,
stood at the roadside a little farther on.

Winter saw him in his rearview mirror. The camera was recording
the oncoming traffic. But then he saw the guy train the camera on him.
That meant he had been caught on the tape; he and the other drivers
headed in the opposite direction were registered, even if they weren't
the ones the police were primarily interested in.

He turned right at the Delsjö junction and continued underneath the
highway and past the recreation area. The sweltering heat kept people
away—nobody in the parking lot or on the grass.

He was about to turn off to the spot where they'd found the woman
when he decided to continue along the old road, underneath the highway that roared right alongside. After barely half a mile he reached an
intersection and turned right into a combined parking lot and bus stop.
He stopped the car and turned off the engine, got out and lit a Corps,
and leaned against the side of the car.

The policeman with the video camera could be an opening. Hadn't the traffic department been sending out night patrols for a while? Early mornings? Cameras that could see in the dark? Testing out heat-sensitive cameras?

And wasn't this test supposed to be concentrating specifically on the eastern districts and arteries?

Winter grabbed the phone from its cradle on the dashboard and called traffic. He introduced himself to the watch commander and asked to be connected to the department chief.

"Walter's busy."

"For how long?"

Winter could see the shoulder shrug, could almost hear the sigh from the other end: why can't this guy call somebody else?

"I asked for how long."

"Who are you, did you say?"

"Inspector Erik Winter. I'm the deputy chief of homicide."

"You can't speak to somebody else?"

"We're involved in a murder investigation, and it's very important that I speak to Walter Kronvall."

"Okay, okay, hang on," the manly voice said, and Winter waited.

"Yeah, this is Kronvall."

"Erik Winter here."

"I was busy."

"You still are."

"What?"

"You're busy with this conversation with me now, Walter. And I'll get straight to the point. I need to know if you had any cameras out around Boråsleden last night, by the Delsjö junction, or anywhere in the vicinity. Early in the morning. While it was still dark."

"Speed check?"

"You'd know that better than I would."

"What's this about?"

"Haven't you heard about the murder yet? We got a strangled woman this morn—"

"Oh sure, I know about it. Despite the communications in this place, I might add."

Winter waited for him to continue. He could feel the sweat around his eyes and where the telephone pressed against his cheek. He sat on the car seat in the shade and wiped his forehead with the back of his right hand.

"You want to know if we were filming in the vicinity, when it was dark. Well, it's possible. Normally we don't have that kind of equipment, but we got some in on loan from the boys in the copter unit to test it out a bit. Heat-sensitive cameras. I'll have to check with the local precinct in Härlanda."

"Can you do that now?"

"Well, I guess I'd better if you're going to have any chance of seeing the footage. If they've been there, that is."

"How do you mean?"

"Don't you know how it works, Chief Inspector? The officers in the video cars peruse the tapes and then rewind them, and then somebody else takes over."

"The tapes are usually recorded over?"

"Sure. We don't exactly have infinite resources over here in the traffic department."

"Then call them, please."

"Where can I reach you?"

Winter told him and hung up, then rose from his seat and walked across the asphalt to the bus timetable. The first departure of the day was at 0500 hours. The final one left at 2343. Yet another lead to add to all the others in the investigation. An investigation is a great big vacuum cleaner that sucks in everything: witness statements and forensic evidence, sound ideas and crazy hunches, most of it completely irrelevant to the case. Eventually you find things that fit together. Then you can formulate a hypothesis.

The phone in his breast pocket rang. He answered with his name.

"It's Walter here again. That was good thinking, Winter. It turns out that they were out last night and this morning in the video cars in the eastern part of town."

"Okay," Winter said. "Were they set up along the Boråsleden?"

"You bet. And a couple of the cameras that were used last night haven't been reused since."

"Is that all the cameras?" asked Winter.

"I'm not following you."

"You said that there were a couple of cameras. Were there more than that being used in the area we're talking about?"

"No, not as I understood it."

"I need to see those tapes."

"Where?"

"Can you get them over to homicide by this afternoon?"

"Absolutely. We have special courier cars set aside just for that kind of thing," Kronvall said, and Winter gave a short laugh.

"Thanks for your help."

"If this solves the case, then we want credit."

"Of course."

"Chief Walter Kronvall of the traffic department provided the crucial assist. Something like that."

"Here at homicide we don't forget our friends," Winter said, then hung up and lingered next to the timetable.

He thought once again about the woman who just a short time ago lay so close by and had been carried there like a slaughtered animal. A victim—and perhaps quarry. Her nameless body was itself a message about what happened. Why? He thought of her half-open mouth and exposed teeth. Like a silent plea. A distant cry.

Winter drove back to the area where the woman was discovered. The grass in the ditch still looked flattened from the weight of her body. He turned around and followed his own tracks with his gaze. It was a long way to carry someone, dead or alive. A dead body was heavy but offered no resistance.

Whoever carried her need not have been a giant. Fear of discovery could make a murderer strong, assuming that he even cared, that is. Or had several people walked there in the sparse light of dawn? More people filled with madness, rage, adrenaline.

She could have been carried over the rough fields, through the fog. Why not?

The police tried to work their way through the terrain within a reasonable radius, but they couldn't go stomping around haphazardly. If there were too many of them, everything became haphazard.

A shot made Winter start. Another shot shattered the early afternoon silence of the forest and disturbed the low drone of the cars driving alongside. The hard sounds sent echoes above the birch trees and across the water beyond. The shooting ranges were back in use.

"And the sun also rises," Ringmar said, knocking on the open door before Winter had had a chance to wring his shirt dry.

"I like the sun."

"When you're ready, the gentlemen of the press are waiting."

"It'll have to be quick. I want to look at these tapes as soon as I'm done."

Winter explained the videocassettes to Ringmar as they walked down the corridors. The representatives of the media looked like they were on their way to the beach: shorts, thin shirts, someone in sunglasses.

Cool guy, Winter thought, and took his place in front of a lectern at the far end of the room.

"We don't know who she is yet," he answered to the first question. "And we may need your help to find that out."

"Do you have a photo?"

"In a manner of speaking."

"What's that supposed to mean?" Hans Bülow from the *Göteborgs-Tidningen* was one of the few journalists Winter knew by name.

"We've taken photos of the victim's body. We don't usually release pictures like that to the public, as I'm sure you're aware."

"But if you have to?"

"We'll get back to you on that."

"But she was murdered?"

"I can't answer that yet. It could be suicide."

"So she took her own life and then drove out to Delsjö Lake and lay down in a ditch?" said a woman from the local radio news.

"Who said anything about her dying anywhere else?" he said.

The woman looked at Hans Bülow out of the corner of her eye. The latest issue of *GT* had an article that speculated about what might have happened.

"We have not yet been able to determine the exact sequence of events leading up to the . . . death," Winter said.

"When will we know whether she's been murdered?"

"Later this afternoon I will be getting a report from the medical examiner."

"Are there any witnesses?"

"I can't comment on that."

"How was the body found?"

"We received a call."

"From a witness, you mean?"

Winter made a gesture with his arms that was open to interpretation.

"Is she Swedish?"

"I don't know."

"Well, you know what she looks like, right? Does she appear to be of Swedish or Nordic origin? Or does she look like she comes from some-where else?"

"I can't speculate on that yet."

"If she doesn't look Nordic, then it's gotta make it easier to speculate where in Gothenburg she may have lived," said a young journalist that Winter hadn't seen before, as far as he could remember.

"What do you mean by that?"

"Don't you know where all the immigrants live?"

Winter didn't answer. He thought of the northern suburbs and thought that that was an oversimplification.

"Any more questions?"

"How old would you say she is?"

"Obviously, we're not sure about that either. But maybe around thirty."

The journalists wrote, held microphones. A summer murder in Gothenburg.

"What are you doing now?"

"An extensive investigation was launched early this morning. We are securing evidence at the site where the body was found and focusing our efforts on identifying the victim," Winter said.

"When did it take place?"

"What?"

"The murder. Or the death. When did it happen?"

"It's hard to say right now. But sometime late last night. I can't be any more precise than that."

"When was she found?"

"Early this morning."

"When?"

"At around four."

"Have you spoken to people who were in the vicinity at that time?"

"We are seeking to question anyone who may have seen anything. Anyone who thinks they may have seen something is invited to contact the police."

"How about motive?"

"Impossible to answer that right now."

"Was she raped?"

"I can't answer that."

"Are there any similarities here?" asked Hans Bülow.

"How do you mean?"

"Are you looking into any other cases, either here or elsewhere, that bear a resemblance to this one?"

"I'm afraid I can't answer that, due to the ongoing investigation."

"So the victim was not already known to the police?"

"I think I just said that we don't know her identity."

"Is that usual?"

"Excuse me?"

"Is it usual for the identity to be unknown? I mean, after this long."

"It's been," Winter looked at his watch, "less than twelve hours since we found her. That's not a long time."

"Sure it's a long time," the journalist in the sunglasses said.

"Any more questions?" Winter asked, knowing that the cool guy was right.

IT RAINED ALL DAY AND SHE SAT AT ANOTHER WINDOW. THE MEN weren't there. She was scared but she was more scared when the men were there. She had cried out once in the car, and one of them had looked like he was about to hit her. He hadn't done anything, but he looked like somebody who hits.

This house was somewhere else; she could see that the trees outside were different. There were no other houses and nobody walking along the road. She couldn't hear the sound of any cars or trains. Once she heard a rumbling overhead that could have been an airplane.

If there were a phone, she could lift the receiver, press the buttons, and speak to Mommy. She knew how.

Maybe the men were out looking for Mommy. They had driven off and come back and driven off and come back again. Now one of them was gone, and the other was also gone, only he hadn't left in the car. She thought that he was in another room, but then she saw him outside the house. It was just a short distance between the house and the forest, and he came out of the forest and looked right at her through the window, and she crawled down from the chair and went in toward the room because she thought it was scary.

She was lying on the floor the next time she thought about anything. She felt sort of sleepy in her head, and there was a strange smell in the room. She looked around, and there was steam rising from a dish on the floor.

"Eat this now."

She rubbed her eyes and looked, but everything was blurry. She rubbed her eyes again. Now she saw that there was a lot of steam coming from the plate.

"It's soup. You have to eat it while it's hot."

She saw shoes and legs and asked for her mommy.

"Your mommy will be here soon."

She asked where her mommy was, but he didn't answer and she asked again.

"Eat your soup now. Here's a spoon."

She said she was thirsty.

"I'll bring you some water if you start eating."

She took the spoon and dipped it into the soup and tasted it, but it was too hot. She couldn't taste anything.

She waited for the soup to cool off. She felt something crinkly in her clothes when she sat on the floor. She thought about the slip of paper she had in the secret pocket of her pants.

"You have to eat now."

She looked down into the dish, but it still looked too hot. She closed her eyes.

Suddenly she felt a pain at her ear and she opened her eyes and saw the hand right next to her. It hurt again.

"I'll pull your ear again if you don't eat."

Then the hand was gone, and she dipped the spoon into the steaming dish again. She started to cry. He would hit her again, pull her ear. Mommy used to smack her, but that was Mommy.

10

WINTER READ THE AUTOPSY REPORT PAGE BY PAGE. PIA ERIKSON Fröberg described each organ in detail.

Strangulation. The woman had been murdered. She had defensive wounds on her arms, her chest, and her face from a sharp instrument. A knife, a screwdriver, anything. There was no evidence of needle marks on her body, but in some of the photographs he could see lacerations in the skin.

Winter thought about what he'd just read. She had had a child, but it was impossible to say when. Nursery school? Day care? School? Babysitter? Playmates who talked about why a friend didn't come out to play anymore? Was there even a child anymore? Or was the child a teenager?

Her body had no scars from operations, but there were small scars on her face, around the ears, and she had at some point in her childhood gotten second-degree burns on the inside of her left thigh. Winter hadn't noticed that in the blue light of the autopsy room.

She was a smoker. Her liver was normal. He had to wait for the results from toxicology. The lab would find any traces of alcohol or drug use there might be.

He was also waiting to hear from the missing persons department of the National Criminal Investigation Department in Stockholm. If she had been reported missing anywhere in the country, Stockholm would identify her.

They hadn't managed to find her among the local missing person reports or criminal-records databases.

The clothes she had been wearing didn't have brand labels. Winter thought of the H&M posters he saw every time he walked down the street and of the poster he might have to put up himself.

She hadn't been wearing any shoes. The police at the body disposal site had found shoes and a whole bunch of other odds and ends from times gone by, but not her shoes.

Her short white tube socks had been wet, or at least very damp. From the grass? It had been relatively dry. From the water? He saw a boat gently gliding through the water, oarlocks wrapped in cloths to muffle the sound.

He rose and stretched his tall body. Fatigue had taken hold of him while sitting.

He walked across the floor to a cabinet and took down a can of shaving cream and a razor from the top shelf and went to the bathroom, where he wet his face and spread the cream on. The light was dim and his eyes glowed in his face, which was like a mask. He leaned in closer and saw that the whites of his eyes had cracked into small red threads.

But the shave perked him up and back in his room he switched on the VCR and TV with the remote. The light of the first film sequence was dim and grainy, and he tried to use the contrast button on the remote to compensate.

The film looked like a photo negative, with the darkness cast in a false silvery hue by the camera's night vision. You could see everything, but the subject took on a surreal quality.

Two cars drove past in the foreground. They came along the road and had not pulled out from the Kallebäck recreation area. The time was displayed in the lower corner of the screen: 2:03 a.m. Another car passed in the foreground, moving toward town. No motion on the other side. The officer who was holding the camera was standing near the top of the hill, hidden from the sparse traffic, with the lens pointing east. Winter could see the side road that led down toward the Delsjö Lake area, but the visibility was poor. The tape kept rolling but no vehicles appeared heading east. Then suddenly a car emerged at the extreme right of the screen, but as soon as he registered the movement, the screen went blank.

He backed up the tape and watched the sequence again. There a car appeared, driving along. There he saw the outline of it. There it went blank.

Winter watched the clip four more times without really seeing anything more than he had to begin with. He removed the tape and inserted the other one into the VCR. Four seconds in, two cars came driving along at high speed from Mölnlycke. He wondered if the drivers were about to be pulled over.

Now he saw a car drive by on the other side and continue beyond the turnoff. Ten minutes had passed since the first time code on the previous cassette.

The camera moved and then stabilized again. The road was empty in both directions. There was a flicker in the right-hand corner of the screen, and a car passed by driving east. Winter saw a turn signal come on, and the car turned off toward Delsjö Lake. He couldn't make out what the make was. He waited and another car appeared on the highway and also turned off to the right. It looked like one of the smaller Ford models, but he was far from certain.

The time ticked away at the bottom of the screen. Several cars passed by from the left, heading toward the city. The camera was steady. Maybe he had a tripod, thought Winter.

Another flash of movement at the bottom of the screen and a car came out from the recreation area. Winter waited until the road was clear again and then rewound the tape.

The car had driven past at three minutes to three, in the direction of town. He studied the sequence again. It could be the same car he had seen coming in toward Delsjö Lake earlier. That was fourteen minutes before. It didn't take more than a minute to drive from the turnoff to the parking lot, one and a half, tops. Just as long to drive back, maybe a little less. That would give someone at least eleven minutes down by the lake: to open the car door, walk to the back of the car, haul out the body, carry it fifty yards, lay it in the ditch, look around, and go back the way he came.

He watched the whole tape through to the end but saw nothing more of interest, so he returned to the sequences where the same car seemed to drive off the highway and back on within the space of fourteen minutes.

"You're still here?" Ringmar had opened the door.

"Come here for a minute, Bertil."

Ringmar walked up to Winter, who pointed at the TV.

"Look at this. Wait a minute. See the car across the road?"

"Is this the tape from Kallebäck?"

"Yes. See the car driving up the hill?"

"I'm not blind. Despite this light."

"Now. See how it turns off toward Delsjö Lake? I'll back it up."

Neither of them said anything while Winter fiddled with the remote. The car came back into view.

"Can you make out what kind of car it is?"

"Well . . . Can you freeze-frame it?"

Winter pressed pause, and the car stopped and jiggled on the highway.

"It could be a Ford. Maybe," Ringmar said.

"That's what I was thinking. Are you sure? You know more about cars than I do."

"No, I'm not sure. But it looks like an Escort. Fredrik knows more about cars than anyone."

"It comes back later on," Winter said, and fast-forwarded the fourteen minutes.

"It's closer, but it's no easier to tell what make it is from this angle," Ringmar said.

"There's someone in the front seat."

"If there weren't, that would be pretty sensational."

"You can just about make out the face."

"You're gonna have a harder time with the tags."

"It's hard but not impossible," Winter said. He turned toward Ringmar. Ringmar saw a strange light in his eyes. Could be the reflection of the screen.

"Someone was in the vicinity of the disposal site after the body was put there. Or shortly before—or at the same time."

"We'll have to track down that car," Ringmar said. But that went without saying, so he continued, "How sophisticated is our equipment for making this footage visible?"

"You mean crystal clear?"

"I mean clear enough to see a few numbers or letters or facial features. And we'll have to speak to the uniform behind the camera. The cameraman."

"We'll have to speak to Beier," Winter said, and just at that moment the phone rang and it was Beier.

"We've got something on the sign," he said.

"The sign?"

"The marking on the pine tree. The red mark, the sign above the body."

"Okay, I'm with you now."

"Did you check with the forestry service?"

"Just a second." Winter put down the receiver and looked through the thin pile of papers on his desk. "Has anyone checked with forestry and everyone else about that marking on the tree yet?"

Ringmar didn't know.

"Not everything has come in yet," Winter said into the phone. "So the answer to your question is still no."

"Anyway, it was fresh."

"How fresh?"

"Could be from last night."

"Don't tell me it's blood."

"No. Paint, acrylic, one of the hundred or so shades of red."

"And it's only on that one tree?"

"Seems that way."

"What's it supposed to be?"

"We're looking into that now, but, to be honest, I have no idea. It could be a cross, but that's pure speculation."

"How many photos do you have of it?"

"Quite a few copies, if that's what you mean."

"Distribute it to all the departments. Could be some gang, youth gang or something."

"Or satanists. Delsjö Lake is not unknown to satanists."

"Delsjö Lake is a big place."

"Let me know when you've checked with the forestry service," Beier said. "If *service* is the proper term under the circumstances."

"Send over a few photos," Winter said. "I was just about to call you, by the way. I have a couple of videotapes that I want you to take a look at."

"Send them up," Beier said, and hung up.

The phone rang again, and Ringmar watched Winter as he listened intently and jotted something down. After he said good-bye he looked up again.

"The guy who owns the kennel over by the bog was woken up last night by a couple of his dogs barking. He went outside and saw a car turn around in front of his spread and drive back out toward the road and the highway on-ramp, or at least toward that recreation area."

"Could he see the car?"

"He had a light on down at the gate, and he's sure it was a Ford Escort."

"That's our car. What time was this?"

"Just before we saw it on the videotape," Winter said, and nodded at the mute TV screen. "He even mentioned what year it was."

"Is that possible?"

"He saw the car in real life," Winter said.

"Now he can see the replay."

"Sometimes I feel like it's the replay you want to be part of," Winter said. "Not the first live recording but the replay."

11

THE NATIONAL CRIMINAL INVESTIGATION DEPARTMENT HAD contacted Winter. He sat with the photo of the dead face in front of him. There were missing women who bore some resemblance to the dead woman, but the similarities weren't enough.

A courier arrived with the photographs from Beier's forensics department. Winter studied the marking painted on the bark. He tried to associate movements with the images. Closing his eyes, he thought about messages: a whole collection of them on file. Sometimes somebody wants to tell us something. Or just mislead us.

Someone knocked, and Winter said come in, and a young detective stepped through the door with a report in hand.

"What is it?" Winter asked.

"I've spoken to the municipal authority and that mark—"

"Thanks." Winter stood up. He recognized the boy but couldn't remember his name, only that he'd joined the unit a month or two ago. This must be his first murder investigation, Winter thought.

The detective held out the report.

"Tell me yourself instead. Have a seat."

The boy sat down in front of the desk and tried to look unperturbed. His forehead was all sweaty and he knew it. The blazer he sported was thin and looked cool but was insane to wear in this weather.

Winter wondered what the boy thought about his vacation-wear cut-offs and T-shirt, his customary dress code having so obviously rubbed off on even the youngest member of the unit. "Can you think in that blazer?" he asked.

"What?"

"Take off your jacket and untuck your shirt. You look hot."

The detective smiled as you might to a joke you didn't understand. He crossed his legs.

"I mean it," Winter said. "One of the perks of working as a detective is that you can dress however you want."

The boy looked like he had decided to be a little tough after all. "That all depends on the assignment, doesn't it? On the investigation?"

"Sometimes."

"Sometimes you've got to blend in."

"Then you're doing a good job of that now."

The boy smiled and took off his jacket. "It's damn hot out there."

"So, what do the authorities and agencies say?"

"They haven't been there—at the dump site. Nobody's marked any trees lately. The land belongs to the municipality."

"What do they mean by that?"

"By what?"

"*Lately.* When were they last there?" Winter bent down and lifted the two sheets of paper his rookie detective had laid on the desk. "What's your name again?"

"Uh, Börjesson. Erik Börjesson."

"Yes, that's right," Winter said, as he scanned the report for the answer he'd just sought. "A month ago. They haven't carried out any forest maintenance around Delsjö for a month."

"No," Börjesson said. "No work like that."

"Have you thought about what it might be, then?"

Winter noticed the boy was surprised by the question.

"Who might have put it there?"

"Yes."

"Fishermen? The fishing club?"

"Have you had a chance to check it out?"

"No, not yet."

"Any other ideas?"

"You mean something that could provide a natural explanation?"

"Something that isn't associated with the murder."

"Kids?"

"Is there anything to suggest that?"

"I, I don't know, actually."

"It could be worth checking out."

"Could have been a couple of lovebirds."

"Uh-huh."

"People who carve their names in the bark and all that," Börjesson said.

"The area is popular among people in search of intimate seclusion," Winter said.

"It could be that kind of sign," Börjesson said.

"Then what would it mean?" He slid a photo over to Börjesson. He looks proud to be here, Winter thought. He's most actively involved in the investigation when brainstorming with the boss. I should do this more often. "What does this inscription or marking, or whatever it is, mean?"

"Aren't they working on that in forensics?"

"I want to know what you think," Winter said. He heard a helicopter whirring outside, caught its shadow as it lifted from the helipad to the west of them and flew past his window. The afternoon would wear on toward evening. The lines for tonight's party would grow longer.

Mounted police would herd people into the pens at Lilla Bommen and Kungstorget. There the people would scream in each others' faces until they fell down dead drunk. The police would dismount and bring in the dog buses to haul piles of unconscious bodies to soiled, empty rooms that lay four double flights of stairs below the room where Winter was now sitting and thinking about his first few years as a law-enforcement officer.

He had sat on a horse and seen the rabble below him, a sea of panic-stricken movement. That was the young cynicism that was so danger-ous to pass along in the years that followed. To see people as a rabble.

Everyone's just scared as hell, Winter thought, and opened his eyes. Börjesson was looking at him. Winter stood and walked over to the window, but he couldn't see through the bright light from the sinking sun to the west.

He squinted and saw banners that cast reflections and shadows. The banners down there were being carried off to yet another confrontation between opposing groups of protesters.

There would be trouble again tonight. The party continued and so did the conflict.

"I think they're connected," he heard Börjesson say.

Winter turned around with blinded eyes. He blinked to get rid of the sunlight in his head.

"I can't say what this is supposed to represent," Börjesson continued, "but it seems like too much of a coincidence for this marking to appear there at the same time as the body."

"Good," Winter said. He could now see Börjesson's face again. The boy looked like a man, or an adult anyway. He'd taken an idea and was running with it, wasn't standing still. "I'm trying to find out if any satanic rituals have been held in that area."

"Satanists?"

"They like the forest. Life in the outdoors."

"It could be something like that."

"Look at this marking again," Winter said, and walked around the desk and stood next to Börjesson. "What do you think it looks like?"

The young homicide detective picked up the photo and held it at arm's length.

"It could be an *H*."

"Yes."

"Or some Chinese character."

"That's a good idea."

"Chinese characters mean something," Börjesson said. "I mean, beyond just a word. It's like a thing. An object."

"You studied Chinese?"

"In high school, for a couple of years. I did humanities at Schillerska High School."

"And became a policeman?"

"Is there anything wrong with that?"

"On the contrary," Winter said. "The force needs all the humanists it can get."

Börjesson gave a short laugh and looked back at the photograph.

"I can compare it to the characters in my books."

"How many are there?"

"Tens of thousands, but only a few thousand are in more common use."

Winter stared intently at the symbol. He had to go back there again and study the contours of the tree. It looked as if the person who painted it on the trunk had followed them. The marking looked like it was part of the tree.

He would have to look at the thing itself, but even now he felt a raw power emanating from the photo, a maniacal force from another world of evil. A message.

Winter shook his head gently. They started again, the connotations swirling in his mind.

To him the marking looked like an *H*. That was also a coincidence. In his mind he had named the woman after the cluster of houses close by: Helenevik.

For him she had been Helene hours before he had made any serious attempt to study the symbol on the tree. Helene. It felt as if the fabricated name would help him find out who she really was.

She was dead and the dead have no friends, but he wanted to be her friend right up until she got her name back.

12

EVERYTHING IN WINTER'S OFFICE WAS BLACK AND WHITE, WITH no shades of gray. The Post-its on the wall opposite his desk were empty rectangles.

Lingering there alone in the silence, he was suddenly very tired—a sensation that seemed to spring from the stillness in the room. He closed his eyes, and his thoughts became vague. He saw a child's face before him and opened his eyes again. He closed his eyes and looked at the face. The hair had no color, and the girl's eyes were looking straight at him. It was a girl.

A reflexive jolt roused him just as he was about to tip over in his chair. Must have fallen asleep, he thought.

He no longer saw the girl's face, but he didn't forget her.

The phone rang.

"So you're back at work." It was his sister.

"Since this morning. Pretty early," Winter said. "I was actually back a bit before that but not for real until now."

"What's happened?"

"'Sounds like murder!'"

"What?"

"Somebo— There's been a murder. It's true. But I was quoting a song by a band I've been listening to, to try to find myself again."

"Coltrane, of course?"

"The Clash. A British rock band. Macdonald—you know, the British inspector I worked with last spring—he sent me a few CDs."

"But you've never listened to rock in your whole life."

"That's why."

"What?"

"It's like—I don't know. I need something else."

"And now you've got a fresh murder on your hands."

"Yes."

"So the assault case, or whatever the expression is, you guys have solved that? Or put it aside?"

"The assault case?"

"Your colleague, Agneta, with the foreign last name."

"Aneta."

"That's the one. Well, apparently she was beaten up, and you know who called me just now?"

Winter saw a swimming pool, a naked man, sun glittering in the water, and he could almost smell the stench of tanning oil again.

"I think so."

"How could you be so stupid as to drive over to that scumbag's house and threaten to beat the crap out of him?"

"Is that what he said?"

"He said that you came over to his house and tried to strangle him."

"I needed information."

"Not the right way to get it, Erik."

Winter didn't answer.

"I haven't heard from Benny in years," Lotta said. "And I could almost say the same about you."

"I'm sorry."

"Sometimes I wonder when it was you stopped being my brother. No, that sounds pathetic. And crabby. I just mean that I need to speak to you sometimes."

"I'm trying." Winter knew that his sister was right. When her life hit the skids, he didn't have a thought for anything other that his own career. Or whatever it is I consider my work to be, he thought. He had been immature. She's right, he thought again.

"But we were speaking about Benny Vennerhag," she said. "He called and complained and asked me to keep you away from him."

"I'll talk to him."

"Why?"

"You know why."

"Can't the police manage without their peculiar contacts on the other side? Or haven't you caught the ones who hurt your colleague?"

"We've caught them. But that bastard shouldn't be calling you."

"Well, at least somebody's calling me."

"Now you're exaggerating, Lotta."

"Am I?"

"I promise to do better. Åke isn't causing any more trouble, is he?"

His sister had gotten divorced from Åke Deventer, and it had been an ordeal filled with bitterness. Now she lived alone with her two kids in the house where they had grown up.

"He stays away, and that means he isn't causing any trouble," she said. "But I had pretty much forgotten the great mistake of my youth, Benny Vennerhag, until I heard his voice yesterday."

"You hadn't even turned twenty-five, I think."

"My God. You're supposed to be considered an adult at that age."

"He must have been rattled."

"What?"

"Benny. I must have scared him."

"You did try to kill him, after all."

Winter said nothing.

"Did it feel good?" she asked.

"What?"

"Trying to murder somebody? Was it a good feeling?"

The room had grown darker. Winter thought about his hands around Benny Vennerhag's jaw. He no longer remembered what it had felt like. They hadn't been his hands.

"Are you there?" she asked.

"I'm here."

"How are you doing, really?"

"I'm not sure. A woman who's no more than thirty years old is dead, and we don't know who she is. That makes me more depressed than I ought to be, at least this early on."

"Why don't you come over here for a bit? It's been months."

Yeah, why not. Everything would still be there when he came back. His anonymous gloomy office at the police station was in that sense bigger than life itself. It was here before he showed up and it would remain after he was gone. "Should I bring something along?"

"No. But you are coming, then?"

"Are you alone?"

"Bim and Kristina are out but only for the moment. They really want to see you, Erik."

Winter thought about his nieces. He was an awful uncle. Awful.

"It's true," his sister said. "They haven't forgotten you."

He walked down the empty corridors of the homicide department. Someone had forgotten to switch off the lights in the situation room. He stood in front of the board and considered his own vague lines and arrows, circles and Xs. He wrote "Helene" next to the circle that marked the spot where the body was found. He wrote "transport" in the empty field to the right of the map and noted the arrival and departure times for the car he had seen on the video. Beier's men were studying the footage now. "We're short on time," Winter had told them.

He thought once again of the lake, the water. How many people owned boats on Delsjö? Had anyone's boat been stolen, even for a few hours? Maybe the fishing club knew.

The possibilities were infinite, the disappointments even more numerous. He thought about the child again. She was like something out of a dream or some kind of a message from a distant and frightening land that he had no choice but to visit. We have to find out your name, Helene.

The parking lot was deserted, and he felt dizzy when he emerged from the police station, like a split-second gap in the middle of his thoughts. As if he wasn't there.

A radio car pulled in, and the man behind the wheel gave him a quick nod. Winter raised his hand and continued over to his Mercedes. The Shell station beyond was an amusement park, a loud glare of neon that gave the surroundings a cheerful tinge. Winter caught a whiff of fried sausages and overheated late summer.

On the other side of the gas station, the traffic was backed up by the cars outside Ullevi Stadium—the whole city was probably gridlocked. Staring stupidly at the keys in his hand, Winter turned back to the front entrance and continued on to the bicycle stand, where he always had a bike parked, in reserve, for situations just like this.

He pedaled past the central train station and on down to the river. Heading west, he had to weave his way through throngs of people milling about the beer tents at Lilla Bommen.

He leaned his bike against the iron fence and walked the short path up to the front steps. It had been months since he was last here, and he'd wondered why that was as he biked through the quiet streets of Hagen, taking in the smell of fresh-cut grass. There were no lights on at the house next door, on the left. Six months earlier he'd investigated the murder of a nineteen-year-old boy who'd grown up there.

The front door of his sister's house stood ajar. He rang the doorbell.

"Go round the back," he heard from inside. He guessed that she was sitting out on the terrace.

He made his way back down the steps and through the grass to the rear of the house. She stood and gave him a hug. He could smell twilight and wine. Her hair was shorter than he remembered and maybe a little darker, and she felt thin around her arms and chest. He knew that she was going to be turning forty in two months, on October 18. He wasn't sure whether she'd be having a party when the big day came around.

"Would you like a glass of wine? Cold. White."

"I'd love one. And some water."

"I didn't hear the car."

"That's because I biked."

"Uh-huh."

"The city is completely clogged."

"The party?"

"Yes. Have you been down?"

"Have you?"

"Not for the purposes of pleasure," Winter said, and smiled.

His sister poured him a glass of wine and left him to fetch some water and two tumblers.

"I bumped into Angela last week," she said once she had returned and sat down next to him. "In a corridor, after the rounds. She was up from radiology."

"Oh yeah?"

"I hadn't seen her in ages. It's as if she's taking after you. Some kind of silence or something. Her not saying anything, I mean."

"About what?"

"About you and her, for example."

Winter waited for her to continue. His sister worked as a staff doctor at Sahlgrenska, and Angela had recently transferred there from a position at Mölndal Hospital.

"The two most important women in my life are doctors," Winter said. "I wonder what that means."

"It means that you're a basket case," his sister said. "But then you're forgetting our mother."

"Oh right."

"When did you last speak to her?"

"The last time she called. Two and a half weeks ago maybe. How about you?"

"Yesterday."

"How is she?"

"I think she's cut back to two martinis before lunch," she said, and they laughed together. "No, seriously. I think Dad's been on her case about it."

"Dad? You gotta be kidding."

"When did you last speak to him, Erik?"

Winter emptied his glass. He saw his hand tremble slightly, and he saw that she caught it.

"When they moved—escaped to Spain."

"I know."

"Now you've had it confirmed a second time."

"Two years. That's a long time."

"He had a choice. He could have done something with his money, for others. And by that I don't mean me or us. It's his money. I have my own."

"Isn't it a heavy burden to always sit in judgment?"

"I'm not a judge. I'm a policeman."

"You know what I mean."

"It was his choice."

"Mom went with him."

"She's not responsible for her actions."

"Oh, for Christ's sake," his sister said, straightening up in her chair.

He reached for the bottle of wine as if he couldn't hear. "Would you like another glass?"

She held hers out, almost reluctantly.

"They have a choice. They could actually return home and face the music."

"And what would that change?"

"It's not about—look, do we have to talk about this now?" Winter said. "Can't we just sit here for a while and drink some wine?"

13

THE NIGHT SANK SLOWLY INTO STILLNESS, UNTIL WINTER couldn't read what was written on the wine label. He drank and the wine tasted of metal and earth. He drank again and when he moved his arm he felt as if he was about to lose his balance.

"How long have you been on your feet today anyway?" his sister asked.

"Well, since four this morning."

"My God."

"Those crucial first hours."

"And now they're over," she said. "Those crucial first hours."

"Just about."

"But the hunt continues."

"If you can call it a hunt."

"Want to talk about it?"

He reached for the glass again but then pulled his arm back, sensing that he wouldn't be able to get another word out if he took another sip of wine. Instead he stood and walked the few steps to the terrace railing and leaned against it. Over by the hedge a playhouse was peeking out from behind a maple tree. Winter had spent endless nights of adventure in there when he was nine and ten, maybe eleven.

Despite a sudden urge to go over there, he stayed where he was. The fatigue was causing him to think of his childhood and its loss. You can have an awareness of a previous life but no more than that, he thought. Soon everything will be plowed into the present.

He turned to his sister. She had pulled a shawl over her shoulders, and it gave her a foreign appearance. A wind from the garden swept through the coarse hairs of his bare legs, but he didn't feel cold.

"There's a child," he said. "This woman who's been murdered, whose name we don't know yet—she's had a child, and that child must be out there somewhere."

"Does that worry you?"

"Wouldn't it you?"

"Sure."

"It bothers me. I've had trouble concentrating because I've been thinking about the fact that Helene has had a child."

"I thought you just said you didn't know her name?"

"What?"

"The murdered woman hasn't been identified. But you just called her Helene."

"I did? I better be careful. I've given her that name in order to—to get closer to her. When I'm thinking."

"Why that particular name?"

"She was found at Delsjö Lake, near Helenevik."

"Helenevik? I've never heard of it."

"A handful of nice-looking houses across the highway, looking out over Lake Rådasjön."

"Helene?"

"Yes. I think of her as Helene. And I think about her child."

He saw Lotta give a shiver, as if more from his words than from the approaching night. "Then you have to find out who she is quickly," she said.

"Of course, but I feel despondent. It's like another descent into hell. Maybe it's just tonight. Maybe we'll have to wait till her landlord calls in and says she's late with the rent."

"That could take a long time."

"Four months," he said and sat down again.

"Have you had a chance to speak to a colleague about your despondency?" his sister asked.

"Of course not."

"Isn't that a problem for you? I mean, not just now, but always?"

"How do you mean?"

"There was a reason why you came here tonight, beyond just coming to see your dear sister. You wanted to express that doubt to somebody else, get it out of your system so you can keep on working."

"Like a confession, you mean?"

"To you it probably is a confession. Whenever you feel doubt it's as if you've committed a sin."

"Bah!"

"That's how it's always been with you."

"I don't know how I should respond to that."

"You should respond by saying that you want to have a normal life too, and that, in turn, will lead to you having someone to talk to about your abnormal life."

"Abnormal?"

"You can't just live one kind of life, twenty-four hours a day."

"I don't. And when I do, it's because I have to." He got up and reeled for a moment. He looked at his watch. He had been on his feet for eighteen hours straight. The crucial first hours. He started to walk.

"Where are you going, Erik?"

"I'm going down to the playhouse. Is the air mattress still in there?"

The owner of the dog kennel over on Old Boråsvägen was dead certain that a Ford Escort CLX hatchback had backed up and turned off in the intersection. It was a '92 or a '93—maybe a '94—probably pearl white. Was he certain? Oh yeah, it had looked white in the glow of the lamp all right, you couldn't know for sure, but one thing was certain, they produced at least a million of that model in pearl white, the man said. "The question is whether it even came in any other color."

"But it couldn't have been an older model anyway?" Fredrik Halders asked.

"Maybe a '91 but no earlier than that. They redesigned the Escort in '91, but maybe you already know that. They made them rounder and more bulbous. And higher. It was one of those."

"But it was a CLX?"

"What?"

"You said it was a CLX. Why not an RS?"

The man looked at Halders as if he'd finally said something intelligent. "So you know something about cars?"

Halders nodded.

"Then you also know that the RS has a spoiler on the trunk. This car didn't have no spoiler on the trunk."

"Could you make out the plate number at all?"

"I didn't have a notepad with me, but it began with the letters *HE*."

"*HE*? No numbers?"

"It was hard to see, and letters reflect the light better than numbers."

"Really?" A complete nutcase, but good eyes and good at cars, Halders thought to himself. He nodded again and noted it down on his pad. "Anything else?"

"You mean, did I see anything else?"

"Yeah. See or hear anything."

"Which do you want me to say first?"

"Did you see anything other than just the car?"

"No driver anyway. The light was angled so that it was all blacked out on the driver's side."

"No passengers?"

"Not that I could see."

"Where did the car come from?"

"I don't know. But it hightailed it off toward town after it had been in there and turned around."

Halders scribbled in his pad again.

"So it must have come from the other direction," the man said. "From the direction of the lake or Helenevik, right?" Halders looked up from his notepad.

"Well, it's possible the driver just drove the wrong way, or changed his mind, or just decided to go for a drive out to that intersection and then turn around and drive home again," he said.

Fucking moron, Halders thought.

"Aha," the man said. "Now I understand how you police work." He gestured at his forehead with his index finger. "I would never have thought of that myself, know what I mean?"

"Did you hear anything?"

"Other than the sound of the car?"

"Yes. Before, during, or after."

"Which do you want me to say first?"

Halders sighed audibly. "It's getting late, and we're both tired," he said. "I'm not tired."

"So you saw nothing else unusual yesterday evening or last night?"

"That would've been difficult anyway, know what I mean?"

"I don't understand."

They were on the front steps of the man's house and Halders could see the wire fence of the dog pen glinting beyond the corner of the cabin, illuminated by a lantern that hung on the wall. The kennel owner himself was short and sort of lumpy, and he'd immediately assumed a defensive posture toward the tall Halders, as if preparing to repel an attack.

"I didn't understand that last bit," Halders repeated.

"It would've been difficult to notice anything seeing as there was so much coming and going from your guys' cabin the whole night, know what I mean?"

The man's habit of ending all his statements in that way was starting to piss the hell out of Halders.

"You mean the function that took place yesterday at the police department's recreation lodge."

"Or the *beer* lodge, know what I mean?"

"Were you disturbed by it in some way?"

"Can't say I was. But there was a lot of traffic."

"Cars, you mean?"

"Well, that's traffic, know what I mean?"

"No pedestrian traffic?"

"Not that I saw. But there have been festivities up at your beer lodge during which the guests have ended up scattered all over my land in the small hours of the morning. Once there was this plainclothes officer and a woman with barely a stitch on who decided to bed down for the night in the moss behind the foxhounds over yonder." He jerked his head toward the corner of the cabin.

That might well have been my fortieth birthday bash, Halders thought to himself. "But nobody was running around in the night last night?"

"Not that I heard. But you ought to speak to your buddies."

"We're in the process of doing that."

"That's a good idea, know what I mean?"

"But you're sure about the car?" Halders was amazed at his own patience.

"I already told you, know what I mean? We've gone into all sorts of detail here, know what I mean?"

"Well, thanks for all the information. If anything else comes to mind, anything at all, then do get in touch, know what I mean? Even if it's something that happened earlier, someone who passed by more than once. Anything. You know what I mean?"

He parked the car outside the police station and walked along the stream. Outside the city hall a couple was drinking something out of transparent plastic cups. That's not raspberry juice, Halders thought to himself, seized by an urge to grab the cups out of their hands and arrest them—kick up a real stink over some petty shit. Society ought to send a clear message: zero tolerance. Every little goddamn crime should be treated as a crime. Anyone riding a bike without a light should lose their license. Anyone caught drinking in public should be sent to jail. That's what they did in New York. The city would calm down. The country would calm down.

Everything and everyone would calm down, except me, thought

Halders. The more I think about calm, the angrier I get. How far would I go if society gave me the go-ahead for my brand of zero tolerance?

He waited together with a thousand others to cross over Götaleden and suddenly found himself crowded together with ten thousand others on the Packhuskajen quay. The fireworks began. Halders's head was popping. He bought a mug of beer and sat at the very end of a long table and scowled at a man opposite him. The man moved after a few minutes.

Halders raised his gaze to the sky and saw the fireworks explode. The light reflected in people's faces. Their foreheads looked like they were tattooed and their cheeks and chins were stamped with symbols that he couldn't decipher. He emptied his mug. He thought of Aneta in her white bed at the hospital. The bad thoughts brewed.

Winter had crawled into the playhouse and lain down on the air mattress. It was only partially inflated, and he felt the grain of the floorboards in the small of his back. Maybe there was old air inside the mattress, some that had remained in the hard corners. Maybe he was lying on air from his childhood.

He reached out his arms and felt the walls on both sides of him. He fell asleep.

WINTER BIKED HOME AT DAWN. HE HAD MADE AN ATTEMPT AT around midnight, against his better judgment.

"Go lie down in the guest room," his sister said, and that's what he'd done.

Now the streets were being swept clean after the night, water flowed over the asphalt, and he nearly fell off his bike while illegally cutting across Linnéplatsen.

In the apartment he kicked off his sandals and bent down for the newspaper. The *Göteborgs-Posten* had covered the murder with restraint, without a lot of speculation.

Helene was without a name, a cold body in cold storage in a white zippered bag. It was Friday morning, twenty-four hours after he had seen her face for the first time. He tried to remember her features, but they melded together with other lifeless faces he'd seen.

The sun climbed onto the roofs of the buildings on the other side of Vasaplatsen. Winter adjusted the blinds and took out beans and a mill and ground the African coffee, its aroma wafting in his face, invigorating him even before it was brewed.

He put butter and cheese on two French rolls that he had bought at the local bakery on the ground floor of the building. The butter was cold in his mouth. He ate the cheese by itself, two thick slices. Streetcars rattled past below, and a seagull took off from the balcony with a shriek and darted awkwardly past the kitchen window. Winter drank his coffee and heard the flap of its wings in the early morning stillness.

The meeting was a short one. Winter took off his jacket and hung it on the back of the chair, rolled up his sleeves, and brushed away something from his pant leg.

Cerruti, Sara Helander thought. Cool. Quality.

"So we still don't know who she is," Winter said.

"We're going through that community today—what's the name?" Fredrik Halders said.

"Helenevik," Bertil Ringmar answered.

"There'll be seven of you," Winter said.

"Wow."

"That's as many as we could scrape together."

"I meant that's a lot," Halders said. "I'm impressed."

Winter looked at him but said nothing. Fredrik was starting to have increasingly obvious problems with his attitude. Is that how it is to grow old? To step across the magical crest at forty and slowly slide downhill?

"How many of us are going to be working with our fellow officers?" Bergenhem asked.

"What do you mean?" Carlberg said.

"The little party the guys over at investigations had," Helander said.

"Can't they investigate that themselves?" Halders asked.

"What the hell do you mean by that?" Janne Möllerström asked.

"Investigation . . . investigations department."

"Cool it, Fredrik," Winter said.

"You and Börjesson handle the party animals," Ringmar said to Bergenhem.

"Some of them are doubtless a little tired," Bergenhem said.

"They're not the only ones," Helander added.

Everyone in the room—all twenty-four of them—suddenly thought of the upcoming weekend. Many of them would have planned the season's big crayfish party for later that evening or Saturday night. Would they have the energy to have a good time? Would they even make it home? How much overtime was the brass ready to give them?

"Tired? Who's tired?" Winter said, and yawned and waved auf Wiedersehen to the group. There was a tie-up at the door as everyone tried to get out at the same time.

Winter took the stairs up to forensics and went in through the double doors that protected the department from unwanted visitors.

He was let through. Immediately to the right was the laboratory section—the evidence lab with two employees, a firearms examiner, and a chemist to analyze narcotics and clothing and do the chemical processing of fingerprints.

A few men were sitting in the new coffee room. The National Center for Forensic Science had come through with a substantial sum of money for the department just minutes before the premises were to be deemed inadequate. Beier was able to refurbish and expand the single lab into a rough lab, where materials were brought in; a room for clothing and fiber analysis; a chemistry and toxicology lab; the trace evidence lab that Winter had just walked past; a fingerprint lab; and an isolation room, since they didn't want to put the clothes from the victim and suspect in the same room.

Impressive, Winter thought. He hadn't been here for a while. Beier came striding down the corridor. "Want some coffee?"

"You bet."

They walked back down the corridor, and Beier shut the door behind them.

"What should we start with?" he asked.

"The car."

"That's some blurry footage."

"But it is a Ford?"

"We think so."

"Escort CLX?"

"Maybe. Probably."

"Could you see anything more of the driver?"

"Jensen is sitting with it now, trying to peer through the blur, but he's not very optimistic, nor am I."

"Can you tell whether it's a man?"

Beier threw out his arms. "You can't always tell even when the pictures are sharp."

Winter drummed his fingers on the desktop. "And one more big question: the plate number."

"We may have found something there," Beier said. "Three letters. HEL or HEI."

"How sure is that?"

Beier threw out his arms again. "We'll keep at it," he said. "But in the meantime you can get to work on these, if you've got the manpower." He poured out the coffee, and Winter drank without registering its taste.

"We know that this car may have been in the vicinity of the dump site when the body was left there," Winter said.

"That's right," Beier said.

"That's something to go on."

"All you have to do is track down all the Ford Escorts in the city. Or the country."

"All the CLXs."

"You don't know that."

"No, but that's where I'm gonna start. That case I worked on last spring, in London—my colleague there told me they were looking for a car and all they had to go on was the color and maybe the make. This is better."

"Maybe."

"Of course it's better, Göran. I can really feel my optimism growing just sitting next to you."

"Then maybe I'd better rein it in."

"What do you mean?"

"I don't have anything new on that strange marking on the tree. Or whatever you wanna call it."

"This kid in my department suggested that it might be a Chinese character."

"Well, that would make things easier."

"Exactly."

"Then there are just a billion Chinese to bring in for questioning."

"You've forgotten all the Westerners who know Chinese," Winter said.

"I suggest you start there," Beier said.

They sat in silence for a short while, sipped their coffee, listened to the noisy ventilation system. Winter almost felt cold in the chilled air. We're probably the only two police officers in the whole building wearing ties today, Winter thought, noting that Beier's leaned toward burgundy. He loosened his own. Beier didn't comment on it.

"I'm sure it's connected to the murder," Winter said.

"Why?"

"It's just a hunch, but it's a strong one."

"Positive thinking, you mean."

"It's too much of a coincidence that someone would paint on the tree at virtually the exact same time."

"Maybe she took part in a ritual."

"No."

"You're sure?"

"That little inlet may have been a haunt for satanists and other fanatics, or maybe even still is, but she didn't take part in that kind of thing."

"Maybe she didn't have a choice."

"It would have been noticed. Someone would have heard something."

"Like our colleagues from the investigations department."

"That department has some of the most keen-eyed officers on the force."

"Regardless of the state they're in?"

"A police officer is always prepared."

"For what?"

"For the worst," Winter said, and they both became serious. "It's often been shown that the choice of location is not random. A murderer selects his spot."

"I agree with you. I think."

"We have to ask ourselves why she was put there. Why she was lying at Delsjö Lake. Then, why at that particular end of the lake—"

"Proximity to the road," Beier interjected.

"Maybe. Then we have to ask ourselves why she was lying exactly in that spot. Not five yards this way or that."

"You really go in for the mise-en-scène."

"The mise-en-scène involves movement; it's the opposite of standing still."

"That was beautifully put," Beier said.

Halders preferred to wander the path along the shoreline on his own. The houses slept soundly and impassively atop the hillside.

The area reminded him that he was a poor homicide detective who would never be anything else. He would never make inspector, but he didn't know whether or not he was bitter about it.

If he was in the right place at the right time, his fortune would be waiting for him there. They would shake hands and return to headquarters, and the police chief would invite him up to his office and at the same time call out to Winter to say, "Now you can just hand everything over to inspector Halders here . . ."

He began the door-to-door inquiries at one of the houses close to a school he didn't know the name of. He rang the doorbell and heard the chime echo through the cavernous interior. There was an awning above the door that shaded him and caused the sweat on his forehead to roll more slowly down his face and linger on his eyelids. When the door was opened by a woman in a robe, he blinked and bowed his head. She was dark haired, or it may have been just the intense sunlight that was streaming in from the open doors behind her.

"I'm sorry to bother you. I'm from the police," Halders said, and held out his police ID. "Homicide department."

He fumbled with his wallet.

"Yes?"

"We're conducting an in—"

"Is it the murder on the other side of Boråsleden? I just read about it.

We were talking about it a moment ago," the woman said, and a bare-chested man in swimming trunks suddenly appeared behind her.

"It's just routine. We have to ask everyone in the vicinity if they've seen or heard anything within the last twenty-four hours."

"When should we be counting from?" the man asked. "My name is Petersén, by the way." He held out his hand. Halders shook it.

"Same here," the woman said. "Denise." She smiled and held out her hand, and Halders squeezed it gently.

"Halders," Halders said.

"Come in, by the way," the man said. He followed the couple to an outdoor patio that was paved with what might have been mosaic tiles.

"Would you like a refreshment?" the man asked, and Halders answered with a yes.

"A drink? Gin and tonic?"

"I'm afraid—"

"A beer?"

"That would do nicely."

The man walked back inside the house, and the woman sank into a folding chair that looked complicated. She nudged a pair of sunglasses to the tip of her nose and seemed to look at Halders. He looked back. She dangled one sandal on her foot. The sandal was red, like the fire in the sun.

"I'm happy to be of service in the meantime," she said.

Don't let your imagination run away with you now, Halders thought. Try to keep a little blood up in your head.

The man returned with a tray and three bottles of beer.

15

WINTER HAD FORGOTTEN ABOUT BENNY VENNERHAG, FOR THE moment, when he called.

"I heard you solved it—the attack on your colleague."

"Where'd you hear that?"

"You haven't become naive, now, have you, Inspector?"

Winter thought of his hands around Vennerhag's jaw.

"I'm still in pain," Vennerhag said.

"What?"

"The brutality of the police force. What you did to me the other day? I could—"

"I may need your help again soon," Winter said mellifluously.

"I don't like that tone in your voice," Vennerhag said. "And in that case it'll have to be over the phone." He waited but Winter said nothing more. "What do you need help with?"

"I don't know yet, but I might be in touch soon."

"What if I leave town?"

"Don't."

"I'm not allowed to leave town?"

"When did you last leave town, Benny?"

"That's beside the point, Inspector."

"You haven't been outside the city limits in four years, Benny."

"How do you know that?"

"You haven't become naive, now, have you, Master Thief?"

Vennerhag snickered. "Okay, okay. I know what it is anyway. I read the papers. But I don't see how I can be of any help to you when I don't know anything about it. Who is she, by the way?"

"Who?"

"The dead woman, for Christ's sake. The body. Who is she?"

"We don't know."

"Come on, Winter. There's no such thing as an unknown body any-more."

"Maybe not in your world."

"What do you mean by that?"

Winter was tired of Vennerhag's voice. He wanted to end the con-versation.

"I honestly don't know who she is," he said. "I may end up needing your help. And you will help me then, won't you, Benny?"

"Only if you're nice."

"The police are always nice."

Vennerhag's laugh cut through the phone line again. "And every-body else is mean. How's Lotta doing, by the way?"

"She told me that you called and complained."

"I didn't complain. And it was for your own good. What you did was out of order. It may be hot as hell, but you keep your emotions in check."

"Don't call her anymore. Stay away from her."

"How far away? You said I wasn't supposed to leave town, re-member?"

"I'll be in touch, Benny," Winter said, and hung up the receiver. His hand was sticky.

He stood and pulled off his blazer and hung it over the back of the chair, then rolled up the sleeves of his white shirt, missing his summer outfit of T-shirt and cutoffs. Donning an expensive suit of armor for work sent out signals. What signals were those?

"They're signals of weakness," his sister had said the night before. "Anyone who has to take cover behind an Armani or Boss suit isn't really comfortable in his own skin."

"Baldessarini," he had said. "Cerutti. Not Armani or Boss—that's what you wear when you're working on your car. Could just be that I like to be well dressed," he had said. "That there's nothing more to it."

"There is more to it," she had said.

And he had told her: About the fear that took hold of him when he came close to evil's darkest core, about how that fear had intensified his own fragility like a bubble expanding with air. The knowledge that he couldn't do anything else with his life, didn't want to do anything else, became a burden when he knew what that involved. When nighttime came around he couldn't set aside the day, just take it off and hang it up like one of his jackets and pull on a comfy tracksuit and think about something else. That goddamn Cerutti suit stayed with him all the way into bed.

But there was also something else there. His beautiful clothes were at the same time a form of protection against the apprehension that constantly threatened to force its way into his body.

"That could be one interpretation," she had said. The problem was that his exterior seldom helped with his interior. "Think about that when you're ironing your armored shirts," she had said in the waning night that was moving toward morning.

The surface of the water was a sparkling layer of silver, with glints that looked as if they had been strewn by hand across the lake. It stung Winter's eyes when he looked to the north.

He walked along the wooded path to the edge of the bog. Crickets were chirping all around him: the sound of intense prolonged heat. A faint breeze brought with it a damp smell from the nearly dried-out bog holes within the dark terrain. Winter saw no one moving around in there, but he knew there were police officers combing the lakeside for clues and people who lived along the water's edge.

It was nearly twelve o'clock. Few cars could be heard from the highway above and beyond him. From where he stood, beneath the trees, he could count up to twenty different shades of green. Even the rays of sunlight shone green. The very sky to the east was green through the leaves and between the branches. Only the symbol painted onto the bark, eight inches from his nose, was red. Winter took it for just that, a symbol. A symbol for what?

Winter heard a noise behind him and turned around. The outline of a man was moving in his direction. When the silhouette stepped out of the sunlight, Winter saw that it was Halders.

"So you've got the time to stand around here, huh, boss?" Halders was wearing short sleeves, his shirt hanging outside his trousers, and his face was partly in the shade, but Winter could see the sweat glinting on the high forehead that continued upward into Halders's close-cropped skull. "This is a pleasant spot, sort of still."

"Did you come from Helenevik? I didn't hear a car."

"It's standing right there," Halders said, and turned around and pointed behind him as if he wanted to prove that he hadn't trekked three miles in the intense heat. "I guess I had the same feeling you did. That I wanted a look at the place, seeing as I was in the area anyway."

Winter didn't answer. He turned his gaze to the tree. Halders came closer.

"So this is that damn marking. Couldn't some kids have daubed it up there?"

"Sure. We just need to get that confirmed."

"And it's definitely paint?"

"Yes."

"There's no way it could be blood?"

"No."

"But it may have been intended to be blood," Halders said. "I mean, to look like it was blood and that we should think of it as blood."

"That's possible," Winter said. "How were the folks in Helenevik?"

"Nice and friendly."

"Oh yeah?"

"A couple in this huge house over there tried to invite me in for drinks."

"That was nice, but they didn't succeed?"

"I told them I was on duty."

"You might have missed an opportunity to find out something really important."

"About what? You want me to go back?"

Winter shrugged his shoulders and smiled.

"There was something else. But it's probably my imagination. Might have gotten hold of the wrong end of the stick, so to speak," Halders said.

"Yeah?"

"Nothing. Otherwise, going door-to-door around here has produced about as little as you might expect. No one's seen or heard anything."

"The kennel guy heard and saw something," Winter said.

"He's a nutcase."

"They're sometimes the ones that prove the most helpful."

They both heard the sound of an outboard from the lake. A plastic boat with a ten-horsepower motor came from the north and steered in toward the inlet fifty yards from where they were standing. The motor cut out and the boat glided into shore, outside the cordon.

They could see two boys climb out, and Halders headed over to them along the path. He returned five minutes later with the two of them, who looked to be in their lower teens. They were carrying at least two fishing poles each, as if they refused to leave anything behind in the boat. Winter had heard Halders ask them why they'd left their boat there. They had said that it was their spot. Their usual spot.

"There wasn't a boat there early yesterday morning," Winter said.

"No, it was gone," one of the boys said and both looked down at the ground.

"What did you just say?" Halders said, and the boys seemed to tremble inside their life vests.

"When was the boat missing?" asked Winter and discreetly gestured to Halders to back off.

"This morning," said the one that was doing the talking.

"You came here this morning and noticed that the boat was missing?"

"Yes."

"When was that?"

"Eigh—quarter past eight, around there."

Winter eyed his watch. That was exactly four hours ago.

"What did you do then?" Halders asked.

The boys looked at each other.

"We went looking for the boat, of course."

"With all your gear?"

"What?"

"All your goddamn fishing gear," Halders said. "Did you lug all that stuff around with you when you went out looking for your boat?"

"We left it here," the talkative one said softly.

"Where did you find the boat?" Winter asked.

"On the other side," the boy said, and gestured toward the water through the branches.

"So it was just lying there?" Halders said. "With the motor and everything."

"No. We always take the motor with us."

"How about the oars? Do you take those with you too?"

One of the boys, the one who hadn't yet spoken, started to giggle nervously and fell silent after two seconds.

"So someone could have rowed the boat?"

"Yes."

"Didn't you have a lock on it?"

"It's busted," said the boy who had giggled. He had regained his ability to speak.

"Busted," Halders repeated. "Does that happen often?"

"It hasn't happened to us before. But others," the boy said, and made a gesture that included all the other boat owners around the Big and Little Delsjö lakes.

"What did you do when you found the boat?" Winter asked.

"We rowed back here and put the motor on, and then we went out fishing."

"You didn't notice anything strange or out of place in the boat when you found it?" Halders asked.

"No. Like what?" the boy said, but Winter could see what he was thinking.

"Anything that didn't belong there," Halders said.

"Not that we could see."

"Nothing lying around, no leaves or anything?"

"We probably didn't check that carefully. But the boat's right over there," the boy said, and nodded toward the path and the boat beyond.

"I'm sure you understand that we have to borrow your boat for a while and examine it," Winter said, and thought of all the time that had passed.

"No problem," the boy said enthusiastically, as if he were on the verge a great adventure.

They walked back to the boat. The bottom of the plastic skiff was covered in four inches of water.

"Have you bailed out any water since you found it?" Halders asked.

"No."

"Good. Where are the fish, by the way?"

The boys looked at each other again and then at Halders.

"We threw them back 'cause we felt sorry for them this time."

"Good." Sports fishermen lie in a thousand different ways, Halders thought. Even the young ones are damn inventive. He bent forward and peered along the inside of the gunwale.

"What's that under the oarlock?" he said, and pointed. "Come closer so you can see. There. The left one, four inches above the water."

The boys looked, but neither of them said anything.

"It's not something you recognize?" Halders asked.

"It looks like some kind of sign," one of the boys said, acknowledging the little red spot of paint on the boat's dirty yellow interior. "Or something. But it wasn't there before."

16

THERE WERE NO WINDOWS DOWN THERE, AND SHE DIDN'T KNOW if it was morning or evening. The light from the lamp sort of stopped halfway up in the air and then a little bit fell on her. She could barely see her hand when she held it in front of her.

She wasn't cold anymore because she had been given two blankets and warm water that they had made sweet. After she drank the sugar water she must have fallen asleep, and when she woke up it was as if she didn't know if she had been asleep. It was so strange, but it was also good because she wasn't scared when she was sleeping. You couldn't be scared because you weren't there.

Now she was there again and she heard a noise from up on the roof. She would have liked to scream out "I want my mommy!" But she didn't dare. Maybe the man would come with more sugar water, and then she'd sleep again.

Nobody had hit her again. She didn't think about that at all. Now she thought about the summer and that it was warm under your feet when you walked on the street or in the sand. They had walked in the sand when they came over on the boat. When they had driven onto the boat it made such a terrible clanging sound, and some men waved to them to drive deeper into the boat's belly. Then she had walked in the sand—it wasn't long after—and Mommy had sat with her awhile, and then she had gone swimming, and Mommy had stood there at the edge of the water, and then Mommy had gone and bought something to drink from a man who was standing on the beach. It was a funny small bottle and the drink tasted like lemon.

It was ugly down here, she could tell. There were no tables or chairs, and she sat on a mattress that smelled bad. She had first tried to hold her nose up and turn away, but that had been hard, and now it didn't smell anymore, or only when she thought about it.

Now she crinkled the slip of paper a little inside her pant pocket. She didn't dare take it out and look at it but she had it, like a secret, and that was scary but it was good too.

Then she thought that her mommy was dead. She's dead and I'll never get to see her again. Mommy would never be away for this long without saying anything, or calling, or writing a note that the men could show her and read to her.

Her whole body gave a start when the door up above creaked open.

Now she saw the legs of the man as he came down the stairs. She kept her head down and only saw his legs even when he came up to her and the mattress.

"We're leaving."

She looked up but she couldn't see the man's face because the light was shining right on him. She tried to say something, but it came out like a squawk from a crow.

"Get up."

She pushed off the blankets and first rose to her knees and then stood, and one of her legs hurt because it had been underneath the other one and had fallen asleep.

Now she tried to say something again. "Are we going to Mommy?"

"You don't need to bring that with you," the man said, and took away the blanket that she had under her arm. "Let's go."

He pointed toward the stairs, and she started walking, and he followed behind her. She had forgotten how high the steps were, and she almost had to use her hands and feet to ascend them, like a mountain climber. Her eyes hurt from the sunlight that poured through the open door. She closed them and then looked again, and it became darker and easier to see because someone was standing in front of the light in the doorway.

17

STURE BIRGERSSON HAD BEEN DISCREET. HE'D STAYED IN THE
background, as usual, and directed his gaze upward, for vertical contact
with the powers above. But now the department commander was calling on his deputy.

Winter knew Sture had delayed his trip into the unknown: when
he took off on vacation he always disappeared somewhere, but nobody
knew where. Many wondered, but Birgersson himself never said a
word. Winter had a telephone number, but he would never even consider using it.

With the window open, the boss's smoke drifted outside and pol-
luted the area all the way to the Heden recreation grounds. His face was
carved out of stiff cardboard, spotted by the sun where the light came
in from the left. His desk was empty except for the ashtray. It's just as
fascinating every time I come here, Winter thought. Not a single shred
of paper. The computer is never on. The cabinet looks like it can't even
be opened anymore. Sture sits there smoking and thinking. It's gotten
him far.

"I've finished reading it now," Birgersson said. "There are a lot of
leads."

"You know how it is, Sture."

"I can only remember one previous case where we didn't know the
victim's identity within the first twenty-four hours."

Winter waited, pulled out his cigarillos, lit one, and took a first drag
while Birgersson looked like he was searching through memory files in
his brain. You can't fool me, Old Man, Winter thought. You know damn
well if there's been one case or more than that.

"Maybe you know better than I do?" Birgersson said, looking his
immediate subordinate in the eyes.

Winter smiled and leaned forward over the desk and tapped off the ash from his Corps. "There's only one case, as far as we can tell."

"In living memory, I mean," Birgersson said.

"If we're both thinking about that guy at Stenpiren, I hope that was a one-of-a-kind event," Winter said.

A man had fallen into the water and drowned, and when they tried to find out who he was, they discovered he hadn't been reported missing anywhere in the country. He'd been wearing a tracksuit, had no money in his pockets, no keys, no ID card, no ring with an inscription—nothing. They barely managed to get his fingerprints after all the time he'd spent in the water, but that didn't do them any good either. He was, though buried now, still unknown to the world.

"That one also took place during the Gothenburg Party," Birgersson said. "Reason enough alone to pull the plug on the damn thing, stop the madness."

"Some quite enjoy the party."

"Don't give me that, Erik. You detest the sight of big groups of people drinking beer out of plastic cups and trying to convince themselves they're having a good time. Or letting themselves be convinced they're giving a good time. And look what happened to our Aneta. The Gothenburg Party! How's she doing, by the way?"

"She's having a little difficulty chewing, I guess." Winter had tried to block out any thoughts of Aneta. But that was the wrong way to go about it. "I'm planning to pay her another visit soon as I can."

"Humph. I hope she comes back soon, for the sake of morale. Her own, that is. And I like her. She's not easily spooked, especially not by me, and that shows moxie."

"Yeah, you're pretty scary, Sture."

"What's all this about a mysterious symbol?" Birgersson was a boor about changing the subject.

"I don't know." Winter perched his cigarillo on the edge of the ashtray. "I really don't know. Earlier I guess I had pretty much set it aside, but then Fredrik and I were down by the lake, and, well, you read the report."

"That must have strengthened your belief in the importance of intuition when working on an investigation," Birgersson said. "That you were on the scene when the boys appeared."

"I literally was on the scene. I had a sudden impulse to head out there and it led me to the right spot."

"How do you explain, then, that Halders went there too? I don't think our good friend Fredrik can even spell *intuition*."

"It's not an easy word to spell. Have you ever tried it yourself?"

Birgersson smiled and waved it off. "So you were on the scene. But what good did it do you?"

"What do you mean?"

"The daub of paint in the boat doesn't prove anything."

"Of course not. But it's the same paint as on the tree."

"Maybe the boys did it themselves."

"Then they're good liars."

"More and more people are getting better at lying. That's what makes police work so variable, so fascinating. It keeps you on your toes at all times, don't you find? Everyone lies."

"The boys may have done it," Winter said. "Or more likely other boys, or anyone at all who wanted to leave a sign behind. Or someone who's just pulling our leg."

"Or else it's something a hell of a lot more sinister."

"Yes."

"Then it'll be either a lot more difficult or a lot easier," Birgersson said. "Know what I mean?"

"A maniac."

"Either a maniac with a purpose, who's satisfied and lost interest and is waiting for us, or a maniac who has only just gotten started."

Winter said nothing. He heard no sounds from the courtyard or from within the building. Birgersson's face was hidden in a patchwork of shadows and blinding light.

"I cannot stress enough how important it is that we identify this woman," Birgersson said.

Helene, Winter thought to himself. Mother and murder victim.

"And where the hell are her children?" A mind reader, Birgersson. "If there are any."

Winter cleared his throat cautiously, suddenly disgusted at the taste of smoke in his mouth, as if the stuff had shown its character as toxic gas.

"I could release photos of her dead face. I'm considering doing that, by the way."

"What? How do you mean?"

"A public appeal, like a poster."

"With her dead face?"

"That's all we have."

"Out of the question. How the hell would that look? Imagine what people would say."

"They might say something that would help us."

"We're going to find her anyway," Birgersson said. "Find out who she is."

"We're doing everything we can."

"I know, I know. But it's—I don't quite know how to put it, Erik. It's as if you have too many lines of investigation from the get-go. Too many directions."

"What do you mean?"

"Well, maybe sometimes you're too conscientious, Erik. Maybe you see too many alternative solutions during the initial phase. Your brain springs into action, and the manpower gets spread thin."

"So what you're saying is that it would be better to have a more plodding, dull-witted cop in charge of this?" Winter crossed his legs.

"No no."

"Well what do you mean, then? We're following up the lead on the car and the marking on the tree, and we're questioning people who either live or have been in the vicinity. We're checking up on the cars that were parked there during the night, and we're devoting all our resources to finding the woman's name."

"Okay, okay."

"I could issue a public appeal, but you think that would be inappropriate."

"Not me, primarily."

"No. It's primarily those biggest and most insurmountable of obstacles that we come up against in this line of work—namely, timorous superiors who don't know and don't understand. And I'm not talking about you."

"You're a superior yourself. Next in line to the throne, some say."

"Not for much longer. I'm not dull witted enough."

"Just forget I said that, Erik. All I meant is that we simply have to move forward. But you said something about the cars. That's good—it's concrete."

"A hundred thousand identical models of Ford. Yeah, that's concrete."

Birgersson didn't hear. Maybe the meeting was over. Then, "You had a good idea there. The night camera, the car."

"Don't start buttering me up now."

"But it could lead somewhere."

"We're doing the best we can. And one way or the other we'll solve this. I can feel it. Intuitively."

Birgersson looked up from fiddling with his pack of cigarettes. "I don't suppose any of our fellow officers partying up at the lodge heard or saw anything? The guys from investigations?"

"Bergenhem hasn't reported back yet. But if so, someone ought to have been in touch by now—on their own, I mean."

"Don't try to fool me into thinking you've suddenly gone naive, Erik. How long does it usually take to get your memory back after a night at the lodge?"

"Don't ask me. I've never had one."

18

THERE'D BEEN FOUR CARS IN THE PARKING LOT DOWN BY THE
lake. The thefts of the two reported stolen—both out of gas—seemed to
have been carried out in accordance with standard rules of the industry,
except that the spot where they'd been dumped was an anomaly. The
owners claimed not to have any connections to eastern Gothenburg.
They also had alibis.

Then there was the problem of the other vehicles. One of the owners
had contacted the police just yesterday. The other they had to go find.

Bergenhem drove through the Högsbo industrial zone and parked
outside the Högsbo Hotel.

It smelled of bread and burnt flour from the Pååls baking factory a bit
farther on. Feeling sick to his stomach at the enveloping aroma, he set
his foot down on the asphalt and silently tapped a rhythm.

When a man emerged from the building and walked down the half
flight of steps to the parking lot, Bergenhem climbed out of the car.
The man walked the twenty paces up to him. Bergenhem took off his
sunglasses, and the man's face brightened up along with everything
else around him. The smell of bread returned. It got stuck between
his fingers. Bergenhem reached out, and they shook hands. The man's
name was Peter von Holten. He was a few years older than Bergenhem—
maybe a bit over thirty, with sharp features, but it may have been the
light.

"I'm the one who called," Bergenhem said.

"Shall we take a little drive?"

Von Holten had insisted that he not be visited at his job. Bergenhem had assured him that was okay. Sometimes they could be accom-
modating.

"There's a little park over by the Pripps brewery," von Holten said.

They drove south and pulled over next to a big bush at the side of the road. They sat on a bench. Now it smelled of beer from the brewery, and Bergenhem wasn't sure which was worse.

He suddenly longed for the scent of his four-month-old daughter.

"So you haven't reported your car missing," Bergenhem said.

"Who could have imagined this? That my car would end up in the middle of a murder investigation?"

"What was it doing there? Why did you put it there, I mean."

"It was a mistake," von Holten said, "and I can explain. But it's a—humph—it's a little delicate."

Bergenhem waited for him to continue. A dozen seagulls passed close above their heads, staggering in loose formation as if they'd been intoxicated by the beer-filled gusts of wind.

"I'm just surprised as hell that the car is still there," von Holten said. "That wasn't the idea."

Bergenhem nodded and waited.

"Here's the thing. There's this girl that I meet up with sometimes, and the night before last we went out to the lake because it's a nice place to be on a warm summer evening. And then afterward . . . we decided that she would take the car." Von Holten rubbed his mouth and then removed his hand. "I'm married," he said, as if that explained everything.

"So your girl was supposed to take the car? Do I have that right?"

"Yes."

"What's her name?"

"Is that necessary?"

"Her name? Of course."

Von Holten said a name, and Bergenhem wrote it down in the note-pad he'd brought with him from the car.

"Where does she live?"

Von Holten stated an address. "She lives alone."

"How did you get back from there yourself?"

"I walked."

"Along the highway?"

"There are walking paths back into town. And I don't live far from Delsjö Lake. Takes about an hour and a half by foot."

"I know. But why was she supposed to take the car?"

"We do that sometimes. She doesn't have a car and, well, I have another one, and this one's a company car that my wife doesn't keep track of."

"But she didn't take the car?" Bergenhem said.

"This is fucking insane."

"Why? Surely you've spoken to her."

"That's just it," von Holten said. "I haven't managed to get hold of her these past few days. Nobody picks up, and I went over there and left a message in her mail slot, but she hasn't—"

"What does she look like?" Bergenhem felt his blood beginning to pound between his temples. "What does"—he looked in his notebook—"Andrea look like?"

"Brown hair, pretty dark, normal features, I guess. Attractive, of course, I think, but it's difficult to describe someone. Maybe five and a half feet tall." Von Holten looked at Bergenhem. "You don't mean to say you think that . . ."

"What?" Bergenhem asked.

"That Andrea is the one who . . . who died out there?"

"Why didn't you come forward with this information before?"

Von Holten started to cry. He rubbed his mouth again and squeezed his eyes shut. "It can't have anything to do with her," he said with his eyes still closed.

"You must have read the news or seen it on TV."

Von Holten opened his eyes and directed his gaze at the trees or the seagulls whose mocking laughter Bergenhem could hear above and behind them.

"I guess I didn't really want to take it in, or think about it. I have a family and they mean a lot to me."

Bergenhem said nothing.

"I know what you're thinking. But you've got to think about what you're doing at a time like this."

You've got to think about what you're doing before you drop your pants with a stranger, thought Bergenhem. "That's right," he said. "Think about what you're doing."

"It was wrong," von Holten said with a weary voice. "Of course I . . . I would have come forward, but I thought that sh—that Andrea would be getting in touch. There's another explanation, or something else that caused me to wait. I wasn't expecting to hear from her for a while, and I had no way of knowing that the car was still down by the lake."

"Was she going to borrow it for an extended period?"

"She was going to make a trip down south and be away for a few days. Maybe that's just what she's done, come to think of it," von Holten said, with a face that brightened.

"Only not in your car," Bergenhem said. "Your car's still there."

"Sweet Jesus."

In Winter's office they showed the photographs to von Holten, and he threw up over Winter's desk. Winter grabbed the photos before they were hit by the witness's stomach contents.

"Go get a bucket and a cleaning rag," he said to Bergenhem.

The lover threw up again behind Winter's back as he poured a glass of water from a pitcher on the cabinet. His blazer was hung up safe and sound. He returned to the desk and held out the glass to von Holten. Then Bergenhem returned and the two of them calmly wiped up some of the spew that had run over the desk. Meanwhile, the witness pulled himself together. The stench remained, but nobody thought about it after a while.

"What awful images," von Holten said.

"Do you recognize this face," Winter said.

"No," von Holten said, and averted his eyes from the photograph that Winter was holding in front of him. "That was the most awf— How can anyone recognize a face like that? It's not . . . it's not human."

"It's a dead human being," Winter said. "It's the face of a dead woman."

"I don't think it's Andrea," von Holten said.

"Are you absolutely sure about that?"

"Sure about what?" Von Holten looked like he was about to be sick again.

They waited.

Von Holten closed his eyes. Suddenly he threw up again, into the bucket that Bergenhem had set on the floor. Most of it ended up in the bucket. "I'm not sure of anything," he said with heavy tears in his eyes. "Do you have a towel?"

Bergenhem had fetched a towel and handed it to him.

Von Holten wiped himself across the mouth. "I don't think that's her, but who can tell for sure? I don't know what to say."

"Did Andrea Maltzer have any distinguishing marks?" Winter asked. "Birthmarks, scars—like from an accident."

"Not that I know of. Is that something I ought to know?"

"We would like you to come with us and take a look at her," Winter said as gently as he could. "It's important, as I'm sure you can understand."

"Do I have to?"

"I'm afraid so," Winter said.

"Can I wash myself off?"

Winter nodded toward Bergenhem, who accompanied von Holten to the toilet.

The light was blue. Even the white was blue. The skin of Winter's body drew taut from the cold in there, and his sweat froze into a crust on his skin. He ought to have been cold on the inside too, but he wasn't.

There was a clattering as gurneys with dead people were pushed to and fro in the corridors outside. There were more dead people here than living. This antechamber to the burial grounds was a place where the dead lay but had no peace. They waited.

Helene's face glowed mutedly beneath the fluorescent tubes in a hue that had no equivalent in the world of the living. Von Holten had shook when they rolled out the gurney, teeth chattering as if he had turned to ice.

Winter looked at him now, not at the murder victim. Von Holten looked down and his face changed. He suddenly appeared happy, a movement in his face that was impossible to hide. Winter could see that he tried, but there was no way.

"It's not her," he said.

"No?"

Bergenhem gazed at Winter, who gazed back.

"I'm absolutely sure that's not her," von Holten said.

Winter eyed the woman's face. The stark white light from the ceiling kept shadows away from her. This was exactly what a person looked like who had neither a name nor a past. Maybe a future, he thought. It all depends on me—whether we track down her future within a reasonable period of time. She could lie here for a year or she could get a decent burial. God, how I hate this room.

Outside, the frozen film melted away in the sun, and Winter's skin became supple and moist again. The effect caused the whites of von Holten's eyes to become bloodshot, like he'd just been punched hard in the face.

"We need to know everything there is to know about your mistress," Winter said. "Andrea Maltzer."

"Does my wife have to know about this? About Andrea?"

Winter didn't answer. He drove in toward town and stopped at a red light.

"I'll give you my full cooperation," von Holten said. "I'll do anything you ask."

"Tell us what you know, then," Winter said.

———

"What a fucking piece of work," Ringmar said.

"One among thousands."

"Man is a weak vessel."

"So now we have a disappearance connected to the murder," Winter said. They were sitting in Ringmar's office, drinking black coffee that scalded the mouth.

"Could she have seen something?"

"Could she have seen *it*?"

"Could she have surprised someone?"

"Could she have sat there in the car, thinking about her future?"

"Would someone have turned into the parking lot if there was someone sitting there in a car?"

"Would they have been able to tell?"

"Could she have tried to drive off but been too afraid?"

"Could she have gotten curious?"

"Could she have been assaulted?"

"Could she have been abducted?"

"Could she be involved?"

"Could she be guilty?"

"Could she have taken the first bus in the morning?"

"Could she have had other reasons for not taking the car?"

"Could she really be who she is?"

"Could she just be a fabrication by that von Holten character, you mean?"

"Can we find that out within half an hour?"

"Yes," Winter said. "And it's already done. There is an Andrea Maltzer at the address that von Holten gave us, and there is a telephone number and nobody answers when you call. Or opens the door when you knock. Börjesson went by there and knocked."

"We're going in then, right?"

"I'd like to wait until tomorrow, if she hasn't gotten in touch, that is."

"What for?"

"There's something that doesn't add up here."

"You can say that again."

"She doesn't fit in," Winter said. "We have to concentrate."

"What do we call what you're talking about? Nonwishful thinking?"

"I'll read through everything again," Winter said. "She'll get in touch tomorrow at the latest."

"What makes you so sure about that?"

Winter didn't answer. His gaze moved from the paper in front of him to Ringmar. "Have we finished running the fingerprints from von Holten's car yet?"

"No. Quite a few people used it. It was his company car, and he lent it to others as well."

"Other women?"

"That's not what he says," Ringmar said. "Other people. Work related."

19

FROM WHERE SHE WAS LYING, THE WORLD SEEMED FAR AWAY
through the tinted windows. The day looked the same from early morning till nightfall, but the evening came more quickly now, and for half
an hour the grayness lifted, and before it turned black outside, the sinking light sliced into her room and blazed on the wall. For just a short
moment it flared up and then disappeared into the wallpaper without a trace. In that sense they were beautiful evenings. Aneta Djanali
started to feel whole again. The long periods of languor became fewer,
the hours when she'd sort of drift in and out of dreams. She began to
long for voices. She listened to the orderly who spoke an exciting mixed
language.

She sat in bed and Winter sat next to her. She pointed at the wall and
mumbled.

"Yeah, very nice," Winter said.

She nodded and pointed at the portable CD player that lay next to
her on the bed.

Winter took out a little bag from his inside pocket. "It was the last
one they had at the record store. They didn't have that Dylan album you
wrote down, so I took the liberty of buying a record by a new band that's
really got something special."

Aneta Djanali pulled out *London Calling* from the bag and looked at
Winter quizzically. "U Wrascch?"

"Yes, the Clash."

"Ew and?"

"New band? No, I guess it's not a new band." Winter smiled.

Aneta Djanali wrote "1979!" on a pad of paper and handed it to
Winter.

"Time flies," he said. "But they're new to me. Macdonald told me

about them. In fact, he even sent me the album. Guess he didn't think
we had stuff like this over here among the glaciers."

While he spoke, Aneta Djanali slipped the disc into the CD player,
pressed play, and pulled on the earphones: "London calling to the
underworld . . ." She moved her body back and forth to the music and
beat the rhythm with her fist against the covers to show Winter that she
understood how good it was and how happy she was to be able to sit
here and relish something she had left behind centuries ago.

"Have you listened to any of the other songs on the album?" she
wrote on her pad.

"Not yet," Winter said. "That first one requires a lengthy evaluation."

"Here's one called 'Jimmy Jazz,'" she wrote.

"Really? Let me see."

She handed him the disc and wrote, "That ought to suit you." Then
she handed him the earphones and Winter listened.

"That's not jazz," he said.

Aneta Djanali gripped the head of the bed firmly so as not to laugh
her reconstructed jaw out of joint.

"But you haven't seen the other album in the bag," he said. "That's
real jazz, and a good album for someone who hasn't listened to much
music from the underworld."

She pulled out a CD with a close-up of a black face on it and then held
up the album cover and wrote, "Wow, a compact mirror!" on her pad.

Winter burst out laughing while Djanali pretended to study herself
in the face on the album cover.

"Lee Morgan," Winter said. *"Search for the New Land."*

She put down her mirror and wrote, "How's Fredrik doing?"

"Not too good without you. Apparently, the two of you have some
kind of chemistry that feeds on mutual animosity."

"Hit the nail on the head," wrote Djanali. "Between a darky and a
skinhead."

"He's a good skin."

"Keep an eye on him."

"What?"

"He could go off the rails. Not doing too well."

"He's not the only one."

"Shouldn't be writing this. But he's," she hesitated with her pen, "nervous, desperate."

"You know Fredrik best of all," Winter said.

I'm not so damn sure about that, she thought. And now my hand
hurts. I've been talking too much.

She leaned back against the mountain of pillows and closed her eyes.

"You're tired." He rose and patted her blanket. "Don't forget Lee Morgan, now."

Outside, he breathed in the night air. It smelled of salt and sand that had been baked at high heat for months. That's no Scandinavian smell, he thought to himself. At least not this late in the year. What will all the Mediterranean tourists think?

An ambulance drove slowly by and pulled in front of the entrance to the ER. Two orderlies wheeled up a gurney, hauled a body onto it from the ambulance, and pushed the gurney in through the double doors that were suddenly radiant portals in the darkness.

Winter drove home and parked in the basement garage and then sat at an outside table at the Wasa Källare restaurant. He drank a beer and listened to, without deciphering them, the conversations at the handful of tables.

Right in front of him the empty streetcars rumbled past and on across Vasaplatsen. Once he saw a face in one of the cars that he thought he recognized, like some vague memory. The waiter took his glass and asked if he wanted another, but he said no and lit up a Corps. He could see the smoke halfway across the park.

He took out his cell phone and turned it on. He had three missed calls and saw on the display that one of them was from Angela. Here I go, he thought, and punched in her number.

20

HE BIKED TO HER STREET, UP ON THE HEIGHTS OF KUNGSHÖJD.
Angela pressed up close to him for a second and then pointed toward the balcony. Standing on the table were water and wine, and something that smelled of herbs and salt.

They sat there and saw the sea silhouetted black against a lighter sky. The roofs appeared sprinkled with ash in the moonlight.

"So you got back yesterday?" Winter asked.

"Like I said."

She was wearing a soft shirt and shorts, hair in a ponytail, no make-up, and Winter thought about women's finely chiseled features when he saw her profile against the pale stucco.

"What have you been doing?"

"Sitting out here mostly, as it happens. Yesterday you could see all the way down to the sandbars and those charter boats that take out sports fishermen. I could see them rolling and pitching."

"It makes me seasick just thinking about it."

"It didn't me." She took a sip of her water. "It was soothing."

"Sounds wonderful," Winter said.

"I thought of us."

Here it comes, thought Winter. We only managed a few minutes of idle chitchat. "How was your mother?" he asked.

"Wonderful," she said, "until we started talking about us."

"It's not as bad as all that, is it? And was that really necessary?"

"What?"

"To have a long discussion with your mother about us. We can reason it out ourselves, can't we?"

"Reason it out? Since when did you ever want to reason anything out?"

"I'm considered to be quite reasonable." He dipped a stalk of blanched celery into the cold dip made of sardines and black olives. It tasted salty and bitter, delicious. "This is really good."

She looked at him without saying anything.

He wanted to be there in the moment with her, but when he bent forward over the bowls again, he saw Helene's face as it had looked in the dead blue glow of the morgue. "I'm sorry," he said.

"Well, it's not like this is the first time. And I'm not saying that to sound like a cop's wife sitting up at night waiting."

"I'm the one who's waiting in this case," he said.

She took his hand as he reached for the glass of water.

"What are you waiting for, Erik?"

What was he waiting for? That was a big question. Everything, from the name of a murder victim and a murderer to eternal peace of mind. For the triumph of good over evil. And for her.

"I waited for you today," he said.

"Maybe mostly for my body," she said.

"I resent that. I want all of you," he said, and squeezed her hand.

She let go of his and drank again. A wind came in from the north and snatched a napkin from the table and took it down into the shaft below the balcony. Winter could see the napkin disappear like a butterfly into the shadow of the moon.

"Your mind is so often somewhere else."

"I know. You're right, but not all the time."

"But right now."

"It's this case—"

"You know I'm not asking you to change jobs. But it's everywhere, covering everything like a layer of dust—on us and over everything around us."

"Not dust," he said. "There won't be any dust on us, since I keep stirring it up all the time. Any comparison you like, only not that."

"You know what I mean."

"I can't help it, Angela. It's a part of me. And of the job or whatever you want to call it."

He told her how he'd seen Helene's face just now, in the middle of a meal. He wasn't looking for it. It had sought him out.

She didn't ask anything about Helene, and he knew that was a good thing. Maybe later, but not now.

"You sometimes carry around images of your patients in your mind," he said.

"It's different with you."

"I can't help it," he repeated. "And it helps me."

"Does it? The great magical inspector? Eventually it'll drive you— It could take over. More and more."

"Eventually it'll drive me crazy? Maybe I'm already crazy. Crazy enough to do police work."

"The fight against evil," she said. "Your favorite topic."

"I know—it's pathetic."

"No, Erik, and you know that's not what I think. But it can get to be too much sometimes, so big, you know?"

What was he supposed to say? Crime is an army. He was a policeman but he wasn't cynical. He believed in the power of good, and that was why he spoke about evil. It was impenetrable, like observing the enemy through bulletproof glass. Anyone who tried to comprehend it with reason went under. He was starting to realize this, but he still had the urge to get in close in order to defeat that monster. If you couldn't use your goodness and intellect to confront evil close up, what were you supposed to use? The thought had flashed through his mind before—a thought that was like a black hole right in the middle of reality, terrifying: that evil could be fought only in kind.

"There's nothing to wait for," Angela said when their breathing had calmed.

His head had exploded into a white light as he once again experienced the sensation where the boundaries between body and soul and body and body disappear, and they were united into a single whole for a few seconds while the white light lasted.

After that came the languorous exhaustion. Then the voice returned.

"What are we waiting for?" she repeated. "I want to throw out those damn pills."

He couldn't answer. Anything he might say could end up wrong, so he unfolded himself from the bed. "I'm going to get something to drink."

"Get back here!"

"I've got to have something." He pulled on his shorts by hopping on one leg at a time, then stepped out onto the balcony to fetch glasses and bottles. The wind from the early evening was gone. It felt as if it had grown warmer, warmer, almost, than inside the room.

He raised his gaze and the sky was empty. It might have been one o'clock or two. He could blame work and cycle home, but that would be cowardly. To say that he wanted to spend an hour hunched over the PowerBook, basking in its pleasant electronic glow, would be true in a way, but it sounded insane.

He carried two glasses filled with equal parts white wine and water into the kitchen, but there was no ice left in her freezer, so he walked back to the bedroom and handed one to Angela.

"So tell me what we're waiting for," she repeated. "I'm tired of this arrangement."

"What arrangement?"

"Everything." She drank thirstily. "I don't want to live apart anymore."

"It was your idea from the beginning."

"I don't care whose idea it was. And that feels like years ago, back when we were both young urban professionals."

"We still are."

"You're thirty-seven, Erik. You're nearly forty. I'm thirty."

He drank and heard a car driving at high speed down on Kungsgatan, going toward Rosenlund. Could be a taxi or a private car on its way down to the hooker strip along Feskekörka. Sometimes the johns produced a heavy flow of traffic below her window, but tonight had been quiet. He wondered why. The conditions were perfect.

"It may sound silly, but playtime is over," she went on. "You know I didn't make any demands before, but I am now."

"Yeah."

"Is there something wrong? We've been together for almost two years and at our age that's a long time for an LAT relationship."

"You want us to move in together?"

"You know what I want, but that would be a start."

"You and me, in an apartment?"

"That is what moving in together usually involves."

He had to let out a giggle, like a little kid. The situation was untenable, awful. He was being held to account for his desire to live on his own and have her within comfortable reach, within biking distance on a warm evening. She was right; it was as she said. Playtime was over.

"You have to choose sometime," she said softly, as if to a child that can't make up its mind. "This is no surprise to you, Erik."

"We could always see more of each other."

"So you're not ready?"

"I didn't say that."

"This is the only chance you'll get."

21

WINTER LEFT KUNGSHÖJD UNDER PRESSURE FROM THE SUN. HIS black glasses dampened the pain in the crown of his head.

Angela waved from the balcony as he turned down the hill. He had been given time to think it over, but that was really the wrong way to describe it. He couldn't think of the right way, so he didn't.

"She hasn't gotten in touch," Ringmar said after morning prayer. "Should we go over there?"

Winter thought for a moment. As the head of the investigation, he had the discretionary authority to "bring in a person of potential interest for questioning." They couldn't just barge into somebody's house, but they could bring someone in for questioning who was important to the preliminary investigation and hadn't come in voluntarily. He looked in his papers. Andrea Maltzer lived on Viktor Rydbergsgatan. Nice address.

"Okay. Let's go over there."

They drove across Korsvägen. Someone merging into the traffic circle in a hurry had not paid proper attention. Two damaged cars stood at a nasty angle, and a uniformed officer was sorting out who was at fault together with two men whom Winter guessed were the drivers. The police sergeant was a man in his fifties, and he looked up as they edged past, then nodded in greeting. Ringmar raised his hand through the window.

"Sverker," Winter said.

"We did a lot of shifts together," Ringmar said. "Sweet youth in uniform."

"I haven't seen him for a while."

"He was sick. Cancer in one of his legs, I think."

"I may have heard something about that," Winter said, and drove up the hill at Eklandabacken.

Winter scanned the facades along the street, once they'd passed the church, and pulled up in an empty parking spot opposite Andrea Maltzer's address. The building was tall and the street was in shade. The entryway was broad and austere, the air inside cool from stone and marble. A statue at the foot of the steps depicted a naked woman pointing upward with one finger.

"Looks even nicer than your lobby," Ringmar said.

The locksmith was waiting for them in a rattan armchair by the front door and stood to say hello.

"Second floor," Winter said. "Let's take the stairs."

The polished tropical hardwood and the lush plants on pedestals made him feel like he was wandering through a managed jungle.

The locksmith got everything ready.

"I'll ring the doorbell first," Winter said.

He rang again and heard footsteps and thought they were coming from somewhere else. The doors were massive—impossible to hack your way through with an axe. You'd need a chainsaw and battering ram, with Fredrik at the front.

There was a rattling inside, and the door was opened by a woman who could be the same age as Angela.

She's calm, Winter thought. This is a surprise for her. She's simply exercised her right to have a private life and disappeared for a few days.

"Yes?" the woman asked.

"Andrea Maltzer?"

"What's this about? Who are you?"

"The police," Winter said, and produced his ID card. She studied it. The locksmith eyed Winter, who gave him a nod, then disappeared down the stairs.

"What do you want?" Andrea Maltzer repeated.

"Could we come in for a moment?"

"Are you also a police officer?" she asked Ringmar.

"Sorry," Ringmar said, and showed her his ID.

She gave his badge a quick glance and looked at Winter again. She had a face sprinkled with freckles that had grown in number this summer, he guessed. She looks young and fresh, more or less like Peter von Holten when he's not throwing up all over my desk. Can't she find someone who isn't already married? She looks tired, but not worn out.

"Would it be all right?" Winter nodded toward the apartment.

"It's all right," she said, and they stepped into the foyer. She lead the way into a living room that resembled one Winter lived in for a period in his life, white stucco and windows that opened out onto a balcony,

which already looked searing hot in the morning sun. The balcony
door stood open, and Winter saw an empty cast-iron table beneath an
umbrella.

She was wearing a tank top and a pair of shorts that were wide and
long and looked comfortable. Summer wear, even though it was almost
September.

Tomorrow I'll wear shorts again, Winter noted. There's no way to
cloak yourself anyway. He thought about his sister, who'd called yesterday and invited him over again. He didn't know why. He'd call her back
when he had the time.

"I suppose I ought to offer you coffee or something, but I'd like to
know what this is about first," Andrea Maltzer said.

They asked her what she had been doing at Delsjö Lake. When do
you mean? They were as specific as they dared be. Then? She had wandered off awhile after Peter left. Why? She needed to think, and Winter
heard Angela's voice.

Andrea Maltzer had needed to think over why she was seeing a married man "on the sly," as she put it. Taking his car would have been
"compromising." That was the word she used. She sat in it for a while
and then went over to the café and waited for the cab she'd called on her
cell phone. They took down all the details, and she shook her head when
they asked if she had a receipt—which would have been off the books
anyway, if she'd had it. They could check up on that phone call. Winter
believed her. People did strange things and perfectly natural things all at
the same time. Scratch von Holten, maybe. Fine by me. Winter asked if
she'd noticed anything whatsoever while she was sitting there.

"When I was alone? After Peter was gone?"

"Yes." He could then ask about what they had done together, if they
had paid much attention to their surroundings. "It's important that you
think about it. Anything at all could be of help."

"I can put on some coffee while I think about it."

"Before you do that," Ringmar cut in, "could you tell us where you've
been for the last few days?"

"Here," she said. "And one other place, but mostly here, I think."

"We've been trying to reach you," Ringmar said.

"I didn't want anyone to reach me," she said. "I unplugged the answering machine and switched that off." She nodded at the cell phone on the
living room table. "And I haven't read the paper or listened to the radio.
Or watched TV."

"What for?"

"I thought I explained that."

"Didn't you hear the doorbell?"

"No. I must have been out then."

"You didn't get any messages from anyone?"

"Peter came by and slid an envelope under the door, but I threw it away."

"What did he write?"

"I don't know. I threw it away unopened."

"When?"

"Yesterday. It went out with the trash, in case you're wondering."

Winter nodded. It wasn't hard for someone to stay out of sight if they wanted to. It was even their right.

"I had a few vacation days left."

Winter nodded again. He wanted to leave, but they weren't done yet.

"Anything else you'd like to know?" she asked when neither Winter nor Ringmar spoke.

"What you saw, if you saw anything," Winter said.

"I was going to think about that in the kitchen," she said.

"That's right," Winter said.

He looked around after she left the room. Two framed photographs stood on a paint-stripped cabinet. No picture of Peter von Holten. One of them was of a wedding couple, possibly her parents—the picture looked like it had been taken thirty years ago. Classic matrimonial attire though. No sign of flirting with that era's flower power.

The other photo was a black-and-white outdoor scene with no people in it—a house somewhere in the archipelago. The house might have been red and it was situated a short distance above a rocky shoreline. He could make out portions of an out-of-focus jetty in the foreground. There were no clouds behind the house. To the left was a sign warning of an underwater cable. There was a stonework stairway, as if carved from the rock, leading from the jetty up to the house.

He recognized it. He had seen this cabin himself, from the sea. You could sail around the promontory to the left and into an inlet three hundred yards farther on and hike up a hill lined with wind-battered juniper trees. Just behind the hill, on the lee side, was another house, which had belonged to his parents when he was a kid. He was twelve when they sold it, and he had sailed past it a few times since then but rarely gone ashore. He missed it now.

Andrea Maltzer had returned to the room and saw him in front of the photo. She said the name of the island.

"I thought it looked familiar," Winter said. "My parents had a house there, but that was a long time ago."

"My parents bought the place a few years back."

"I guess that explains why I didn't recognize you," Winter said, and turned around. A tray stood on the table, and she had sat down and was eyeing him strangely. "I mean, there were no little kids there back then."

She smiled but said nothing. Winter sat opposite her. She gestured toward the tray and Ringmar did the honors. Winter suddenly felt impatient, even more restless than usual. The photograph from the island had affected him. There was no room in his head for personal memories right now. Something had led him here too. He didn't believe in coincidences, never had. Many crimes were solved by chance, or what might be referred to as coincidences, but Winter didn't believe in them. There was a purpose. Chance had a purpose.

"That's my refuge," she said. "That's where I am when I'm not here. Like yesterday."

"Do you remember anything from the night we're talking about?" Ringmar asked.

"I remember that I saw a boat," she said. "Out on the lake."

"A boat," Ringmar repeated.

"A white boat or beige. Plastic, I assume."

"Was it far out?"

"It was a ways out on the lake. I saw it when I climbed out of the car—when I decided that I'd borrowed Peter's car for the last time."

"Describe exactly what you saw," Winter said. "As best you can."

"Like I said. A boat out on the water that appeared to be lying pretty still. I didn't hear anything. No motor."

"Did you see an outboard motor on it?"

"No. But if there had been an outboard, I wouldn't have seen it in the dark anyway." She put down her cup.

"No sound of rowing? You heard nothing?"

"No. But I could see that there was someone sitting in the boat."

"Some*one*? One person, on their own?"

"It looked that way."

"You're not sure?"

"It was too dark to be sure."

"Would you recognize the boat if you saw it again?"

"Well, I don't know. But I remember the shape of it, the size more or less."

"What did you do then?"

"What do you mean?"

"How long did you stand there?"

"Five minutes maybe. I guess I didn't think much about it; people go out fishing at night too, don't they?"

"I don't know," Ringmar said. "I don't fish."

"And the boat stayed out there while you were standing by the car?" Winter asked.

"It seemed to be lying there completely still."

"Can we just go over the times again, as precisely as possible?" Winter said.

22

THE PUBLIC APPEAL BORE FRUIT. PEOPLE CALLED IN AND JANNE Möllerström was one of the ones who took the calls. Many had seen something, but no one had been in the vicinity. That's just how it was. "There's somebody out there somewhere," as Möllerström expressed it. Winter liked that kind of optimism. It was in line with his spirit.

Winter had drawn up the text, and they'd printed posters that would hang in the residential neighborhoods until they were ripped down. No photograph. The caption read, "Police seeking information!" The copy explained that a murdered woman had been found on Thursday, August 18, at 4:00 a.m., in the vicinity of Big Delsjö Lake and Black Marshes. It gave a description of her and the standard, "The police are interested in speaking to anyone who . . . ," et cetera; and a little farther down, "If you have any further information, please call the telephone number listed below." And farther down still: "Let the police determine what may be of interest." A strange sentence, if taken out of context, but Winter left it there. He signed it, "District CID, homicide department," in order to avoid any misunderstanding, and at the bottom added, "Grateful for any tips!" The prose had an exuberant quality to it, which he disliked. But maybe that meant the poster would have an effect.

"Find anything in the boat?" Halders asked.

"Beier says it's the same kind of paint," Erik Börjesson said. "And it could have been daubed there at approximately the same time."

"Anything else?" Winter asked.

"No footprints in the bilge water, but a hell of a lot of fingerprints, which it's going to take time to go through. And that's putting it mildly, as Beier expressed it."

"Prints from many hands?"

"Seems the boys were only too happy to lend out their boat. Or rent it out, but they're not telling."

"I'll talk to them again," Winter said.

"There were a lot of fish scales too," Halders said. "Seems there are fish in that lake."

"They haven't found any footprints up along the gunwale of the boat?"

"What's that?" Börjesson looked at Winter.

"When you jump ashore, you step off the edge or gunwale. Sometimes anyway."

"I'm sure Beier has checked that."

"Speaking of checking," Halders said. "Stockholm hasn't been in touch? From missing persons?"

"Nothing from Stockholm," Ringmar said. "No report that fits the description."

"Oh, for Christ's sake," Halders said. "There ought to be loads of them right now. Thirty-year-old housewives who've had enough."

"Had enough?" Sara Helander said.

"Who've left the stove," Halders said. "Who've gone off to find the meaning of life."

Winter and Ringmar had been sitting in Winter's office, talking cars, and they returned to this when their colleagues left. Ford Escort 1.8i CLX three-door hatchback, a '92 or '93. Or possibly a '94. Or a '91, a 1.6i. The Road Administration had done a plate search via the National Police Board's central office, beginning with the letters *HEL* or *HEI*. It took twenty-four hours. They'd received lists of all Ford Escorts with those letter combinations, as well as the earlier models, the primitive, flatter ones that were revamped and made more bulbous after '91. They'd also requested a search of all Escort models that didn't have those letter combinations. Beier wasn't certain about the letters—he'd spoken of a possible "optical illusion." No one was certain, not even the kennel guy as it turned out.

If they limited the Gothenburg area to Greater Gothenburg plus Kungsbacka to the south, Kungälv to the north, and Hindås to the east, there were 214 Escorts from between '91 and '94; that is to say, cars that closely resembled each other. That was a lot of cars.

"As always, it's an issue of priorities," Ringmar said.

"You mean this isn't the top priority? Thanks, I know."

"But you feel strongly about this?"

"It is a good idea, admit it." Winter looked up from the lists that lay in shallow piles on his desk.

"It could be worse," Ringmar said. "We could be looking for one of the most common models of Volvo."

"It could be a lot better too," Winter said. "A Cadillac Eldorado."

"Why not a Trabant?"

"Fine by me."

"We can put two guys on it," Ringmar said after a pause. Two police officers could go into the vehicle registration database and pull up every single owner. "And we'll start with all the ones currently on the road."

"Who steals a Ford Escort nowadays?"

"We could always ask Fredrik. His specialty is stolen cars."

"We can take the rentals first."

"And the company cars."

"A Ford Escort? You gotta be kidding me."

"Small businesses," Ringmar said, and Winter smiled. "Sole proprietor."

"And after that, the private individuals," Winter said.

"Of course, there are some you can discount right from the start."

"We'll assign two investigators," Winter said. "Okay. Let them get started."

Winter was thinking of nothing when he knocked gently and stepped inside the office of the district chief.

The asphalt in front of Ullevi Stadium was empty, a sea of black glittering from all the bits of trash that had been chucked from the cars along Skånegatan.

"I just thought I'd find out how things are going," Wellman said. "Or how things are, rather."

"We're doing everything in our power," Winter said, and considered whether he should mention the search through the vehicle registration database.

"Have you read this?" Wellman reached for the newspaper before him. "'Police have no leads,' it says."

"You know how it is, Henrik."

"You— We do have some leads, don't we?"

Winter saw a big bus drive across the sea of asphalt and come to a stop. No one got out. He couldn't tell whether the engine was turned off. "Absolutely," he said. "Surely I don't have to submit a report on that, do I? To you."

"No no. But there's a press conference this afternoon."

"As if I didn't know."

"And of course it's really all bullshit," Wellman said. "All this damn commotion."

"What do you mean?"

"I don't like it when we don't have a name. When we have a name, it's a hell of a lot easier to manage everything. Like a straightforward drug deal or an aggravated assault or a hit-and-run driver."

"You much prefer that kind of thing?"

"You know what I mean."

"If we have more answers from the start, it's easier to come up with leads."

"W— What?"

"You mean that it's easier if everything is easier from the start."

"Now you're parsing words, Erik."

"Was there anything else, Henrik?"

"No. You know your business."

"As long as I don't get disturbed all the time," Winter said.

Still no one had emerged from the bus. Winter saw a woman walk up to it and stop next to the driver's window. It looked as if she was speaking to the driver. He saw how she suddenly took a few steps backward and then turned around and started running away, out toward Skåne-gatan and across the parking lot toward the police station—straight for the building in which he was standing—and he saw how her features became more distinct. She disappeared beneath him. She had looked horrified.

"Excuse me," Winter said, and left the room and took the elevator down to the lobby.

23

THE WOMAN WINTER HAD SEEN RUN ACROSS SKÅNEGATAN WAS hanging halfway through the glass window in reception. Winter could see the precinct commander, with a contingent of five or six men around him, on his way forward. A couple of homicide detectives were loafing next to them. Otherwise the hall and waiting room were filled with the usual mix of bicycle messengers, uniformed patrol officers, reception staff, lawyers, and their clients—a mixture of high and low: junkies on their way up or down, whores, car thieves, shoplifters from all social classes, half-drunken petty criminals, deputy directors who'd been tossed out of bars and returned later with a crowbar, hungover female executives who in frustration had violently resisted the police. Then there were the ones who'd just come by to fill out a form, who were applying for a passport and had lost their way, who'd been missing someone long enough, or who'd just wandered in there, God knows why.

The woman pointed at the bus outside Ullevi. Winter moved closer. He wasn't doing anything just then anyway.

She explained that there was a man sitting in the bus with a little boy and that he was threatening to shoot the child and himself and at the same time blow up the bus. He had shown her the weapon and a string or something that he said he could pull and then the bus would explode.

"Cordon off the area," the PC said to a uniformed woman standing next to him.

Winter could see the order getting passed on, the movement intensifying in the cramped space next to the reception desk, and the police officers preparing to go outside and join up with their colleagues who had been called back from elsewhere in the city. He saw the bus, now from a different perspective. It looked smaller, as if the sun had shrunk it as it stood unprotected out there in the empty square.

"Contact Bertelsen at immigration," Winter heard the PC shout to someone who was already heading off into the bustle. He had now heard enough to know that sitting in the bus was a desperate man who'd finally made a choice, when he no longer had any choice. He guessed it was yet another man who wasn't welcome in Sweden, about to be sent out into orbit around the world, if he survived that long. Yet another space refugee, a stateless human being circling the planet in rusting hulks that never put into port—or in cattle cars that clattered through all the marshlands and deserts of the earth without ever stopping at any its oases. He might shoot himself and the boy, Winter thought. It wouldn't be the first time.

Skånegatan was quickly cordoned off and the traffic redirected. The curious were congregating, as if the tragedy had already been beamed out by the fastest media. And maybe it had. The police station's tasteful lobby was teeming with reporters.

Winter walked out. Onlookers came from all directions and had to be forcibly removed since the police officers hadn't yet managed to get all the cordon tape put up. The Gothenburg Party has been replaced by a new spectacle, and I'm no better than all the other bystanders, he thought, and walked back inside and rode the elevator up to his office, which faced the canal.

He glanced out the window and saw people coming across the grass, a sudden accretion of matter where there had previously been nothing but wind and heat. It was like someone crumbling a loaf of bread in the middle of the empty sea and thousands of seagulls suddenly shrieking down from the sky.

The phone on Winter's desk rang.

"Yes?"

"Bertil here. There are some people shooting at each other over at Vårväderstorget."

"What?"

"The witness who called three minutes ago said that it's like an all-out gang war, and now we have a car out there confirming that shots have been fired."

"Busy day today."

"Did I miss something else?"

"There's a hostage situation out front, or whatever you want to call it."

"I've been on the phone the whol— Are you serious? A hostage situation?"

"A bus. But never mind that now. Have you had a chance to send someone to— Where did you say it was again?"

"Vårväderstorget square. In His—"

"I know where it is."

"Like I said, there's a radio car on the scene, but no one from the department. I don't have a single fucking officer—"

"Let's go," Winter said. "Do you have a car ready?"

"Yes."

They drove out via Smålandsgatan. Winter heard the megaphones and thought about the boy sitting with the man on the bus. Maybe they were father and son. He felt a sudden rage, a nausea that punched at his chest.

"What's going on?" Ringmar was looking in the rearview mirror.

"I don't know much more than you do. Except that there's a man sitting in a bus intent on killing himself and the boy he has with him. There may be other people there too."

Ringmar sounded like he let out a sigh.

"He may also have an explosive device," Winter said.

"And here we are on our way to another corner of the event center," Ringmar said.

Winter looked at him askance just as the radio crackled to life with an update about Vårväderstorget. Four shots had been fired from the roofs of the buildings surrounding the square. And it seemed that two men had been shooting at each other but had disappeared. The police were now searching along the rooftops and on the ground.

"What the fu— Now somebody's shooting again!" the voice was heard to say, and then the radio cut out.

"What the hell." Ringmar pounded on the radio. It crackled but there was nothing intelligible. "That sounded like Jonne Stålnacke."

They drove across the bridge and continued down Hjalmar Brantingsgatan. As they neared Vårväderstorget, Winter made out two patrol cars and people lying on the ground. When they got closer, he realized they were people who had taken cover, but he saw no blood around the cars or the people.

They stopped the car and ran, hunched over, to the two police officers who'd crawled down behind their car. One was holding a walkie-talkie and nodded when he recognized Ringmar and Winter. It was Sverker. A few days ago they'd seen him investigating an accident on Korsvägen. Winter thought about Sverker's cancer and his return to the job.

"Fucking gangsters," Sverker said.

"What happened?" Winter asked.

"Somebody started shooting—that's what happened," the police sergeant said, and suddenly a shot rang out close by.

"It's a fucking war," Sverker said.

Someone started screaming somewhere up ahead. The voice went silent and soon started up again, more softly and drawn out.

"What is that?" Ringmar asked.

Winter stood with his knees bent and slowly lifted his face and peered through the windows of the car. Thirty yards ahead, on the asphalt, lay a uniformed police officer, and he was the one who was screaming—more like shouting now. He's probably been shot, Winter thought, since he seems unable to move. Unless he has chosen to lie still. But he was shouting. Winter saw no blood, but the man was lying at a strange angle with his leg pointing straight out. Now he moved an arm, in a kind of wave. He fell silent.

"Good God, it's Jonne," Sverker said, also looking through the windows. "He moved forward when it seemed like they'd stopped shooting. It's Jonne Stålnacke."

"Do you have a megaphone?" Winter asked.

"In the car. I'll get it." Sverker cautiously opened the door. "We've still got this one from a traffic accident the other day. It ought to be standard equipment."

Winter took the megaphone and called out, "THIS IS THE POLICE. WE HAVE A WOUNDED OFFICER WHO NEEDS IMMEDIATE MEDICAL ATTENTION. THERE MAY BE OTHER INJURED PEOPLE HERE. PUT DOWN YOUR WEAP—"

And then there was another explosion, and Winter dived headlong onto the street and scraped the hand that was holding the device. Someone fired again, from above. The shot seemed farther away, like the one he'd heard before. Maybe they're pulling back, Winter thought. The enemy is retreating. Or was that just one of them? They had been shooting at each other, after all.

He raised the megaphone again and saw that he was bleeding from the knuckles and fingers of his right hand.

"THIS IS THE POLICE. PUT DOWN YOUR WEAPONS IMMEDIATELY. THERE ARE PEOPLE INJURED HERE. THIS IS THE POLICE. PUT DOWN YOUR WEAPONS AT ONCE. WE HAVE INJURED PEOPLE IN DESPERATE NEED OF EMERGENCY MEDICAL ATTENTION. PUT DOWN YOUR WEAPONS IMMEDIATELY."

On the road behind him, an ambulance whined its way closer. Two ambulances. He turned around. The cars had stopped twenty yards away. People were standing along the other side of the road, by the thousands it looked like. Around him lay police officers and civilians who'd happened to be in the wrong place at the wrong time. Or the right place but the wrong ti—

Another shot, but now in the distance like a New Year's firecracker in another neighborhood. The injured police officer mumbled something. He's in shock, Winter thought. He could die.

"We have to go get Jonne," Sverker said. "There could be more people lying out there."

"THIS IS THE POLICE. PUT AWAY YOUR WEAPONS. WE ARE GOING TO STAND UP NOW AND MOVE OUT ONTO THE SQUARE. WE'RE GETTING UP NOW. THIS IS THE POLICE. PUT DOWN YOUR WEAPONS. THERE ARE A LOT OF PEOPLE HERE. WE HAVE TO BRING UP AN AMBULANCE. THERE ARE INJURED PEOPLE HERE."

The ambulances behind Winter honked their horns, backing up his words. People all around gazed at him and at the long and narrow square, the roofs, the shop signs. Sverker held his service weapon in his hand.

"Put that away," Winter said.

Jonne cried out again. No one was shooting anymore. Winter tried to see if there was anyone on the rooftops, but the sun stung his eyes and made the buildings look like they were being corroded by a chalk white light.

"THIS IS THE POLICE. WE'RE GOING TO MOVE OUT ONTO THE SQUARE AND THEN AN AMBULANCE IS GOING TO FOLLOW. WE'RE MOVING FORWARD NOW."

He stood up and, holding the megaphone, slowly walked around the car. Clever idiot. He took a few steps forward, as if walking on thin ice, and continued over toward the injured police officer. Jonne Stålnacke lay still, but Winter could hear a low murmur, as if he were talking to himself.

Winter bent down over Jonne, dropped to his knees. Jonne's face was white like the sky around the sun. His lips were invisible. His groin area was soaked in blood—they hadn't been able to see this when they were crouching behind the car. Winter thought about how clean Jonne's socks and shoes were. The leather shone like a mirror. Sverker jolted up and waved vigorously to the ambulance, which popped the clutch and screeched toward them. It was like a signal to everyone else who was lying down. People stood, but many of them were shaking so badly they had to sit right back down again. Winter heard crying. An entire square in shock. He caught a whiff of excrement from a man who tried to walk toward the street. More ambulances arrived on the scene. A streetcar passed by, as if it had emerged from another world. Uniformed police officers took care of people and looked to see if there were any more injured along with the paramedics and doctors. Stålnacke was carried into the ambulance and driven off. Winter suddenly felt terribly thirsty.

It was so hot, so it was strange that the little girl didn't come outside for a dip in the wading pool. Many days had passed. It had been hot for such a long time now, but she didn't know when she had last seen the girl. Nor the mother, but she wasn't so far gone as not to realize that she couldn't quite keep track of time the way she used to. Elmer wasn't around anymore. He used to wind up the clock or say when it was getting on toward evening. It was hard to know what time it was when it took so long for it to get dark. But now it went quicker because the skies were turning toward fall.

Ester Bergman heard the children's voices through the window she'd cracked open. She didn't believe in keeping the windows wide open when it was hot. It just made it hotter inside. She had a good temperature in there.

The children jumped into the water, but there wasn't much water to speak of. So close to the sea and still they couldn't go there. Perhaps they didn't want to, but nor could they; she understood that much. Perhaps there wasn't any sea where they came from. Desert maybe, mountains and such.

The girl didn't have black hair, and not all the children in the courtyard did either.

She thought the girl lived in one of the units to the left, on the short end of the yard, but she hadn't seen her go in or out of it, because the gable blocked the entrance from view. Maybe it was because the girl had red hair that she remembered her and wondered where she was. A few of the other children had light hair, but none of them had red hair.

The girl had walked past her window on the way to the playground. She never ran.

The girl's mother had light hair and always sat by herself. Perhaps that was another reason why she remembered the girl, because the mother never spoke to anyone. They were never in the courtyard for very long. After a while the mother would take the girl, and they would go back inside again or leave the building altogether. She had wondered several times where it was they went. But what business is it of mine? she had thought.

The mother had smoked, and she hadn't liked seeing that. There weren't many other mothers in the courtyard who smoked, as far as she could tell.

A couple of times over the past week she had thought she'd seen the girl, but it wasn't her. She didn't know what her voice sounded like. And she'd never heard the mother speak to the girl either.

I guess I miss that little moppet, she thought. They must have moved out, but I didn't see any moving van.

24

SHE WAS GIVEN OTHER CLOTHES BUT SHE DIDN'T WANT TO PUT them on. The man said that she had to change clothes when he went out, and so she took off the old ones she'd had on for a long time.

She coughed. She felt hot in her face and on her body.

Where did the dress come from? It wasn't hers, but it didn't look new. It didn't smell of anything.

The man wasn't there. She had the slip of paper in her hand. Was it because they were looking for the slip of paper that she had to take off her pants? They hadn't said anything. She looked around, but there was no place where she could put the slip of paper. She felt inside the dress for a pocket and found one. She'd had a dress before, so she knew to look for it.

She pulled the dress over her head. If she crumpled up the paper a little, it fit right into the pocket and she could sort of put a flap of the fabric over it. She patted it on the outside and couldn't feel the paper.

It seemed like they were back where they had been before, except it didn't look exactly the same. Had the windows been moved? Can you move a window like a table or a chair?

Mommy was out there. She thought about Mommy, but it was hard without getting sad.

"Have you slept?"

She tried to say she had slept, because she thought that's what he wanted her to say. But no sound came out and she had to try again, and then it worked. After that she coughed. She was sweating.

"Sit still," he said, and took hold of her shoulder with one hand and held the other to her forehead. He mumbled something she couldn't hear. Then he said a bad word. "You're hot," he said again, and she coughed again. He shouted something to someone else, and she heard an answer.

"The kid's got a fever."

Someone said something from somewhere else.

"I said the kid's sick!"

She heard something that sounded like another bad word.

He left and she thought about how her dress was a little damp under her arms and along her back because she was so hot. She lay down on the mattress and that felt good, so she closed her eyes. It sounded like the man was back, but she didn't want to look up. Then he took hold of her again.

"You have to sit up and drink this," he said.

She didn't want to, but he lifted her.

"You have to drink this while it's hot," he said, and she opened her eyes and saw the cup. "Then you can lie down again."

She took a sip but her throat hurt when she swallowed. Then it felt a little better, but when she tried to drink again it hurt.

"Does it hurt?"

She nodded.

"Do you have a sore throat?"

She nodded again.

"It'll feel better afterward," he said.

She said that she wanted to lie down. He laid her down and took the cup with him. She closed her eyes. She started to dream.

25

HALDERS ENTERED THE COFFEE ROOM AND POURED HIMSELF A
fresh cup. He sat down at Ringmar's table and lifted his gaze toward the
window. "What a circus."

It was the second day of what the city's tabloids had been calling, among other things, "Terror!" Two hundred thousand issues had
been sold, and there was nothing strange about that. Gothenburg *had*
exploded—at least parts of it. The smart-asses said it had come as no surprise. "To think we're the ones who are supposed to stay one step ahead
of these guys," Ringmar said to Halders.

"What did you say?"

"Surveillance department. We're supposed to have our ear to the
ground. To be monitoring developments. Be a step ahead."

"Who could have seen this coming?" Halders raised his hand toward
Ullevi and the drama that was still unfolding out there.

"I was mainly thinking about Vårväderstorget."

"How's Stålnacke doing?"

"He lost a lot of blood," Ringmar said, "but he'll pull through. He'll
be able to walk."

"The question is whether he'll be able to take a piss again, let alone
be able to—"

"We can't exactly have people everywhere, can we?" Ringmar interrupted.

"And now we're going to spread our resources even more thinly."

"We're going to bring in the ones who shot Stålnacke."

"That seems like a concrete assignment," Halders said. "Something
you can really sink your teeth into."

"How do you mean?"

"The murder at Delsjö is going cold. You know it is. It's going cold,
no matter what Winter says."

"The cars," Ringmar said. "That's something."

"A shot in the dark," Halders said, "but okay. A Ford Escort. That's concrete all right. But more to the point, it's a hell of a lot of work."

Ringmar seemed to prick up his ears when the megaphone bawled again outside. "It's awful," he said.

"What is?"

Ringmar gestured at the window but didn't answer.

The friendly match between Sweden and Denmark, scheduled for that evening at Ullevi Stadium, had to be postponed. The management of the Swedish Football Association had made discreet inquiries with the police about whether the "incident" might be over in time but had been given no guarantees.

The man on the bus was a Kurd, and the boy at his side was his son. After seven years in Sweden, they were going to be deported. The boy had lived in Sweden for six years. The Migration Board was certain the man and his family were from northern Iran, and that's where he was going to be deported to. Turkey was an alternative. The man claimed that he risked being imprisoned or even put to death in both countries, in different ways, for different reasons. Different forms of execution. The state authority, which an increasing number of people dubbed the Emigration Board, displayed pride and emotional zeal for doing what is right and proper. When the man arrived, he was given another name and another nationality because he feared being sent back to the terror. But he had lied, and now he was going to be deported.

Winter stood at the edge of the mass of onlookers. Maybe someone ought to put up some bleachers, he thought. Charge admission.

He knew that the man sitting in that bus, a hundred yards away, had committed an emergency lie to make it into Sweden. Maybe he'd left a job as a consultant and a seven-room house in Diyarbakir or Tabriz just because he felt like trekking through Syria with his family before hopping a cruise to Scandinavia. Perhaps the family was just having a hard time explaining why they didn't want to return to the fertile land they had left behind. There is no room here in any case. Sweden is too built up, Winter thought. The forests are full of towns and densely populated villages.

He closed his eyes and saw a forest in front of him. Water glittered between the trees. Everything was green to his unseeing eyes. He saw a path and someone walking along that path. He recognized himself. He was holding a child by the hand.

He opened his eyes again and everything was black and white. The asphalt was black beneath his feet, and it turned increasingly white as he raised his gaze toward the bus, which stood right in the sun. It must be 120 degrees in there, he thought. Not even a man who's grown up in the hottest country in the world could hold out for much longer. It must be a question of hours, perhaps minutes. Let there be an end to it.

A small negotiating team moved toward the bus. The people all around were very quiet. A helicopter hovered overhead. Winter heard radio and TV reporters speaking nearby. He heard the events taking place in front of him described to him.

Ringmar said something. He'd come outside and seen Winter and was standing next to him.

"What?"

"I think this will be over soon," Ringmar said.

"Yes."

"We might also have a lead on the shooters at the square."

"Was it an internal settling of scores?" Winter asked.

"Depends on how you look at it. Essentially, it's the same desperation we're experiencing here," Ringmar said. "We're headed toward the end of the century and the end of the world as we know it."

His cell phone vibrated in his inner pocket as he stepped out of the elevator.

"Yes?"

"Hello, Erik. I thought it was about ti—"

"Hello, Mother."

"What's going on over there? We just had the newspapers delivered, and it looks just terrible."

"Yes."

"First that murder. And then those people shooting at each other. And now a kidnapping too!"

"There's no kidnapping."

"There isn't? Someone's kidnapped a boy and is hold—"

"They're father and son," Winter said.

"Father and son? I don't understand."

"No."

"Father and son? How awful."

He had reached his office. The phone on his desk rang.

"Hang on, Mother," he said, and lifted the receiver and put the cell phone down. "Winter," he said.

"Janne here. We've received a few more phone calls and letters in response to the poster. You want the copies and transcripts now or are you coming over here?"

Winter considered his office chair. He felt that he needed to sit down for a moment and think about his murder investigation. Möllerström would put together a nice package of all the witnesses' statements. "Send it up," he said. He hung up the receiver and retrieved his cell phone.

"Here I am again," he said to his mother, who was sitting in a house in Marbella. He couldn't hear his father in the background, but he guessed that he was close by, with a glass in his hand and a weary gaze directed out at the dusty palm trees and the foreign wind. Winter didn't really know how the place looked, apart from the photographs that his mother had sent and he'd only glanced at. The house was white and stood next to several other houses in the same style. In one picture his mother sat on a veranda built out of white stone. It looked lonely. The sun behind her was on its way down, the sky so blue that it looked black against the whiteness. His father may have taken the photo, since he wasn't there on the veranda. His mother looked as though she were searching for something in the eye of the camera. She was smiling, but he had looked at the photograph long enough to see that it wasn't a happy smile. She looked like someone who had reached a goal and become confused or disappointed.

"I heard from Lotta that you'd been to see her," she said. "It made me so happy. And her too, I can tell you."

"Yes."

"It means so much to her. She's more alone than you know."

Then why don't you come home? he thought.

"She's coming down to see us in October with the girls."

"That'll do her good."

"It's her fortieth birthday. Imagine."

"A big day."

"Your big sister."

"Mother, I—"

"I don't dare ask you to come down here anymore. It's a crying shame, Erik. We'd so like for you to come down. Your father especially."

He didn't answer. He thought he heard something close to her, a voice, but it might have been a Spanish wind or a Spanish seabird.

"I don't know what to do about it," his mother said.

"You don't have to do anything."

"I can't do more."

"We don't have to talk about it."

"Can't you call next time? On the weekend?"

"I'll try."

"You never call. It's pointless my even asking. It'll be just the same as it always is. How's Angela?"

The question came suddenly. He didn't know what to say.

"You're still seeing each other?"

"Yes."

"It would be nice to actually get to meet her one day."

Ester Bergman stood outside the store and studied the big notice board. They had put it up quite recently. It was the only one she had seen in the area.

Her bag was heavy since she had done the shopping for several days. It had become more difficult for her to find what she was looking for since the store started to stock so many new products that people from other countries bought. Strange vegetables and cans.

She tried to read. The local parish was going to have a sing-along. She'd go and listen, if she had time. The property management company was organizing a party for one of the other courtyards, but it didn't seem to be open to everyone. She wondered why. The police had put up a poster about someone who'd gone missing. It occurred to her that people seem to go missing a lot, and then she thought about the red-haired girl and her fair-haired mother, who were so quiet and still whenever they walked past. Where are they now? she thought again. I miss that little girl. I enjoyed watching her when she played in the sand.

Where had they moved to? She regretted that she hadn't at least spoken to the girl. That's the sort of thing you regret, she thought. There are a lot of things you can regret when you get old. I regret never having had children. It's strange to think about. We couldn't have children, and it might not have been my fault. It may have been Elmer's fault, but he didn't want to get himself examined and I let him decide. I regret that now. What if I'd known that I'd grow old and sit here regretting all the things I hadn't done? All the sins I hadn't committed.

She read the notice posted on the bulletin board again. She had to strain because the print could have been bigger. If they wanted people to read it, they ought to think about not making the letters so small.

When she walked back, she thought once again about the girl who had been so quiet. Why am I thinking about that so much? I've been doing that for a few days now.

On the way back to her unit, she walked past the property management office. A sign outside said "Residential Services." Was that something new? There was also something about a "district superintendent" who manned the office during opening hours. What was a district superintendent? She didn't know, but it must be someone who knew something about the area or the buildings. She could pay a visit to that district super and ask. It's not good to go around thinking all the time. She could ask when that mother and her little girl moved away and where they went.

26

THE TEMPERATURE DROPPED LATE IN THE NIGHT. WHEN WINTER awoke, the air in the apartment smelled different—of green instead of white. It was colder and darker, like a lingering sadness at the long summer's passing, finally expired at a record old age.

He put his feet on the sanded fir floor, its coolness soft beneath the arches of his feet. Then he yawned, a leftover from burning the midnight oil with his head bowed over the PowerBook he could now see through the bedroom doorway, screen still open. Today it was a different apartment. He'd grown used to four months of almost constant sunshine and a home that offered no protection from the light.

In the kitchen he raised the blinds without getting dazzled. The sky had no opening. An invisible rain made the awnings across the park glisten. The streetcars passed beneath him with a sound reminiscent of a ship.

Winter walked back into the living room in his robe and opened the door to the balcony. The wet became more audible, as if he'd stepped out of a wheelhouse and found himself at sea.

He drew air into his lungs, as much as he could manage. It felt good. He felt good. The fatigue from the night before was gone, and he realized that the heavy heat had had an adverse effect on him, on his work.

It was like a depression, he thought. Everything started to crumble to bits. We saw the proof. Things exploded. People went crazy and shot each other. A man and his son were at the end of their tether.

A week earlier, the dramatic standoff outside Ullevi had had an undramatic resolution. The man left his gun on the bus and stepped off, holding his son by the hand. Winter heard that the son seemed happy and perky, waving to his mother, who was standing there—she who had pleaded with her husband.

The family's lawyer had submitted a new application for a residence permit. But the government was following a hard line. Desperation was to be regarded as threat and coercion. Despair, though it may move the hearts of the weak, had no effect on the authorities' judgment.

It was nine o'clock in the morning and it was Saturday. The dizziness had returned for two split seconds on Friday afternoon, so Winter had decided to stay home in the shadows today.

Now the shadows were gone, as was that nagging sensation of losing his footing. He knew he would not feel dizzy again, not for a very long time. I'm more of a northerner than I realized, he thought. Surround me with crispness and cold and I function better.

Winter stepped back inside and lingered by his desk. He looked at the computer screen but didn't turn it on. Last night he'd tried to sort through all the various sidetracks, as if he were working in a rail yard. He'd followed different leads until they ended, then reversed course to see if he could spot anything that had fallen off along the way, in a ditch or in the grass.

A lot of time had been spent following up on every public sighting of thirty-year-old fair-haired women at "mysterious" locations or who'd appeared generally confused or suspicious. Winter had sent all the documentation to Interpol. It was a new tack, and he hadn't received any usable information from there as yet. He didn't think she came from another country. The fillings in her teeth were done in Sweden, even the ones that were done when she was a little girl. She could have been living abroad, but that was another matter.

He'd called up other police precincts throughout the country.

His staff had continued to question the boys about the boat, and they were telling the truth. But their boat had been used for something. Maybe it was the boat that Andrea Maltzer saw out on the lake. If she really had seen a boat. Winter had thought about her, and her lover, von Holten. There was something—he didn't know what it was—something that made him not quite swallow her whole story. Why hadn't she called a cab right away? Had she planned on borrowing the car? Was she there alone? All these questions ran through Winter's mind, and he'd typed them on his screen before the temperature outside had dropped.

Two officers had spent almost a week trawling through the vehicle registration database in search of the owners of the Ford Escorts located within the geographical area he had decided they should limit themselves to. They would start with all the license plates beginning with the letter H. Not even then could they be sure. I don't know, he'd thought to himself the night before, with the blue glow from the screen on his face. Is this therapy? He'd thought about the woman again. Helene with no name. Inside he knew they wouldn't make any progress without her identity. He knew that the others knew.

He raised his gaze from the PowerBook and returned to the kitchen to put on the electric kettle for tea. He poured the leaves into the pot and toasted two slices of French bread from the day-old loaf he'd bought at a convenience store on the way home. He could have pulled on his trousers and shirt and taken the elevator down to the bakery across the park. Why don't I do that, he thought, and left the bread where it was and went back into the bedroom and threw off his robe and put on a pair of shorts and a shirt.

He bought fresh poppy-seed buns and a brioche, returning across the grass and feeling his sandaled toes get wet. Back upstairs he made himself a café au lait instead of tea and squeezed three oranges and poured the juice into a glass. He ate the still-warm bread with butter and cherry jam, and with a boiled egg that he peeled and sliced up and ground black pepper over. He drank two cups of coffee and read the paper. He felt ready for anything.

Ester Bergman cautiously stuck her hand out the window and felt the dampness. It was good for the skin. She kept her hand there long enough that tiny droplets of water formed in the folds of her palm. She thought the world looked dark when the sun wasn't there to wash everything out.

She'd stayed indoors for several days because she hadn't been feeling well. She hadn't had the energy to go to residential services, or whatever it's called. Then the woman from the home-help service had come—the new one whose name she didn't know—and had futzed around the apartment as if she were cleaning. But Ester knew she wasn't actually cleaning, that everything looked almost the same when she left as it had when she arrived. Sometimes she does the dishes even though I've already done them, Ester thought. When she thinks I'm not looking, she takes out the glasses and washes them again, as if I couldn't look after myself.

She may be nice, but she's not family. Ester Bergman had thought about that sometimes, but there was no point in thinking like that. No family was going to drop in for a visit, no matter how much she wished for it. That's just the way it was. An old woman couldn't have a family if she'd had an old man who didn't want more people in the house.

"Seems like you've got a little fever, Ester," the home-help woman had said, and put her hand on her forehead.

"I'm lying here thinking about something."

"Oh yeah?"

"Do you notice the people who live around this courtyard?"

"How do you mean, Ester?"

"Do you recognize them, you people who work around here, visiting with old people and such?"

"You mean, do we recognize our clie— the ones we go to visit? Of course we do."

"No no. I mean the other people around here. The others who live here."

"The others?"

"The children and the others on the street! The children and their mothers!"

"Are you thinking of anyone in particular, Ester?"

"No, never mind."

"Tell me if you're thinking of anyone special, Ester."

It's always Ester this and Ester that with this woman, she'd thought to herself. She was getting a headache from hearing her name all the time. "There used to be a little girl with bright red hair. She would sit out there with her mother sometimes or play while her mother sat near-by. They're not here anymore."

"You haven't seen them, Ester?"

"I haven't seen them for quite a while. I was just wondering if you'd seen them."

"A girl with red hair? How old?"

"I don't know. A little one, five or something maybe."

The woman from the home-help service looked like she was think-ing. I wonder if she really is thinking, Ester Bergman thought. She smells of smoke. She wants to get out of here and have a smoke out on the steps.

"The mother smoked too."

"What did you say, Ester?"

"I said that the girl's mother smoked too. If she was her mother."

"What did her mother look like?"

"She was fair and looked like all young people do these days, I guess."

"She was young, you say, Ester?"

"Everyone's young to me, I suppose."

The home-help woman smiled. She looked like she was thinking again.

"I can't picture them," she said. "But I don't get to see much of the courtyard. We just come in here, after all, and into the entranceways." She appeared to be thinking again. "No, I can't picture them."

"Ester would like some coffee now," said Ester Bergman.

The service woman again placed her hand on Ester's forehead. "Now, you just lie still here while I go fetch the cup."

"I'm not going anywhere."

Then she'd been left on her own again. She thought about this now, as her hand grew increasingly wet. The rain felt good. Old people have a hard time in the heat, she thought. Even old people from other countries stay indoors when it's hot outside.

She pulled in her hand but left the window open. There were streaks running down the pane. It smelled like when she was a child. Through the rain-washed window she could see the children outside.

Suddenly it was as if something struck her hard in the chest. She thought she saw a head of red hair through the window. She leaned forward, then pushed open the window to get a better view. But she didn't see anyone with red hair or anyone else for that matter—there was nothing outside her window right now. Look how I'm behaving, she thought. I'm seeing ghosts.

Aneta Djanali returned home with the fall. It smelled stagnant in her apartment. She opened a window, and despite the total absence of wind she saw a little fluff of dust whirl in the center of the room. The first thing she did was put on some music, and it wasn't jazz.

It was early afternoon, but it felt like evening, when the light is gone and doesn't pierce through everything anymore. This light lingered around things. It was discreet, relaxing for the mind, she thought, pouring herself a glass of whiskey from the bottle on the kitchen counter. The last time she'd poured from it was the evening she was beaten up. It was a strange feeling. She'd sat here with Lis, sipped at a whiskey, and then gone out. Now she was back and sipping another as if it had just been a little parenthesis in time. She drank a little more and grimaced as much as she dared with her patched-up mandible. The alcohol flared up at once and became a little flame that flickered around inside her body, swept down her nerve endings, and flushed out into her bloodstream. Better than painkillers, she thought, and took a little whiskey in her mouth and let it slowly trickle down into her throat. I feel pretty good, she said silently to herself.

ESTER BERGMAN TOOK A SIP OF HER COFFEE, BUT SHE WAS thinking about something else. The young man on the radio had just said that it was eight o'clock. She was all dressed and ready to go. The woman from the home-help service wasn't coming today, and that was a relief.

She lingered outside the office and read the sign, just to be sure. She was a little nervous once she was standing there. Speaking to a stranger about that girl and her mother—it felt silly now. What business was it of hers? It was better to go back and che—

"Mrs. Bergman, you shouldn't be standing out here in the rain," the girl who had come out from the office said. "Can I help you with something? Do you need help with anything from the store, Mrs. Bergman?"

"No. No, thank you," she said, recognizing the girl from her courtyard. They had said hello a few times. "You know my name?"

"Well, you've lived here for such a long time, Mrs. Bergman," the girl said. "We've spoken to each other. My name is Karin Sohlberg."

"Lived here for a long time? Since it was built." That was true. They'd moved here in 1958, when everything was new and filled with light. Elmer had never explained how they had been able to afford it, and she hadn't asked. She hadn't asked about anything at all, and that had been foolish.

"You're getting wet, Mrs. Bergman."

"Could I come in for a moment? There was something I wanted to ask you about."

"Sure. We shouldn't stand out here any longer. I'll take your arm, and we'll walk up the steps."

Inside the desk lamp was on, illuminating a surface covered with papers. She was offered a comfortable chair to sit in.

The telephone rang, but by the time the girl picked up the phone there was nobody there. She put down the receiver and turned to her visitor. This could take a while, and that didn't matter.

"The weather really turned around."

Ester Bergman didn't answer. She was thinking about what to say.

"It really feels nice," the girl said.

"I wanted to ask about those two who were living in one of the units farther up from me. A mother and her daughter."

The girl looked at her as if she hadn't heard, as if she wanted to keep talking about the weather. It used to be old people that talked about the weather—now it's apparently young people, thought Ester Bergman. "A little girl with red hair," she said.

"I'm not sure I understand, Mrs. Bergman."

"There's a little girl with red hair I haven't seen for a long time. And her mother. I haven't seen them and that's why I'm asking about them."

"Are they friends of yours, Mrs. Bergman?"

"No. Do they have to be?"

"No no. But you want to know something about them, Mrs. Bergman?"

"I haven't seen them for some time. Do you know who I mean?"

The girl stood and walked over to a filing cabinet, returning with a thin pile of papers, which she laid on the table in front of her. Then she looked at Ester Bergman again. "This is the list of all the apartments on your courtyard, from number 326 to 486."

"I see."

"You said a little girl with red hair? And her mother? What did she look like?"

"I don't know that she actually was her mother. She had fair hair, but I don't know any more than that. I never spoke to her. Not once."

"I think I remember," the girl said. "There aren't that many girls with red hair, after all."

"Not in my courtyard anyway."

"A single mother with one child," the girl said, and flipped through her records.

"I saw the notice from the police," Ester Bergman said suddenly.

The girl looked up. "What did you say, Mrs. Bergman?"

"There's a notice from the police out here on the bulletin board. They're looking for a young person." She hadn't thought about that before. "They're looking for a woman with light hair."

"They are?"

"Haven't they handed them out to this office? The police? They should have, surely."

"I've been on vacation. The office was closed for a while for renovation. You might still be able to smell the paint, Mrs. Bergman."

"No."

The girl looked in her files again.

"We have a number of single mothers with small children. You only saw the mother with the one child, Mrs. Bergman?"

"The mother had fair hair and the girl had red—"

"I mean, did she have any more children. Or a husband."

"Not that I saw."

"And you don't know which entrance was theirs?"

"No. But it was down a bit from mine."

The girl looked in her files again, flipped through them a ways. "Judging from the apartment numb—" The girl looked up. "I'm looking for possible apartment and personal identity numbers from the list here," she said.

It wasn't the first time somebody had asked about someone who hadn't been seen for a while. Last spring a neighbor had started to wonder why he never saw the gentleman who lived in the apartment just below him, even though the light was on. After a week, the neighbor had come to see the unit super. Karin Sohlberg went over and rang the doorbell, and when no one opened the door, she peered through the letter slot at a pile of mail. Since the man had no family she could contact, and she didn't have the authority to enter the apartment herself, she called the police. The old man was sitting there dead in his chair. Afterward she thought about how she hadn't detected any smell.

She continued to run down the columns on the list.

"Find anything?" Ester Bergman asked.

"It could be Helene Andersén you're wondering about. She lives two doorways up from you." She muttered an apartment number that Ester Bergman couldn't catch.

"Does she have a red-haired girl?"

"It doesn't say, Mrs. Bergman." The girl looked up. "But I wonder if she doesn't—wait a minute." She eyed the list again. "She has a little daughter named Jennie. It actually says so here."

"Jennie?"

"Yes. That might be them. I can't really say what they look like until I've seen them."

"But they're not here anymore. They're gone."

"How long has it been since you last saw the girl? Or the mother?"

"I can't say for sure, but it was a month or so ago. When it was hot. And it was hot for a long time after. And now it's been bad weather for a while too."

"They may have gone away on vacation. Or to visit someone."

"For so long?"

The woman made a gesture signaling that stuff like that could happen.

"I thought perhaps they had moved," Ester Bergman said.

"No. They haven't moved."

"I see. But they're not here anymore."

"I know what we can do. I can go over there and ring the doorbell and see if anyone's home."

"What are you going to say if somebody answers?"

"I'll have to think of something," the girl said, and smiled.

Ester Bergman didn't want to go along, so Karin Sohlberg entered the stairwell alone and walked up to the second floor. She rang the doorbell and waited. She rang the doorbell again and listened to the echo inside the apartment. It was still echoing when she opened the letter slot and saw the little pile of junk mail and other correspondence she couldn't identify. You couldn't see how much was lying there.

She headed back down the stairs and a minute later rang on Ester Bergman's door. The old woman opened up at once, as if she'd been standing just inside the door.

"Nobody's home."

"That's what I've been saying the whole time."

"There was some mail lying just inside the door, but that could have a number of explanations."

"I just want one," Ester Bergman said.

"There's one more thing I can do for you, Mrs. Bergman." And for myself, she thought. I want to know too. "I can go to the district office and see if the rent has been paid."

"You can see that?"

"We're far enough into September now that we can see whether the rent has been paid or if a reminder has been sent out to Helene Andersén."

"I'm mostly concerned about the little girl."

"Do you understand what I mean, Mrs. Bergman?"

"I'm not stupid and I'm not deaf," Ester Bergman said. "You go to that office. That's fine."

Karin Sohlberg walked to the district office in the old central heating facility on Dimvädersgatan and checked on the computer whether Helene Andersén's last rent had been paid. It had, on the second of the month. Technically one day late, but it had been a weekend. In any case, the rent had been paid at the post office less than two weeks ago. Just like usual. Helene Andersén apparently always took her preprinted payment slip to the post office and paid first thing. Many people did this, and most of the tenants in the area used the post office at Länsmanstorget, thought Karin Sohlberg.

Ester Bergman had said the mother and the girl had been gone a long time. That sort of measure was relative. Old people could say one thing and mean something else. In that sense perhaps they're not much different from anybody else—but to them a week can feel like a month. Time could pass slowly and yet all too quickly. Karin Sohlberg had sometimes thought about the elderly who sat there all alone with their thoughts, with so much inside of them that has to come out or else get bottled up.

She stood outside her office again. It was past opening hours. She tried to remember the face that belonged to the apartment, but she couldn't recall seeing anyone with fair hair. Maybe a little girl with red hair, but she couldn't be sure. She'd just had a long vacation with a lot of different faces around her.

Ester Bergman wasn't confused. Her eyesight may not have been what it once was, but it was still sharp in its way. She wasn't the type to go around jabbering about things for no reason. It must have taken her a long time to decide to come to the service office. What she'd said—that the little family hadn't been there for a long time—might well be true. The question was what this meant. The rent was paid. But that didn't mean they had to live there every single day.

She may have met a man, thought Karin Sohlberg. She met a man and they moved in with him, but she's not ready yet to let go of her apartment because she's unsure. She doesn't trust men because she's been burned before. Maybe. Probably. It's probable because it's common, Karin Sohlberg thought, glancing down at her left ring finger, where a thin band of white skin still shone against her tanned hand.

She walked over and looked at the notice. It was laminated, which suggested the police wanted it to be able to hang there through all kinds of weather. At first she didn't understand what the connection was to this area, but then she thought about Ester Bergman: If she can see a possible connection, then I suppose I can too. But still, the rent was paid. She read about the missing woman again then unlocked the door to her office. She didn't have time. If she remained sitting there, someone was bound to come in and then she'd have even less time.

She walked back to the courtyard and entered Helene Andersén's stairwell and stood once again at her door and rang. The echo of the doorbell chime never faded out completely. Through the letter slot she could only see the brightly colored junk mail and a few brown and white envelopes. They look like bills, but I can't be sure, she thought. But I can be sure that nobody in there has opened the mail for quite some time.

She didn't see any newspapers, but that didn't mean anything. Many people couldn't afford a morning paper anymore, or had given it up for something else instead.

Eventually it felt strange standing there, sort of spooky—as if she expected to see a pair of feet come toward her. She recoiled with that thought and returned to the courtyard and looked up toward Helene Andersén's kitchen window. The blinds were drawn, and that distinguished her window from those adjacent, above, and below. During the heat wave, the blinds in all the windows had been down, but now the window she was looking at was virtually the only one.

She exited through the building's main entrance and tried to locate Helene Andersén's window from the outside. It wasn't difficult, since the blinds were down on that side too. It was a natural thing to do when you went away. After half a minute she had that same unsettling feeling and closed her eyes in order not to see a shadow suddenly appear in the window. My God, here I am getting myself all worked up, she thought, and looked away in order not to see that movement, the shadow. It was a powerful sensation, this dread, as if she'd lost her skin in a split second. Then it was over and she was herself again.

Sohlberg felt foolish as she rang the doorbell of the Athanassiou family in the apartment immediately below. Mr. Athanassiou opened the door, and it was a familiar face. She asked as simply as she could about the woman and the girl upstairs. The man responded by shaking his head. They hadn't seen them for a while, but who could know when the last time had been? No, they hadn't heard anything. They had always been quiet up there, the whole time they had been living there. The girl may have run around a little sometimes, but nothing they had reason to complain about. My ceiling is someone else's floor, after all, the man said, and when he pointed upward, Karin Sohlberg thought about the Greek philosophers.

She was drawn to the notice board again but stopped at Ester Bergman's window when she saw the old lady through the glass. Mrs. Bergman opened the window, but Sohlberg said nothing to her about the rent having been paid. Perhaps she wanted to keep the mystery alive a little longer for the old lady. Maybe I want to keep it alive for myself too, she thought.

Now she stood in front of the notice board and wrote down the phone numbers for the district CID's homicide department.

At the window, Mrs. Bergman had said she wanted to write a letter to the police. Could the young lady help her?

"If you would like to contact the police, Mrs. Bergman, then maybe you can call them," Sohlberg had answered. "I could help you."

"I don't like the telephone. Nothing gets said."

28

SITTING WITH ESTER BERGMAN WHILE THE RAIN BEAT AGAINST
the kitchen window, Karin Sohlberg imagined that this, more or less,
must be the old lady's world. Or was that a preconceived notion? She
was often here in the kitchen, at her window. She must notice quite a lot
in her world of faces and voices that she saw and heard but didn't know.

The shouts from the children sounded far away. Sohlberg could see
them moving in the playground like blurred little splotches of color.
When the rain came, the colors came too, she thought, and turned away
from the window toward Mrs. Bergman. "What should I write, then?"

"Write that we're wondering where the mother is, and her little
girl."

"Perhaps we should mention the notice about the dead woman."

"You can write that we read it on the bulletin board. And that the
mother is fair haired."

"Yes."

"Don't forget to put down which courtyard it is."

"No."

"You don't need to put down my age."

Karin Sohlberg smiled and looked up from the sheet of letter paper
Mrs. Bergman had taken out of a beautiful writing desk in her living
room. "No, we don't need to write your age."

"You can write down the age of the mother and daughter."

"I'll start now."

"Don't forget to say they've been gone since well before the rains
came."

"Maybe we don't really—"

"I know what you're trying to say. But I know that to be the case."

"Yes."

Karin Sohlberg thought to herself, What right did she actually have

to write her way into Helene Andersén's private life? Maybe she wanted
to be left in peace. That was normal. And the girl wasn't old enough that
she had to be in school.

It occurred to her that she could ask around to find out if the girl had
been attending day care or nursery school in the area. But was that her
job? Or was she just curious?

"You can sign it with your own name if you want," Ester Bergman
said.

"Why would I do that, Mrs. Bergman?"

"You'll do a better job of talking to the police when they come here
in their cars."

"But you're the one who's most convinced that they've been gone a
long time."

"I still say you'll do a better job of talking. And I don't like it when
too many people come here in their cars and with their dogs. Or horses,
for that matter."

"I don't think there'll be that many. Maybe just one or two, asking a
few questions. And it might take a while before they come. If they come
at all."

"Why wouldn't they?"

Sohlberg didn't know what to say. She looked outside, as if hoping the
mother and her red-haired girl would walk past holding hands. "How
about we say that I'll be with you when you speak to the police? I can sit
next to you, Mrs. Bergman."

"I guess we could say that."

"Then I'll seal this and send it."

"Read it to me again."

As she read she thought about how it would end up at the bottom of
some pile. The police must receive hundreds or thousands of tips like
this about missing people.

Winter pulled a report from the increasingly voluminous preliminary
investigation, a pile of papers that grew on his desk. He sat wearing his
blazer and worked with the window open.

There was a grand total of 124 white Ford Escort 1.8 CLX three-door
hatchbacks dating from '91 to '94 with license plates beginning with the
letter H in the districts of Gothenburg, Kungälv, Kungsbacka, and Härryda. Peculiarly, none began with HE.

He'd sat again for a long time in front of the blurred video footage
and was sure the first letter on the plate was an H. There was no doubt
in his mind.

One of the cars on the new list was the car on the screen. What had it been doing there?

It really wasn't a manageable number, 124, even if he had, along with the plate numbers, the name, address, and personal identity number of all the owners.

Of the 124 cars, 2 had been reported stolen at the time of Helene's murder. One had been found, badly parked with a bone-dry gas tank, in the parking lot in front of Swedish Match. There was no sign of the other.

Questioning people about their whereabouts at certain times in their lives was always a process of elimination—of listening and, on the basis of what was said, deciding who was lying and how much and, possibly, why.

The most problematic were those who lied, not because they had done anything illegal—their actions may well have been immoral, unethical, or deceitful toward someone close to them, yet nothing that was against the law—but because under no circumstances did they want to reveal what they had done in secret. They'd rather let murderers go free.

He felt restless. He wanted to wander out into the field again but instead played Coltrane on his portable Panasonic perched on a bench by the window. Still, "Trane's Slo Blues" brought him no peace. He tapped the rhythm against the edge of the desk with the middle finger of his left hand and looked through the files while Earl May busted out his bass solo from a studio in Hackensack, New Jersey, on August 16, 1957. Winter had never been there. You have to save some things for later.

His thoughts drifted to "Lush Life," and for a few seconds he became absorbed by the powerful melody. Janne Möllerström stepped into the room just as Red Garland began his piano solo.

"Well, isn't this cozy," Möllerström said.

"Yes."

"What is it?" Möllerström nodded toward the CD player.

"The Clash."

"What?"

"The Clash. A British rock—"

"That's not the Clash, for Christ's sake. I've got the Clash."

"Just yanking your chain. Can't you hear who it is?"

"All I hear is some nice piano. And here comes a trumpet. Must be Herb Alpert."

Winter laughed.

"Tijuana Brass," Möllerström said. "My dad liked it too."

"Really."

"Just yanking your chain," Möllerström said. "Since you're the one listening to it, I'll hazard a wild guess that it's John Coltrane."

"Naturally. But I don't suppose that's why you stopped by."

"I have a letter here that I think you should look at," Möllerström said.

"Okay." Winter took the Xerox and read it, then turned his gaze back to his registry clerk. "What makes you think this might be something?"

"I don't know. Maybe because they're two of them—that older lady and the girl writing on her behalf, so to speak."

"There's something hesitant about it."

"Exactly. Or restrained, as if they're doing their duty or something. Not trying to get attention."

"Not wackos, you mean?"

"Yes."

"The one who wrote the letter—Karin Sohlberg—she's added that we can call her if it's worth investigating. That's what she writes, 'worth investigating.'"

"I saw that."

"What do you think, Janne?"

"About what?"

"Is this letter worth investigating? Should we call her?"

"That's why I came by."

"Good." Winter reached for the telephone.

It wouldn't be the first time in the past week they'd gone out to speak with the family of someone who'd been reported missing, only to discover a natural explanation for the "disappearance." The most natural one being that no one had disappeared. In the most drastic instance, a young woman had been in the hospital without her neighbors knowing about it.

"Hello? Karin Sohlberg? This is Inspector Erik Winter at district CID, homicide division." He waved at Möllerström to turn down the volume. "Yes, we received the letter. That's why I'm calling. Leave that for us to decide. It's never wrong to be vigilant. But Ester's the one who's particularly concerned? That could be a good thing. Yes. One should always care about others." Winter nodded to Möllerström to turn off the music completely.

"Helene Andersén actually hasn't been seen for a while," Karin Sohlberg said on the telephone from Hisingen.

Winter thought at first that he had misheard. That it was his own thoughts he had perceived, that the old dreams were suddenly back

again. He saw his Helene, her face in the obscene light over the gurney.
"Excuse me?" he said. "What did you say her name was?"

"Helene Andersén. She's the one we're concerned about, but I didn't
want to wri—"

"So this woman that you haven't seen for a while, her name is
Helene?" Winter felt that the incredulity in his voice was far too obvious. He had spoken gruffly, his throat constricted.

"Is there something wrong? Was it a mista—"

"No no," Winter said. "It's just fine. We'll be happy to come out and
talk with you about this. Could we meet," he looked at his watch, "in
half an hour? In the courtyard you referred to in your letter?"

"Do you always proceed this way?"

"Excuse me?"

"Do you always investigate things this promptly?"

"The important thing is to meet up and talk about it."

"In that case we can do it at my office," she said. "It's just next door.
You'll see it when you come up from the parking lot." She gave them an
address. "Should I ask Mrs.—Ester Bergman to come here?"

"No. We'll come by and talk with you, and then we can go to her
house together." Winter thought for a moment. "Could you let her know
that we would like to ask her a few questions today? It won't take long."

"She's probably a little anxious about that. That a lot of people might
come, for example."

"I understand. But it'll just be me."

"She has this image of uniforms and dog leashes. And dogs too, for
that matter."

"It'll just be me," Winter repeated. "A nice young man who'd love to
come in for a cup of coffee."

Halders tried not to think about whether the man sitting in front of
him was lying because he was just nervous in general or because he had
something to hide. It was nothing big, just little lies that flickered in the
corner of his eye every time he shifted his gaze. It was easy to see. Each
time he told a little lie, he looked away. Halders wondered if they should
be clearer in their questioning. Have a clearer intention.

"I haven't been part of that gang for ten years."

The man had come straight here from his auto repair shop, and
Halders noticed thin strips of oil and other crud underneath the man's
nails, and that was a likable quality. Overall, he was a likable guy, apart
from his furtive gaze.

"What gang?" Halders asked.

"You know. You've spoken about it before."

"I didn't say anything about a gang."

"Then it was somebody else. But I'm clean. I keep my head down."

"Can you ever really steer clear?"

"Of course you can. There's so much fear propaganda."

"You're saying it's propaganda?"

"I'm saying it's exaggerated."

"But you still keep your head down."

"It sounds like I'm under suspicion for something."

Halders didn't answer the man, whose name was Jonas Svensk.

"Am I?"

"I just want you to tell me about Peter Bolander," Halders said.

"He works in my repair shop, and that's all I can tell you about him. You'll have to ask him."

"He, on the other hand, is under suspicion," Halders said.

"I know that he's been arrested in connection with that shoot-out on Vårväderstorget, but I also know that he says that he wasn't there," Svensk said.

"He was seen there. Holding a rifle. And when we came to see him at his house, his Remington was gone."

Svensk shrugged his shoulders. "Rifles can get stolen. That's what he says too. And he looks like a hundred other guys. But I don't know either way. I'm not here to defend him for something I don't know if he's done or not. He was off work that day, I already told you. And I certainly wasn't there. I've got an alibi."

Halders didn't answer.

"It's not a crime to hire people," Svensk said.

"No."

"I used to be a member of Hells Angels. Peter might also have been. But you can't accuse me of anything. I'm not a member anymore. It was a sin of my youth."

"Okay."

"And if you think this is a gang showdown, then you're mistaken."

"Why would we think that?"

"Isn't that what you think?"

"That it was a showdown between gangs?"

"Yes."

"Or an internal showdown?"

"Well, I don't know."

"It's hardly a secret, even for someone who keeps his head low, that there have been showdowns within the Hells Angels in Gothenburg."

"I may have seen something about it. But wasn't that the Bandidos?"

Halders wondered once again why Svensk was playing dumber than he was.

"You might want to check out the Arabs."

"The Arabs?" Halders said.

"Check out the Islamists," Svensk said. "I think they're the ones who were shooting at each other. They've been a bit restless this summer. You know that too. And just look at what's happening in Algeria now."

29

RINGMAR DROVE ACROSS THE GÖTAÄLV BRIDGE. THE RAILROAD cars stood enveloped in fog along the Frihamnen docks.

"I have a feeling we've driven this way before," he said.

"It wasn't that long ago," Winter said. He was tense with thought about what might be awaiting them in a little while. He needed a cigarillo and stuck a Corps in his mouth without lighting it.

They approached Vårväderstorget. The fields alongside Rambergsvallen Stadium appeared to be floating above the ground like an extension of the Lundbybadet swimming complex. Everything Winter saw was enclosed and fenced off, as if enormous walls of water had been lowered from the sky and surrounded his field of vision, held in place by clouds.

Vårväderstorget was barely visible.

"It feels like years ago," Ringmar said, and nodded to the left. "Like another age. Or another country."

"It very nearly is," Winter said. "Or was."

"It's a weak lead."

"They've behaved themselves for a long time. Maybe the pressure has to get released somehow."

"Maybe it was because of the heat."

"Leather jackets are hot when it's ninety degrees out."

"Hells Angels show up in suits these days." Ringmar glanced out of the corner of his eye at Winter's graphite-colored Corneliani suit and the Oscar Jacobson coat that lay in his lap.

"If they show up at all," Winter said. "They're like British football hooligans."

"How so?"

"You never see them anymore. But they're still there."

"We've got a close eye on our Angels," Ringmar said. "At least we thought we did."

They turned up onto Flygvädersgatan and found their bearings from a sign that said "North Biskopsgården." Off to the right, Winter could see the enormous tenement blocks, the top floors of which disappeared into the low sky. The buildings were so tall they seemed to move away from him.

The satellite dishes on the building sides were like uncovered eyes looking toward outer space, or ears that had been turned into steel to home in on voices and movements in countries that the people here dreamed their dreams about, or open mouths that called out for answers, thought Winter.

Karin Sohlberg was waiting outside the office in a raincoat. Winter was surprised by her Asian features, since on the phone she sounded like she'd grown up in Gråberget or Lindholmen. And maybe she had. He thought briefly about Aneta and why he'd been surprised just now.

Inside, she invited them to sit, but Ringmar remained standing. She did too, with her raincoat unbuttoned. Winter had sat down in a chair in front of the desk but stood up again when no one else sat down.

"So the September rent for this woman's apartment has been paid," he said. One might well ask what we're doing here, then, he thought. "That was on the first, you said?"

"Yes. Right after the weekend."

"So no reminder was sent out?"

"No, but that's not my depart— No, it takes longer than that. First they check the account. The reminder gets sent out after five or six days."

"And you haven't seen Helene Andersén and her daughter for a while?"

"No. But I'm honestly not sure if I remember them. I haven't been here for very long."

"What was the daughter's name?" Ringmar asked.

"Jennie."

"How do you know that?"

Sohlberg mentioned the tenant lists she had, and indicated with her hand that they were lying on her desk.

"And this old lady lives there too?" Winter asked.

"Yes. Ester Bergman."

"Then let's go," Winter said. "Is there a locksmith nearby?"

Sohlberg nodded.

The entrance was longer than Winter had expected, which must mean the apartments were long and narrow.

It was a large courtyard—impossible to see across to the other side in the fog. Maybe this is how it always is for Ester, Karin Sohlberg thought. Right now I'm seeing what she sees.

A few children were playing on a tangle of monkey bars in the middle of the courtyard. A child shouted something, but Winter couldn't hear what. The shout didn't reach very far, perhaps because of all the buildings.

They turned left into a second doorway. Winter read the names on the board just inside: Sabror, Ali, Khajavi, Gülmer, Sanchez, and Bergman. Two apartments per floor. They walked up the first half flight, and Karin Sohlberg pressed the bell. Winter noticed Ringmar's grave expression. We feel the same way, he thought. Damn it! I said I'd come alone. But then the old lady opened the door as if she'd been standing just inside waiting for the ringer to sound.

They drank a cup of boiled coffee that clutched at the gut. Winter accepted the offer of a refill and caught a look from Karin Sohlberg. It smelled dusty and sweet in the apartment, as it did in old people's homes.

"So you haven't seen Helene and her daughter for some time, Mrs. Bergman?" He was trying to sound gentle.

"I didn't know what her name was."

"The girl's name is Jennie," Winter said.

"She had red hair," Ester Bergman said.

"Yes."

"What's happened to them?"

"We don't know," Winter said, leaning forward. "That's why we're here."

"Well, surely something must have happened—otherwise you wouldn't be here."

"We received your letter, Mrs. Bergman, and that's why we're here."

"Are you really a police officer?" Ester Bergman squinted her eyes at Winter.

Winter set down his cup. "Yes."

"You're so young," Ester Bergman said. Still wet behind the ears, not that you can see them. He could do with a haircut. Aren't policemen supposed to have short hair? The other one has short hair and he's older. But he's not saying anything. "You can't be much older than her."

"Than whom?" Winter asked.

"Than her. The mother with the fair hair."

"So they haven't been here since it turned . . . Since the weather changed? Since the hot weather ended?"

"They weren't here then either," Ester Bergman said. "It was hot and I sat here at this window and didn't see them."

The stairwell smelled of liquid cleanser. Like in the other entrances, the walls at the bottom were of rough-hewn brick that gave way to yellow plaster. Winter read the list of names: Perez, Al Abtah, Wong, Andersén, Shafai, Gustavsson.

The second floor. Andersén. His temples were throbbing and he saw that Bertil noticed this. What Bertil didn't know was that he had christened the dead woman Helene a long time ago. But he understood. And hadn't asked why. Bertil was also clutching at straws in this investigation, as if he could feel them in his hands.

He nodded to the locksmith. They climbed the stairs and stopped in front of a door where a child's drawing hung a few inches above the nameplate inscribed "H. Andersén." Winter bent down a little. The drawing was of a ship on water. The sky was divided in two. It was raining to the right of the ship and to the left the sun was shining. The ship had round windows and in one of them you could see two eyes, a nose, and a mouth. The mouth was a straight line. A bit farther down, in the water, the girl had written "jeni."

Winter straightened and rang the doorbell, the noise so piercing he gave a start. Or else it only sounded that loud inside his head.

He pressed it again and heard the chime disappear, as if into the fog at the other end of the apartment. Ringmar stooped and lifted the hatch to the letter slot with a gloved hand and tried to peer inside. He saw colors from all the junk mail and the corners of envelopes.

Winter rang the doorbell a third time. It was the same sound, and he suddenly wished himself away from there. He closed his eyes and swallowed, and the pounding in his head subsided again. He nodded to the locksmith, and the man turned the key he had ready in the cylinder. There was no deadbolt above.

The door opened outward. They saw the little pile of papers on the carpet inside and the darkness of the hallway. A window was visible in the far room like a dim rectangle of light. Winter asked the others to wait and then stepped into the apartment after putting on the plastic shoe covers he'd removed from his coat pocket. In the silence he heard a humming from the refrigerator that he could now see to his left through the kitchen doorway. It smelled of silence in there and of dust that had

collected in the stagnant air. He continued on. To the right was a door
that was closed, while straight ahead lay what had to be the living room.
Winter's concentration was like an iron hand clenched tightly around
his brain. His gun was chaffing in his armpit more palpably than ever,
and he felt a powerful urge to draw his weapon. He looked at the closed
door, then moved cautiously through the open doorway and into the
living room. He saw a couch and table and armchairs. A small glass cabinet and a TV. A chest of drawers. Dead plants on two narrow shelves
beneath the windows. A carpet on the floor. A painting of an Indian
woman on the wall above the couch. Winter backed up and drew his
weapon. He stood in front of the shut door and pressed down the handle
and opened it with a jerk, in the same moment pressing back up against
the wall in the hallway. He leaned in toward the room. It was long and
narrow, with two beds at either end, the smaller one against the far wall.
Along the short wall next to him were wardrobes, one with the doors
open. The wall above the little bed was stapled with drawings. The window was closed and the room was hot—summer had remained trapped
inside here. The sun still shone in several spots above the girl's bed.
It was raining in a few of the drawings. In others there was both rain
and sunshine. I wonder what that means, Winter thought. He turned
his gaze toward the larger bed. Next to it stood a little bedside table
that held a telephone and an empty glass. There was a newspaper lying
there too and a framed color photograph of a fair-haired mother with
her red-haired little girl. Winter moved closer. The woman in the photo
was smiling a little smile that barely showed any teeth, and that was
Helene. He thought, as he stood there in front of the little frame, that
death hadn't done all that much to her face. Helene was Helene. They'd
finally made progress in the hunt for her killer, but he felt as yet no
satisfaction as a hunter. It was only now that it really began—this investigation that had been in the process of closing. Helene had been given
back her name. The little girl was smiling in the photo, wider and more
openly than her mother. The girl's name was Jennie, and she wasn't
here. At first Winter had felt relieved that he hadn't fou— But before he
could finish thinking that thought, it gave way to another almost just as
unspeakable, unthinkable. In the hunt for the killer they would also be
searching for the child. They had had a body without a name, and now
they had that name. But they now also had a name without a body. The
thought struck him hard and wouldn't leave him.

30

OFFICERS FROM THE FORENSICS DEPARTMENT'S CRIME SCENE
unit swabbed ninhydrin on the newspaper that lay on Helene Andersén's bedside table and applied the chemical to other loose objects. The
ninhydrin method allowed them to lift fingerprints that were left long
ago. Salts and proteins from people's sweat penetrate paper and stay
there, like a handshake through time.

Prints on steel could not be polished away. They were like etchings.
There were even methods for finding fingerprints on wet paper.

The officers dusted the apartment's surfaces with the black charcoal
powder Winter knew Beier didn't like. The iron in the powder rusted
when it became damp and left ugly marks.

The three technicians searched for prints by the light switches,
around doors, tables, and other surfaces that hands may have touched.
They dusted with powder and then waited for it to fully adhere to the
print residue, which they would then lift using tape.

The danger was not actually getting the print onto the tape, which
sometimes happened when it was too firmly attached. In the few in-
stances where this seemed likely, the fingerprint was photographed
before an attempt was made to lift it. The photographer always used
black-and-white film.

Karin Sohlberg was crying. Winter sat opposite her in the residential
services office.

"Ester was right," she said.

"Yes."

"What's she saying now?"

"I'm going to speak to her shortly."

"How awful." Sohlberg blew her nose. "That little girl and everything."

"You don't remember her?"

"I feel like I'm completely confused now. But I can't really remember. Maybe later."

"Well, I'm afraid we'll have to ask you to help us with the identification later."

"What does that mean? Do I have to accompany you to—to the morgue?"

"Yes, I'm afraid so. We're going to have to ask the old lady to come too. I'm sorry."

She thought quietly for a moment. "I know it sounds strange, but I haven't been here very long, after all, like I said. And maybe they were the kind of people who kept to themselves. Or the mother anyway."

"Kept to themselves?"

"Some people are a little quiet or don't attract much attention."

Winter knew what she meant. Loneliness could cause a person to withdraw. Loneliness and poverty. Winter was born into a poor family, but suddenly, while he was still a child, there was money. He'd spent his first years in one of the innumerable high-rises in the outskirts of Gothenburg. It was a world he still remembered.

Karin Sohlberg blew her nose again. A small group of onlookers had gathered outside the entrance to Helene Andersěn's courtyard, fifty yards away, on the other side, and followed a football game between two girls' teams.

"So her rent is paid," he said. "Do you know anything more about that?"

"No, nothing other than that's what I got from the computer at the district office."

"So you could only see that the rent for that specific apartment was paid?"

"Yes. On the computer."

"Paid using a preprinted rent slip?"

"Yes, or with a regular deposit slip. Manually, in other words."

"And Helene's rent could have been paid either with the rent slip sent out from your office or a regular blank deposit slip?"

"Yes."

"But you don't know which it was?"

"It's not specified. The computer only indicates that it's been paid."

"But if someone paid without the preprinted rent slip—that is, with a blank deposit slip, manually or whatever—then you would have a copy?"

"I think so."

"And someone would have had to write her name in order for you to see that it's specifically for that apartment."

"It's enough to just write the apartment number."

"Is there someone at this district office now?"

Sohlberg checked her watch. "Yes, I think so. Lena is the one who handles that and she should be there. I can call and check."

Winter nodded, and she punched in a number on her desk phone. He waited while she spoke.

"She's there," Sohlberg said, and put down the receiver.

Winter called Ringmar on his cell phone and learned that Bertil was about to start the interview with Ester Bergman. He hung up and slipped the phone into his blazer's inner pocket.

Outside, one group had dispersed and another had formed, closer. Winter saw the dark faces, perhaps from Southeast or East Asia. Like the woman walking next to him. He hadn't asked about her background.

"There are a lot of nationalities in this area," he said.

"Over fifty percent are non-Swedish," Karin Sohlberg said.

Winter looked down at her. She was a full head shorter.

"But I am," she said. "Swedish."

"I didn't ask."

"South Korea," she said. "Adopted, though some call it abducted."

Winter didn't comment.

"I know who my real parents are," she said.

"You haven't been back there?"

"Not yet."

Lena Suominen was waiting for them at the district office. She had already taken out a copy of the deposit slip that was used to pay Helene Andersén's latest rent: 4,350 kronor for a 750-square-foot, three-room apartment.

Winter looked at the paper.

"So this is a copy?"

"Yes."

"Where is the original?"

"Of these manually filled-out slips?"

"Yes."

"At the direct deposit processing center, I would imagine. In Stockholm. Just like the preprinted slips. They end up there too."

Winter looked at the copy in front of him. Someone had written the property management company's seven-digit direct deposit number, 882000-3, and then another number in the box for messages to the payee. There was no reference to name or address.

"Is this the apartment number?" he asked, and pointed at the three digits on the copy.

"Yes, 375. That's the apartment."

"So you don't have to write the name?"

"No."

"Is it usual for tenants to pay their rent this way?"

Lena Suominen looked as if she was smiling, or maybe it was just a movement in her face. "Well, of course, there are those who lose their rent slips and call here asking for the direct deposit number. And then we give it to them. But that's a different number."

"Excuse me?"

"For manual direct deposits—that is, for a blank payment slip filled out by hand—we use another number."

"This one, you mean: 882000-3?"

"No. That's the property manager's regular one."

"So it works anyway? Someone making a payment can use this number for the manual payment slips as well?"

"Yes."

"But then you'd have to know it—copy it from a regular rental slip, for example." He was talking to himself. "Does this number apply to all your apartments in Gothenburg?"

"Yes."

"How many are there at North Biskopsgården? Apartments, I mean."

Lena Suominen thought for a moment. Around fifty years old, with a wide intelligent face, she spoke with a Finnish-Swedish accent that softened her formal tone. "Approximately twelve hundred."

"And many of your tenants pay their rent at the post office, I understand? Even with the preprinted slips?"

"Yes."

"And some by direct deposit from their personal accounts?"

"Yes, and some don't use the rent slips since they can't pay the whole rent all at once. Unfortunately, that's how it is, and that's problematic for them as well as for—"

"They pay in installments?"

"Yes, well, at least in a first installment. Sometimes that's all we get."

"Is that common?"

"Increasingly common."

Winter thought again about loneliness and poverty. How did it feel when you'd paid only part of the rent for your apartment? Did you stop going into the living room?

"And sometimes you can't see who's paid. You can't read the name or the address or the apartment number. But money's come in."

Winter read the copy he was holding in front of him. So they might be able to find the original at the post office's direct deposit processing center up in the capital. They would have to call them up and ask them to find it and put it in a plastic bag. It was a lead.

At the very bottom of the slip was a string of numbers. Winter could identify the payment date—the first weekday in September, just as Karin Sohlberg had said earlier. By then Helene Andersén had been dead for thirteen or fourteen days.

He couldn't decipher the other numbers.

"What's this?" He held out the copy and pointed.

Suominen took the paper, and he saw Sohlberg standing next to her.

"That's the post-office code number," Suominen said. "I think the same figures appear on the receipt they give to the person making the payment."

"You don't have the phone number of the post office, by any chance?"

"No."

"Hand me that telephone book behind you," he said. "The one with the pink pages." He looked up the number to the Länsmansgården post office, and a woman answered after two rings.

"Hello, my name is Erik Winter and I'm a homicide inspector. We're investigating a crime, and I was wondering if you could help me with a few factual details. No. Just a fact— No, you'll do just fine, I think. It's about the code numbers that appear on your recei— Yes, that's right, the series of num— No, I just want to ask you about one I have he— *Please*, just listen to me now. I have a question about the following numbers." He eventually managed to tell her what those numbers were and where he had obtained them.

He listened.

"So the first one refers to the type of transaction? The 01 indicates that this payment was made by direct deposit? Thank you. The four subseq— Yes, immediately following. The *P* number? The post office where the payment was made. That number indicates where the transaction took place? I have the number here. I'll give it to you again. Can you tell me where it is? Get it then. I'll wait."

Winter moved the receiver a few inches away from his ear. "These first four numbers say where the payment was made," he said to the two women. "She's gone to get some kind of reference catalog." He heard a voice in the receiver and put it up to his ear again. "Yes, 2237, that's right. Mölnlycke! Are you sure? Yes, those are the numbers. And then the oth— Okay, what does that me— The cashier, you say? So these numbers, 0030, indicate which cashier handled the transaction? So this number combination indicates that the rent payment for the apartment with this number was made on September 2 at the Mölnlycke post office at this particular cashier's service window? Is that right? Thank you."

Winter was on his way into the courtyard when his cell phone vibrated in the inner pocket of his blazer.

"Winter here."

"Bertil here. Where are you?"

"On my way into the courtyard. You?"

"Outside the apartment. Andersén's apartment."

"I'll be there in one minute."

Ringmar was waiting in the stairwell. "Beier's team says someone's been inside her apartment recently."

"What does that mean?"

"Probably sometime within the past few weeks. After her death."

"How can they know that?"

Ringmar shrugged his shoulders. "They're wizards, aren't they? But I think they said something about the dust. Stay tuned. They also say it looks like someone rummaged through all the stuff in there and then tried to put it back more or less the way it was."

"That sounds clumsy."

"Could be a red herring. The vic— Helene Andersén may have had some kind of special system for organizing her stuff."

"Or else someone was in there and rummaged around and wasn't particularly worried about it being discovered."

"There's going to be one hell of a commotion when this gets out," Ringmar said.

"Then we'll have to see to it that it doesn't get out," Winter said.

"How do you mean?"

"A few days from now, someone might walk into the Mölnlycke post office and pay the rent again. We're going to be there waiting for them."

"My God," Ringmar said. "I wonder if it's even possible. I'm a bit surprised that there aren't a few TV vans parked out here already."

They conducted an internal search for Helene Andersén, now that they had her name. Yet another round of searching, only this time with better chances of success.

In a few days we'll release her name and distribute a real live picture of her, thought Winter. There are photos of the little girl too, on her own and together with her dead mother. If we don't get any response, that means we've come across the loneliest people on earth. They've existed but almost only in name.

All the different agencies had to be contacted. Winter hadn't gone through the mail that was lying in the hall, but the technicians had yet to find any letters from the social services. Perhaps they had disappeared together with the rental slips. Still, there were other ways to find out if she was receiving money from the state or from a job. Soon they would know.

She had a telephone. Winter remembered it, on the little bedside table. Now that they knew her identity, they could pull her phone records and get some history. She'd chosen to have a phone in order to speak to someone.

31

THE POST OFFICE'S DIRECT DEPOSIT PROCESSING CENTER HAD A
special department for dealing with "police matters." A man answered
reluctantly. Winter explained.

"Then you're screwed," the post-office official said.

"Excuse me?"

"The slips are discarded after two weeks or something. Didn't you
say this rent was paid more than three weeks ago?"

"Yes."

"So you're screwed."

"You better do something about that attitude of yours, you smug son
of a bitch. I'm investigating a murder and I want my questions answered.
So, what do you mean when you say that the slips are discarded?"

"They're shredded."

"And that happens after two weeks?"

"Sometimes after a few days. It depends on how much we have
to do."

"Then what's the point of sending them to you in the first place?"

"I really don't know. I've asked myself the same question. We don't
have any space here, after all."

"So there's a possibility that a consignment of canceled deposit slips
sent over to you from some post offices still hasn't been processed?"

"Not for three weeks. Unless it's ended up at the very bottom or something, or we've been short staff—" Something had suddenly occurred to
him. "We actually have been understaffed for the past few weeks. So it's
possible we did fall behind. Where did you say the payment was made,
again? Gothenburg, I know, but which office? Can you repeat the direct
deposit number and the amount? And the apartment number as well."

Winter realized he was speaking to someone who hadn't initially
been listening. He repeated what he'd said before.

"Hang on," the drawling voice said, like one of those jazz musicians who come down from Stockholm for a gig at Nefertiti's. They play better than they speak.

There was a fumbling sound in the receiver, and the voice returned.

"Can you hang on a bit longer? There might be something else here."

"I'll hang on," Winter said.

"I've got it here."

"You've found it?"

"Yes, actually. I'm surprised myself."

So I wasn't screwed, thought Winter. "I want you to put that slip into a new envelope right away and put it in a safe place. Lock it in a cabinet."

"Okay."

Winter looked at his watch.

"Are you going to be there for another two hours?"

"Yes."

"Another police officer will be by there within the next two hours to pick up the envelope. He'll ask for you," Winter said, and looked at the name he'd written down. "Ask him to identify himself."

"Okay."

"And thanks for your help. I apologize for swearing at you before. Good-bye."

He pressed down on the cradle and waited for the dial tone and called Stockholm again, getting a security consultant who asked if he could call Winter back in half an hour.

He put down the phone and stood up, his left shoulder blade stiff from sitting while speaking on the telephone. Much of his time was spent in stiff positions on the telephone. He ought to do calisthenics in his office. Tonight he would go to Valhalla and sit in the wet sauna, if he had time for it. A sauna and a beer at home and the silence and his thoughts. He ought to call Angela. He ought to—

The phone rang, blared. The tone was turned up loud so that he'd be able to hear it if he was out of the office but still close by.

"Okay," the security consultant said. "This is proving a little complicated. We have routines when it comes to payments made to a blocked account, but flagging a specific payment, well, that's actually something new."

"There's always a first time," Winter said. "But what can we do?"

"What you're asking for is for some kind of a trace to be put on a specific payment that's going to be made at the Mölndal post office at the end of this week, lasting up to the second weekday in October."

"Mölnlycke," Winter said.

"What? Yeah, Mölnlycke. Okay. But it's too little time to be able to fix the computers and cash registers to respond to specific inputs on the screen, and we actually can't do it anyway, because all we have to go on is the apartment number. In the best case."

"Isn't that enough?"

"The system won't let us put a trace on that. And if we were to go by the direct deposit number, then some five thousand people, or however many there are, would find themselves subject to an investigation."

"I see."

"There is one thing I can do for you, although it is highly irregular. I can send out a memo to all the different post offices, asking them to try to keep an eye out for these numbers."

"How do you do that?"

"I'd rather not go into that if I don't have to."

"But you can get that out right away?"

"Yeah, pretty much. But like I said, it's highly irregular. Last time was a few years ago when we tried to stop a currency exchange. It's really only supposed to be used in cases of extreme importance. Top priority."

"This is."

"I realize that. But, well, that's what we can do."

"Good."

Winter imagined millions of computer screens receiving the security consultant's electronic memo. He thought of the office in Mölnlycke. He'd never been in it, had barely even set foot in the district that lay six miles east of the city. But there was a small chance that someone would come back to pay the rent again. If they could just get some discreet surveillance equipment put in place. And not just use the existing security system but also have someone there on the spot. One or two police officers. That is, if there even was any equipment in Mölnlycke. A camera. He noted something down on the pad in front of him.

"But there are other ways too," the security consultant went on. "You could speak to the postmaster in Mölnd—Mölnlycke about putting up notices for the cashiers at each of the cash registers. So they have the number and maybe reac—"

"Yes, I understand," Winter said. "I've sort of thought of that."

"Uh, okay. But that's a right-to-privacy issue. Like a search warrant. The post office needs a written request from a prosecutor."

"Or from the person in charge of the preliminary investigation," Winter said. "And that's me."

"Sure. I'm just saying you can put a trace on that payment if the people at that office know what the deal is."

"Thanks for all your help," Winter said. "I'm very grateful."

"Then I'll send out my letter. In case something happens somewhere other than in Mölndal."

Winter pressed down the cradle button again and waited for a dial tone. With his left hand, he flipped to the number in the phone book and called the post-office security department in Gothenburg. A man answered.

"Bengt Fahlander."

"Hi. Erik Winter from the Gothenburg Police Department here. I'm investigating a murder."

"Hi."

Winter explained the background and asked a question.

"We've got a camera at Lindome but not in Mölnlycke," Fahlander said. "Mölnlycke hasn't had any equipment like that for quite a while."

"Why not?"

"Well, the usual. The offices facing the greatest threat get the surveillance equipment. That's some fifteen offices in the district. Like Lindome. They were robbed a number of times, and in the end we took the initiative to install a CCTV camera."

"But not in Mölnlycke," Winter said.

"No. But that wouldn't make any difference anyway," Fahlander said.

"What do you mean?"

"The video footage. In certain extreme cases we might be authorized to hold on to it for a month, but almost without exception it's erased after two weeks. Wiped clean, discarded, you might say."

What is this goddamn obsession with discarding everything? Pretty soon there wouldn't be anything to go on when you wanted to search back in time. Two weeks back and you hit a brick wall.

"So even if there had been a camera in Mölnlycke, the video footage for the day you just mentioned—that film would have been erased," Fahlander said. "But Mölnlycke used to have a camera. For quite a while, I think. Then things calmed down. Crime moved away, you might say."

"To Lindome," Winter said. "But now it's returned, and I would like to set up a camera again."

"Now?"

"Today, if possible. As soon as possible."

"You have to submit a formal applic—"

"I know what has to be submitted and to whom. But this is extremely important. And it's gotta happen quickly."

"You're talking surveillance of a public place," Fahlander said. "That means there have to be signs put up informing the public that the premises are under video surveillance."

Whose side are you on? Winter wondered. But of course the postman was right. "Of course," he said. "Maybe the old ones are still there. Otherwise we can take care of it."

"Would it be possible to do it a little discreetly?" Fahlander asked.

There were more police officers in the situation room now than when the investigation began what felt like two hundred years ago. It was hot and damp. Ringmar was just opening a window. Winter hung his blazer over the swivel chair and turned to face the group.

"So we're going to be doing something highly irregular over the next three days—a discreet door to door in North Biskopsgården, but only as part of the preliminary investigation. We keep quiet about the other stuff."

Ringmar stood up and continued. "If anybody asks what we're doing there, we just say that we're slowly making our way through the whole city, searching for the woman's identity."

"Her key," Bergenhem said. "The one who paid her rent has the key to her apartment."

"That's right," Ringmar said. "Either someone has gone in there and looked around thoroughly for something or Helene Andersén kept her things in an odd sort of order."

"What else is missing?" Sara Helander asked.

"Her rent slips," Winter said.

"So the crime—the murder—wasn't committed in her apartment?"

"Not as far as Beier's men have been able to determine."

"Would that be realistic, given how far it is to Delsjö Lake?" Börjesson asked.

"Would what be realistic?"

"For her to have been murdered in her apartment and then taken down to Delsjö Lake."

"In terms of time, it might be possible, but so far we haven't found any evidence in her apartment to suggest that."

"Didn't it attract a lot of attention when we found out where she lived? Enough that the secret could already be out?" Halders asked.

"There were a few curious onlookers, but it's not unusual for the police to come calling," Ringmar said. "I didn't say anything to anyone anyway." He looked at Winter, who shook his head. "We have to hope our witnesses will keep their oath of confidentiality."

"How do we deal with the press, then? It would be strange if they didn't pick up the scent," Halders said.

"I haven't heard anything yet," Ringmar said.

"It would be strange," Halders said, "if they didn't already know something."

"I'll handle all contact with the press," Winter said. "I've spoken to Sture and Wellman."

"That's a damn good idea," Halders said. "I would have given the exact same order." He saw that Winter understood that he was serious.

"So where are we now?" Helander asked.

"I've spoken to the post office in Mölnlycke," Winter said. "The camera's all set. We might even get two. We're going to try to give the impression that it's always been there."

"Who's going to be in position inside the post office?" Bergenhem asked.

"I was going to suggest that you do it," Winter said.

"Me?"

"We need to have someone who looks as ordinary as possible," Halders said.

"Yeah, well we can't have someone who scares away the customers, can we?" Bergenhem said, and turned toward Halders. "When do you want me to head over there?" he asked, turning back to Winter.

"Now. I'll talk to you just as soon as we're done here. And you will be relieved."

"How's the search going?" Bergenhem asked.

Winter gazed at his database expert.

"Nothing so far," Möllerström said. "We're still working through the central criminal-records database."

"Has surveillance gotten busy on this yet?" Halders asked. "With the latest, I mean? The names."

"Of course," Ringmar said.

"There's always an informant who knows something," Halders said. "Take the shoot-out at Vårväderstorget. That could get solved using your stoolie. Someone knows somebody else who knows something more."

"I know," Ringmar said.

Winter took the floor again.

"We're waiting for the list of everyone she's called."

"Then it's in the bag," Halders said.

She may have only called out for pizza, thought Helander, but she didn't say it.

Winter felt the team's impatience, the urge to work and the frustration at having to wait for documents and lists and results to provide a little guidance for the way forward. Another name could pave the way to greater clarity. A new address. A fingerprint. He thought of the technicians leaning over their instruments.

"How's it coming along with the fingerprints from her apartment?" Bergenhem asked.

"Her daughter's are there, we presume, since there's a set that belongs to a child," Winter said. "There were at least two other unknown sets of prints. In addition to Helene's, of course."

"At least?"

"That's what we know so far. There's also a partial print. But they're not done with the whole apartment yet. Then there's the basement storage room."

"What do you mean by partial?" Bergenhem asked.

"According to Beier there's a partial fingerprint on a dresser drawer, I think he said it was. I don't know how big it is yet, or whether it's big enough to be used to establish full identity at some point. Forensics doesn't know yet. But it's there."

"Was it a torn glove?" Helander asked.

"Probably," Winter said, and looked at her. "That was good thinking. There was a piece of fiber next to the print. It could come from the apartment or from anywhere, but someone may have torn a little hole in their glove. Against the edge of the drawer. That's where the print is."

32

WINTER PARKED THE CAR NEXT TO FRISKVÄDERSTORGET AND walked north. Thin paper blew across the square toward the southeast. The morning was dry, no rain. Outside the ICA supermarket someone had tipped over a trash can, and three headless bottles lay on the ground. People walked past saying words Winter heard but didn't understand.

Two police officers he barely knew were there. They weren't wearing uniforms, but they stood out in the surroundings, strangers in a foreign land.

He went over and said hello. Before them lay the remains of a small fireworks rocket, in red and gold paper with blackened tasseled edges that were slowly being eaten away by the wind gusting from the northwest. The spent paper canisters rolled back and forth.

"Probably another damn ethnic group celebrating its own damn New Year," one of the officers said, and gestured at the ground. The other sniggered. "Or else they have to set some off every day, to remind them of home back in Kurdistan."

"What was that?" Winter said.

"What?"

"What you said just now. About the New Year. And Kurdistan."

"What's the big deal?" He turned to his partner. "It was just a joke, right?" He looked at Winter. "You got a problem or something?"

"It wasn't funny," Winter said. "I can't have officers with prejudices against the people who live here working this assignment. This investigation is way too important."

"Oh give me a—"

"I don't want you here," Winter said. "Get out of here."

"This is craz—"

"I decide who does what around here. And I'm ordering you to go back to the station and report to Inspector Ringmar. He'll assign you new duties. I'll call him."

Winter had already started walking away and called Ringmar as he walked. Ringmar answered after the second ring, and Winter explained.

"You can't do that, Erik."

"It's already done. You'll have to try to send down a couple more guys. We need them."

It sounded like Ringmar sighed.

"What should I say to those two jugheads when they show up?"

"Just give them something else to do. Put them on the cars."

"Yeah, maybe they're better suited to that," Ringmar said. "Assuming none of the owners is of foreign extraction."

As Winter neared Helene Andersén's apartment he heard children's voices. The temperature had dropped during the night, and on his way into the shop that lay a hundred or so yards from Karin Sohlberg's residential services office he zipped up his leather jacket.

Immediately upon entering he caught the smell of exotic herbs and spices. The shelves to the right were filled with glass jars of pickled foodstuffs and tin cans containing southern European and oriental dishes.

A sign with "Halal" written on it hung above the meat counter, which was half-filled with sausages, lamb shoulder, and tripe. The vegetable counter was stuffed to the brim with ten different kinds of bell peppers, big spotted tomatoes, strange-looking root vegetables, thick bunches of coriander, and other fresh herbs. The selection was bigger and more interesting than in any of the delicatessens in the city center or the indoor market.

Had Helene ever bought anything here?

Sometime over the course of the day, one of his investigators would come by and ask questions. Winter left the store, and the guy behind the counter looked up, and Winter nodded.

He walked past Karin Sohlberg's office, which was closed. She'd called in sick, and he could understand that. Unfortunately, the police couldn't call in sick after a distressing experience, and it was never enough just to get the rest of the day off. What they had was Hanne, and Winter suddenly missed the sound of her voice, or perhaps it was her words.

Hanne Östergaard was a priest from Skår who worked part-time as a healer of souls at the Gothenburg Police Department. She tried to speak to the men and women who had gone through difficult experiences or had seen the consequences of them. The police turned out to be just as vulnerable as anyone else, and more often than not they carried their scars with them for a long time. Forever really.

Hanne had combined a vacation with a leave of absence in order to attend university, and she hadn't been at the police station since the end of spring. Winter had spoken to her twice during the summer, but that had been by phone. Perhaps she would feel under too much pressure when she came back. That was sure to be the case. A part-time fellow human being and hundreds of scared police officers. An inspector who feared the worst for the coming weeks. He thought about the girl again, Jennie Andersén. He couldn't keep those horrible thoughts at bay.

He stood in the courtyard, facing the building. They had staked out the apartment but avoided other forms of surveillance. The kitchen window was a dark rectangle against the light-colored brickwork. Black pigeons clung above and below, as if to signify that the silence within was forever. The pigeons sat clustered around her window, hugging the wall as they moved along—like winged rats, thought Winter. He entered the house and continued up to the door. Jennie's drawing of the rain and sun was still there, an apt depiction of the past six weeks. He saw the ship in the drawing and thought of the boat in Big Delsjö Lake. They hadn't made any more progress there. Had Helene Andersén and her daughter had access to a boat? Why else would the girl draw a ship or a boat—there were more drawings like it above her bed. When Beier's men went through the apartment, they found even more children's drawings, enough to fill a big paper sack.

Winter opened the door and stood in the hall. Someone had been here after Helene's death. Was it just the rental slips he had come for? Winter pictured a man in order to focus his thoughts more clearly. They hadn't found any personal letters—no surprise since there wasn't a soul in the world who'd come asking for Helene Andersén when she'd disappeared. Or her daughter either. How immense could loneliness be? He carried the thought around with him in rooms that smelled of mute sorrow.

They knew the murder had not been committed here, so where had it taken place? In the vicinity of where the body was found? She had made a journey from the northwestern part of the city to the Delsjö lakes in the eastern expanse where all urban development came to an end. Had she made that trip of a dozen or so miles on her own? Had she already been dead?

Winter stood in the kitchen. He heard the sounds from the pigeons' throats outside the window. A child's drawing was attached to the refrigerator door by a magnet in the shape of a sailboat. The technicians had chosen to leave it there, and Winter wondered why.

The drawing showed a car with faces in the front window and the back. The car was white. It was raining in half the sky, and in the other the sun was shining. Winter had glanced at the drawing the first time he was here, yesterday. He now saw that the face in the front was drawn in profile and that there was a beard hanging off the man's chin, like a goatee.

My God, he thought, and felt his blood rise to his head.

The face in the backseat had red hair in pigtails.

Someone with a beard driving a car that the girl is riding in, he thought. He thought of all the drawings they had removed from the apartment. Good Lord, he thought. The girl has drawn everything she's seen and experienced. All children draw. They draw what they're going through since they can't write it down.

Jennie's drawings are her diary, he thought. We have her diary.

He still felt the blood in his face and told himself that he needed to stay calm, that it was just one lead among many others, perhaps not even a lead at all. Still he felt the excitement. *He* hadn't come there for the drawings. It's not the first thing it occurs to you to take away, especially not if you've seen a child draw and know that all children draw, and when you're trying to make it look like you haven't been inside the apartment, you know it would look bare without any children's drawings.

He's seen her drawing, thought Winter. He knows her. He knows this little family. Take it easy. Remember what Sture said about being too meticulous. The man with the beard could be somebody else—a friend. Or a taxi driver, or just any man from her imagination. I'll have to go through her drawings one by one. How many are there? Five hundred? Is it usual to hold on to that many? Don't ask me, he thought, I know nothing about children, and then, just as quickly as he thought that thought, he saw Angela's face in his mind's eye.

He stood still in the kitchen. There could be more from the basement, where Helene Andersén had kept a storage room without an apartment number or name. That wasn't unusual. After a while they'd found it, locked with a little padlock. It contained a few boxes of clothes, a pair of children's skis, and a chair.

WHEN SHE LISTENED, IT WAS AS IF THE SAME CUCKOO WAS SIT-
ting out in the forest hooting to her—at least for a few hours today and
yesterday too. *Hoo hoo, hoo hoo,* it cried, like it was far away beyond the
trees.

Her hair was wet and her clothes too. She had spread out her dress
underneath her, like a sheet, and it had gotten wet. She felt cold sometimes and pulled it on over her trousers and shirt, and then she felt hot
and took it off again. The men came and looked at her when they thought
she was asleep—only she was awake, but it was almost like being asleep.
She was dizzy the whole time and she had all these goose bumps on
her body, like when you've been swimming and the wind blows on you
before you've put a towel around yourself.

The man, the one who always came up to her, brought some pills that
he wanted her to swallow. But she couldn't. He called to the other man.

"She's not swallowing."

"Tell her she has to."

"It doesn't do any good."

"You'll have to dissolve them."

"What?"

"Dissolve them in water and it'll be easier for her to swallow. Or put
the powder in a cup of hot sugar water."

The man had bent forward and laid his hand on her forehead again.

"She doesn't feel so hot now."

"Maybe she doesn't need them."

"What?"

"The pills, for Christ's sake."

"I think she needs them."

"Then do what I told you."

She'd tried to swallow the glass of water, and it tasted bad. Then she dozed off and heard sounds from outside, like a rumbling or a chugging, and then they were gone. And she listened for the cuckoo, but you couldn't hear it anymore after the chugging came. She waited for the cuckoo, who was maybe always there.

She thought to herself, I'm not going to be here for long. I'm going to be at home in my new bedroom where it says Helene on the door. My name is Helene, and the men haven't said it once, so I'll just have to say it myself. She whispered and it hurt her throat, but she whispered Helene one more time and then it became lighter and all red in her eyes and then she thought she heard the cuckoo again.

PART 2

HE HEARD THE SOUNDS OF THE FOREST, BUT THEY WEREN'T like they were before. Nothing was like that former calm. He barely heard the wind anymore.

She had stepped out of the past like a greeting from the devil. He'd tried to fend her off during that first call. You've got the wrong number, miss.

That voice. Like something that wasn't supposed to exist anymore, that wasn't meant to be heard.

He had done what he could to forget. The others who could talk were gone.

Afterward, while he could still hear her voice, he had looked down at his hands and shut his eyes, and still those hellish visions taunted him. The house and the wind from the sea that blew right through that damned house. He had done what he had to. Though he'd planned it, he'd thought it wouldn't be necessary—but then he understood that he had to do it. His hands did it.

This was the second time he'd driven to the bus stop and picked them up. It wasn't the closest stop, but she understood why. Perhaps she was the one who'd suggested it. He was afraid now. He hadn't been able to hang up when she called again. Come alone, he'd said. She refused.

No no no—who said anything about that? he'd asked. She eyed him with a crazed look that he recognized in himself. Terrified of what was going to happen, he'd looked up at the ceiling, thought about how he had one way out. It had been there the whole time. One option. Fear had stopped him.

There was screeching above their heads. It was the second time she'd come alone, and he didn't know if she knew everything. As they walked through the field down to the other glade, animals ran off into the trees. She'd turned her face toward him, but he hadn't wanted to look into her eyes. A shout came from far away and suddenly he wanted the child there. Next time she'd bring the child with her.

The sweat running down into his eyes blinded him, and he couldn't hear any cars on the road. It never got really dark. He tried to blink away the sweat. Her arms . . .

When he turned around, he saw a white boat floating on the surface of the lake, without sound, as if it were waiting. She seemed to be following it with her eyes, her head turned to the side, but the boat lay still, trapped in the late-night fog. He couldn't see anyone in the boat, and when he turned around again, for the last time, the surface of the water was empty and black.

34

THE APARTMENT WAS LOCATED IN A BUILDING WITH A VIEW
out toward Black Marshes. There was nothing outside to suggest that it
housed a private day care with three rooms and a kitchen.

The architecture struck Winter as frozen music, crystallized chords,
which carried a rough beauty within its walls but kept everything con-
fined within. Nature was right up alongside it, but apart.

He'd received instructions from Karin Sohlberg, but she didn't want
to accompany him. He walked in through the building's front entrance
and rang the doorbell of the apartment to the left in the stairwell on the
first floor. The door, covered with children's drawings, was opened by a
man who could have been seventy years old or eighty. He was wearing
a brown khaki shirt and broad suspenders fastened to gray trousers that
were big and comfortable. He had a white mustache and thick white
hair, and Winter thought of a Santa Claus who had shaved off his beard
and descended to live among humans for good. The old man was holding the hand of a little boy who was sucking his thumb and staring wide-
eyed at the long-haired blond police officer in a black leather jacket.

"Hello," Winter said, as he bent down a few inches toward the boy,
who started to cry.

"There, there, Timmy," the white-haired man said, holding his hand.
The boy stopped crying and pressed his face against the man's pant leg.

"Well, good afternoon," Winter said, and held out his hand. He introduced himself and his reason for being there. The search for a missing
person. Two missing persons, he thought. A child and a murderer.

"Ernst Lundgren," the man said. He was tall and slightly bent forward. He must have been nearly seven feet tall when he was young,
Winter thought.

"Could we speak for a moment?" he asked.

Lundgren turned around. Winter had heard children and adult

voices, and he now saw several elderly people busy helping the children put on their coats.

"We're just on our way out, as you can see," Lundgren said. "In ten minutes or however long it takes, it'll be quiet in here. If you can wait that long."

"Certainly," Winter said.

"We couldn't just sit here and do nothing, seeing how difficult things are for them," Lundgren said. "The young mothers, that is."

Winter nodded. They sat in the kitchen. Through the window he could see the little troop move across the road and in among the trees. It might have been ten children and four adults.

"There are a lot of single mothers with small children living around here," Lundgren said. "They have no jobs and no child care and hardly even any friends. Many are stuck in their loneliness and never get out of it."

Winter nodded again.

"It's dangerous," the day-care manager said. "Nobody can survive for very long under those conditions."

"How long have you been running this day care?" Winter asked.

"About a year. We'll see how long we can keep it going. It's not really a proper day-care center, in the strict sense of the word, if by that you mean an institution."

"So what is it, then?"

"It's a few old fogies trying to help the young and desperate, to put it bluntly." Lundgren nodded toward the coffee machine. "Would you like a cup?" Winter accepted the offer, and Lundgren stood and prepared coffee for himself and Winter, then sat back down at the table. "Some of these poor girls don't know which way to turn. They need, well, for want of a better word I guess I'd have to say alleviation. We try to provide them with a little alleviation in their daily lives."

"Uh-huh."

"That means a young mother can leave her child here with us for a few hours and go off to the hairdresser or into town to be by herself for a bit. Or just go home and take it easy."

"Yes," Winter said. "I think I understand."

"Having the chance to be by themselves for just a little while a couple of times a week," Lundgren said. "Can you imagine what it's like never to have a moment to just be by yourself?"

"No," Winter answered. "I'm more familiar with the opposite."

"What did you say?"

"The opposite. Spending too much time by myself."

"Aha. But you see that's also a problem these girls face. They don't get to socialize with anyone their own age." Lundgren rolled up one sleeve of his khaki shirt, and Winter saw that the hair on his arm grew like white moss all the way down to the middle of his knuckles. "And don't forget that some of them have more than one child."

"Are there many wanting to come here?"

"A few, but we can't handle any more. We'd need a bigger apartment and there'd have to be more of us, but we're already dependent on charity as it is. No doubt the municipal authorities see us as pirates. Fine by me."

"You're doing a good job," Winter said.

"You gotta do something before you die. And it's fun. It's the most fun I've had for a long time."

Winter finished his coffee. It was still warm.

"There's always a lot of crap being said about the city's outlying suburbs, but one thing is true," Lundgren explained. "There's a hell of a lot of loneliness in areas like this. The little lonely people are being pushed out to the margins. It's strange out here. On the one hand, you've got the immigrant families, who after all do have a sense of community. It can be a little fragile sometimes. But still. And wedged in among them you've got these young Swedish mothers with their little kids. Almost never boys. Young girls and their children. It's a strange mix."

"Yes."

"And many people keep their distance." Lundgren's eyes were still fixed on the group from the day care outside. "That may be why I haven't seen this woman you're asking about. Helene, was that her name?"

"Yes. Helene Andersén. The little girl's name was Jennie."

"I don't recognize it. Of course, I can ask my staff, or whatever it is we're called."

"It's possible," Ringmar said, eyeing the big pile of children's drawings on the table in Winter's room.

"A diary," Winter said. "It could be like a diary."

"Then we'll have to get lucky."

"Luck is often a question of seeing the opportunity when it presents itself," Winter said. That was a real smart-ass remark, he thought to himself.

"And you think that opportunity lies here." Ringmar held up a picture depicting a lone tree in a field. The drawing was divided in two. Rain. Shine. "There's both rain and sunshine in this one."

"It's like that in a number of the drawings I've seen so far," Winter said.

"Seems like a case for a child psychologist."

"I've thought about that too."

"And then there are the locations."

"And the figures."

"This can really give you the creeps. I was thinking about my own kids' drawings. What stuff like that can mean."

"The fact is that kids draw a lot, right? And what is it that they draw? They draw what they see. What we have lying here in front of us is what she saw."

"Rain and sun and trees," Ringmar said. "A boat and a car. Where is this taking us?"

"Well, we can at least go through them, can't we? Beier isn't finished with all the drawings upstairs."

"What else does he have to say?"

"They're just test firing the rifle into the water tank."

"Aha. Does the rifle match up?"

"He doesn't know yet," Winter said.

They had empty shells from the shoot-out at Vårväderstorget and a suspected weapon. Beier had procured similar ammunition of the same make and fired it into a water tank in order to compare the bullets with the casings.

"What are you thinking about?" Ringmar said.

"Right at this moment? A bullet traveling through water, and a motorcycle crashing through a roadblock somewhere in Scandinavia."

"I'm thinking about the little girl," Ringmar said. "And the mother."

"I'm still waiting for the reports from child services," Winter said. "And the hospital."

"She seems not to have any family or friends."

"Sure she did. We're slowly getting closer to them. It won't be long."

He grabbed his jacket from the chair and put it on.

"Where are you going now?" Ringmar asked.

"I thought it was about time I agreed to meet with a reporter. Don't you think?"

"Go and get a haircut before you meet the press. Birgersson mumbled something this morning about a Beatles wig."

"He's still living in the good old days," Winter said, heading toward the elevators.

Hans Bülow was waiting at a bar in the center of town. It was getting dark outside, and the candles on the tables were lit. People on the Avenyn were walking briskly, on their way home or out.

"Can I buy you a beer, seeing as you've taken the time?" Bülow said.

"A Perrier will do just fine."

"You're increasingly becoming one of those straight-edge types."

"Do they drink Perrier?"

"Water. No alcohol."

"Straight edge?"

"Yes."

"Sounds good," Winter lit up a Corps. "It has a ring to it."

"They don't smoke either."

Winter looked at his cigarillo.

"Then I guess I may as well have a light beer. Hof on tap, if they've got it."

Bülow went over to the bar and came back with two tall glasses. He nodded to a familiar face and sat down. "That's a colleague of yours, isn't it?" he said, and took a sip from his glass.

"Where?"

"Behind me, off to the right. The one I said hello to."

Winter looked over the reporter's shoulder and saw Halders's close-cropped head. Halders didn't turn around. Winter couldn't tell if he was sitting with anyone.

"You know Halders?"

"You kidding me? As a reporter embedded at the police station, you get to know the forces of good," Bülow said.

"And you count Halders among them?"

"He's got the best reputation of anyone."

"With whom?"

"With the press, of course. He doesn't put on an act. If he has nothing to say, he doesn't say anything."

Winter took a sip of his beer.

"So what's going on?" Bülow asked.

"We're still trying to determine the dead woman's identity. And possibly looking for a child as well, but we don't know for sure. It scares me."

"What if I say that you've found her?"

"You can say whatever you like. But what do you mean? Of course we found her."

"Her identity. That you know who she is. But you don't want to release it."

Winter sat silently. He took another sip of his beer, to keep himself occupied. The bartender played music at two-thirds volume. It sounded like rock.

"Why not, Erik?"

"I agreed to meet with you because I want to sort out a few things," Winter said. "But there are certain questions I simply cannot answer."

"For reasons pertaining to the ongoing investigation?"

"Yes."

"By virtue of the statutory confidentiality of the preliminary investigation?"

Winter nodded. Halders still sat with his back to him. Perhaps it's a doppelgänger, thought Winter.

"Paragraphs 5:1 and 9:17 of the Swedish Penal Code," Bülow said.

"Are you a lawyer too?"

"It's enough to be a legal reporter."

"I see."

"So what can you tell me, then?"

35

IT WAS DARKER NOW. WINTER WAS BACK IN HIS OFFICE. BÜLOW
was ready to hold off on writing certain things. You owe me a favor, he
said when they parted. I just did you one, Winter had answered.

The music from the CD was louder than the other sounds in the
room. Michael Brecker was blowing ice-cold notes from the tenor sax
on "Naked Soul" from *Tales from the Hudson*.

He thought about Helene's face and body. Her soul had left her body.
Thinking about her name now was no different than it had been before.
He had known. How had she let him know? How had she communi-
cated her name to him?

He picked the topmost drawing from the pile on his desk. It showed
a figure, who might be a child, with its arms reaching upward. There
was no ground. The figure was hovering in the air.

Winter studied the next image. In the middle of the picture, a car was
driving along a road that went through trees. There were no faces in the
windows of the car, since it didn't have any. The car had no color, was
white like the paper. The trees were green and the road brown. Winter picked up the next drawing, which also showed a car. It was driving among houses that were drawn like tall blocks with windows that
were irregularly square. The road was black. Winter flipped through
the drawings until he found another with a car in it. It was driving on
a brown road. In five drawings the car was driving along a black road.
The cars were uncolored, left white like the paper. He saw a person with
red hair in one of the windows. None of the cars had any drivers.

He looked for any letters or numbers on the cars. She had written
her name, "jeni." She could recognize and copy a letter or a number.
Weren't there five-year-olds who could read and write fluently?

He closed his eyes. The music helped his concentration.

He opened his eyes and laid the drawings with cars in them to the right. There were also other vehicles—something that looked like it could be a streetcar, in some of the drawings. The carriages were long and lined with windows, like the high-rises he had seen earlier, only lying down. One drawing showed something that could have been a streetcar seen from the front. The number 2 was drawn at the top, above a large window.

Winter laid the drawing aside and looked for more streetcars in the pile. After ten drawings, he found one. It didn't have a number. He flipped past a few more and saw the number 2 written on yet another streetcar, only this time on the side. A face with red hair could be seen in one of the windows. Eyes, nose, mouth.

Checking his watch, he reached for the pink commercial section of the telephone book and looked up the number for the public transport information center. The office at Drottningtorget was still open. He called and waited. A woman answered. He asked about the route of the number 2 streetcar, was told, and hung up.

It fit. That number 2 passed North Biskopsgården. Clearly they would have taken it. Maybe on a daily basis. Or else the number 5, which he'd learned also went through there. Maybe he would see a 5 in the drawings. He'd started sweating, a thin film he could feel from his hairline to his eyebrows. He stood and went out to the toilet without turning the light on and splashed cold water on his face.

The telephone rang. He walked over to the desk and picked up the receiver.

"Winter."

"It's Beier here. I figured you'd still be there."

"What is it?"

"I don't know. But there's a slip of paper that's centuries old. Or pretty old, anyway."

"A slip of paper?"

"A piece of paper with something written on it. We took everything that was in her storage room back with us, including two boxes of clothes. One of them had some children's clothes in it, and we found this slip of paper in the pocket of one of the dresses."

"I see."

"It's an old dress and an old slip of paper."

"You've already been able to determine that?"

"Yes, but no more than that. We haven't started analyzing it yet, so we haven't established exactly how old it is."

"You sound like a doubtful archeologist."

"That's just what you are in this job. But coming up with a precise age is very difficult. So, what's it gonna be? Do you want to come up and take a look at it? I'm leaving pretty soon."

Winter looked at the drawings that he had started to sort into piles. He felt interrupted. "Should I?"

"It's up to you. It's not going anywhere. But—it's a little odd—I'm feeling some kind of vibes here."

"Intuition," Winter said.

"An impulse," Beier said.

"Then I'd better come up."

"So, what do you say?" Beier said.

Winter looked at the dress and the slip of paper lying next to it on the illuminated examination table. The dress could be Jennie's, but it had an old-fashioned feel to it, as if it belonged to another time. Winter couldn't say which one, but that kind of thing wasn't hard to establish.

The paper was four by four inches and looked like it had been folded a thousand times. It was yellowed with age and seemed incredibly delicate. A Dead Sea Scroll, thought Winter. "It certainly looks old," he said. "Do you have the copy?"

Beier handed it to him.

"It's still legible," he said.

"Is it ballpoint?"

"Felt-tip, we think. But don't ask me anything difficult yet. We're going to check it out, just like everything else. If there's any point."

"Well," Winter said. "People hang on to old stuff sometimes. There's nothing unusual about that per se."

"No."

"Then they get murdered or disappear and suddenly we're poring over their personal effects."

"That's when a child's dress becomes interesting," Beier said. "Or a piece of paper with a mysterious message."

Like a cry from the past, thought Winter. He held the copy in his hand. Written on it was "5/20." On the line below was a dash about a quarter of an inch long followed by "1630." The third line read "4—23?" and after that came a blank space of an inch or so and then "L. v—H, C." The C had been circled. On the right side of the paper were lines that looked to Winter like some kind of map. Next to one line, in the upper left-hand corner, was something that could be a cross or short lines.

"This could be a map," he said.

"The horizontal lines start next to that *C*," Beier said.

"It could be a road. A street or a country road. Or just a line."

"It could be anything," Beier said.

"One of them ought to be the time; 1630, that's a time."

"And 5/20 could be a date," Beier said. "May 20."

"The twentieth of May at four thirty," Winter said. "What happened then, Göran? Can you tell me what you were doing then?" he said, deadpan. "Well. We'll just have to think about it. Can you determine how old they are? The dress and the paper?"

"That all depends. The older a piece of paper is, the easier it is to find out how old it is. But this isn't a hundred years old." Beier looked down at the slip of paper again. "So the margins we have to work with are smaller, since the methods of manufacturing paper won't have changed much over such a short period of time. We'll have to check with paper manufacturers about watermarks and such. We'll have to look at the quality of the paper."

"But nothing more?"

"We can't do a full chemical analysis here, if that's what you mean. Fingerprints, yes. Maybe. Age, no. For that you'd have to hand it over to the National Center for Forensic Science. That is, if they can handle stuff that's just ten or twenty or thirty years old. Otherwise there might be other experts."

"I see."

"If it's worth the trouble."

"Right."

"With clothes it's a little different. Here, for example, we have a label, which makes the job a lot simpler. I don't recognize the name of this particular clothing manufacturer, or whatever it is, but that doesn't make a whole lot of difference if it's closed down. Of course it's easier to pin down the age of a piece of fabric. That we ought to be able to do here."

"Maybe the slip of paper is from the same time," Winter said.

"Possibly. But we don't know that, of course."

"How about fingerprints?"

"There are some, but that's all I can say for the moment."

The dress in front of him could belong to the girl, to Jennie, but he didn't think so. He was convinced it had been Helene's, but he didn't say that to Beier. She had worn it when she was about the same age as her daughter is now, so about twenty-five years ago. That's when it's from, thought Winter. The early seventies. On the cusp of my own teenage years. She wore this dress, and maybe she put the slip of paper in there at some point. Or someone else did, at a completely different time. Perhaps her daughter. The question is why. The question is also whether it has any significance for me. I think so. Yes. I think so.

"If you can determine the age of this paper, I think it would be helpful," he said.

36

WINTER PARKED BELOW THE KONSUM SUPERMARKET IN MÖLN-
lycke and walked the narrow arcade. There was one shop that sold both
perfume and health food. Granola with a scent of musk, he thought to
himself.

To the right lay the post-office entrance. He stood next to the doors
and studied the open square, about seventy-five yards across, like a park.
Immediately to his left was the big Konsum supermarket complex.
Kitty-corner to that was Jacky's Pub. To the right of him the open arcade
led east, and he could make out a sign for the Sparbanken savings bank
and another that said "Flowers." Anyone leaving the square normally
headed to the left or right, to access the parking areas or the other shops.
He stepped out into the square and turned around. The windows of the
post office covered maybe twenty yards of the facade. Sitting down on a
bench, he still had a clear view. He got up and walked to the pub. It was
closed but would open in three hours. He turned around. From there
he could see the entrance to the post office. Behind him was a window,
and inside he saw a counter and bar stools. He guessed that he could sit
in there and still see the doors to the post office.

Stepping through those doors, he first entered a vestibule with all
the post boxes: 257 of them. You had to push open another door to get
to the service windows. Good, thought Winter. It took longer to come
in but also to get out.

He knew that nobody had paid the rent for Helene Andersén's apartment yet. Unless it had been done within the last hour, in which case
they had failed.

In the center of the service area was a large desk. Three people were
leaning over it and appeared to be filling out forms.

One of them was Bergenhem. He looked up and gazed indifferently at Winter, or at something next to him, and then peered back down at his form.

Attached to the wall four yards up, between the sign for banking services and service window 1, was a CCTV camera. Winter looked into it, briefly. It was well positioned and an unremarkable gray like the wall, except for the black eye that moved slowly.

The other camera was placed above cashier 3, next to a sign that said, "Our advice costs nothing."

Winter hadn't noticed the sign by the door stating that the premises were under CCTV surveillance. That's good, he thought again. I didn't notice it and maybe no one else will either.

Winter saw that the thick blue-gray carpet by the door had a fold in the middle of it, and he knew that Bergenhem had arranged for that in some discreet way.

Two women with children around their legs were chatting. Others were writing or staring straight ahead. There were about the same number of women and men in there. None of the adults had beards or glared suspiciously at the cameras.

Maybe this was it after all, Winter thought. Maybe this was the time. If he sticks to the program, then it'll be tomorrow, but anyone can change routine.

The ladies manning the cash registers were working calmly and professionally. They wore navy blue post-office blazers with pinstriped blouses. There were lines at each window even though everyone had taken a ticket.

Each cashier had a slip of paper marked with the numbers. Everyone knew the deal. No customers were jumping the line, demanding quick service to distract attention. If that happened, they would all be extra vigilant.

Winter drove in toward town, past Helenevik and through the tunnel beneath the highway. He turned off into the parking lot and climbed out of the car. There were two other cars there. He heard a motor out on the water but could see no boat. The sky was reflected across the whole lake. Sky and water were one, and he was blinded by light as he drew closer.

Beneath the trees or in the water, thought Winter. We'll have to drag the lake soon if we don't find anything on land. The boat that woman, Maltzer, says she saw. That could have been the boys' boat. There were a thousand fingerprints on it from five hundred people. It was a popular boat. Made the boys a bundle. But it had no prints from Helene, so it was useless as evidence for the moment. Still, it did have a red daub of paint.

The symbol was there on the tree—the marking that could be a Chinese character and that resembled the letter *H*.

A boat steered slowly into the inlet a ways, then turned back out again in a wide circle. Winter made out two people in the boat. One of them was wearing a cap and held a fishing pole out over the side, and Winter thought he saw the wet fishing line flash for a moment in the light from the sun that now seemed to be coming from below.

"They're not done with the deposit slip yet," Ringmar said. He scratched the bridge of his nose and seemed at the same time to be sucking on a tooth.

"Stockholm sent it over by car, like you asked."

"I didn't ask. I ordered."

"They had a car coming down here anyway."

"That's their way of alleviating the shame of having to obey orders from Gothenburg."

"Do you have a complex?"

"Not me. But Stockholm does."

Ringmar continued scratching. Bertil's nose is becoming paler, thought Winter, as if he has cut off its blood supply.

"One thing's for sure, though—that slip definitely has prints. There could be prints from thirty different people on it. And those are just the ones we can actually identify."

Winter felt the excitement but also the doubt. The one who paid the rent would most likely have worn gloves, just in case. But you never know.

What they were certainly going to find were traces of the innocent fingers of the post-office staff.

"By the way, there was an incident out at one of the motorcycle clubs just now," Ringmar said.

"It's escalating."

"I wonder what's going on. And here we were thinking peace had taken hold."

"We trusted the motorcycle-borne youth," Winter said.

"Most of them are older than you are." Ringmar scratched himself again. "Something's gotten them rattled," he said.

"You can say that again."

Ringmar knew Winter was referring to the shoot-out at Vårväderstorget. "On the other hand, it's not the first time the Angels have taken potshots at each other in the midst of us mortals. It's part of their business model."

"You mean—"

"Terror is their business model. It's good to spread fear."

"Except for the ones that get shot."

"Jonne's gonna be all right, thank God."

"We'll have to see if we can get our hands on Bolander again."

"He's gone to ground."

"An underground Angel," Winter said. "Just like the devil. A fallen angel."

"Speaking of shoot-outs, that Kurd was sent home today. So we have finally carried out the good edict of the state."

"I know."

"Poor bastard. You think he hoped to be indicted for threatening to shoot himself and the kid?"

"For unlawful threat? I don't know. We don't fall for that anymore. He'd have had a chance only if he'd actually succeeded in doing what he said he was going to do."

"Then we would have taken it seriously."

Or if he'd had a slick lawyer to get him a stay by entering an insanity plea, thought Winter. But there was no sign of that, of course. The man had behaved completely normally, possibly a little overwrought, but perhaps there were reasons for it that they didn't understand.

"I'm sure he'll be happy," Ringmar said.

Winter was busy working his way through the pile of Jennie's drawings when the phone rang. He lifted it with his right hand and held a picture of a sparse forest and open sky in his left.

"You seem to have stopped going home altogether," his sister said.

"Hi, Lotta."

"Do you have a bed in that office?"

"It hasn't reached that point yet."

"Can you get away for a few hours next Saturday?"

"What's happening then?"

"A little party. I think I mentioned something about it earlier. I'm turning an even number of years. Far too many."

"Weren't you going to Marbella?"

"I see you've spoken to Mother."

"Or the other way around."

"I'm going later. So, what do you say?"

"Where is it?"

"Here at my place. If that makes any difference."

"Saturday night?"

"Yes, from about six on. Nothing formal, some punch and then dinner. No assigned seating. If you want, you can sit in the kitchen."

"In that case."

"Good. I'll put your name down."

"I really don't know if I can, Lotta."

"I see."

"I'll come if I can. Maybe."

"You can't damn well spend every waking hour investigating! Not to mention the few you're asleep, knowing you."

"I'll do my best to be there next Saturday evening. At six o'clock."

"The invitation includes Angela, of course."

"Angela," Winter repeated.

"Your girlfriend or lady friend or whatever you want to call her. Remember her?"

51

BEIER RETURNED FROM SUNDSVALL ROSY CHEEKED.

"There was a scent of snow in the air," he said from his office chair.

"It's not like you were all the way up in Kiruna," said Winter, sitting opposite him.

"Norrland is Norrland. They're very particular about that up there."

"Have you discussed it with Sture?"

"I just got here, as you well know. And Sture doesn't like talking about his northern roots."

"Maybe he's hiding something."

"Aren't we all?"

"Which leads me to the reason for my visit."

"You're quick. I expect it's the usual demand from homicide. 'You must have something.' But I haven't had time to speak to the team since returning from my educational trip."

"When?"

"Give me an hour."

The telephone in Winter's jacket pocket rang when he passed through the security gate leading out of the forensics department.

"Winter."

"Hi, Erik."

"Good morning, Mother."

"We read in the *GP* that some madmen opened fire on a square in Hisingen."

"That was ages ago."

"We took a trip to Portugal with some close friends of ours, and when we came home we went through the pile of newspapers, and then I thought I should call and ask you if you were involved. The newspaper didn't say anything about that."

"I wasn't involved in any way."

"That's a relief."

Winter walked down the steps, meeting Wellman outside the elevators on the fourth floor. Wellman nodded and stepped in through the elevator's steel doors.

"Are you there, Erik?"

"I'm here."

"It's so awful about that woman getting murdered."

"Yes."

"You still don't know who she is?"

"No."

"How dreadful."

"Guess I'd better—"

"Lotta has postponed her trip down here."

"So I heard."

"You've spoken to her?"

"Yes. Just now."

"You saw her?"

"It was on the phone."

"She wants you to go see her more often. But I guess I've already been on your back about that."

"Yes."

"Now, she's going to have a little party anyway to celebrate her big day. You're not going to miss that, are you?"

"No."

"Promise? Lotta needs her little brother."

"I know. We have to look out for each other up here while you two are occupied elsewhere."

"Don't be like that now, Erik. We've talked about that. Your father has tried . . ."

Winter was standing in his office. He looked at the CD player and the desks covered with drawings. It was quiet.

"Someone's trying to call me on my work line," he said.

"I can't hear it ringing."

"It blinks. Good-bye, Mother."

He hung up and walked over to the window and picked up a CD case from the sill, took out the disc, and slipped it into the player.

Beier called down to Winter.

"Come up here right away, please."

"What is it?"

"Just come up as quickly as you can."

Winter passed through the security gate and entered the fingerprint lab, where Beier and Bengt Sundlöf were waiting. The slip with the map or whatever it was, and the codes or whatever they were, was lying on a table.

"One thing is clear now," Beier said. "There are two sets of prints from Helene Andersén here."

"What do you mean?"

"As a child and as an adult."

"As a child?" Winter said.

"Yes. They're the same lines, only smaller. She held this slip of paper when she was a child of around four or five."

"So she's the one who held on to it. Why?"

"It's your job to find that out, Erik," Beier said.

"So then we do have at least some kind of time frame for the paper."

"I didn't say that," Beier said. "We know that she held it in her hand about twenty-five years ago."

"Are there any other prints on it?" asked Winter, and he looked at the paper that seemed younger now that he knew more about its history.

"That's where it gets trickier," Beier said. "We can see some traces of fingerprints but only partials. I can't help you there yet."

"Okay."

"You want us to continue?"

Winter blew air out through his mouth and thought. He studied the faint characters and lines.

"Maybe she had a reason for saving it. I don't know. I really don't know, Göran."

"I'm only asking because we have a whole apartment's worth of evidence to go through. And this isn't exactly the only case we're working on."

"Keep working on this one whenever you get a little time left over, then." Winter eyed the slip of paper again. "But what can you do with the partial prints?"

"For us to be able to conclusively establish identity, there have to be twelve points of comparison, minimum. You follow me?"

Winter followed him, in theory. But practically was another matter. The computer didn't know what a fingerprint looked like—it simply registered the ridge endings, bifurcations, and dots.

There were twenty fingerprint experts in Sweden. Two in Gothenburg. One of them was Bengt Sundlöf and he was still standing there next to Beier and Winter.

"It does kind of give me itchy fingers, so to speak," Sundlöf said of the slip of paper.

"A challenge," Beier said.

"You sit there and peer into those two microscopes and search—and make sketches."

"For days on end," Beier said. "And get bad back pains from working so intensely in a hunched-over posture."

"And you carry on like that until you find twelve points that match," Sundlöf said.

"Know what you say then?" he asked Winter.

"Bingo?" Winter said.

"We're going to help you," Sundlöf said. "You appreciate knowledge and experience despite your youth and long hair."

"In France they require a fourteen-point match for a positive ID," Beier said.

"Maybe we're taking risks up here in the north."

"The Americans have the largest fingerprint database in the world, naturally," Sundlöf said. "The FBI has millions to choose from and compare to. They once found a seven-point match. Only they were different people!"

"I think I've lost you now," Winter said.

"They had two sets of prints, and seven of the minutiae points in the two fingerprints were identical," Beier said. "They were completely identical. And yet it turned out they came from two different people. No one's ever found so many matching points in two separate individuals. Never."

"Not yet anyway," Winter said. "So twelve gives us a pretty good margin, then?"

"You can be pretty sure," Beier said.

"Then do the same with the print on the drawer in Helene's apartment," Winter said.

"That's a partial print," Sundlöf said. "And a faint one, probably deposited through a tear in a woolen glove, judging from the fiber sample. We're analyzing that right now."

"So, difficult in other words?" Winter asked.

Beier and Sundlöf nodded simultaneously.

"How about the others? In the apartment?"

"We're still working at it, Inspector," Beier said.

"I'm sure you'll find all there is to find," Winter said, and took a step toward the door. "Thanks for the lesson, by the way."

Winter passed through the security gate. He wanted to get back to his office to go through the drawings, to sort them.

He also wanted to study his copy of the slip of paper again. Here in forensics it was as if the numbers and letters had become more distinct, the lines longer, sharper. It meant something to him. It was a map.

It had meant something to Helene too. Or had she simply forgotten the slip of paper twenty-five years ago in that pocket, after some kind of game? It was possible—for those who believed in coincidences.

But she hadn't written the numbers and drawn the lines herself. It was a grown-up's hand that had guided the pen.

He felt warm and the inside of his head felt sort of swollen. A cold shower was in order.

38

THE LIGHT OVER THE SQUARE WAS JUST AS HARSH AS ON PRE-
vious days, though the air had grown warmer. Winter was sitting on
one of the benches, eyes trained on the entrance to the post office. He'd
been sitting there for half an hour and was about to stand. It was a quarter to one. Lots of people were walking in and out through the doors
along the arcade—the time of the month when salaries and pensions
were paid out and bills came due. A group of men were waiting outside for the doors of Jacky's Pub to open. I'll go in there later, Winter
thought. I can see from in there.

Sara Helander had relieved Bergenhem an hour and a half ago and was
sitting on one of the benches by the window, with a brochure on the art
of borrowing.
    She glanced down at it and tried at the same time to keep an eye on
what was going on over at the service windows. She could see them,
but perhaps she ought to stand. I'll rest my legs a minute longer, she
thought.
    She'd lifted her gaze and stood when she saw the women at win-
dow number 3 raise a hand. Helander quickly moved closer, crossing
between a baby carriage and a child. The woman behind the counter
looked pale, as if she was about to fall off her swivel chair. She lowered
her hand and pointed toward the doors.
    Helander saw the light signal flashing at short intervals above the
service window, like a reminder of her negligence. A man as broad as
the poster above him had already positioned himself in front of the window, expecting to be served. Helander thrust him aside, thrashing her
way forward, intense nausea surging in her chest.
    "What the he—"

"He was here!" the woman behind the glass said. "I tried to catch your eye. He was here thirty seconds ago. Didn't the light go on?"

Reflexively Helander looked up once again at the angry signal from the warning light mounted above the service window. Fuck, I'm gonna get fired! Oh my God, I didn't even think . . . But she pulled herself together.

"Was it the same number?"

The woman held up a deposit slip.

Helander grabbed hold of the little woven basket on the counter. It was half-filled with slips.

"Put these somewhere safe," she shouted, and tried to squeeze the basket through the far-too-narrow gap beneath the window. "Open up and put these inside!"

"He went ou—" The woman in navy blue and pinstripes felt her voice crack.

I bet he fucking did. Helander almost tripped over the fold in the carpet but regained her balance and avoided breaking her nose against the shatterproof glass.

Winter was just lighting a Corps when he saw Sara Helander fly out through the doors of the post office and look around wildly.

Something's gone wrong. He threw away his cigarillo and ran to where Helander was standing. She saw him.

"He was here!" she said breathlessly. "The cashier processed a deposit—"

"Which way?"

"I don't know."

"When?"

"Just now. A few minutes ago. I'm sor—"

"Forget about that now. What does he look like?"

"I don't know. It happened so fa—"

"Bergenhem is eating over in the bar. Go over there and tell him to come over to the post office right away, to the room at the back where we've got the video machine. You come back here with him. But first call Bertil and tell him to send over two cars with extra manpower. I'll call the officers watching the parking lots."

He dialed a number for one of the cars stationed at the western parking lot and spoke into his cell phone.

"They're standing by," he said, and hung up. "We'll see if we can't pick him up."

Damn it, he thought to himself. "I'm going inside to check the CCTV footage. Come as quickly as you can. Which window was it?"

"Number 3."

Inside the post office, life went on as usual. The postmaster was waiting by the door to the back room.

"I'll go in and rewind the tape," Winter said. "He was in here. Have someone relieve the girl at window 3 and send her back here to the video room."

"But I've got no one else!"

"What's the matter with you? We're investigating a mur—" But he calmed down. "Look, just close it or sit there yourself if you have to. I want her in here immediately."

The camera was connected directly to the video recorder, which was connected to a monitor in a room with no windows. Winter stopped the machine and looked at his watch. He rewound the tape to a half minute before the time Helander had put down that the man had been there. The woman from window 3 came in. Winter pressed play. The film scraped to life and the interior of the post office appeared.

Winter had chosen the camera location at the very back of the premises, and from there it looked like a thousand people were gathered. The woman now standing next to him could be seen in angled profile close by. A female customer left the window. A man wearing a baseball cap and a long, heavy jacket was next in line and then stepped forward.

Winter saw the man drop his slip in the basket on the counter, like a reflex action. Winter couldn't see his face—just his profile, at an angle, from behind.

"That's him," the cashier said.

"Are you sure?"

"Of course it's him. He was wearing that same cap," she said, as if the footage they were watching wasn't a replay but a live take in a reality show.

Winter saw how the man handed something over and how the cashier took it and shifted her gaze in front of her, still angled down, and how she then looked up at the man and seemed to look past him. Winter followed that gaze right across the room to Helander, who was sitting on a bench, looking down at a brochure.

The light above the service window started flashing. The woman said something to the man.

"I tried to keep him there, but he didn't want a receipt."

The man in the cap left the counter and moved toward the door. The cashier raised her arm and waved her hand. Another man stepped up to the window and looked at the cashier gesturing. Winter saw how Helander jumped up and forced her way up to the window. The man in the cap walked out through the double doors without tripping over Bergenhem's fold in the carpet.

Bergenhem and Helander had entered and were standing next to the cashier.

"My God," she said. The idiot's caught on film, she thought when she saw herself.

Winter stopped the tape and backed it up. The man in the cap came back into frame.

"That's him," Winter said. He won't be the only one out there with one of those fucking caps, he thought to himself. But his has some big, pale lettering on the front.

"Yes, that's him," the cashier said.

Winter spoke on his cell phone, repeated the description.

"They're searching for him," he said to Helander and Bergenhem as he held the phone to his ear, waiting for someone else to pick up. "Hello? Yes, seal everything off. Forge— What? No, no sirens for Christ's sake. And don't forget the bus station. Yes. The bus station. Send someone over there *now*!"

He hung up and headed for the door.

"Is Bertil bringing more men?"

"Yes," Bergenhem said. "What do we do now?"

"You all know what he looks like." Winter checked his watch. "Less than ten minutes have passed since he was in here. He may have jumped into a car and driven off, but there's a chance he's still around, and we've got the big parking lots and the bus station covered. I don't think he suspects anything. And call Bertil again, right away."

"Okay," Bergenhem said.

"He's still here," Winter said. "I think he's still here. One of the female officers has taken up position outside the doors to Konsum. I want you to go into the department store and see if you can spot him. And if you do, call me and go outside and wait there with the others."

He looked at Helander. "You come with me."

She didn't answer as he hurried her out of the post office.

"You circle around the edge of the square, to the left, and we'll meet up at the corner over there," Winter said.

He entered the savings bank and came out again. The man in the cap wasn't in the flower shop, nor was he in the Bella Napoli Pizzeria. Not in the real estate office on the corner.

"Nothing," Helander said when they met.

They walked down the pedestrian tunnel. They walked past the newly built high school and stood in front of the cultural center. To the left Winter could see a bridge over a stream. The path forked in two after the bridge, and then again farther on, and once more after that. He thought about the fingerprint, his heart pounding.

They entered the cultural center and continued through the library and the other public spaces. They saw two teenagers wearing caps.

"He was at least forty," Helander said.

"Yes."

They went out and the wind hit them from the left. They continued into the wind, half-running. Up ahead lay the bus station. Winter could see the back entrance to the supermarket and the parking lot below, toward the street. Fredrik and Aneta—back on duty—moving around among the cars. Halders's scalp was self-illuminating.

There were police officers standing by the buses. He could make out Ringmar speaking to Börjesson. Bergenhem approached from the arcade next to Konsum and shook his head when he saw Winter. We're all here, thought Winter, the whole hardworking team, but what good is it?

He continued west across the bus station. On the other side of the road was the health clinic, and in front of him was yet another big parking lot. As he drew closer he saw a man, thirty yards away, leaning forward to unlock a red Volvo 740. He was wearing a black cap with white text and a green oilskin coat that Winter could only see the upper part of since the man was standing on the other side of the car. Winter started to run.

The man looked up, black cap pulled down over his brow. He was wearing a red scarf. It's like watching a black-and-white film transform into color, Winter thought as he ran.

The man saw him and turned around to see if anything was happening behind him, and that's when the others approached. A police car tore out from the bus station and accelerated toward him. The blond guy in the leather jacket sprinting toward him was now shouting something. He threw himself into the car and jammed the key into the ignition, and the Volvo roared to life. When he sent the car surging backward, the guy in the leather jacket clung to the door, but then flew off when he popped the clutch and shot forward. It would have worked if the back end of a cop car hadn't smashed right into his front on the exit ramp and then been dragged halfway across the damn street on the hood of his Volvo before he finally came to a stop. He couldn't get the door open, so he threw himself to the passenger side and stepped out onto the asphalt, which was when that goddamn skinhead came at him and barreled into his stomach skull-first, and the air just exploded out of him and he crumbled to the ground after two steps, and the skinhead flew onto him again.

"You okay?" Halders asked.

"Just a little scratch," Winter said, peering at his elbow through the hole in his leather jacket. "Nice work, Fredrik."

"So that's him," Halders said, and looked at the man sitting in the backseat of one of the radio cars.

"He's the one who paid the rent."

"Has he said anything?"

"Not a word."

"Guess we'll have to torture him," Halders said. "This is just the beginning. Aren't you happy, Winter?"

"Happy?"

"It could have all gone to shit."

"We'll have to wait and see."

"Come on, this is a big breakthrough for homicide. Look at him. He knows he's going to come clean."

"Nice takedown there," Winter repeated. "I'm going to have a quick chat with Sara before we head back."

Halders nodded and walked toward Aneta and the car. It looked as if he were going for a stroll.

Helander was waiting by the station building.

"I was negligent," she said. "Criminally negligent."

"We should have practiced a bit," Winter said. "But there's no guarantee it would have turned out differently anyway. There were a lot of people in there and he was quick."

"Bullshit."

Winter lit up a Corps. It tasted good. "Okay. But we had a preparedness that worked."

"He wasn't suspicious," Helander said. "Not even when you came running toward him. Isn't that strange?"

"We'll have to see what he says and who he is," Winter said. "If his name matches what his driver's license says—that is, if he's got one." He took a drag and studied the smoke that followed the wind up toward the sky.

THE MAN'S NAME WAS OSKAR JAKOBSSON AND HE HAD HIS own registration number at the station. They'd pulled the fingerprints from the slip and compared it to the ten-print database and the system found a match. Oskar Jakobsson had a criminal background. Nothing big.

He'd done time for larceny and battery against friends and had been convicted of car theft, and he had done stuff they didn't know about, Winter thought as he sat in front of Jakobsson, who looked worried but not desperate. He was prepared for a detention lasting twelve hours and maybe longer, but not a lot longer. He claimed that he knew what he had done, but not why.

"Of course you help someone out when they ask you. Of course you do."

Beneath the baseball cap his hair was dark brown and disheveled. Jakobsson had declined the offer of a comb, but had said yes to coffee. He had a scar above his chin, like a proper criminal who's had broken bottles shoved in his face in his time.

"You're happy to lend a hand?" Winter asked.

"People help me out."

"Tell us again from the beginning."

"From when?"

"From when you were asked if you'd be willing to help out."

The tape recorder was turning on the table between them. The interrogating officer, Gabriel Cohen, sat next to Winter and was silent. No one else was in the room. There were no windows. The ventilation system droned from the walls. When Jakobsson asked if he could smoke, Winter said no.

"I'd just parked," Jakobsson said.

Winter wondered how the man had managed to drive a car around for months without getting stopped. He'd never had a driver's license. The car belonged to his brother, who seldom drove.

"When was that?"

"When was it I parked? Last month. Unless it was the end of the month before that. At the same spot in the parking lot where I was standing this time. Maybe a luck—"

"What were you going to do?"

"Do? I was going to do some shopping."

"Where?"

"At the Terningen supermarket. My brother wanted some *snus*, so did I, and a loaf of bread and some potatoes."

"Okay," Winter said. "You've just locked the car and are about to walk away from it. What happens then?"

"She comes up to me after I've turned around and maybe taken a step or two."

"You didn't see her before?"

"No."

"Did you see this woman after you parked but before you got out of the car?"

"No. Not that I remember."

"So you got out of the car and took a few steps. What happened then?"

"Like I said. She came up to me with that damn envelope."

"She had an envelope?"

"Yeah."

"What did it look like?"

"What are you asking about that for? You already have it for Christ's sake. You took it from the glove compartment."

"Did it look like this?" Winter held up a white A5 envelope. "Go ahead and take it."

Jakobsson held it in front of him. "It's the same size, but this one was brown."

"She came up to you, you say. You say she had the envelope. Could you see it? Was she holding it out in the open?"

"Yes."

"Did she say anything?"

"She asked me if I wanted to make a little cash. Well, she didn't say 'a little,' come to think of it—she just asked if I wanted to make some cash."

"What did you say?"

"Nothing. I guess I must have just stared at her."

"Describe what she looked like."

"There wasn't a lot you could see. Black sunglasses and a hat, so I couldn't see any hair, but she wore a shirt and pants. That's what I remember."

"Was she white?"

"What do you mean, white?"

"What color skin did she have? Was she white or black?"

"Well, she wasn't a black person, if that's what you're asking. She had a tan, I guess, but the shades were so big they covered almost her whole face."

We'll have to return to this later, Winter thought. He's got more to tell us about her appearance. "What did she say?"

"I just told you, she asked if I wanted to make some cash."

"What did you answer?"

"Nothing. I stared at her like a fucking idiot. It's fucking creepy, someone just popping up out of nowhere like that and handing you an envelope."

"What did she say then?"

"She said that I could make some cash if I did her a little favor, and then she told me what it was—that I was to go to the post office at the end of every month and pay this rent and write down the number of the apartment. That was it."

"What was the envelope for?"

"That's where the money was, for Christ's sake. And a paper with the depo—direct deposit number and the other number."

"Where's that slip of paper now?"

"I threw it away."

"Why did you do that?"

"I remembered the number. I have a good memory for numbers, see. And of course I wasn't so stupid as not to realize that it had to be something a little shady. In which case you shouldn't hang on to any little slips of paper. Never keep slips of paper—that's my motto."

Jakobsson looked as if he was going to smirk, and Winter felt the skin tighten around his scalp. He was full of impatience, but he kept it suppressed beneath the calm that was necessary for him to be able to make it through the interrogation.

"Say the number," Winter said. "The direct deposit number."

"What?"

"You've got a good memory for numbers, right. You said earlier that you had to pay two rents and that you had received five thousand for your trouble. Then you must remember the number."

"Three rents," Jakobsson said, "and I got ten thousand. Talk about a memory for numbers, huh?" He looked at Cohen, who nodded. "This guy doesn't even remember if it was two or three rents." Cohen nodded again.

"Okay," Winter said. "Let's hear the direct deposit number, then."

Jakobsson stared at the tape recorder. The air-conditioning droned, and finally he cleared his throat. "Damn it, it's this interrogation. It makes me nervous. It's not so strange. You don't even remember how many rents it was."

"You don't remember the number?"

"Sure I do, just not right now. I have to pay another rent, don't I? Then I gotta remember."

"Where is the money?" Winter asked, well aware of the answer.

"Are you kidding me? You think I've got it in the bank?"

"So where, then?"

"Spent, Mr. Chief Inspector. Consumed, you might say. And a long time ago."

"What was the number you were supposed to write on the payment slip at the post office?"

"What?"

"You were supposed to write another number too. What was it?"

"I'll know it when I'm standing there."

"You won't be standing there anymore."

"No. But you know what I mean. When I have to remember, I do. It's kind of like this motto I've got."

"Do you have any idea what this is about?" Winter said, edging closer to the table.

"Nobody tells me anything."

"This is about murder and kidnapping."

"What's that got to do with me?"

"You're involved."

"How the hell can I be involved? What did you say—kidnapping? Murder? What the f— You guys know me, well, not you maybe, but ask some of the other officers in the building. Go on! How the hell can anyone think that Oskar Jakobsson would be involved? Jesus fucking Christ."

"Where's the slip of paper?"

"I told you I threw it away."

"Where?"

"In the garbage, for fuck's sake. At home."

"When?"

"When? Ages ago. When I got the stuff from the woman."

Winter decided to reveal something else to him about the reason for their interest, and at this Cohen stood up and went to get some coffee. Jakobsson then said he was dying for a smoke, and Winter took out the pack of Princes he had bought and handed it to him, lighting Jakobsson's cigarette and a Corps for himself.

"I might have it at home," Jakobsson said.

"So you didn't take it with you when you were going to pay the rent at the post office? You've got to help me out here a little," Winter said.

"Okay, okay. I threw it away afterward."

"You threw it away? When?"

"After I paid it. There was a wastebasket in that room you walk through before you get to the section with the service windows. I threw it away in there."

"Why did you throw it away? You had another rent to pay."

Jakobsson exhaled and gazed at the smoke rising to the ceiling.

"Why did you throw it away?" Winter repeated.

"Okay, okay. I didn't have to pay any more rents."

"You didn't have to pay any more rents?"

"I said, no. You were right before, although you didn't know it. I only had to pay two rents."

"Are you telling me the truth now?"

"Yes."

"Why should we believe you now?"

Jakobsson shrugged his shoulders.

"I guess 'cause of what you told me," he said. "That's some heavy shit. That's not something you want to be involved in, hell no." He looked around for an ashtray, and when Cohen nodded to a plate where some buns had been, Jakobsson flicked off a long pillar of ash. "I'm not involved. I haven't done anything."

"Why are you lying about this woman, then?"

"What the fuck is this now? I'm not lying, am I?"

"You told us that she came up to you when you got out of your car. Is that right?"

"Yeah."

"You stood there facing each other, and she handed you the envelope and made you this offer?"

"Yes."

"What did she say?"

"Oh for Chri— How many times do I have to tell you? She asked if I wanted to make some cash and do them a favor at the same time."

"Them?"

"What?"

"You said 'them' now. What do you mean by that?"

"I did? I don't mean anything."

"You don't want to help us, Oskar. Should we break it off here and continue when you've had a chance to think it over?"

"I don't need to think it over."

"You want to continue?"

"You're asking and I'm answering. That's how it always is. Ask me a good question and I'll give you a good answer."

"This isn't a game," Winter said. "There's a four-year-old girl somewhere out there who may still be alive, and we've already wasted a lot of time."

She wasn't five. They'd been able to establish that Jennie was four and a half.

Jakobsson was silent. The cigarette butt lay crumpled in the dish. Winter held his extinguished cigarillo in his hand.

"How this ends might depend on you," Winter said. "You understand what I'm saying?"

"Can I have another cigarette?"

Winter handed Jakobsson the pack and let him light one himself.

"Everybody knows that I would never have anything to do with murder," Jakobsson said. "Everybody knows."

"Did you do it?"

"Do what?"

"Kill the woman?"

"What the fu—"

"Just tell us and you'll be doing us both a favor."

"Oskar Jakobsson a murderer? People would laugh—"

"Where did you meet this woman?"

"What?"

"The woman you say made you the offer. Where did you meet her?"

"Christ, you guys are too much. I told you, the parking lot."

"I don't think you're telling the truth. Unless you tell us where it was, I can't believe anything else you say."

Jakobsson looked at Cohen, who nodded encouragingly.

"Okay, okay. *Fuck!* There was this coffee shop there, and I got a call beforehand."

"A call? A phone call?"

"Yes."

"From whom?"

"From her. The woman I met later in the coffee shop."

"She called you?"

"Yes."

"Where were you then?"

"Where was I? At home, of course. I don't have a cell phone."

"Were you alone at home?"

"When I got the call? Well, my brother may have been out. I can't remember."

"What did she say?"

"That she had a proposal and that I could do her a favor and . . . For Christ's sake, we've been over this a thousand times."

"What do you mean?"

"She said what I said she said, only it was someplace else. At the coffee shop."

"Which coffee shop?"

"Jacky's Pub."

"That's a coffee shop?"

"To me it's a coffee shop. Coffee's the only thing I drink there. The beer's too damn expensive, and anyways I've quit."

"Who suggested that you meet there?"

"I did."

"Are you sure about that?"

"Nah. Maybe it was her. It's so . . . Can we take that break soon? This is tiring me out."

"We'll break soon," Winter said. "Try to remember who suggested that you meet there."

"It was her."

"What was the first thing she said?"

"I can't remember a damn thing anymore."

"What's her name?"

"No idea. I told you several times before we sat down here. I'd never seen her before."

"You know her."

"No way."

"Why else would she get in touch with you?"

"Fuck if I know."

"You said before that you're happy to lend a hand."

"I said that? Well, maybe that's why she got in touch."

"Are you known for lending a hand?"

"Don't ask me. But that could be the reason, like I said. She heard from somebody that I'm a good guy and she called me."

"Who might she have heard that from?"

"What?"

"That you're a good guy?"

"A hundred people at least," Jakobsson said.

"List them," Winter said, and took out a fresh notepad from his inside pocket, along with a stubby pencil.

"You're out of your . . . I gotta go to the toilet."

"In a minute."

"You don't get it. If I don't get to a toilet in one minute, it won't be much fun for anyone to sit in here."

"What's her name?"

"I said I don't know. You can continue questioning me in the toilet if you want to but I can't—"

"Give me a name."

"I don't know *for fuck's sake!*"

"Who might have tipped her off that you're ready to lend a hand?"

Jakobsson didn't answer. He'd risen up to a half-standing position, and they could tell from the dark spot spreading out across his jeans that perhaps for the first time during the interview he had spoken the truth.

40

RINGMAR READ THE TRANSCRIPTS FROM THE SESSION WITH Jakobsson. He too was struck by its significance, by the possibility that they were suddenly making progress. It was like catching a whiff of something you knew would smell a lot worse when you got closer.

"I don't think he knows what he's involved in," Ringmar said.

"He's a pretty tough character."

"Not that tough," Ringmar said. "Not for this. Jakobsson is small time."

"Möllerström is working on his circle of associates."

"There must be a lot of them," Ringmar said.

"Not as many as you might expect."

"That all depends. Did you know that Oskar used to ride a motorbike?"

"Yes," Winter said, "but it's hard to believe."

"He was in a biker gang. Some local chapter of the Hells Angels, but even they kicked him out, I think."

"I can hear the rumbling throughout this investigation," Winter said.

"What did you say?"

"Nothing. The sky's rumbling."

Ringmar sized up his younger superior. Winter had dark circles under his eyes, and in certain lighting he almost looked as if he were wearing war paint. His long hair reached his shoulders.

"Maybe I'm reading too much into it," Winter said. "Maybe Jakobsson is just an innocent bystander."

"Innocent messenger," Ringmar said. "But there are no innocent messengers."

Winter flipped through the printouts. The words struck at him from the paper. Over the last two or three years, he'd come to read interrogation transcripts with a vague feeling of dread, as if they were fiction taken from a reality he couldn't penetrate. The exchanges were fiction and sport at the same time, and both parties knew it.

"He says that the woman could have been forty or twenty-five."

"That may be because of the sunglasses," Ringmar said. "That is, if she was wearing any. Or if she even exists."

"It's not unusual to have a proxy," Winter said. "Someone like Jakobsson gets an assignment from someone who got it from someone else who in turn was contacted by the prime mover. The murderer."

"Yeah, standard criminal procedure," Ringmar said.

"So we have to work our way backward along the chain," Winter said.

"If all he did was that one service, and didn't think any more about it, then he would have said so straight off."

"Yes."

"That means he knows whoever it was that gave him the job. The woman, if it is a woman."

"Could be."

"We can't even say for sure that there was any money involved."

"No."

"We'll have to put the screws to him again," Ringmar said. "But let him go empty his bladder this time."

The nationwide APB had been issued. Wellman defended the delay and did a good job of it. Winter might see Wellman in a different light after this.

Everything from the past month came back. Winter could see his own investigation described in different varieties of newspaper prose. He read the newspapers and set them aside. Bülow's article was fairly well informed, but that wasn't so strange given that Winter had provided the facts. It was an agreement of sorts.

Winter had agreed to take part in a press conference the next morning. Tomorrow, not earlier.

Sitting alone in his office, he reached for the drawings, but first he closed his eyes so his mind would be as dark and still as possible.

They dragged Delsjö Lake. They walked through the forested areas along the water's edge again. They were able to be more candid when they questioned the neighbors.

Photographs of Helene Andersén's apartment had been disseminated through the media and printed on posters. They went through the census register. Helene Andersén had lived in the apartment at North

Biskopsgården and before that in an apartment in Backa. Jennie had been born at Östra Hospital. The father had been listed as unknown. Helene had taken care of her child on her own from the start.

She'd been in contact with the social services or, rather, the other way around. They had evaluated her and visited her home, but she was apparently deemed fit to look after her little daughter. No one that Winter spoke to remembered anything.

She had no job and she was not getting any support from the welfare office. It didn't make any sense. She had an unblemished credit history. Not even someone who lives simply can manage that. Winter opened his eyes again. She had money coming in from somewhere. She had stated in her tax returns that she had a minor sum of money put by, but they didn't find any accounts or safe-deposit boxes. They had more to do there.

There were 145 Anderséns in the Gothenburg telephone book, but none had thus far been in touch.

Helene had had a telephone installed three months before, and she wasn't registered as having had one before that.

It was October now, and her service had started on August 10. She'd bought a telephone, but they didn't as yet know where. A twenty-nine-year-old woman who may have gotten her first phone ever. Why did she get a phone? Why had she decided not to have one earlier?

Something had happened that caused her to need a phone, thought Winter. She needed to get in touch with someone, maybe quickly if necessary. Was she afraid? Had she bought it for protection? Had she been told to be reachable?

Seven days after her phone was hooked up, she was dead. She'd made two calls, both to phone booths. One was at Vågmästarplatsen, which she had dialed at 6:30 p.m. on the evening of August 14. The other booth was at the bus terminal at the Heden recreation grounds, which she'd called the following evening, August 15.

Helene had in turn received three calls, two immediately preceding the calls she'd placed herself and from the same phone booths. Someone had apparently been waiting there for her to call back. Why?

The third call came from a number that was registered to an apartment in the Majorna district. Someone had phoned at four thirty on the afternoon of August 16. The conversation had lasted one minute. The dialer was a woman named Maj Svedberg, and she had no recollection whatsoever of the call. August 16? Had she even been in town? Could it have been when she dialed a wrong number? A child had answered and then a woman, and it was a wrong number. Whom had she intended to call? The public dental service, actually, and if they wanted to check her story, she had the number for the dentist, but she didn't know anything about this other number.

They checked the number for the dental office, and it was identical to Helene's except for one number.

"Check up on her," Winter had said to Möllerström.

The pile of Jennie's drawings had become smaller, and Winter continued to go through them. He could see that some were more accomplished or more detailed. It wasn't clear whether this had to do with age. Perhaps sometimes the girl just grew tired of drawing.

There were recurring elements: boats and cars, faces in a window a few times. A forest or just a few trees. A road that was brown or sometimes black. Sun and rain, nearly always sun and rain. Always outside. Winter had yet to see a single drawing of an interior.

He held up a drawing depicting a house with a pointed roof and a Danish flag on top.

A Danish flag, thought Winter. White cross on a red background. The house stood in a field indicated by a few green lines. The house had walls that were white like the paper.

Over the next half hour he worked his way through the rest of the pile of drawings, and found another with a Danish flag.

Two drawings with a Danish flag.

More than twenty of a boat on water.

Three drawings of a car driven by a man with a black beard that grew straight out from his chin.

He laid the two Danish flag pictures next to each other on the desk and studied them, one at a time. He searched for the signature "jeni" and suddenly stiffened. The drawing on the left was signed "helene." He looked for the signature on the other. It was in the lower right-hand corner: "helene" again. He swallowed and started to go through the piles in front of him. One of the drawings of the car was signed "helene." You couldn't tell it apart from the other two. Five of the drawings depicting boats were signed "helene" in the same childish scrawl as "jeni." The motifs were the same, their execution seemingly identical.

This is one of the spookiest things I've ever experienced, thought Winter.

In the back of his mind was something else that he had noticed as he'd sorted through the drawings over the past half hour—something recurring, something he hadn't reacted to, like a spot in a corner that you only vaguely register but don't ascribe any importance to.

He went back to one of the desks with the sorted drawings. One, two, three, four, five, six, seven . . . There. It was the path that went from the bottom of the page to the top. It was possible that it was a road, since it gently wove its way past a few trees before ending up at a house that had a door and a window but no roof.

The pages felt stiff in his hands as he sifted on. There: The road leading up from the bottom of the page. The house with no roof, a window to the left of the door. To the right of the house—like a vertical rectangle with an X at the top—was a double cruciform.

Winter looked at the first drawing again. The same little barely visible box in a dead corner, with diagonally crossed lines.

A windmill, he thought. It could be a little windmill that she's drawn.

Both drawings were signed "jeni."

"I brought along a basket," Angela said, and held it up for him to see.

"Is it Friday?" Winter asked.

"Friday evening, eight o'clock."

"Then I can't leave you standing out here on the doorstep."

"You could come outside."

"And miss the trumpet solo? Here it comes now."

"Sweet."

"Well, come inside, then, before it's over."

"You weren't surprised, were you?"

"No, it's just that I was—"

"Sitting and working? Or thinking? Forgot that I was coming?"

He didn't answer, took the basket and set it down on the floor and helped her with her coat, which was heavy and smelled divinely of her and pungently of the street along Vasaplatsen.

"I haven't been here for a long time," she said as they stood in the living room.

"Me neither."

"So I've realized."

"May I?" Winter grabbed hold of her and pulled her out onto the wooden floor, which bounced varnished reflections from the glow of a lamp over by the windows.

She bent her face a little backward and looked at him. "What's this?"

"Donald Byrd."

"I mean *this*. This dance. It's a surprise."

"Life's full of surprises."

"What's gotten into you? Have you been drinking?"

"Quiet now and follow my lead," Winter said.

He swung her around, in a right turn, when Trane came in after

Byrd's solo, and then Byrd came back and he drew her more tightly to him and continued the right turn.

They danced. She couldn't remember when they had last done that. It was nice. It was just a good way to start a Friday evening. Dancing and the wine she had brought along and the langoustine and white . . .

They continued to dance until the music ended, then moved to the kitchen. She took out the food while Winter prepared dry martinis in a shaker.

"When did you last have a dry martini?" she asked.

"Was it five years ago?"

She looked at him. His face seemed sort of chipped along the edges, paler than the last time they had seen each other. His shirt was open at the collar, and she could see the sinews in his neck. He looked up from his shaking and smiled.

"Are you celebrating something, Erik?"

He stopped moving the ice-colored cylinder and set it down on the kitchen counter.

"More the opposite really."

"What's that supposed to mean?"

"I felt that I needed something else."

"Something other than that awful case you're working on?"

"Well, yes, something that glittered and sparkled a little differently. Like that," he said, and nodded at the shaker.

"Well, pour it up," she said. "Here are the glasses."

He poured and they drank.

"Shall we set the table and sit down and talk about this past week?"

"Let's do yours," Winter said.

"You're probably the one who most needs to talk," she said.

41

IT WAS SUMMER AGAIN WHEN HE STEPPED OUT THE FRONT DOOR before eight o'clock, the shadows from the houses still bearing traces of the past night's darkness. A street cleaner dragged itself along the asphalt on the other side of Vasaplatsen and sucked the last of the morning haze into its rotating bristles. A van delivered fresh bread to the Wasa Källare restaurant. Winter took in the smells. He was hungry. He'd drunk a cup of coffee and that was it. Angela had continued sleeping.

He walked across Kungstorget. The market stalls were being set up for the day. Crates of vegetables and fruit were carried out from trucks to their spots on the stands. He went into a shop on the other side of Kungsportsplatsen and ordered a café au lait and two French rolls with butter and cheese. He sat down by the window and watched the tabloid paper's city office across the square opening for the day. A young lady had put up headline posters. He couldn't read them from where he was sitting, but he could guess what they said. Up to now the media reports had brought in hundreds of tips, perhaps thousands. Winter had worked with them as much as he could bear and tried to take seriously anything that seemed worth being taken seriously. There was a desire to help but also a fear of what had happened. Of what might happen again, what might happen to me.

He got up and walked north to Brunnsparken and stood at the number 2 stop. Jennie had drawn a streetcar with a 2 at one end. It was likely she had ridden on it, most likely together with her mother, Helene.

They'd questioned the streetcar drivers, but no one recognized the faces of the people they drove through the city. Perhaps it was a form of security. It was an insecure job. They had also shown photographs around North Biskopsgården but nobody knew anything; no one recognized anyone.

A series of photos of the girl had been taken in a studio at Vågmästarplatsen a year ago. The photographer remembered doing it but nothing more. The few other photos of Jennie they'd found in Helene's apartment were taken with one or more cameras that they hadn't found.

Someone had taken the photos of Helene and of Helene with her daughter.

There were seven or eight that had been taken relatively recently, in addition to the studio photos. Two had dates printed on them and that could prove helpful.

There were no photographs of Helene as a child.

Winter looked around. A dozen or so people were waiting for the streetcar. The number 2 arrived, and on an impulse he boarded, together with four men who might have been Ethiopians and a drunk who was Swedish.

He got off at Friskväderstorget, and the sun filled the ears protruding from the sides of the buildings. The satellite dishes seemed to swivel back and forth, homing in on sounds from a native land. He heard music, coming from somewhere, which sounded like John Coltrane with a hookah and a fez. Turkish jazz, he thought. It really swings.

Ernst Lundgren was out with the children in the playground outside the building that housed the pensioners' day-care center. The tall old man bent down in a way that would either strengthen his back or soon snap it in two.

"Anything new?" he asked when Winter said hello.

Winter told him the latest.

"Well, we still don't have anything here," Lundgren said. "She didn't belong to our little flock."

"And none of the other parents recognize her?"

"The mothers? No, not a one."

"She seems to have been one of the loneliest people in the world," Winter said.

"There's nothing strange about that. Nothing surprises me."

"I didn't take you for a cynic."

"I'm not cynical. I'm just not surprised."

"About the loneliness?"

"She wasn't the only one," Lundgren said. "There's a whole bunch of them. You could safely say that they're in the majority."

The apartment smelled of wood and wind.

"I've cleaned the house," Angela said, holding a glass of wine in her hand. "A proper housewife."

"Apart from the glass of wine," Winter said.

"Want some?"

"No. I'd prefer a gin and tonic, seeing as you've started the drinking."

"You're the one who's started. You never used to drink, but now you've started."

"It's never too late."

She followed him out of the kitchen.

"I've been here all day," she said.

"That's more than I've ever managed."

"It's quite a nice place. If you like, I can show you around."

"Where's dinner?"

"What?"

"Dinner's supposed to be on the table!" Winter shouted, and pointed at the round table by the window.

"Let's eat out," she said.

"Spoken like a true housewife. But if we're going out, I want to jump in the shower first." He started unbuttoning his shirt.

She'd been busy over by the sink and now brought him his gin.

"How's it going, Erik?" She helped him off with his shirt and held it between her hands.

"Well, how's it going? It's moving forward, I guess, but I'm worried as hell about the little girl. You know as well as I do what the chances of finding her are."

"I've been thinking a bit about what you said about her. Have you checked with all the ERs?"

"What exactly are you asking, here, Doc? If we've checked the hospitals? Well, of course we have."

"Helene? I mean, the mother."

"Helene? What are you talking about?"

"If she doesn't have family—if no one has been in touch—she still must have grown up somewhere."

"As soon as we got her name, which was just recently, we contacted all the institutions and agencies under the sun. That includes foster homes, orphanages, and stuff like that too."

"Okay. I was sitting here today thinking about Helene as a child. When she was little, like her own girl. Jennie, is it? Okay. Maybe she isn't at some hospital, Jennie that is, or you don't know yet. But maybe the mother was admitted to the hospital when she was a child. Or was brought in to the ER for some reason. Helene, I mean. I know you've been thinking about that name. Andersén."

"Yeah," Winter said. "Keep going."

"Well, say a little girl named Helene something was brought in for some reason years ago. If she was, then there must be a record of it."

42

WINTER MET BERGENHEM IN THE PARKING LOT OUTSIDE POLICE headquarters. He was on his way in, and Bergenhem, who had the afternoon off, was carrying his daughter on his back. Winter walked behind Bergenhem, and Ada looked at him wide-eyed.

"We've met before," he said.

"As recently as yesterday," Bergenhem said.

"I wasn't talking to you."

"Oh."

"How's it going?" Winter ran his finger along the baby's cheek. It felt like something soft that he couldn't remember.

"It's going good," Bergenhem said.

"I'm still not talking to you."

"She's lost her power of speech," Bergenhem said. "You've made an impression. Could you lift her out, by the way?"

Winter raised his hands toward the infant. Ada began to squeal.

"She doesn't want me to."

"She's just testing."

"Okay." Winter lifted her up, and Ada stopped her screaming. "What do I do now?" He held her close.

"Nothing," Bergenhem said.

Winter kept his unpracticed grip in place, and the little girl ogled him.

"I've heard that kids like Ada here can get it into their heads that it's no fun to go to sleep at night," he said.

"Where did you hear that?"

"I must have read it somewhere."

"Ada has never heard about that."

Winter stole a glance at Bergenhem. The detective was ten years younger than him. Or was it eleven? Right now it felt the other way around. Lars has knowledge in a field where I don't even qualify as a trainee. Lucky thing Angela isn't along.

Winter set the child gently on the ground.

"See you this afternoon," he said.

The desk in Birgersson's office glistened. The department chief was smoking with the window open, but Winter left his cigarillos where they were, inside his jacket pocket.

Birgersson's face looked fried in the sunlight coming in, as if he'd held it over a fire. "The dragging of the lake has attracted every journalist in the country," he said.

"That may be a good thing."

"Now you've got more material than you can shake a stick at."

"Better make sure I don't get too conscientious, then."

"Are you still upset about that?"

"Yes."

Birgersson smiled and tapped his cigarette into the ashtray that he had taken from his drawer.

Same old procedure, thought Winter.

Birgersson cocked his head like a dog that's just detected a sound. "Hear that? The bikers are out in force."

"They're fewer now that the heat's gone."

"But it's come back, hasn't it?"

"Not to the same degree."

"This damn shoot-out at Hisingen. What's his name? Bolander. Can't we nail him somehow? I don't like how he got off scot free."

"You know how it is, Sture."

"They can just stay put over in Denmark," Birgersson said. "It's a Danish phenomenon. Maybe southern Swedish."

"American," Winter said.

"The Danes have the worst of it," Birgersson said. "I heard about Ålborg. They shot at each other outside the station. Outside the railway station!"

Möllerström met up with Winter at the situation room. He was excited.

"Sahlgrenska Hospital issued an appeal for information," he said. "In 1972, October. They're a little unsure of the exact date."

Winter thought about Angela in her white coat in a ward where someone lay in bandages.

"About a child?"

"About a girl who came in. Alone, somehow."

"Sahlgrenska?"

"Yes, apparently the child was in a pretty bad way."

"And that was Helene," Winter said, and at once Möllerström looked disappointed that Winter had interrupted his chronological account.

"Yes," he said tersely.

"What happened?"

"What I know now is that they put out an appeal for her . . . no, I mean for her family, asking them to come forward, and that someone recognized the girl quite soon afterward."

"But no family," Winter said, and Möllerström looked disappointed again.

"No."

"It's the same pattern," Winter said. "That's what I'm saying."

"Neighbors from Frölunda recognized her."

"And that's when she got a name?"

"Yes. Helene. Helene Dellmar."

"Dellmar?"

"She lived with her mother in an apartment in Frölunda, and their name was Dellmar."

"But it wasn't her mother who'd gotten in touch?"

"No."

"So where is she?"

"I don't know," Möllerström said. "Nobody seems to know."

Winter held the copy of the slip of paper between his fingers. The young Helene and the grown-up Helene had both held the original. Those were the conclusive prints. Had the child's sweaty hands caused those specific prints to leave a more indelible impression behind than the others?

"So it was found in the dress in the box in the basement?" Ringmar asked. "The same one she was wearing when she was brought into the hospital?"

"I don't know. It doesn't say here."

"Is there anyone who'd know?"

"I don't know, Bertil. That's yet another question that needs an answer."

"I'm just thinking about the dress, if she was wearing it. What happened to it afterward?"

"Yes."

"It's unlikely she asked for it back herself. From the hospital."

"Well, that's a good question."

"So, questions: Where did that slip of paper come from? When did it end up in the dress pocket? How long has it been lying there? Who put it there?"

"Another question," Winter said. "What does it mean?"

The apartment smelled of garlic and herbs.

"I've cooked dinner," Angela said, with a glass of wine in her hand. "A proper housewife."

"Apart from the glass of wine," Winter said.

"Want some?"

"No. I'd prefer a gin and tonic, seeing as you've started the drinking. No, scratch that. I don't want any right now."

She followed him out into the kitchen.

"You were right."

"Right? About what?"

"A little girl named Helene something was brought in for some reason years ago. There was a record of it."

43

THEY HAD SLEPT TOGETHER, AND WINTER FELT THAT DIVINE fatigue in his body, like a creative fatigue that took over from the destructive one. His body was supple, rejuvenated. The last few days it had been a tool, easily abused.

"You're thinking about the girl," she said.

"Yes. But not like before."

"How do you mean?"

"You know how it goes up and down. One moment you see possibilities and the next only obstacles."

"Sounds like a good description of life."

"And of work, unfortunately. Earlier today I was feeling discouraged."

"You're thinking the worst."

"I'd rather not say that."

"There's hope," she said. "You've said so yourself several times before."

"There's hope in the sense that this isn't a classic disappearance where a child goes missing from a playground and we think that some bastard's taken her. In those cases there's rarely any hope. We seldom find the child, unless a psychopath confesses and takes us to the grave."

"But here that's not the case."

"No. What we have here doesn't follow the typical pattern. There may be hope. Or else something worse than we've ever seen."

"Don't say that," she said. "Or maybe you need to."

He didn't answer.

"You should speak to somebody—other than your fellow detectives on the force."

"Yeah. Maybe you're right."

"Well. I'm listening."

"But there's something else as well." He propped himself up on one elbow. "There's a great loneliness that rests over this case. It's taken a long time to find out her name and where she lived, and to get the suspicions about a missing child confirmed. If it hadn't been for an old lady, we would still be fumbling around looking for a viable lead. You know what I mean? An enormous loneliness. We have her name but we still don't know more than a few small fragments about her past."

"More is sure to come in now that you've gone out with it in such a big way, with a public appeal and the APB or whatever you call it."

"Yeah, that's true. Or is it? That's what I mean. That awful loneliness that seemed to surround her life."

"Yes."

"No one to speak to. You know? Like you and I are speaking now."

"Like you and I," she repeated. For how much longer? she thought. I can't bring it up now. It's impossible and he knows it, if he's thinking about it. He looks more vulnerable than I've ever seen him. Younger, and it's not just the hair. It's not the right time for an ultimatum. Maybe in an hour. Or two days.

She raised her arm and ran her hand through his hair.

"How long are you going to let that grow?"

"It's growing all the time."

"Just no ponytail. It doesn't suit you."

"Okay."

"The only man I ever thought looked good in a ponytail was your colleague from London."

"Macdonald."

"Are you in touch with him at all, by the way?"

"Macdonald?"

She nodded. She had taken her hand away from his hair.

"Just the odd postcard. I might give him a call. Maybe he can give me some advice."

"Cross-border cooperation."

"It wouldn't be the first time," Winter said, and swung his legs over the edge of the bed. He twisted his body and looked back at her. "Angela."

"Yes?"

"We found out that Helene may have spent a short time at Lillhagen for depression."

"Oh."

"One of my men looked through the records, and it could be her. Under another name. Then she was discharged and never came back."

"That's common nowadays," Angela said.

"That they don't come back?"

"You know that yourself. How things are now. The psychiatric hospitals are closing and people are being discharged and don't come back because there's nothing to come back to."

The call came after the morning briefing. Winter took it in his office and he was prepared. He had expected something as early as yesterday, possibly even the day before, if he was lucky. They already knew about the orphanage, and he was sitting there with the name of the one who was supposed to call in front of him. They had known for a few short minutes, and it was as if Louise Keijser sensed it.

"I'm calling about Helene Andersén," she said.

"Where are you calling from?" Winter asked.

"Helsingborg. I spoke to someone from the police down here and they said that I should contact you."

"Yes. We've just been informed about that."

"I am—or was—her foster mother. One of them, I should say."

"Just talk about yourself," Winter said. "You recognized Helene Andersén?"

"Yes."

"In what way?"

"Well. I saw the photograph in the *Helsingborgs Dagblad*, and then they spoke about it on TV. And I guessed that it was Helene." There was a pause. "I live in Helsingborg," she added.

"When was the last time you saw Helene?"

"Oh, it was many years ago."

"Many years ago? How many?"

"We haven't had any contact in . . . It must have been, let's see . . . It was long before Johannes died—that's my husband. Helene moved away from here some twelve years ago. I've got a record of it here somewhere. I can look it up."

"But you recognized her from the pictures in the newspaper?"

"Well, I didn't know that she had a girl. They looked so alike in the pictures."

"I would like for you to come in to see us, Mrs. Keijser. Could you do that?"

"Come up there? Travel to Gothenburg, you mean?"

"Yes."

"Well, I'm getting along in years, but of course I can take the train, if need be."

Winter eyed his watch. "It's still early. We could book you on a train and call and let you know. We'll meet you at the station and can arrange for you to spend the night in a hotel."

"I have friends in Gothenburg."

"Whichever you prefer, Mrs. Keijser."

Helene had been placed in three different foster homes. As far as he knew, she'd never been adopted by anyone. She spent a brief period at an orphanage when she was four, after which she was at Sahlgrenska Hospital in Gothenburg, critically ill with pneumonia. She'd been left on a couch in an empty waiting room by some unknown person. No message. Just the little girl, who suddenly cried out in her delirium.

All this he now knew. The girl had been mute for weeks, and it had taken time before they were able to identify her as Helene Dellmar. Her mother's name was Brigitta Dellmar.

The woman had by then been missing from her home for three weeks.

She had lived alone with her daughter, Helene.

The apartment was at Frölunda Square.

It had had thirteen tenants since then.

Brigitta Dellmar was known to the police. She was arrested in 1968 in connection with a fraud ring but had been released for lack of evidence. She had been pregnant. Her name was mentioned in connection with the robbery of a branch of Handelsbanken in Jönköping in 1971, but she had only been questioned regarding her relationship to one of the men involved. He'd served four years for another robbery, but the police had been unable to tie him to the one at Jönköping.

The man's name was Sven Johansson. That's the Swedish equivalent of John Smith, Winter thought when he read through the pile of documents from Möllerström.

Sven Johansson. He died of lung cancer seven years ago. Was he Helene's father? Why was her name Andersén? There was no Andersén in the files, but he was still missing the name of one of the foster families.

The mother had disappeared and never returned. Brigitta Dellmar. That's how it was. History repeated itself. It was peculiar but not unheard of. The daughters of single mothers sometimes have children with men who then disappear. Disappear. You can't simply disappear. We find everyone we go looking for. We found Helene and now we've found her mother and we're going to find her father and her husband. Jennie's father.

We're going to find Jennie.

"It's a long way down to the street," Halders said, and peered out the window in the living room. "I can see all the way to the army drill hall."

"Does it make you feel dizzy?"

"Yeah. I always feel dizzy when I see the Heden recreation grounds."

"Bad memories?"

"Bad ball control," Halders said, and turned back in toward the room. Aneta Djanali was crouched in front of the CD player.

"What sort of music do you listen to when you're relaxing at home?"

"I don't relax."

"What do you listen to when you're not relaxing?"

"I borrowed a few jazz albums from Winter, but I grew sick of it. He doesn't ever get sick of it."

"No."

"I saw him sitting in a bar with Bülow the other week. Suspicious."

"Bülow?"

"The journalist. At the *GT*. Runs around at the station, trying to look important."

"Like you, then."

"Exactly. Just like me."

"What were you doing at that bar?"

"Relaxing," Halders said. "I don't relax at home. I relax at the bar."

"Must cost a bit."

"Winter didn't look like he was relaxing."

"So tell me what you like, Fredrik."

"Does it make any difference?"

"I'm curious."

"You think it's gotta be white power music?"

"Yeah."

"WAR stuff, huh?"

"Only when you're relaxing."

"You really are curious, aren't you?"

"I'm interested in widely diverse cultures," she said. "Yours. And mine."

"Bruckner," Halders said.

"What?"

"Bruckner. That's my kind of music. Te Deum."

"My God, that's worse than I thought."

"Wagner. I'm a Wagner man."

"Don't say any more."

Halders looked out across the city again. "It's a long way down. The people look like ants."

"More like beetles."

"Cockroaches. They look like cockroaches."

"Fredrik. Try to relax for a moment."

"I told you I only relax at the bar. Wanna go out?"

"Get away from that window, Fredrik."

"You afraid I'm gonna jump?"

"I didn't say that."

"But the thought crossed your mind?"

"It did occur to me, yes."

"You're right."

Winter parked in front of Benny Vennerhag's house. A dog barked like crazy from the neighboring yard, and he heard the rattle from the running leash.

The entrance lay in shadow. He rang the doorbell and waited, then rang the bell again, but no one opened. He went back down the steps and turned left and started along the plaster wall.

There was no longer any sun reflected in the water of the swimming pool. Nor was there any water. The pool was a hole of blue cement, and if anyone dived into it, they'd kill themselves.

Benny Vennerhag was trimming bushes. He turned around in half profile and saw Winter but kept on trimming. Scattered at his feet lay piles of branches and twigs. He wiped his forehead and put away his loppers. "I thought I heard something."

"Then why didn't you answer the door?"

"You came in anyway."

"I could have been somebody else."

"That would've been nice."

"Don't you have the impression we've had this conversation before?"

"Sure," Winter said. "But now it's even more serious."

"I agree."

Winter moved in closer.

"You're not planning on becoming violent again?" Vennerhag said, and raised the loppers.

"Do you know a Sven Johansson?"

"Sven Johansson? What kind of name is that? You might just as well ask me if I know John Smith."

"Bank robber. Among other things. Died of cancer seven years ago."

"I know who he was. I was just thinking. It was a bit before my time, so to speak, but Sven wasn't unknown. Not to you either, so I don't understand why you're coming to me."

"He may have had a relationship with a woman named Brigitta Dellmar. Does that name mean anything to you?"

"Birgit. Dell . . . No. Never heard it before."

"Brigitta. Not Birgitta. Brigitta Dellmar."

"Never heard it."

"Are you being totally honest now, Benny? You know what this is about?"

"Broadly speaking, but not what these names have to do with your murder."

"And the little girl's disappearance."

"Yes. The child is missing, I hear."

"Brigitta Dellmar is the dead woman's mother."

"Uh-huh. So, what does she have to say?"

"She's disappeared, Benny. Gone."

"Well I'll be damned. That's a lot of disappearances."

"Two disappearances."

"Disappeared, huh? Guess you'll have to put out an APB."

"She disappeared twenty-five years ago."

"That shouldn't make her much more difficult to find."

"Really?"

"People tend to leave traces behind. Especially if they've been together with Sven Johansson."

"You'd better tell me everything you know."

"Will that be enough to satisfy you?"

"I have a few more names," Winter said.

44

DRAGGING DELSJÖ LAKE HAD PRODUCED RESULTS. WINTER
left the moment he got the call, and it was as if he were blind to the traffic, the sky was so clear. Once he could see parts of the road again he
grabbed for his sunglasses.

A child's shoe lay in the grass along the water's edge. The shoe was
filled with rocks, as if the intention was to make it sink. It could have
been lying in the water for a month or more, or less. It could belong to
anyone and no one, but Winter knew.

They had found a lot, but nothing belonging to a child until now.
The discovery had been made north of the promontory that narrowed
into a finger that pointed out the spot where they should look.

Winter felt a dread, frozen sensation that took partial control of his
faculties. They ought to break off the dragging before they all went
insane. What would the shoe be followed by? He saw the faces of the
men and women, and they all said the same thing: that the girl lay down
below.

Louise Keijser was sixty but looked older.

"I'm grateful you could come, Mrs. Keijser," Winter said.

"It was the least I could do. If I had known . . ."

Winter said nothing. He waited for her to sit down in the chair.

"If I had known. I'm almost glad that Johannes isn't alive." She took
out a handkerchief and dried the corners of her eyes. "I was so sad on
the train."

"How old was Helene when she moved out?" Winter asked.

"Eighteen. When she came of age. We didn't want her to go, but
what could we do?"

"When did you last hear from her?"

"It was—it was several years ago. Before she had a child." She took out her handkerchief again. "I didn't know about it. But perhaps I already mentioned that." She blew her nose cautiously. "The little girl looks like Helene. Not the same hair, but otherwise you can see that it's the sa— How awful. You know nothing more? About the girl?"

"No," Winter said. "We can talk about that later, but right now I'd just like to ask you about Helene. Is that all right?"

"Yes. Certainly. Excuse me."

"How long did she live with you, as part of the family?"

"It was just Johannes and I—but nearly three years. I've brought records with me, if you'd like to see them. From social services and the like."

"Three years," Winter repeated. "And not much contact after?" He made his voice stable, calm. "You said it's been a number of years since you last heard from her."

"Yes. It sounds strange, of course—awful—but that's how it was. We tried but she, she didn't want anything to do with us." She raised her handkerchief to her face again. Winter could see small specks of black in the corner of her eyes where the thin mascara was being dissolved by her tears.

"Can you describe your relationship with Helene when she was living with you? How did you get along?"

"Well, I always thought she was a very special girl, with her background and everything. But we always got along well. She was very quiet, of course, and sometimes Johannes tried to bring up, well, what had happened, but she wasn't up for it, really. It was mostly Johannes who tried. For me it worked better to have that silence in the house."

"First she moved to Malmö," Winter said. "That much we know."

"Yes. It's not that far away, and we saw each other a few times. But it was never very good. We tried to invite her over, but she didn't want to come. She came once, but it was as if she had never been in the house. It was strange—or it sounds strange anyway—but somehow that sort of fit in with how she was."

"She then moved here, to Gothenburg," Winter said. "She lived at three different addresses in Gothenburg."

"We never received a moving card. Not when she moved away from Malmö. We tried to call her, but she didn't have a telephone."

"No."

"She didn't like telephones. She didn't want to speak on the phone. Don't ask me why, I'm no psychologist, but you might find something about it in the files there."

"What files?" Winter asked.

"The evaluation that the child psychologists carried out on her, or, rather, that they started to. I don't think they ever really followed through with it."

"We're waiting for that material."

"You won't find it under Andersén," Louise Keijser said.

"No."

"Her name was Dellmar back then. Did you know that?"

"Yes."

"Her name was Dellmar when she lived with us too. I don't know when she suddenly became Andersén. Do you know? Do the police know?"

"A few years ago. She changed her name four years ago."

"Why?"

"We don't know."

"Maybe when she had her baby? Is the father's name Andersén? I mean the father of Helene's little girl. Her name's Jennie, isn't it?"

"We don't know that either," Winter said. "That's why we're asking so many questions."

"The father's unknown? How awful. And he hasn't been in touch with you?"

"Not yet."

"How terrible. That's just what happened with Helene. She had to grow up without knowing who her father was."

"Did you talk to her about it?"

"About her father? No. She didn't want to, or else she couldn't. I don't know how much you know about her problems—her clinical picture or whatever you call it."

"I'm listening," Winter said.

"As I recall, Johannes and I were the third foster family. I'm suddenly a little unclear on that point. But she had gaps in her memory from when she was little, and when she would recall something it would cause her a great deal of distress, and then it would disappear again, as if it had never been there. She was very much alone in that sense. Alone with herself, or however you want to put it. We tried to help her, but it was as if she was surrounded by gauze."

"Didn't she ever talk about what had happened to her when she was little?"

"Never. And nothing about what happened afterward either—that is, after she ended up in the care of others."

"She never asked about her mother?"

"Never. Not that I heard, or Johannes either. Of course, you can ask someone else, but we never spoke about it. I don't know if she knew."

"Excuse me?"

"Did she know? What did she know? Do you know that?"

"No. Not yet."

"And now it's not possible anymore," Louise Keijser said, and covered her eyes with her handkerchief. "It's too late."

"Maybe we can uncover a few answers," Winter said.

"Just so long as you find the little girl," Louise Keijser said. "I feel somehow like a grandmother." She looked straight at Winter. "Is it wrong of me to feel like that?"

"My God," Ringmar said. "You mean to say that Brigitta Dellmar's name has come up in connection with this case?"

"Yes. Möllerström dug up everything there is on her, and an APB was put out on her back then," Winter said.

"Sven Johansson too?"

"He was questioned but they couldn't tie him to it in any way. He had a watertight alibi."

"But her name was in there?"

"Several witnesses were able to identify her from the photographs. A few of the robbers were Swedes—that much they knew. And one of the employees had seen a child."

"What the hell are you saying? You mean they brought a kid along? For the actual robbery?"

"I don't know for sure, but several witnesses testified to that fact. It's all in there."

"Good Lord. Where's this taking us?"

"To a solution," Winter said. "It's yet another complication that will lead to a solution."

"Or a dissolution," Ringmar said. "She had the child with her?"

"It's possible."

"It boggles the mind," Ringmar said.

"Do you remember the case?"

"Yes, but only vaguely. Now that you mention it. An officer was killed, if I remember correctly. That's probably why I remember it at all."

"An officer and two of the robbers."

"Jesus Christ. Yeah, that's right."

"At least three of them got away. Along with the child, if the information is correct."

Ringmar shook his head and picked up the incident report but held it without reading it. "You don't bring a child along on an armed robbery."

"Maybe something went wrong," Winter said. "Could have been anything. Maybe the mother was supposed to be the driver and had to go anyway when nobody came to look after the child. I don't know."

"Danske Bank in Ålborg," Ringmar read. "Monday October 2, 1972. Danske Bank, on the corner of Østerågade and Bispensgade. At five past five in the afternoon."

"Yeah," Winter said. "No customers but plenty of staff inside the bank, working with money."

"Plenty of money."

"Seven million."

"A big haul in Ålborg."

"Big anywhere. And there's more."

"What?"

"Helene was there."

"What?"

"At about the same time we learned all this stuff, we also got everything else connected to the name Brigitta Dellmar."

"Obviously."

"It was the name that suddenly opened everything up for us. We had nothing on Helene Andersén, but we do on Helene Dellmar."

"What do you mean, she's been here? Helene has been here?"

"She was prepped for questioning and then questioned, when she was Helene Dellmar." Winter fixed his gaze on Ringmar. "You look like you've seen a ghost, Bertil."

"Just heard about a ghost, more like."

"It's just that I learned about this a few minutes before you did."

"What did you get to know, for Christ's sake?"

"We've got the files here. When the girl ended up at Sahlgrenska Hospital, or afterward, I'm talking about the four-year-old Helene now, right? There were suspicions coming from Denmark and they managed to tie her to her mother—who may have disappeared in connection with the robbery."

"How did they identify her?" Ringmar asked. "At the hospital, I mean, or afterward, when she was questioned, or whatever. How could they make the connection with her mother?"

"They put out a description. And it appears some neighbors got in touch."

"We'll have to get that confirmed. Anyway, so they spoke to the girl here, at this station? Who was the interrogating officer?"

"Sven-Anders Borg, it says."

"He went into retirement about five years ago."

"But he's still alive, right?"

"Still clear in the head, as far as I know. But he could hardly have been expected to sound the alarm about this."

"If we had gotten a name earlier."

"I'll give him a call," Ringmar said.

"Ask him to get down here as soon as he can." Winter read the file while Ringmar dialed, but he was distracted by the call.

Ringmar covered the receiver and turned to Winter. "He's got a pain in his leg, but we're welcome to come by and see him. He lives in Påvelund."

The light over the river was stronger than ever. They drove along Oskarsleden, and the cranes on the other side were ablaze in the glare from the Kattegat. Two ferries met out at sea, and Winter thought about Denmark.

"She drew a Danish flag," he said to Ringmar.

"Who? Helene?"

"Yes. And her daughter, Jennie. They drew Danish flags."

The distance between the ferries was growing. The larger one continued out across the sea.

"What the hell are you talking about?"

Winter described the two different signatures.

"Have you sent them in for analysis?" Ringmar asked.

"On their way."

"Christ."

Winter followed the ferry's westward progress. It grew ever smaller.

"Maybe they went there," Ringmar said. "To Denmark. Anything's possible now."

Aneta Djanali introduced herself and Halders, and the man in the doorway invited them in. The house looked a hundred years old. Through the windows she saw the forest and beyond it a field. Two horses walked along the edge of the clearing with their heads bowed down to the ground. They were chestnut and sleek. There was a serenity in what she saw.

"Nice view," she said.

The man followed her gaze as if it were the first time he had seen the forest and the field. They knew from their search at the Swedish Road Administration that he was sixty-nine years old. They had names,

addresses, and personal identity numbers. According to the vehicle registration database, he owned a white Ford Escort with plates that began
with the letter *H*. That was what they knew about this man. But he
looked like a nice old man. Georg Bremer's head was as bare as Fredrik
Halders's, but he had a mustache that was dark and didn't look dyed. His
shirt was light blue and open to a neck wizened with age. He wore black
trousers held up by a brown belt.

He seems almost withered, Djanali thought.

Bremer continued to look out through the window, and his profile
hardened suddenly when the sun disappeared. Seconds later the sun
reemerged from behind a cloud and the light softened his face again.

That was strange, thought Djanali. The shadow sort of sliced off
his jaw. How silly. I've become obsessed with jawlines since getting
my own smashed.

"We've been trying to get in touch with you," Halders said. "Don't
you listen to your answering machine?"

"I've been away for a while. Got home yesterday and just haven't
gotten round to it."

Damn courteousness, thought Halders. We shouldn't bother calling ahead. We ought to come barging in just when the family is sitting
down to dinner and ask what the hell Daddy or Mommy's car was doing
in the vicinity of Delsjö Lake in the dead of night. Make people choke.
On their shame if nothing else.

"It's about your car," Halders said. "It's just routine, as I'm sure you
understand."

"Don't you want to take a seat?"

"Thank you," Djanali said.

She sat down on a couch that was green and worn. Halders remained
standing, as did their host.

"What about my car?" Bremer asked.

"You drive a white '92 Ford Escort?"

"A '92? Is that when it's from? I really don't know. I'll have to look at
the registration."

"See, we're checking up on the owners of a certain type of car, who
might be able to help us solve a case."

"What case is that?"

"A murder."

"And a Ford Escort is involved?"

"One was seen close to where the body was found on the night
in question. We're hoping that the driver of that car may have seen
something."

"Like what? And where?"

Halders looked at Djanali, who sat in the couch with her notepad.

"The night we're talking about was August 18," Halders said. "Back when it was still hot summer."

"That's not something you forget. I sweated half to death out here."

"Guess we pretty much all did, every man jack of us." Halders eyed Aneta again. "And woman."

"I was here then anyway," Bremer said. "And so was the car."

"Okay," Halders said.

"I didn't see any car out front," Djanali said.

"It's been at the shop since last Friday. Started leaking oil like a sieve. You can probably see for yourselves out there on the driveway."

"When did you take it in to get fixed?"

"Day before yesterday. I tried to have a look at it myself, but it's probably the oil pan. And I get dizzy if I spend too much time under the car."

"But you said you were away yesterday?"

"Yeah, so? What is this, an interrogation?"

"No no. I was just wondering since it's a little out of the way—you need some kind of vehicle to get out here, don't you?"

"Well, you sure don't walk all the way from the bus. But I have a motorbike that I dust off from time to time. It's out in the barn, if you want to have a look-see."

"Where is the car?" Djanali asked.

Bremer named the repair shop.

Djanali wrote down the address. "That's pretty far away from here," she said.

"That's how it is sometimes. You gotta go to the ones that offer the best prices."

"So you've checked around?" Halders asked.

"Well, you pick up on these things. Found it through a friend of a friend, you might say."

"How far is your closest neighbor?"

"You gonna ask me about their cars too?"

"We didn't see any houses on the way here."

"I guess there are a few out in the forest at the end of the road, but I'm pretty much on my own out here. There's a farm to the right a few miles up the road. I think it's more of a summerhouse. I knew the last owner, but the new ones I only wave to a few times a year when I see them."

45

SVEN-ANDERS BORG OPENED THE DOOR, PROPPED UP ON A crutch.

"Been playing football?" Ringmar asked.

"I wish. Bad circulation. If it continues like this, they'll probably have to take it off." He looked down at his left leg.

"It's not that bad, is it, Sven?"

The retired homicide detective shrugged. "And now I'm back in horrible reality. Guess you better come in."

They walked through the hall and into a room lit up from the garden out back. Unwashed windows couldn't block out the sunlight, only dampen it. Dust swirled in the air. It smelled of tobacco and fried onions. A radio was speaking in some other part of the house.

Borg sat down heavily on one of the armchairs and waved to the couch opposite. "Have a seat, guys."

They sat and Ringmar started to speak.

"I was thinking about it," Borg cut in. "It's one hell of a case. A real nightmare investigation. Nothing at first, then everything all at once. You don't even have time to sort through all the stuff."

"No," Ringmar said. "We were talking about that on the way out here."

"Had I known before, I would have gotten in touch. Maybe I would have made the connection between the name, Helene, and that last name. What was it again? Dellmer?"

"Dellmar."

"Dellmar. Right. But you haven't released it."

"We haven't had the chance," Winter said. "We're busy sorting through everything, like you said."

Borg sounded like he sighed, then looked up at the ceiling and then at Ringmar. "Here's more or less how the whole thing went down. We heard about the kid being left at the hospital—well, and then we got the name of the mother. Dellmar, that is. And she had a record. Once we had her name we started looking, but she wasn't at the apartment out in Frölunda and nowhere else either. Vanished into thin air."

"So she's been missing ever since," Ringmar said. "And you never found any leads, as I understand."

"In a way we had a lot to go on," Borg said. "That robbery didn't exactly go down without a trace."

"So she was identified in connection with that," Winter said. "How certain were you?"

Borg looked at Winter as if the young dandy had asked a trick question. He'd left the force before the kid had made inspector, and maybe that was just as well. "How certain? Guess you'd better ask the Danes that. What can I say, of course we believed it. How certain is certain? I don't know if it's possible now to get further than we did. There was no video surveillance back then, but a couple inside the bank saw the car drive off and saw the woman. She'd turned around or something. I'm a little rusty on the details. You'll have to look that up for yourselves in the files."

"Of course," Ringmar said.

"How did you tie her, Brigitta Dellmar, to the robbery?" Winter asked. "It wasn't just because of the child, was it?"

"In part, of course. She was critical. But we followed the usual procedure when we got the call from Denmark. Started checking through our list of known criminals over here. She was among them, after all, though not one of the worst, you understand. A ways down the list, and I guess we hadn't made it down that far when we were contacted by Sahlgrenska."

"And you knew, of course, that there was a child involved over there. In Ålborg."

"Well, it was in the report," Borg said, "but it was by no means certain. In any case, the neighbors got in touch when they recognized the girl, and then we got right on it."

"I see," Ringmar said.

"Then, of course, it took a while to make the connection with the robbery in Denmark."

"Yes," Ringmar said.

"And by then she'd disappeared, of course," Borg said.

"Yes," Ringmar said.

"Executed," Borg said.

"What?" Ringmar's face had gone pale.

"Executed, of course," Borg said. "Or possibly scared out of her wits. Or, as a third alternative, dead from injuries that we didn't know about, but that she might have sustained during the robbery."

"How was it that there were police on the scene," Winter asked, "so soon after the robbery?"

"Something to do with the bank's alarm system going off *before* the whole thing had really started. Something strange having to do with a short circuit or one of the employees—no, it was something technical. You'd better check about that with the Danes too, if need be. But a patrol car arrived on the scene just when the whole thing began, and the rest, as they say, is history. One hell of a history."

"So what you're saying is that she could have been killed by one of the other robbers?"

"Why not? Two of them escaped with her. They had the money. Then they dropped off the kid, because maybe there were certain things they weren't willing to do. I don't know. But I do know she never got in touch. She had a kid, after all, right?"

Ringmar nodded.

"You know those hard-core biker gangs were really staking out their territory big time around then, after a bit of a soft start. We never managed to prove it, but there's no doubt they were the ones behind it."

"I read about that in the file," Winter said.

"That Dellmar woman had those sorts of contacts," Borg said. "We did what we could to follow her sad life back in time, and she'd flirted a bit with the local bikers. How innocent it was then, I don't know."

Ringmar nodded again.

"But she wasn't there later, as far as we could tell. The Danes worked at it from their end, but she was gone. Just vanished. And then this fairly well-known biker thug pops up in Limfjorden, or wherever the hell it was, and when the bank cashier gets a look at him, she says she's sure that he's one of them!"

"You have a good memory, Sven," Ringmar said.

"There's nothing wrong with the circulation in my head," Borg said. "It's getting clearer now as I'm thinking about it."

"But no one ever managed to tie that guy to the robbery?"

"I don't know. No. But we knew. Deep down we knew. He was Danish and disappeared at the time of the robbery and eventually turned up floating facedown in the water, like a dead fish."

"Yeah."

"Well. Then the kid ended up here in Gothenburg, and we had good reason to suspect that she had actually been along when it happened. There was a reason to try to speak to the girl. A number of reasons. So we did."

"We read the transcripts," Winter said.

"Well, then you've seen it for yourself. She didn't actually say anything. She was clearly distressed by what had happened, that was obvious. But what exactly that was—you'll have to talk with a psychiatrist about that. We had one sitting in back then. Have you spoken to him?"

"No," Winter said.

Borg stretched out his left leg and massaged it. The sun had gone behind a cloud and the dust moving about the room disappeared with it.

"But you've read it yourself. There's a section in there where she may have been trying to talk about how she'd been in some house or in a particular room. Maybe a basement somewhere for a while. The Danes talked about a house where they'd been."

"They?" Winter asked. "The robbers?"

"Who else are we talking about?" Borg said. "I'm talking about the robbers. They had been in some house outside town. Preparing. Planning. You'll have to ask the Danes about that." Borg started to rub his leg again. "Could be that's where they hid out again afterward. The ones who were still alive, that is. A little while longer. Maybe the child was along. I don't know. Maybe the mother. We never found out."

"You found out a fair bit," Ringmar said.

"Most of what I've said you could have read in there yourselves. But you've got to speak to the Danes again."

"Yeah."

"Maybe it wouldn't be a bad idea to go over there."

"Yeah," Winter said. "I'm starting to see that."

"There's one more chilling aspect to this, if you guys want to torment yourselves some more. At least I think there is. But I guess you've already seen it."

"What are you talking about, Sven?" Ringmar leaned forward.

"In my day there was no such thing as video cameras, but back when this whole thing was going on we were testing out filming the questioning sessions in Super 8. That footage should still be lying around somewhere. Have you checked it out?"

"There's a film?" Winter said.

"Of the questioning session. Tapes get recorded over, I guess, but maybe that film of us speaking to little Helene is still there."

"There's no mention anywhere," Ringmar said.

"That we were filming? Or that we saved the film?"

"Neither," Ringmar said. "This is the first I've heard of it in connection with this case."

"Well, you weren't with us back then," Borg said. "I guess someone was sloppy and forgot to enter it or something, or else the film was simply discarded. That kind of thing does happen, far too often, unfortunately."

They found the film among a group of cassettes containing stuff that had been transferred from Super 8 to video and then forgotten. There was an index, but not with the Dellmar case file.

They took the cassette into Winter's office and popped it into the VCR. Ringmar made a gesture that looked like he was crossing himself. Winter felt a hood of steel slowly being screwed tight around his head.

Borg entered the frame, younger and with better circulation. The room could've been any in the station, at any time. Not much had changed.

The child sat across the table with barely more than her face visible. She said a few words and looked straight down at the table and then up and directly into the camera, and at Winter and Ringmar. The pressure around Winter's head mounted. That was perhaps the most appalling thing about it—sitting there with the answer sheet, knowing how things had turned out, and making this awful trip back in time, clutching the answer sheet like some kind of bridge spanning the long divide.

He thought about Helene's face on the gurney.

"I don't know if I can fucking handle this," Ringmar said.

Winter saw the girl get up from the chair, and he wished that the tape had been destroyed.

Ringmar stood up.

"Now let's go out there and find Jennie," he said.

46

WINTER READ THE TRANSCRIPT FROM THE CONVERSATION THE child psychologist had with Helene. The experienced psychologist, who was now deceased, had tried to find something in her memory that she didn't want to—or was unable to—talk about. It made short and painful reading, and as in the film, it was clear that she had been traumatized.

The assessment didn't reveal much either. There was a note about the girl's need for conversational therapy at the psychiatric clinic—continuing into adulthood. What would happen then? Winter wondered. Wasn't that when the nightmarish memories worsened?

They hadn't found anything to indicate that Helene had had such conversations as an adult. There'd been no follow-up as she became older, other than a routine checkup a few years after the event. Winter made a note about the foster parents at the time.

He read: "When she reaches adulthood, she may become aware of the ordeal she shows clear signs of having experienced, but it's possible that she will only be able to recall a few specific images."

Winter considered the lonely woman living with her child in the apartment he had wandered around in, and where he'd felt such a powerful sense of fear. There were few memories there. The memories were sealed, like hatches.

Long-repressed memories could open into an abyss.

There were examples of patients who'd had memory lapses in the middle of conversations. Suddenly the patient could become someone else. Memory disorders could cause a patient to split the self into different identities, Winter had read.

"Consciousness wants to protect the person from the memory of unbearable experiences." It was an awful sentence. What was going on in the mind of a person like that? Had Helene been like that? The cursory investigation into her fate hinted at it, but Winter couldn't find anything conclusive.

It was raining again, pattering rhythmically against the window-pane. Winter looked for a moment at the childish drawings attached to the wall opposite him. They showed flags, windmills, men in beards driving cars. It was raining and the sun was shining. The sky is displaying different identities, he thought.

"Once they reach their thirties, people who have been subjected to severely traumatic experiences as children can gain increased awareness of their ongoing torment." Yet another awful sentence. "Once awareness returned, these people could find themselves in another place."

She didn't know how she got here.

Different identities. He read the words again: "another place."

Was it possible that had happened to Helene? Who, then, had taken care of her child?

It struck him now that they hadn't established the time of the daughter's disappearance. They didn't know when Helene and Jennie had been seen together for the last time. Had the child disappeared before Helene? Had Helene been aware of who she was? Maybe she'd been confused for a long time. Was that possible?

He made a note that he should speak to Ester Bergman again.

Halders switched on his bathroom light and leaned in closer to the mirror. His hair had started to grow out on the sides and he decided to go to the barbershop over the weekend and let the machine trim it down again.

He thought about running a bath, but that felt like a lot of effort. He thought about going out and sitting down at Bolaget and ordering a beer, but it was so far away. He thought briefly about making himself something to eat, but he didn't have the energy.

Damn it, he thought. I barely have the strength to go into the bedroom to lie down.

He thought about calling somebody, but he couldn't think of anyone he wanted to speak to or who would want to listen. It would be Aneta in the case of the former.

He went to the kitchen and opened the refrigerator and took a bottle of beer from the shelf in the door.

He sat down in front of the TV, with the remote in his hand. He debated whether to switch it on.

"We can't hold Jakobsson any longer," Ringmar said.

"I realize that," Winter said. "It's . . . Shit."

"All he's done is pay somebody else's rent," Ringmar said.

"We'll have to keep him under surveillance."

"After this, he'll go to the liquor store and disappear for two weeks."

"I think we can tie one of them to the weapon and the shoot-out," Winter said.

"Excellent," Birgersson said. "Bolander?"

"He's not saying anything, of course, but he was there."

"I still don't understand why they did it. Unless it was yet another crazy display of power."

"You might not be far off."

"Or a reminder of power, though I guess that's the same thing. In any case, it nearly cost us one of our officers."

"Yes."

"There's been trouble down in Malmö again," Birgersson said. "Seems those bastards were in the process of building up some scheme. There's something really scary about this gang. Especially the control they have over their own."

"It's a little calmer in Denmark right now."

"Speaking of which—I spoke to Wellman and he gave us the green light."

"I'll go as soon as I've read through a little more of the material they sent over," Winter said.

Halders entered Winter's office with the expression of someone pissed off as hell and yet at the same time a bit relieved.

"We can cross one of the leads off our list," he said.

Winter was already standing. "Let's hear it."

"That marking on the tree. It was as I suspected. Did I mention that? Some punk kid put it up there."

"Some punk kid?"

"The boys with the boat were, as you know, a little reluctant to help us out by remembering who they'd lent their boat to. There were quite a few of them."

"Uh-huh."

"Okay, okay. Two boys—younger than the ones with the boat—had borrowed it, and they're the ones who put the marking on the tree."

"Did they come in here and say so?"

"Like I said, we've worked our way through the list now. I spoke to one of them on the phone, and what he said sounded a little strange, so I went over to his school to chat with him. He was having one of his apparently innumerable free periods."

"He confessed?"

"Came straight out with it. Said it was just a goof they got into their heads to do."

"When did you find this out?"

"Just now, damn it. I know, it's taken time to go through all this but it's not like we didn't have other things to—"

"Did we get round to checking whether there are any similar markings by any of the other lakes?"

"Yes. So far we haven't found anything."

"And he knew that we were looking for information about this?"

"He hadn't seen it," he said.

"Is he lying?"

"Of course he is. But I doubt he's lying about the marking."

The evening was dark and mild as Winter biked across Sandarna and through the center of Kungsten. Långedragsvägen was lit with dim streetlights. You could feel and hear the sea in the wind.

The road outside Lotta's house was crowded with parked cars. He heard the party through the open windows. Bim and Kristina had put a sign that said "Happy Birthday Mommy" above the open door, which was festooned with balloons and left ajar. The daughters had chosen white and blue. Winter removed the rubber bands from his pant leg and walked up the few steps.

He took a deep breath and stepped through the doorway.

Standing in the front hall were people he'd never met. He nodded to the three in the kitchen entrance and hung up his leather jacket on top of three thousand others. He smoothed out his jacket and stuffed his polo shirt down the back of his black pants. He was carrying a present under his arm.

"Erik!" Lotta had come out into the hallway from the kitchen.

"Hiya, sis."

"So you made it after all!"

"I promised. And I wanted to."

She hugged him and stroked his cheek. She smelled like the evening outside and faintly of wine.

"Happy birthday," Winter said, and held out his present.

"There is a standing order that all presents be put in a pile and opened at the same time to the cheers and adulation of the masses," Lotta said, and took the present.

"When?"

"Oh come on, what kind of a question is that?"

"Sorry."

"It was the girls' idea."

"Come on. You like it too," Winter said. "Being in the spotlight."

"But Angela couldn't come," Lotta said.

"She was on call and got paged."

"Well, that's a shame. She called me."

"Really?"

"She said to say hello to you. Seems I'm acting as go-between for you guys."

"It's not that bad. It's better."

"What do you want to drink?" She waved toward the kitchen. "There's wine, beer, and the hard stuff."

"No water?"

"On a day like this? Of course not."

"Uncle Erik!" Bim and Kristina grabbed hold of Winter and pulled him out into the kitchen.

47

THE MORNING WAS PALE AND THE SUN SLOWLY DRAGGED THE
day up from behind the rooftops in the east. Winter drank coffee with
milk and read the papers. Michael Brecker blew hard through the apartment, but at low volume.

The worst of the commotion has settled, Winter thought, reading
District Chief Wellman's statement about the preliminary investigation. Wellman was good at saying something in public when there was
nothing to say.

The commotion was down to three columns on the first page of the
news section and a short lead-in on the front page. Brigitta Dellmar was
unknown to the press, or at least they weren't writing about her. Oskar
Jakobsson was known, since his arrest in Mölnlycke, but his identity
hadn't been released.

There were some differences here and there, Winter thought. The
Danish press wasn't very particular about protecting the names of the
people involved.

He thought again about Brigitta Dellmar. Had her name appeared in
Danish newspapers back when it happened?

They'd kept quiet about the Danish connection, but it wouldn't stay
that way for long. Perhaps it might be to their advantage to leak some
of the information, but Winter wanted to head over there first, to build
up a picture of what happened, perhaps even to get a *feeling* for what
happened.

It was becoming increasingly obvious that what had transpired in
Ålborg played a role in the murder that had recently happened here, maybe even a decisive role, like a long shadow reaching from the past into the
future, like a distant cry or a voice. Helene's voice, or her mother's, and in
a ghastly repetition of history, also that of the girl, Jennie.

———

It was nearly twelve o'clock, and the sun shone into the room through the big windows. Winter had opened the balcony door to the sound of the sparse Sunday traffic. A flock of seagulls passed by engaged in eager discourse in the wind.

He studied the photograph in front of him. Brigitta Dellmar. The photo had been taken three weeks before she vanished. She disappeared on October 2, 1972, sometime just after five in the afternoon, and this photograph was taken in a studio in west Gothenburg three weeks before that, almost to a day. It was found in her apartment in Frölunda. Hers and Helene's. Was there any particular reason why she'd had her picture taken at that time? She seemed to be looking past the lens at something standing next to it. Her gaze was lowered. Was she looking at her daughter? Was Helene standing there and consequently also in this photograph?

There was a clear likeness between mother and daughter. Their mouths were broad and their lips full. Their eyes were spaced widely apart. Their hair was blonde, their cheekbones high. They were beautiful women. They disappeared at the same point in their lives.

Jennie had inherited her mother's and grandmother's face and someone else's hair. What sort of person could abandon their child? Where was Jennie's father? Was he dead? Who was Helene's father? One of the men killed during the robbery? Or did he disappear? The man found floating in Limfjorden?

Who was Helene's father?

Hidden within that question was part of the solution to the riddle— that much Winter realized. Perhaps even the entire solution. The past cast its stark shadow over the future.

Brigitta wore a tight-fitting sweater typical of the time, but the photo cut off where the shoulders gave way to the arms. Her face was angled slightly downward in the photo, as if she couldn't hold her head higher. It wasn't a furtive look, but Winter got that impression. There was something evasive in her posture. She was alone in the photo. No props. The studio she was sitting in glowed with a harsh loneliness. The picture was black and white but there wouldn't have been any color in it anyway, thought Winter. He didn't think in color when he thought about Helene's mother. When he saw Helene, he thought in red and in the ice blue that hovered mutely in the cold rooms of the morgue. When he imagined Jennie, he saw in black.

Winter biked across Heden and saw students playing football in the mud.

A fax was waiting for him in the basket in his office. His Danish colleagues were looking forward to his arrival. They may well have meant it. The unsolved robbery and killing of an officer had plagued the Ålborg police over the years.

"When are you going?"

"Tomorrow morning, with the catamaran."

Ringmar poked in his coffee cup with a spoon.

"I have to go, Bertil. It feels like I can do more good over there than here right now."

"I think you're right. It's just that, well, it's as if you're going over there to confirm that this thing happened, while we keep on working without finding the right lead." Ringmar looked around. "We're starting to shrink down to a skeleton crew. Even the search for the little girl is going cold. People are hanging their heads."

"I don't know what to say. I'm not hanging my head. You're not hanging your head." Bergenhem entered the coffee room. "Lars isn't hanging his head."

48

WINTER DROVE ON BOARD AND PARKED IN THE SEACAT'S BELLY.
He locked his Mercedes and gripped his briefcase and wandered up to
the passenger deck, standing at the stern as the catamaran put out to
sea. The remains of the devil's hour floated across the river from the
south and disappeared among the run-down buildings by the northern
bridge pylon.

He went inside and passed through the bar. The wrinkly ones were
already in position, with their first beer of the day. Smoke wafted in
clouds across their faces, which were slowly becoming smoothed out
by the alcohol.

Winter sat in an armchair in a lone row of seats facing the windows. The catamaran accelerated when it reached Dana Fjord and he
saw how the sun hit the cliffs with a sharp glare. The archipelago was
all nuances of rock, which shone in the early morning sunlight and was
transformed into steel and earth and granite. The sky pushed the thin
clouds downward and outward.

Two boats met and their red sails slid into one another over a sea of
congealed lead. The world was reflected through the window. These
were northern waters, increasingly viscous as winter approached.

He took the E45 to Ålborg and turned off toward the city, following the
tunnel underneath Limfjorden. It was years since he'd last been there
and the city seemed bigger than he remembered it. The route in passed
through docks where the warehouse buildings blocked the sun. The
steam from the distillery turned the sky white, as if it had been chalked.

Winter parked outside the railway station and walked straight across
John F. Kennedy Square to the Park Hotel. His room was small and
infused with the sour smell of tobacco. It looked out onto a dark courtyard where a pile of boxes was stacked halfway up the wall and stood

level with Winter's room. There was a low humming from the ventilation system that clung to the wall outside his window like ivy made out of aluminum. The sound reminded Winter of the vibrations from the catamaran.

He took his bags and went back to the antique elevator and rode it down to reception.

"I want another room," he said to the young clerk, who nodded as if it was to be expected for a guest to return like that five minutes later.

"We don't have any more single rooms," he said.

"Then give me a double."

"That'll cost—"

"I don't care what it costs," Winter said. "But I want one on the third floor, with a view." He gestured through the lobby and out toward Kennedy Square.

The guy at reception studied something on the counter in front of him and then turned toward the board behind, where the keys hung from row upon row of hooks fixed on red felt. I crossed a time zone in the middle of the Kattegat and have landed in the nineteenth century, Winter thought, closing his eyes. When he opened them again the young man was holding out a key.

"You're in luck," he said. "Third floor, double room, facing the square."

The room seemed clean. Winter went up to the window and through the thin curtains saw the square below and the state railway building on the other side of it. Two soldiers stood outside the station, as if guarding his car from the buses driving back and forth. Winter saw a man pass by holding a hot dog and he felt hungry. There was a bar in the station building, level with his Mercedes, so he pulled the door closed and left the key with a new man behind the counter. Outside the sun stood right above the square. It was still a warm October.

Winter ordered two red *pölser* sausages in a bun, with roasted onions, and a Carlsberg Hof. He stood at a bar table and started eating. He was alone inside the bar. It smelled of bacon and other fried food and malt.

Diagonally off to the right was the bus station, and in the adjacent parking lot stood four motorcycles, as if chained together in the middle of the entrance. The owners were standing next to them and talking. They wore black leather and blue denim and black boots with sharp heels—all men with black beards and hair as long as Winter's. Two had a ponytail. All were drinking beer. The cars were forced to skirt around the campsite the biker gang had set up, but Winter didn't hear or see any of the drivers honk their horns and tell them to get the hell out of the way. What he saw was just a natural part of city life. Perhaps this was a place where everyone lived happily side by side.

Winter finished off his lunch and went out to his car. Following directions from the guy at the hotel, he drove around the block and back onto Boulevarden from the right and parked on the one-way street alongside the hotel. He got out and locked the car and walked back across the square, past the station. The motorbikes had disappeared in a low rumble that could still be heard above the fjord. Winter followed Jyllandsgade for two blocks, and the police headquarters loomed up on the left like a futuristic palace of coal and silver.

Inside the police HQ everything was black leather and steel and marble floors. The walls of glass brought in the city.

He reported his arrival at a short counter to the right, where a uniformed officer asked him to have a seat in a steel chair and wait.

Instead he walked into a big airy public reception area where the counter was at least fifteen yards long. People were standing at pulpits, filling out forms. This place is full of space and light, Winter thought, conjuring in his mind the cramped hovel in Gothenburg that was supposed to accommodate all the citizenry in need of assistance from the police.

He went back to the big hall, and a woman in a black shirt and black jeans was standing at the counter, next to the uniformed officer. She was thin and had thick, slicked-back fair hair. Winter could see a pack of cigarettes sticking halfway out of her left breast pocket. She had blue eyes, which he could detect because the light was reflected in them from the glass walls. She seemed even younger than he was. It can't be possible for someone in such an exposed position to be younger, Winter thought, as he took the hand that was held out to him.

"Welcome, Inspector Winter."

"Thank you, Inspector . . . Poulsen?"

"That's right. Michaela. So now we can dispense with the titles."

She followed Winter's gaze out through the glass wall. "Pretty sleek, huh? I'm not talking about those wrecked railcars out there. But this building. The police station."

"I'm impressed," Winter said.

"We're all impressed," Poulsen said. "We're impressed by the audacity of our superiors. We're short on computers, but we've sure got a beautiful building to not house them in." She looked at Winter. "Is this the first time you've been here?"

"No. But the last time was many years ago."

49

THE HOMICIDE DEPARTMENT'S OFFICES CONSISTED OF LONG corridors and small rooms—akin to Winter's workplace in Gothenburg in that respect.

She showed him into a chamber at the far end of the corridor. Inside was a computer on a table and some binders on a desk. There was also a telephone. Through the window he could see the local Alcoholics Anonymous.

"If you Swedes can help us with this old case, we'll be thrilled," Michaela Poulsen said. "I wasn't around back then, of course. But there are people here who haven't forgotten. Jens Bendrup is one of them, and he'll be happy to speak to you as soon as you like."

"Thank you," Winter said.

"No problem. It was a nasty business."

Poulsen sat down on one of two austere chairs by the window. She waved her hand toward her hair, as if to push away bangs that weren't there. The black-and-white border tartan jacket she'd popped into her office to grab took on another color in the glow from outside. Her eyes were just as blue when they met Winter's.

"That's what I'm here for," he said. "It would be great if you could fill me in on a few details."

"Let's bring in Jens first," she said, and stood up and walked out.

From the desk Winter picked up a binder with a registration number on its spine. He counted five binders and also some brown A4 envelopes that might contain photographs or other materials.

When he looked up, Poulsen was back with Detective Jens Bendrup. Casually dressed in a shirt and sweater with jeans, he was a burly man, broad across the neck but shorter than Poulsen. Winter guessed he had only two or three years left to go before retirement, and he smelled of cigar smoke when Winter greeted him—along with a whiff of the two beers he'd had with lunch.

"Welcome to the scene of the crime," Bendrup said.

"I'm grateful for the reception."

"I need a smoke," Bendrup said. "This is your room, so I guess it's your call."

Bendrup had pulled out a cigar that looked life threatening and Poulsen nodded. "The boss is usually restrictive," Bendrup said, waving toward Poulsen with the match he'd just used to light his cigar. "Better do the same while you have the chance."

Winter shook his head and let his Corps remain where they were in his jacket pocket. He would relish the secondhand smoke. Bendrup sat down.

"A young police officer sacrificed his life," Bendrup said, and his face was no longer soft. "I was the one who had to deliver the news to his fiancée, and that's something you never forget. She was pregnant as well."

"What happened?" Winter asked.

"It was an inside job, of course, but we were never able to prove it. Maybe that's what bothers me the most." He drew in and blew out some smoke, and Winter thought about a locomotive. "But there was seven million in there that afternoon, and the ones who came for it knew about it."

"Wasn't the bank locked?" Winter asked. "It was after closing, wasn't it?"

"It was officially closed, but the door was still open," Bendrup said. "Everyone blamed everyone else. But that's not what makes me think it was an inside job. You see, back then it wasn't that usual to lock the doors. Not here in good old Denmark anyway."

"That's why they could just walk in," Poulsen said. "The money was there, and four men entered. Black stockings over their faces, of course. Three marched straight in and one remained by the door."

"You know that? Precisely?"

"There was a camera," Bendrup said. "This may seem, for the most part, like something out of the 1800s, but there was a camera in the bank. So we could see."

Winter nodded.

"And then all hell broke loose," Bendrup said, and sucked on his cigar, which glowed in front of his face.

"As it turned out, we were already on our way over there before the crooks even stepped back out across the threshold."

"So I understand," Winter said. "How did that happen?"

"It's the sort of thing that only happens to fools and geniuses," Bendrup said.

"A group of morons from the electric company was putting new wiring in the vault and tripped the alarm to the police station, which also stood right here but wasn't quite as beautiful."

Winter nodded. Poulsen was leaning against the desk. A truck had pulled up outside the window and was revving its engine. Someone called out. Winter heard a train. The truck suddenly rattled and went silent.

"Meanwhile, the staff was sitting there with seven million in used bills. We called, course—well, not me because I wasn't on duty—but they called and didn't get any answer because those idiots managed to cut the phone lines at the same time that they set off the alarm. So there was no answer, and the first car careered down Østerågade and arrived right in the middle of the party. Or just as it was ending. The robbers were on their way out, and the police car came screeching to a stop on Nytorv and Søren Christiansen was first out and the first to get killed. The robbers brought guns with them, see. AK-4s that rip a body apart even if you're a bad shot." Bendrup fixed his eyes on the window and then on Winter. He sucked at his cigar, but it had gone out while he was talking. "Jesus Christ. With a bit of imagination you can still see the stain left by Søren's blood."

"But there was return fire, right?" Winter asked.

"Yes. The officers who'd arrived with Søren took cover behind the car and opened fire. Just then another car came up from Ved Stranden—I can show you later, when we go down there—and those officers saw what was going on and more or less took the bastards from behind. There was more shooting. A few of the guys called it the 'Bonnie and Clyde case' afterward," Bendrup looked at Poulsen. "But not me. It was too serious to joke about."

"Two robbers died," Winter said.

"One died on the spot. A bullet in the eye that must have been a lucky shot. The other was still alive when it was over, but he was in a bad way. We thought he'd make it, but he died without ever regaining consciousness. The doctors said he'd had something called a fat embolism. Know what that is?"

"Vaguely," Winter said.

"Same here, but I learned a bit about it. He'd been hit in several places, and the resulting fractures caused bone marrow to enter the bloodstream, which in turn caused a clot that resulted in his death. It was—well, disappointing. We had no one to question."

"No," Winter said. "The others got away."

"They got away. Two men and the driver and maybe the kid. The driver was a woman. Two detectives and a uniformed officer swore they'd seen a child's face lying on the floor of the getaway car when the doors were opened before they took off."

"They were sure of it," Poulsen said. "Just as sure as they were that the driver was a woman."

"Brigitta Dellmar," Winter said.

"Apparently she was later identified as such," Poulsen said.

"She was unknown here," Bendrup said.

"So they got away." Winter kept his voice neutral.

Bendrup looked at him suspiciously. "That's the story, in broad strokes. The epilogue is that they hid out in a holiday home in Blokhus. And that the third robber floated up in the fjord a few weeks later. At least it's believed that it was him. He was buddies with the two who died. Or one of them anyway."

"What was their connection to the biker gangs?" Winter asked.

"Well . . ." Bendrup tried to light up his cigar again.

Winter waited. Michaela Poulsen, irritated by the noise, walked over to the window. It quieted down just as she looked out.

"Well, the organization was being built up here back then. They'd come over from California, like the Beach Boys and all kinds of other crap. Somehow they got a stronger foothold here in Denmark than in other European countries. I think. In any case, there were a few trail-blazers, and two of these hapless bank robbers were among them. At least two. But that's about all we know, which, of course, isn't the same thing as what we think."

"So, what do you think?" Winter asked.

"We think—or I think anyway—that it was a straightforward attempt to raise funds. Seven million was a lot of money back in '72. Anyone wanting to build up a strong organization needs capital. Bear in mind that the Danske Bank heist wasn't the only one that took place at the time, nor the first. It was probably just one in a series of planned robberies, even if it was the biggest. And the bloodiest."

"Supporting that theory," Poulsen added, "is the fact that one of the robbers was probably killed by his own—"

"How do you mean?" Winter asked.

"He was executed since he was no longer needed. That may sound shocking, but things got pretty nasty around here. Or else he was weak—according to their definition, that is—a weak person whom they couldn't trust."

"Or else they simply had a falling-out over something," Bendrup said. "They may just have been hired hands. Connected to the organization, yes. Sent out by the gang leadership, no. Could be."

"You said they may have had a falling-out," Winter said. "Over what?" He felt a cold surge through his head and hair. Suddenly his pulse was racing.

"I can almost see what you're thinking," Bendrup said. "I can see it now. And it's not a very nice thought."

"Is it possible that the woman and the child had to disappear?" Winter asked.

"Well," Bendrup said. "I've thought a lot about it, and that's one potential explanation. Either there was an order handed down from above that the weak had to be gotten rid of, or else something happened between the robbers afterward. Maybe the men fought over the lives of the woman and child. Perhaps all their lives were in danger. Maybe it was just a coincidence that things turned out the way they did, but I don't think so. All you can say for sure is that it was a nightmare."

"Turned out the way they did?" Winter asked. "You mean that the one guy was murdered?"

"Yeah. He was shot, but why him?"

"Okay," Winter said, and lit up a Corps. "They escape and get away. They hold out somewhere. Maybe others in some organization know where they are, maybe not. Then something happens. It's possible they've already gone their separate ways, but let's assume that one of the men is killed in the presence of the others. That leaves a man and a woman and possibly the child. The woman is from Sweden. They manage to make it back to Sweden—"

"Yeah, fucking hell," Bendrup said. "We did what we could, but that wasn't good enough. They must have had contacts and been taken across by some smuggler."

"Or else they got themselves a contact," Poulsen said. "They had money, after all, right?"

"If there was any money left," Bendrup said. "With them, I mean. The money might already have been in the coffers."

"But if the girl was actually along during the robbery, and we also know that she came to Sweden and was eventually found at a hospital in Gothenburg," Winter said, "then the question is, who else made the trip over?"

"Maybe no one," Bendrup said. "It's not unthinkable that the woman and the last remaining man, if we call him that—that they're dead too. That they died soon after the robbery. Executed."

"Or else they came across too," Poulsen said.

"So the last man was never identified?" Winter asked.

"No. He may have been a Swede. The woman was Swedish. The man might have been Swedish too."

"Then why did they come over here in the first place?" Winter said. "Why did they specifically take part in this robbery?"

"Maybe there was a sister organization in Gothenburg, but we never managed to determine that," Bendrup said. "That is, after we heard about the child and the hospital and the connection to Brigitta Dellmar. And that she'd been seen during the heist."

"You found no link between her and any of the Danish men who were killed?"

"Nothing. Nor with anyone else in the fledgling organization. But there may have been. Maybe cross-border love. Just like cross-border collaboration. Spread the risk."

"We really searched for them," Poulsen said. "The woman and the man."

"She's never been heard from again," Bendrup said. "And she had a little child, after all. That really points to only one possibility."

"So, what was the deal with that house? Where was it? I can't remember the name from the file."

"Blokhus. On the North Sea. It's a seaside resort."

"You were able to establish that they'd been in a house there?"

"According to some witnesses, they had. We checked out the house, but it was empty. Empty as a tomb."

"Of course this was long after the robbery," Poulsen said.

"What?"

"They'd picked the lock or something and gotten inside. Or else they'd had a key. No one saw anything suspicious back then. The house was a bit isolated, given that there were no year-round residents. Now it's different, but back then there were nothing but holiday homes along the whole street. They left no trace behind. Then the owners came along a few weeks later and continued renovating the house, which they'd already been in the process of doing for some time. New wallpaper. Fresh coat of paint. And finally someone living up the road reacted to all the commotion following the robbery. In other words, it all went very slowly."

"How did they connect the robbers to that specific house?"

"They found something," Bendrup said. "The owners of the house, that is." He stood and picked up the binders. He found the one he was looking for and started flipping through it. "They were busy working on the house." Bendrup put down the binder and picked up another one. "It should be here."

"It was really just a small slip of paper wrapped up in a little child's sweater," Poulsen said. "It was when they were getting started on the flooring and were about to access the crawl space underneath. There was a loose floorboard in the corner, over by the window. Lying inside was a sweater, and that slip of paper fell out when they picked it up. It was a slip of paper with symbols on it. Like a map."

"Here it is," Bendrup said, and held out the binder. Winter felt sick to his stomach and excited at once. "Don't you feel well?"

Winter shook his head. He took the binder. Lying in a plastic folder was a copy of the same map, or message, as the one he had studied several times in Gothenburg, with the same letters and numbers and a similar drawing that could be a set of instructions or anything at all: 5/20, —1630, 4—23?, L. v—H, C.

"I recognize this," he said, and explained the connection to them.

"Good God," Poulsen said. She'd removed her jacket.

"Well, we never managed to decipher it," Bendrup said. "But this is a step forward nevertheless."

"Did you find any fingerprints?" Winter asked.

"Mostly from those who touched the stuff afterward," Bendrup said. "But we did come up with one set that belonged to Andersen."

"Andersen? I haven't seen anything about an Andersen in the files," Winter said.

"What? Oh shit, sorry, I was unclear," Bendrup said. "The robber we later found, the one who was floating in Limfjorden, his name was Møller and that's how he appears on all official documents, but when we checked with his buddies here in town, it turns out he had some kind of a code name, and that was Andersen. They all had double names, every one of them."

Winter's mouth was dry. He had trouble swallowing, but he felt that he had to swallow before he could speak. "The dead woman in Gothenburg, her name is Andersén," he said. "Helene Andersén. She adopted that name a few years ago. So she may well have been that little girl."

"Good God," Poulsen repeated.

"When did you find that out?" Bendrup asked. "Her identity, I mean. That name. Andersén."

"Just a few days ago," Winter said. "Everything's gone so quickly after that. Didn't you get the name from us? My registry clerk was supposed to send over most of the material ahead of my arrival."

Poulsen looked at Bendrup.

"Jesus fucking Christ," Bendrup said. "I've been off work for the past three days and only came back this afternoon. The stuff was lying on my desk. It must have been there since it arrived, without anyone taking a look."

"That's my fault," Poulsen said. "I should have checked the mail earlier. But maybe we've made some progress here after all." She eyed Winter. "If you'd like, we can all head downtown now so you can have a firsthand look at where it happened."

"But first we're going to have a beer," Bendrup said.

50

WINTER AND BENDRUP EACH SAT WITH A CARLSBERG HOF AT LA Strada opposite Danske Bank, on the corner of Østerågade and Bispensgade. Michaela Poulsen was drinking a club soda with lemon. They were alone in the bar, but there was a lot of hustle and bustle on the pedestrian street outside.

The bank occupied a building that looked as if it might have been a church erected in the late Middle Ages, though it had been a bank for as long as anyone in Ålborg could remember. The stones in the walls were rough-hewn. The windows were large and appeared to have been there for centuries. A telephone booth stood next to the gaping entrance, just opposite them, across the pedestrian street.

"I wonder how many times they walked past here and planned that job," Winter said, turning to the Danish homicide detectives.

"It could have been done by others," Bendrup said. "Or just one of them."

"We also believe that the driver—the woman—first tried to drive east along Nytorv, but that way was blocked off," Poulsen said. "I'll show you when we go outside."

"You mean that the escape route across the bridge wasn't planned?"

She made a gesture with her hand. "It may have been, but perhaps from a different direction. We don't really know. What I mean is that maybe everything wasn't planned down to the last detail."

"But the idea didn't just occur to them as they happened to be walking past," Bendrup said.

The bank was closed, and they were alone in there with two of the staff. The commotion outside the window intensified apace with the onset of evening. Winter reconstructed the events in his head, while Bendrup and his boss recounted and pointed.

They'd rushed in with their black masks, a repeat of so many robberies in the criminal history that united all countries.

Outside, the young police officer had been gunned down. Christiansen. And two of the robbers. Their names and background were in the files that Winter had brought along from the police station to read in his hotel room.

Bendrup indicated where people had stood and where they had fallen. Everything eventually flowed together from all different directions, and Winter felt the fatigue take hold, his consciousness dulled like the daylight that was seeping away into the walls of the buildings on this street corner of the world where people had died for money. Or was there something else too? He wondered if it might have been for an idea—an awful concept of power and control, of naked terror.

"And heading north," Bendrup said.

Winter followed his gesture past something that seemed to be a copy of a British pub.

"We took off after them, but I already told you that," Bendrup said. "It started to get dark, like it is now. It was almost the same time of year."

Winter wished himself back at the hotel. An hour's sleep and then work and a bit of food. He needed to be alone again.

"Well," Bendrup said. "Is there anything else we can show you? That you want to see right now, that is."

"Not right at the moment," Winter said. "You've been very forthcoming, I must say."

"Out of pure selfishness," Bendrup said. "You solve the case, and we get the glory."

"Of course," Winter said. He was starting to get a little tired of Bendrup's chatter.

"Well, maybe we're trying to be a little more professional than that," Poulsen said. "Let's get going, then. We can drop you off at the hotel."

"I'd prefer to walk," Winter said. "It's not very far, is it?"

"Not far at all," Bendrup said. "Just follow this street and it'll take you straight to the square next to the station. Kennedy Square. That's where your hotel is."

Winter raised his hand in farewell and started walking. "I'll come by tomorrow morning."

Poulsen waved and nodded.

He had dozed off for a while and was awakened by the sound of motors. Eventually you barely notice it, Michaela Poulsen had said. It gets to be like living next to a railroad. Here he had both. Motors and trains.

He got out of bed and walked to the window. The room was half in darkness from the encroaching evening and half in light from John F. Kennedy Square, which was patchily lit from there to the station building, where two motorcycles stood revving their engines. After a few minutes they drove off to the right.

There was a rumbling from bus traffic at the far end of the square. To the right he could see the dim light from the Mallorca Bar. Two men staggered in and another staggered out.

Winter drew the curtains and took off his clothes and left them in a pile on the floor.

The water in the shower reached the right temperature almost immediately. He stood there for a long time before he lathered his body and rinsed the suds off with his face pointing into the stream.

There were still a lot of people on the streets in the center of town as Winter headed south along Boulevarden. He met with fewer as he neared the station. The evening was so mild that he could walk with his jacket unbuttoned.

Two men were standing outside the Boulevard-Caféen, opposite the hotel, but they went inside the bar when he drew closer. The windows were open and he heard the murmur of voices. Winter walked across the street and glimpsed a man through one of the windows. He lit a cigarillo as he walked, which allowed him to glance at the window of the bar, and the man was still standing there, with the half darkness behind him and half-hidden behind the thin curtains.

It might not be, thought Winter. But if those are the same men who were standing outside the Jyske Bank, talking over a hamburger, when I was there, this city isn't actually very big.

He was standing next to his car now. He opened it and pretended to rummage around in the glove compartment. The man remained standing in the window, but his silhouette had moved, as if to follow Winter's movements more closely.

Winter stepped out of the car, rounded the corner, and went into the hotel. He was handed his key. The elevator had gotten stuck somewhere, so he walked quickly up the stairs and waited in the hallway outside the door until the timer switched off the hall lights. Then he opened the door to his room and slid from darkness into darkness and shut the door at once behind him. The room was silver from the illuminated square and streets outside. Winter went down on his knees and crawled across the floor.

When he was below the window, he crawled off to the side and slowly stood up, concealed by the thick curtain that hung there. He heard a shout from the Mallorca Bar and saw a man move along unsteadily. He couldn't see the door to the Boulevard-Caféen, but he waited and saw the man outside the Mallorca joined by another drunken lout, who shouted in Danish.

Then something moved in the right of his field of vision and he backed up a few inches into the room, but not far enough to prevent his seeing.

The two men came into view, moving away from the street and across the square. Winter saw that it was the same men he'd seen just before, outside the bar. He was certain he had also seen them up by Nytorv. More than certain, in fact.

The men looked up at the window as they walked past on the sidewalk below. They can't see me, thought Winter. One of them kept his gaze fixed on the window, and Winter stayed still.

Then they had passed.

The most foolish thing now would be to go down and follow them, he thought. I don't think they know that I know.

51

THE SOUNDS SEARED WINTER'S SLEEP LIKE RED-HOT COALS,
waking him from a state of deep unconsciousness. No dreams tonight.
The exhaustion from the day before had taken its toll and given him rest.
He lay still for two minutes and primed himself to get up, opening his eyes
to a room washed out by the morning light from John F. Kennedy Square.
As he climbed out of bed, the room began to vibrate from what he now
identified as one hell of a racket coming from outside. For a second, he
thought it was motorcycles, but the sound was different. He checked his
watch. It was 6:30. Just then the alarm clock on the bedside table rang.

He drew the curtains and saw a tanker truck parked next to the
phone booths, with thick hoses feeding from it into the ground. Sometimes the local sewage cleaners know when you've checked into a hotel
and make a point of getting to work outside your window at the crack
of dawn, he thought. But I was getting up anyway.

The sky encased his field of vision like dirty steel. The buses in front
of the station departed with early-rising unfortunates. There were
still soldiers in front of the station. Maybe it's a permanent posting, he
thought.

The vibrations ceased seconds after the racket, and the sewage cleaners pulled levers and pressed buttons and headed off for breakfast.

Winter could now take in the sounds of early morning, delicate and
clear.

He was escorted to his temporary office on the second floor by a uniformed officer who didn't say a word. Michaela Poulsen came in a minute later.

"I'm being followed," Winter said.

"I'm not surprised," she said. Winter noticed that she didn't ask if he
was sure. "Your arrival was no secret, after all."

"Who are they?"

"Who's following you? To know that I'd have to see a few faces."

"Then I guess I'll have to invite you out for dinner tonight," Winter said. "You'll have to discreetly glance over your shoulder."

"Okay. But it'll have to be after eight."

"Could be that one of the gangs over here got a message from Sweden," Winter said.

"Or an alarm," Poulsen said.

"Yes. An alarm. That could tell us something. And there's something else," Winter said. "The name Andersen. Or Møller. The one who wound up dead afterward."

"Kim Møller."

"Let's call him Kim Andersen. I read up on him yesterday in my hotel room. I couldn't quite get my head around it. He seems to have been a reluctant member. A reluctant biker. There wasn't much in there."

"And he wasn't known to us before."

"First time?"

"First and last."

"Are you talking bank robberies now?"

"The more serious stuff, yeah."

"His parents weren't especially forthcoming, as far as I could tell."

"They were terrified," Poulsen said. "Literally scared to death. The father died a few months later, and while it could have been his heart, it may well have been something else."

"Is the mother still living?"

"Yes." Poulsen looked at Winter. "Do you want to question her? That is, do you want us to question her again?"

"Where is she?"

"At home, I think."

"Can you set it up?"

"We can try. If she doesn't want to, we'll have to go see a judge."

"Try contacting her at home," Winter said.

Poulsen left the room and returned five minutes later. "No answer and no answering machine."

"Do you have the address?"

"Yes, but that's not a good idea. If we just show up on her doorstep, she's liable to just deny everything. And if she was afraid back then, she's afraid now too. We've had some contact over the years."

"Is she being watched? By them, I mean."

"I would think so."

Winter was alone in the room, studying the slip of paper that resembled the map he had first seen on Beier's desk in Gothenburg, a copy of which he'd brought along and was now holding up for comparison. The handwriting was different but the message was the same. The lines were scrawled in the same directions. The letters and numbers could be references to times and quantities. People or money? Or both? Initials of places or names? On the desk before him and in the files on the computer were fragments of answers. As soon as he got home, he could sit down with all the documents and other materials and very slowly work his way through the preliminary investigation from August 18 to today. He looked at the photo of Kim Andersen that glistened through the plastic pressed over his face. From October 2, 1972, up to the present, thought Winter. Andersen's face was alive and seemed painted with a heavy burden that could have been anything. Winter knew it was taken the year before Andersen died. He was a member then, in one way or another. He had a Harley 750. His eyes were black and his chin was in shadow. The shadow fell from the left and made his face indistinct. Winter knew what he was looking for, but he couldn't find any direct resemblance to Helene Andersén in Kim Andersen's youth of twenty-five years ago.

He drove across the bridge and turned left on Vesterbrogade. This was the route Brigitta had driven. Helene sat in the back or lay pressed against the floor. Or was held there. How frightened had the child been? The mother? Had she known where she was going? According to Bendrup, a few witnesses later came forward saying they'd seen a Fiat driving at high speed between the high-rises. The high-rises gave way to detached gray stone houses when the street turned into Thistedvej.

The traffic thinned out when fields began to open up along the roadside, and Winter could hear the wind. The light was transformed as he went from city to countryside, a paler hue now spanned the sky to the west, where the sea lay. Before Årybybro he looked to the right and saw mile-long stretches of tree-lined country roads rambling through ploughed fields.

One ran parallel to the road that he was driving on. He looked to his right again: a flash of movement among the trees, keeping pace with his own. He looked again: the movement continued when the roads ran side by side through the Store Vildmose marshes. He guessed it was three hundred yards to the tree-lined road that paralleled his. The sun broke through the sky. His gaze returned to the road in front of him. There were no cars ahead, and he saw none in his rearview mirror. He looked to the right again, and now he was certain. The polished chrome of two motorbikes caught the sun at rhythmic intervals as they passed tree after tree.

Then the trees came to an abrupt end, as if an artist had tired of drawing them and lifted his pen from the paper. At that same moment, the motorcycles disappeared from view. Winter drove another half kilometer, but there was no longer any parallel movement. He slowed down suddenly and pulled into a parking space at the side of the road. With the engine running, he tried to see the line of trees in his rearview mirror. He saw the end of it and how it meandered back the way he'd come. They must have stopped right at the last tree, thought Winter. They knew how it looked. Maybe they didn't notice that I'd spotted them. Perhaps it wasn't *them*. I've got to stay calm.

He continued on, at Pandrup turning left toward Blokhus.

The resort town looked at first like a cautiously inhabited year-round community, but the impression of life dissipated the closer he got to the sea.

Winter turned right at an intersection and stopped two hundred yards farther on, in front of the Bellevue Hotel—all wood and glass that shook in the wind gusting from the sea, across the sand dunes that abutted the hotel. The balconies were abandoned zones waiting for the next season. A pennon was being ripped to shreds on one of the house's yellow timber-framed towers.

He removed a piece of paper from his jacket's inside pocket and read it.

They'd been seen leaving Blokhus on a path that ran between the dunes just as it does now.

He climbed out of the car and the wind lifted his hair up, slapping the collar of his jacket against his throat. Sand from the beach had been swept across the street like snowdrifts. It grew higher and ever closer to one of the few open shops, where clothes on hangers waved armless greetings from empty sleeves.

This is a ghost town, thought Winter.

A new square marked the center of Blokhus. There was a Cowboyland and a Sky Bar, whose windows were just shadowy black holes. Outside another clothing store, dresses and jackets swelled to twice their size in the wind. Winter saw no seabirds. Perhaps the grotesque scarecrows on the hangers in this town scared the shit out of birds.

The house lay behind the square, on Jens Bærentsvej—the third to the right on the dirt road that led to the sea across wind-battered grass.

The plasterwork was gray and spotted, and the house was more like a garden shed than a home. There was an extension on the back of it that might be a room. There was no fence. A rusty lawn mower stood in the center of the little front yard, as if abandoned in miduse.

It was here. It was here, he thought to himself again. They had been here. Helene had been here. The little girl that was Helene had been here. And someone else besides. Maybe her mother, maybe not. Maybe her father, maybe not. Kim Andersen. Maybe a father. Thou shalt obey thy father. Honor thy father. Our father who art in heaven, thought Winter.

Had he been murdered here?

During the drive back to Ålborg, Winter thought about how much the Danes had been able to accomplish in their forensic examination of the house back then. The technicians found traces of Helene, but not of anyone else except the owners.

He would have liked to have gone right in, but that was an issue for the judge in Hjørring. The house had changed hands three times.

When he reached the tree-lined stretch again, all was still. The setting sun covered everything in gold leaf, and Winter put on his sunglasses for the drive into town. He parked outside the black police headquarters, which he thought looked more and more like a spaceship that had landed in the midst of this Danish urban agglomeration.

Michaela Poulsen was still in her office. The glow from her computer screen gradually caught up with the fading sun.

"Beate Møller wasn't interested in being questioned," she said, as she saved a document in the word-processing program and looked up.

"Not even in having a talk?"

"What she actually told us was to go to hell, using only slightly more genteel language."

"I see."

"Her son has never done anything bad. He's only had bad things done to him."

"Where does she live?"

"Why do you want to know? You're not thinking of doing something foolish?"

"Never while on duty," Winter said, and Poulsen laughed.

Winter asked about the things he had been thinking about in the car on the way back.

Poulsen listened. "I don't know who owns the house now, but that can be checked out. If we've got enough to establish probable cause, we can get a search warrant from the judge in Hjørring. Where leads are concerned, I think it's all there in the binders in your office. And I'm sure forensics conducted a thorough search of the house."

"Even underneath the new wallpaper?"

"I don't know about that specifically, but we can quickly find out. We can check with the National Center for Forensic Science in Copenhagen."

The phone on the homicide inspector's desk rang. She lifted the receiver and listened.

"It's for you. From Sweden."

52

WINTER HEARD RINGMAR'S BREATHING FROM ACROSS THE KAT-
tegat before the man had even started speaking. The receiver crackled
as if the phone line were swinging in a storm.

"Hi, it's Winter."

"Hi, Erik. It's Bertil. I called your mobile but you didn't answer."

He picked up his mobile phone and looked at it. "It looks completely
normal."

"I'm not talking about how it looks. But how it sounds."

"Something must have happened to it," Winter said, and brought up
the call list on the display. Nothing since he'd arrived in Denmark.

"Oh well. We're speaking now anyway. And we haven't found any
Møller here," Ringmar said. "No one who fits, anyway. Not yet. But
that's not why I'm calling."

"Okay."

"We've really had our hands full over the past twenty-four hours,
sifting through all the tips about the girl—well, you know all about that,
of course, but we have a couple of interesting ones here. One came in
just an hour ago. A bus driver at Billdal says he's sure that he's seen the
girl on his bus."

"Alone?"

"He says she was accompanied by a woman. I've only spoken to him
on the phone. He should be showing up here any minute."

"When did he see the girl?"

Winter heard the overloaded phone line crackle again.

"He was going to try to remember on the way over here. He's checking his driver's log. It's too early to tell. But it was a long time ago."

"How long?"

"Months. Could be in connection with the murder."

"Or before."

"What?"

"Nothing. We'll have to discuss it later, when I get back."

"When are you coming back?"

"Tomorrow evening, I think. I really ought to stay longer, but I can always return."

"How'd it go today?"

"I think the biker gang, or gangs, over here are keeping an eye on me. Somebody is."

"They're following you?"

"Possibly, but I think they want me to know about it. Or else they screwed up."

"We're working on that lead," Ringmar said. "It's gotten stronger."

"What's happening otherwise?"

"Halders had something—no, I think that had to do with the shoot-out. I don't know, in that case it's in the interrogation file. But I don't know if I have time to read it to you right now, with everybody calling in with their information. You can read it later. It's your job. You can't go on eating *smørrebröd* forever."

"I haven't had a single bite."

"Then there's no reason to stay on. If you're not planning on eating those tasty *smørrebröds*."

"Good-bye, Daddy," Winter said, and hung up.

A female police officer showed him the way out. He walked down the stairs. It was past sundown. Iron clanged against iron in the freight yard across Jyllandsgade. Winter followed the street westward toward his hotel.

He hesitated outside the entrance to the Park Hotel and instead headed left across Boulevarden. No one was standing in the window of the Boulevard-Caféen this time. He walked up a chipped stairway and opened the door to the beer hall. It smelled at once of alcohol and the smoke that enveloped its two large rooms in a great haze. The few tables by the windows were empty. Winter sat down and saw the hotel's facade through a windowpane that was smeared in fat. He couldn't see the window to his room. Few of the windows in the hotel's facade were lit up.

The bar was located in the far room, and a few old men sitting at a table in front of the counter were in the midst of a sing-along about faith, hope, love, and alcohol. A woman wearing a white blouse and black skirt was sitting at the table, eating a meal. When she saw Winter sit down, she stood and wiped her mouth with a napkin that was fastened to the waistband of her skirt. The old men turned their heads toward Winter and then turned back again in midsong. The woman came up to his table. He ordered a Hof. She went back and fetched a bottle from a large refrigerator behind the bar and returned to Winter with the opened bottle and a glass. He paid the few kroner it cost.

He grabbed the bottle by the neck and drank it like a Dane, and realized as he drank how thirsty he was.

Sitting at a table at the very back of the bar was a man in a brown coat, with a beer and a bottle of aquavit in front of him. He was staring straight at the bottle of liquor and never moved his head except when he drank. Winter saw his elbow rise up at an angle at regular intervals. A professional. When the woman finished eating, she rose and fetched another beer for the man in the coat without his having made any sign that Winter was able to see. Winter finished his beer and stood up. The old men were still singing. No one seemed to pay any attention to him.

Michaela Poulsen called from the lobby. It was shortly past eight. Winter was ready and walked down the steps under the desolate landscapes that hung in frames on the walls.

They followed Boulevarden, which turned into Østerågade. There were a lot of people out. Winter heard Swedish and German. A street troubadour sang about eternal youth in an open square to the left and had just started "Knockin' on Heaven's Door" when they walked past.

The wind tore at Winter's hair at the intersection of Bispensgade.

"I always feel a strong sense of dread right here," Poulsen said.

"I can understand that."

"Come to think of it, I often feel a sense of dread in this job."

"I know what you mean."

"Now I'm going to keep looking straight ahead while I speak to you, because I think there's a guy standing over there by the bookstore who's more interested in us than he is in the books in the shop window."

Winter felt he had to make an effort not to turn his head to the left. He looked at the dark stone walls of the bank in front of him. People passed behind them on the sidewalk as they stood with their backs to La Strada.

"Do you recognize him?" he asked.

"It's hard to tell from here, but I doubt it. They wouldn't be stupid enough to send a celebrity after us. A celebrity to me, that is."

They moved a bit to the side and gazed at the Jyske Bank.

"So let's get back to talking about what we were talking about just now," Poulsen said. "Do you remember what it was?"

"The strong sense of dread we feel in our work," Winter said.

They continued looking at the Jyske Bank but in silence.

"I can now inform you that the guy over by the bookstore has gone," she said. "You don't have to look, but we can walk over there now. I'm starting to feel stiff from standing here."

They passed the bookstore. Mannequins stood unclothed in the windows of the Nordjylland fashion house and gazed out with glassy eyes. The bookstore was displaying new books by best-selling Danish authors.

"He's either been reading Ib Michael or Susanne Brøgger," Poulsen said.

They continued along Bispensgade to the entertainment district around Jomfru Ane Gade. It was difficult to make headway among all the people moving between the restaurants and bars. Music was coming from every direction. Winter thought about the Gothenburg Party. It was the same atmosphere here, filled with an anxiety that was both hard and soft, or of that same old search for calm.

"Shall we grab a table somewhere, seeing as we've confirmed that we are being watched?" Poulsen asked.

"Let's do that."

"There's a pretty good brasserie in the next street. Or should we try to force our way into the thick of things right here?"

"Might be best to be in the thick of things," Winter said. "It's easier to observe us without our seeing."

"He's been walking behind us for the past few minutes," Poulsen said.

Winter looked around. A hundred brutal neon signs pummeled his eyes: "L.A. Bar," "Fyrtøjet," "Rock Nielsen," "Down Under Denmark," "Café Rendezvous," "Faklen," "Rock Caféen," "Duty," "Jules Verne," "Sunrise," "Dirch på Regensen," "Fru Jensen," "Gaslight," "Pusterummet," "Corner," "Jomfru Ane's Dansbar," "Giraffen," "Musikhuset," "Spirit of America."

They went into Sidegaden. The slogan for the place was: "The night belongs to us."

Poulsen ordered two bottles of Hof, and they squeezed together in front of the bar.

Winter was about to say something but was cut off by his Danish colleague.

"He walked past and now he's walking past again."

Winter raised the bottle to his mouth and turned his head slightly. He saw people out on the street and that was it.

"I don't recognize him," Poulsen said. "But that bastard's certainly keeping an eye on us."

"What conclusions should we draw from that?"

"I suppose you should feel honored. And that this is serious. I think your arrival has stirred up a bit of dust."

"We've gotten closer to something."

"Yes, and it both frightens and pleases me."

"Now we're going to find the last man in the group," Winter said. "The group that visited the bank."

"You think he's still alive?"

"Yes. He killed Helene Andersén and he killed her father."

Poulsen gripped her half-finished bottle of Hof and looked at him. "After twenty-five years. Why?"

"That's what I'm trying to work out."

"He could have done it right away."

"No. That may have been the intention, but it didn't work out. Maybe Kim Andersen got in the way."

"What happened to the mother, then? Brigitta."

"He killed her too," Winter said. "He killed Kim Andersen and Brigitta Dellmar and the child was taken to Sweden. The idea was to get rid of any connection."

"So why kill Helene after all this time?"

"I don't know. Something happened. Something has happened. She found out something. She got to know who did it. She confronted him. The man who killed her mother and father. I've been looking for a single murderer all along."

"And another child," Poulsen said. "It's a horrific situation." She set her bottle down on the bar. "They're all possible theories. But the question is still whether our bikers are more than just indirectly involved."

"Look at the guy following us."

"Maybe they know," Poulsen said. "But the question is whether more than just the original gang of five was involved in this from the beginning."

"Six," Winter said. "You're forgetting the child, Helene."

"Where's your murderer, then? Did he go along to Sweden or is he still in Denmark? Maybe even here in Ålborg?"

"He may have just walked by out there on the street," Winter said.

"I don't know. The murder in August in Gothenburg doesn't necessarily point to him living permanently in Sweden, but he was certainly there then."

"If it is a he," Poulsen said.

Winter nodded mutely.

"Or there's another possible theory," she said. "That there's still just one survivor left from that bank robbery—and I'm counting all six—but that it's a woman. Brigitta."

Winter nodded again.

"I think your face just went pale," she said. "I'm probably just as pale as you are. That's an even more horrific thought."

"That would have meant having her own child killed."

"Maybe she had no choice. Maybe she didn't know. You know as well as I do that we're treading along the very brink of human misery here."

"Yes," Winter said, "that's part of the job."

"But it's also just a theory," Poulsen said.

THE RAIN AGAINST THE WINDOW WOKE HIM BEFORE THE ALARM.
There was no sky out there to light the path through the room from the bed to the toilet.

Winter swung his legs over the side of the bed, and as he walked toward the john he stubbed his toe against the bedside table. It happened once every season.

He swore and sat down to massage his toe. The pain shrunk to a dull ache, and he stood up in order to take care of his pressing need.

When he was back in bed, he looked up at the ceiling and thought about Beate Møller, whom he hadn't seen. Is that what he would end up doing? Would he drive out to her house in the east of the city only to park a ways off and see her walk in and walk out?

He wouldn't be alone. There would be another car parked out there or a motorbike that he would be able to see, or not. It would be a provocation. Perhaps from both sides. The woman would end up caught in the middle. What good could come of that?

Better to let Michaela speak to her, he thought. I'll probably just screw things up.

"We have two unsolved murders gnawing at our souls," Jens Bendrup said, as he sat on the desk in Winter's office. "That wander like ghosts through the passageways of the soul."

"Excuse me?" Winter raised his gaze from the computer screen.

"Old, unsolved murders," Bendrup said. "Not to mention a couple of old armed robberies. Are you aware that the statute of limitations has run out on the Danske Bank robbery? It's twenty years. Anything requiring a minimum sentence of eight years has a twenty-year statute of limitations here in Denmark. The same goes for murder. But stuff like that loses its meaning now that we're linking the past and the present together, right?"

"What unsolved murders are these?" Winter asked.

"One of them, I believe, is a biker killing," Bendrup said, "but as usual it's impossible to find the evidence to back up the suspicions."

"What happened?"

"A twenty-four-year-old woman was found with her throat slit in a toilet stall at the railroad station. She had a ticket to Frederikshavn in her purse. The train was scheduled to leave a half hour later, but she wasn't on it. That was fourteen years ago, in '84.

"At some point every year, I take out the case file and go through it. The Jutte case. Her name was Jutte, the girl who had her throat cut at the railway station. It's my case—I have the whole preliminary investigation and now it's even being transferred to the computer. Maybe that'll improve our chances. I never forget. The case is going nowhere, and I can't forget."

"No new leads?"

"Little things pop up every year, of course, but nothing solid to go on. Then there's Pedersen from Ringsted who calls every so often to confess. He confesses to everything, but I guess you get that kind of thing too."

"Yeah." Winter switched off his computer. "So you think that this murder of Jutte can be tied to the biker gangs?"

"To the Bandidos," Bendrup said. "She was what you might call a passive member. Her boyfriend was a mechanic and a passive member too. But there's no such thing when you're dealing with these people. Maybe that was the message we—she—got in that damn toilet stall. But it wasn't her boyfriend who did it."

"Any other suspects?"

"Nothing solid or substantial."

"You mentioned another murder," Winter said.

"What? Yeah. A Mrs. Bertelsen. Four years ago. She was at a restaurant of the cheaper variety, left on her own, and disappeared. Eight months later somebody's pet grubbed up a skeleton in an empty lot down by the docks. We found no personal belongings. Nothing. She was buried naked, and when we dug her up she was more than that. She'd been reported missing, and we ID'd her by her teeth. But that's as far as we've come."

Winter thought about Helene. He saw the lake. The narrow ditch like an open grave. The mossy ground. A seagull that shrieked a warning.

———

There was one more thing he wanted to do. First he called the Seacat office in Frederikshavn and changed his ticket, getting one of the last available seats on the 1515 boat home. He'd checked out from the hotel, and his suitcase was in his car parked in the lot opposite the Alcoholics Anonymous. It was just past noon.

Winter walked down the corridor to Michaela Poulsen's office. The door was open. He saw her through it, hunched over her desk. Her hair was hanging loose today. He knocked on the door, and she looked up and waved him in.

"I'm leaving now," he said.

"Right. Anything new on the home front?"

"Maybe. A bus driver claims he saw the girl. Could be. And then I'm dying to read through the preliminary investigation again."

"So you said yesterday."

"But we'll be in touch soon again?"

"I hope so," she said. "I'm trying to arrange to speak to Beate Møller. To start with. Then I'm going to speak to the judge, and the current owner, about the house in Blokhus." She looked down at the papers in front of her and shook her head. "Once I've waded through all this mess."

"What is it?"

"It's a mess, literally. A mess of hooch! We found eighty thousand liters of the stuff on a farm halfway to Frederikshavn. Eighty thousand liters! That ain't hay."

Winter sat alone in a room on the ground floor with a sign that read "Newspapers on Microfilm" on the door. He placed the rolls of film in the machine and then stood to open the window of the stuffy room. Outside lay a pedestrian crossing, and the crosswalk man was glowing red. Even after he'd hitched open the window, it was still red. He read the first page of the *Aalborgs Stiftstidende*. It was dramatically typeset, with the news about the bank robbery plastered across more than half of the front page: "GUNMAN KILLS OFFICER." The subheadings told of the other deaths.

Jens Bendrup was interviewed, and Winter couldn't help but smile at the young Bendrup with long hair and flipped-out sideburns. All the men he saw in the photos had flipped-out sideburns on October 3, 1972.

Bendrup lied a little and spoke the truth where necessary. Winter sat there knowing some of the answers. Bendrup's superiors spoke about what little they knew. "You always have to keep one last card up your sleeve," Bendrup had said to Winter that morning.

In this case, they had truly done just that. The question was whether there was one, and where.

Winter continued reading but found nothing of any greater value than what he already knew. He stopped scrolling the film, and the blurred lateral movement halted before his eyes. He felt slightly nauseous. It may have been from the air in there and also the film in the reader, the different speeds that made it feel as though he were sitting in a car and staring out at the passing countryside printed on paper.

He walked over to the window again. The little crosswalk man was still red and the crossing long abandoned by the city's pedestrians.

Winter walked back to the microfilm reader and sat down. He slowly scrolled through the past, the events of the day. What had it been like? How had it been when Helene and Brigitta were here? Had Brigitta read the same thing he was reading now?

He continued his slow journey through the time machine. Denmark was the world's largest exporter of beer in 1972. An illustration showed how Ålborg's infrastructure was likely to look in 1990: subway, a raised monorail around a city that the artist seemed to have modeled on something taken from the Liseberg Amusement Park. Mass transport by helicopter. Winter envied that era's faith in the future. He had been twelve years old back then, also on his way somewhere, and could always be found in the playhouse at the bottom of the garden in Hagen.

England's manager, Alf Ramsey, was sticking with his old stars for the 1974 World Cup qualifier. There was a picture of Bobby Moore, and young Ray Clemence, and a twenty-one-year-old Kevin Keegan with sideburns that were even more flipped out than Jens Bendrup's had been seven pages earlier.

Paul and Linda McCartney started writing "The Zoo Gang," and the students' abuse of power at the universities was squelched.

The flickering of the racing screen made Winter's nausea worse. He looked at his watch. Time to quit and head north. He'd kept scrolling the film forward as he looked down, and when he looked at the screen again, he'd landed on a local page about Pandrup and the surrounding area. The name Blokhus was in the headline of an article that seemed to be covering the building of the big hotel he'd passed on the deserted square the day before.

There was another article about Blokhus on the same page. If Winter understood the headline correctly, it had something to do with reclaimed land. There was a photo taken from a spot just off the square. The photographer was standing on a street called Sønder i By. Winter studied the car.

He stiffened. He knew exactly where the photographer was standing when he took the picture, which was supposed to illustrate land-use zoning and partitioning from the street on down to the sea. Winter read the lead-in. He read the caption that explained the partitioning and the piece of land in question. There were seven or eight houses in the photo that showed the full length of Jens Bærentsvej. Winter knew which street it was because he recognized the third house on the right-hand side of the dirt road that led to the sea across the wind-battered grass. The plasterwork was gray and spotted, and the house was more like a garden shed than a home. There was no fence. No sign of life in the windows. The photograph could have been taken anytime within the past twenty-five years, but Winter knew that it had been taken in conjunction with the article, as generic accompanying artwork. He knew that. The pressure mounted in his head and his midriff. A car was parked on the road outside the crooked house. The distance was fifty yards or more. Two figures could be seen in front of the house, on their way in or out. You couldn't make out their faces, but it was an adult and a child.

He had deliberated with himself and then driven to Frederikshavn. Before, he'd called straight to Michaela Poulsen and told her about the photo in the *Aalborgs Stiftstidende*.

"It must be possible to find out when it was taken," Winter had said.

"Of course. I'll contact the newspaper. And the photographer, if he's still alive."

"Would you please send me a good enlargement of it as quickly as possible? So we can continue working on it."

"Of course," she'd said again.

The wind grabbed at his hair. He was standing on deck, watching as Denmark grew smaller and disappeared. Dusk fell over the sea. It had stopped raining in international waters. Winter felt as if he had a fever, a heightened heart rate. They were halfway home. He went into the bar, which was full of glazed-eyed people who continued the drinking they'd started hours ago in Frederikshavn. A few of them were sitting in wheelchairs, which was convenient for anyone who really wanted to get tanked, he thought.

Mountains of bottles and cans took form on the tables. People's contours seemed to dissolve, he thought, and become part of history in such a way that more and more of them now seemed to resemble some kind of medieval troupe of jesters or lepers.

The smoke smudged out the features of the bar guests still further. Winter went out again, to get enough fresh air to feel like smoking a Corps. The catamaran passed Vinga. Wild ducks flew black against the evening sky while the lighthouse swept cones of light across the water. He smoked and felt his pulse drop. They passed Arendal. The big North Sea ferries slammed against the Skandiahamnen docks, reminding Winter of the walls of high-rises around North Biskopsgården—only the satellite dishes were replaced by a thousand eyes peering up toward outer space.

The drawings glowed on the wall of his office when he switched on the desk lamp and the ceiling light. The Danish flag in the depictions had taken on new meaning.

The road still ran through forest.

A windmill moved its vanes.

The streetcars went somewhere.

Ringmar knocked on the open door and entered. "Welcome home."

Winter turned around. "Thanks. How's it going?"

"I should be asking you that."

"How'd it go with the bus driver?"

"It could have been her."

"I had an odd experience," Winter said. "I saw a photograph in a newspaper from back then, in 1972, of someone who could be Helene, and all I could think about was *her*." He nodded at the drawings on the wall. "The girl I saw was Jennie."

"That's not so strange," Ringmar said.

"Don't you see? Everything's getting mixed up. Pretty soon I won't know who's who. Or else that's just how it feels at the moment. Maybe I'm just tired."

"You look pale. For Christ's sake, Erik, go home and get some rest."

Halders was drumming his fingers against the desktop. He hadn't done all the work himself, but he was responsible.

The material lay neatly organized in translucent-gray plastic folders. He was the first to see it in its entirety: 124 owners of Fort Escorts with license plates that begin with the letter *H*.

They hadn't arrested anyone. They hadn't even seen anything out of the ordinary. One of the stolen cars had not been accounted for, but the owner had an alibi and a spotless record.

Not everyone had quite so spotless a record. One-eighth of those 124 people had been convicted of minor offenses and occasionally something a little more serious, but Halders had been a police officer long enough to be able to say whether that was a high or low number.

There was something else in the back of his head. It was one of the ex-felons, Bremer. Georg Bremer. The old man had once done time for burglary. Six months twenty years ago. Halders remembered his house out in the sticks. The road through the wilderness. The horses at the edge of the field. The airplanes coming in over Landvetter and Härryda, which sounded like lightning striking.

Christ, Halders thought. What was it? What was it I didn't check? What was it I put off till tomorrow?

He flipped through the folders and read.

It was the repair shop.

Aneta had taken notes. He had written his report, but who had checked out the shop where Bremer left his car for repairs? Should he have done it himself? No. Someone else had been assigned that task. Who was it? It wasn't recorded here. It didn't say the name of the repair shop either. Halders had written down the name. It was something generic, like Joe's Car Repair or something. But the job wasn't done. Or else it was done but hadn't been entered. He checked his watch and called Möllerström, who answered on the third ring.

"It's Fredrik. Can you help me with something?"

Halders sat with his interrogation transcript. Veine Carlberg had checked out the repair shop. Nothing strange about it. The time matched what Bremer claimed in his statement. It was a little odd that he had taken his rust bucket all the way in from the outback, and driven it across town, but the guy who owned the repair shop was an acquaintance.

Still, Halders was also acquainted with the guy who owned the repair shop. He'd brought him in for questioning once: Jonas Svensk. He remembered it, managed to reconstruct most of it with the help of his memory and the report in front of him. Svensk had a past he claimed to have put behind him. Halders hadn't believed him.

Should he talk to Winter about Bremer and Svensk? Or should he check up on it himself a little more first?

He tried to think. They had leads going in different directions, and they had to pull back on one and focus more on something else. Right now it was the lead through the Billdal bus company. During the brief-ing this morning, Winter spoke about the house in Denmark and the connection or the link or whatever the hell you want to call it to that Andersen guy.

Halders thought about it. Bremer had a large plot. Aneta had thought of it as a vacation home.

54

ALONE IN HIS OFFICE ONCE AGAIN, WINTER SLOWLY MADE HIS way through the preliminary investigation while he waited for Michaela Poulsen's call.

The telephone rang, and the switchboard informed him the call was from Ålborg.

"I thought for a while that we'd bungled things even more than I'd thought, and I've turned out to be right," she said.

"Let's hear it."

"The photographer is retired but living. It was the local bureau of the paper that took the photo—i.e., not a professional photographer. Anyway, I've spoken with him and he remembers the story about the land partitioning and all that. But he couldn't remember the photograph itself. I went over there and showed him a copy of the newspaper, but he still couldn't remember taking it, although he must have, he said."

"When was it?" Winter asked.

"He didn't know the exact day, but it must have been shortly before the article was published. The vote in the town council came just before it, and that was three days before the article went to print, so he must have taken the photo during those two or three days."

"Does he have copies?"

"No. That's where the next link in this chain comes in. Every afternoon he used to hand over his roll of film to the pig truck or some other farmers' transport—sometimes to the intercity bus—and it would be developed at the main bureau in Ålborg, where the prints were made. Everything is filed away in the archives of the newspaper. They have it all in good order. I know because that's where I'm calling from now."

"Have you seen a print?"

"They made me a quick print, and I've got the negatives. There are several frames. I'll take them back to the station and let the photographer down in forensics work on them. Once we have some good enlargements, I'll give you a call."

"Excellent."

"I'll let you know," Poulsen said, and hung up.

"Jakobsson has disappeared," Ringmar said. "His brother thinks he's been the victim of a crime."

"The man himself is a crime," Halders said. "He's probably holed up somewhere drinking himself into a stupor."

"But he's gone," Winter said. "He went home the day before yesterday and now his brother has reported him missing."

"What do we think about that?" Bergenhem said to no one in particular.

"We think the worst," Ringmar said.

Halders stayed behind after the late-afternoon meeting. He'd said a few words to Winter beforehand.

"Let's go into my office," Winter now said.

Halders eyed the drawings in the office but said nothing about them. He rubbed his hand over his scalp as if to emphasize the difference between his own crew cut and Winter's long hair. Winter stroked his hair back behind his ears.

"Have you had a chance to go through all the reports on the owners of the cars yet?" Halders asked.

"No. They're lying here." Winter nodded toward the desk piled high with binders and document stacks of varying sizes. In and out trays were a thing of the past.

"There's one name . . ."

Georg Bremer. Winter read his rap sheet while Charlie Haden played a solo from the shadow beneath the window: the volume was on low and Haden's bass was part of the office walls.

Bremer had done time for burglary and criminal damage and had behaved himself while serving out his sentence at Härlanda Prison. No conspicuous drug use. After his release, he disappeared from the world of cops and robbers. He owned a Ford Escort, but that was no crime. He was acquainted with one former biker, as he himself put it. His car may or may not have driven along Boråsleden on the night of the murder. Winter grabbed hold of the lamp and directed it toward his new shelf, where he'd placed the VHS cassette. The sphere of light was reflected in the TV screen.

He walked over to the shelf and pulled out the telephone book, flipping to the *B* section of the Hindås district. There was one Bremer, Georg.

He picked up the phone and sat there with his finger poised over the buttons. No. Better to wait until tomorrow. All he really wanted was to hear the guy's voice. Perhaps determine whether this was yet another distraction that they didn't have time for. And yet he knew he would drive out there the next morning.

"You look like you could do with some sleep," Angela said.

"Give me a hug," he said. "No, on second thought, a massage."

"First I'll give you a hug," she said, and did so. They stood still for half a minute. "Now sit down."

She began to knead his neck and shoulders.

Winter was silent and closed his eyes and felt her strong fists get his blood flowing and make him a little more supple.

She continued.

"I think that's enough," he said. "Now you can fetch my slippers."

"I'm not your housewife," she said. "Masseuse, yes. Housewife, no."

"You wouldn't be able to stand it," he said.

"So we're back there again," she said.

"Angela."

"No. I know that you came home from Denmark with a fresh batch of horrendous things on your mind and that you're searching for that little girl and the murderer. All that, I know. I'm trying to stay out of the way."

He didn't know what to say.

"I don't want to keep going on about it—you know that's not what I want. But now it's serious. It's serious again," she said, and her hands disappeared from his shoulders.

He'd remained seated while she spoke. Now he stood. She was still turned away.

"I'm going home now," she said. "I want you to make up your mind. This can't come as a surprise."

She turned around, and he saw that her eyes were glistening.

"It's always the wrong moment," she said. "You're tired. You have a lot of stuff to work out. But I also have a lot of stuff to work out. We have a lot of stuff to work out. I don't want to be alone anymore. I don't want to."

She walked out into the hall, and Winter called her name but got no answer.

PART B

THE WIND BEAT AGAINST HER FACE AS SHE STOOD ON DECK.
The sun was low in the sky, a line on the edge of the earth. It was the final voyage. Suddenly the rain came, but she only noticed when she shifted her gaze from the day slipping down behind the horizon. There was a lightning flash, and then another, like her own flashes of memory that came just as suddenly and then left behind great gaps in her thoughts, as if she had surged out of a dream and woken up in another life. The shouts remained in her head like echoes.

Seek out evil in order to destroy it. There was a voice inside her. It came back and told her things. Told all!

The courtyard was in darkness. Behind the window stood the old lady, who lifted her hand like a bird raising its wing. She heard a noise from the swings.

The first few days she had paced in circles around the living room table. It was hot, but she didn't open the windows. She had been in the basement and come back upstairs. She couldn't be there.

The sun was here; then it was gone. Everything happened at the same time. I'm cold, Mommy. It'll be better soon. It smelled of night and rain, and then it became easier to move around again.

She had sat with Mommy a long time. She had slept for a while in the backseat and then crawled up front. It was cold there, and Mommy started up the car and let it run for a while and then turned it off again. Mommy hadn't answered when she had asked, and she asked again and

Mommy's voice was hard. Then she went quiet. He stood close to her. He had taken the scissors out of her hands. She had one question left and then no more. The cuckoo called. His hands held her. She heard the cuckoo and its wings beating against the wind. There was a scream from the sky.

55

HALDERS DROVE AND ANETA DJANALI SAT NEXT TO HIM. WIN-
ter was in the back. They turned off the highway and made their way
through the forest.

The clear-cut was in the process of growing back, until the next
time. Old growth survived in narrow reserves. They came to yet another crossroad.

"That's the last one," Halders said, and turned to the left. After about
half a mile, or a little less, the road opened out onto a slope and ended
in front of the house, which was crooked but stable. Winter thought he
recognized it. The garden consisted of the hillside in front, and behind
the house Winter could see the forest and parts of a field. Now he heard
the gloomy sound of hooves against the earth. Horses were running
somewhere back there, perhaps startled by the sound of Halders's Volvo.
They'd parked next to Bremer's Escort. It was covered in mud, hardly
pearl white anymore beneath the crud, since it was being driven on forest roads in late October.

Winter couldn't make out the license plate.

To the left of the house, ten yards away and an equal distance from
the edge of the forest, stood a windmill.

It was yellow and the vanes weren't moving. It was about four and a
half feet high.

Halders knocked on the door, which had a window with a curtain.
No one opened up.

They hadn't called ahead.

"What is it?" The man had stepped out from behind the house.
"You again." He approached them and pointed. "The car's standing
right there, in case you're wondering." He looked at Aneta Djanali and
Halders. "I recognize you."

Winter shook his hand. Bremer was tall and his hand dry. His eyes looked past Winter. He was wearing rubber boots, and Winter saw that one of them had a gash above the foot. Winter knew that beneath the knitted cap on his head the sixty-nine-year-old was bald. His mustache was dark. He was skinny and wizened, as Aneta had said in the car on the way out.

"May we come in for a moment?" Winter asked. He looked up at the sky, low above the glade. "Looks like it's starting to rain."

"A little rain never hurt anybody," Bremer said. "But sure, we can go inside."

Aneta Djanali met Winter's eyes as they stepped up onto the porch. The hall inside was dark. Bremer took off his boots, and the police took off their shoes and followed him into a room with windows facing the back of the house.

Winter looked out, and the horses were gone. He turned toward Bremer and took a step forward. "It's about your car again," he said. "And a few other things."

"What about my car?"

"We're talking to all the owners of this kind of car. To see if maybe they can remember anything else that might help us."

"Help you with what?"

"Aren't you aware that we're investigating a murder?" Winter asked. "And a disappearance in connection with that murder?"

Bremer looked at Halders. "He mentioned something about it."

"Is that all you've heard of it?" Winter asked.

"Maybe something on the radio or TV. I don't know. I mind my own business."

Winter made up his mind when he saw the horses emerge from the bushes. They were moving in perfect symmetry, floating above the high grass.

"Do you know Jonas Svensk?"

"Svensk? Well, he owns the repair shop where I leave my car when it's acting up. Why do you ask?"

"We're in the process of looking into any potential connections here," Winter said, expressing himself as cryptically as he could.

"What connections? What's my car got to do with it?"

"I didn't say anything about that."

"You didn't? You were talking about the auto repair shop."

Winter took a breath. "I'd like you to accompany us back to the police station so we can discuss this further."

"What's this all about? If you think I'm using my car to move around stolen goods or something, you're welcome to take a look."

Winter didn't answer.

"You think you can go around harassing people like me just as you please, huh? I've behaved myself ever since I got out. Ask anyone, you'll see. Is it Svensk? He hasn't done anything. Is it that shoot-out? Is that why you're here?"

"We'd like you to come with us," Winter said.

Bremer looked at Halders and Aneta Djanali as if they had the authority to reverse Winter's decision. He took another step and stopped. It's as if his body is shrinking, Winter thought. His skin is sinking inward.

"For how long?" Bremer asked, suddenly resigned to it.

Maybe he was resigned to it all along, thought Djanali.

Winter didn't answer.

"Six hours," Bremer said, but not to anyone in particular.

Six plus six, Djanali thought. If not more.

Ringmar was waiting. He entered Winter's office when they'd left Bremer alone for a moment.

Winter held up his hands. "I'm just exercising my legal authority."

"I didn't say anything."

"The car's still at the house, along with Aneta. I want you to send someone out there straightaway to pick it up and pull it apart."

"I won't ask if you think they rode in that car."

"Now let's look at the tape." Winter inserted the cassette with the footage of the traffic on Boråsleden.

The car drove past and then came back. There and back.

"If that is him, then he shouldn't be driving toward town but toward his house," Ringmar said.

"He was visiting someone," Winter said. "No. He drove to her apartment."

"Whoever it is," Ringmar said. "After all, they weren't Bremer's prints we found in her apartment."

"It won't be that easy," Winter said. He froze the frame. He pressed play again and froze it again. "There's still a guy sitting in there and it's still a Ford."

"Now we have a car to compare it to," Ringmar said. "That could give us something. We'll have to take apart this film as thoroughly as we're taking apart the car."

"I want everything on Svensk," Winter said. "Everything."

"I want everything about the biker brotherhoods," Ringmar said. "Everything."

"I want to know where Jakobsson is," Winter said.

"Do you want us to search Bremer's house?"

Winter shook his head.

"Too early?"

"We'll wait. I want a search warrant first, and then we'll tear the place apart."

Michaela had been quick, as quick as the photographer and the copyist. The photos were flown to Copenhagen and on to Landvetter.

Winter closed his eyes, wanting to put off opening the envelope for half a minute. He took a drag and stubbed it out. Maybe for good. There was no room for smokers in a modern world.

He lit a fresh cigarillo before he stood and went over to the wall where the drawings hung.

Landvetter. As they were leaving Bremer's, a Boeing jet had roared through the space barrier above Bremer's house. Bremer hadn't shown the slightest reaction.

He'd seen it in one of Jennie's drawings—in her diary. It wasn't hanging on the wall. He went to the desk where the drawings lay sorted into piles, and in the third one from the left, the one containing all kinds of vehicles, there were two drawings with a long cylindrical object floating above the forest and the house. It was a good drawing. Winter could almost hear the roar as the airplane cut through the rain and sunshine.

He sat back down in his chair and opened the envelope. There were five photos. The top one showed the two people level with the house, on their way in. The woman was holding the child by the hand. They were looking straight ahead. You couldn't see their faces.

In the second, they had moved closer to the house. The child was turned toward the camera or in that direction. Perhaps she'd seen the photographer. It was Helene. You still couldn't see the woman's face.

The third photograph was taken closer to the two figures. The girl became more distinct. The woman was in profile. He wanted to put a name to that profile, but he wasn't certain.

There was something else that made him go cold and still. Between the woman and the door was a window, and in that window he could discern a third figure. Winter shut his eyes and looked again, sharpened his gaze. The contours of the figure were still there, behind a thin curtain: a face and an upper body.

He studied the contours. Had they picked up on this in Denmark? Of course they had. Winter rummaged through the envelope and found the accompanying letter, a single sheet that had gotten stuck inside. He read it quickly. She had written about the figure in the window. "We don't know who it is."

The fourth photo was taken seconds later, when the woman and the child had reached the door. The figure in the window was gone. Winter saw the backs of the pair outside.

The fifth showed the house and was the most enlarged of the prints, rough and grainy. It must have been taken about a minute later, maybe, the local photojournalist having taken a break in his coverage of future land partitions. Then he had pressed the shutter release one last time. In the window a man had pulled aside the curtains in order to be able to see more clearly what was going on outside. He did it without thinking, exposing himself.

The man could have been a young Georg Bremer. He had a mustache, a cap pulled down over his brow.

The phone rang. It was his mother.

"Your father's ill," she said.

"I'm sorry to hear that." He slipped the photos back into the envelope and filed the accompanying letter in a folder inside the desk drawer. "What's happened?"

"He was feeling a bit under the weather this afternoon and we asked Magnergår—he's a doctor who lives in the area—to come over, and he thought that we ought to take him to the clinic in town."

Winter tried to imagine Marbella but failed. He had only seen a map of the city on the Internet.

"What's the matter with him?"

"That's where I'm calling from right now. The doctors have examined him and done an EKG, but it didn't show anything."

"He's probably just overexerted himself," Winter said. On the golf course, he thought. He tried to think light thoughts, but the nausea was growing.

"He hasn't overexerted himself," his mother said. "We haven't done anything out of the ordinary."

"No."

"I'm worried, Erik. If something happens, you have to come down."

He didn't answer. Someone rapped on the door. He called out, "Just a minute," and listened again.

"What is it?" she said.

"Just somebody at the door."

"Are you at the office? Well, I guess you must be since it's only evening."

"Yes."

He heard footsteps walk away outside his door. She said something.

"Sorry, Mother. I didn't hear what you said."

"If something happens, you have to come down."

"Nothing's going to happen. You'll just have to take it easy for a while, that's all. No more spur-of-the-moment trips to Gibraltar."

"You promise, Erik? You promise you'll come if he gets worse? I spoke to Lotta, and she also thinks you should come. You both have to come."

"I promise," he said.

"Now you've promised. I'll call later this evening. You can call too." She told him the number to the clinic. "I'm going to be here the whole time."

"Maybe you'd better come home soon."

"I have to go now, Erik."

He sat with the cell phone in his hand. There was a rapping at the door again. He called out, "Come in," and Ringmar appeared in the doorway.

"His sister lives on Västergatan," Ringmar said, and sat down. "That's in Annedal."

Winter checked his watch—nearly six o'clock. Georg Bremer had reluctantly mentioned his one relation, his sister, Greta. Nothing about anyone else. They could keep him for the rest of the evening, and shortly after midnight they'd have to let him go. It was pointless to go to the prosecutor now.

"Seriously, Erik."

"Seriously?"

"We've got to let him go."

"He can go at midnight. How's it going with the car?"

"They're going at it hammer and tongs."

"I don't want to speak to him anymore right now," Winter said. "We let him go home, and the day after tomorrow we haul him back in again."

"Are you sure about that?"

"No."

"Want to know what I've been waiting to happen for the past month?"

"Tell me."

"For the girl's father to get in touch. Christ. His ex is dead and his daughter is missing. We're searching, and the whole country knows about it. But he doesn't get in touch."

"Maybe he can't."

"I've thought about that, but I'm not sure. He may be dead, sure."

"Or afraid."

"Fear feels like a recurring theme in this investigation."

"Or else he doesn't know that he has a child."

Ringmar changed position. "It's not easy to trace her past," he said. "It virtually doesn't exist."

"There you have it," Winter said. He sat up straighter. "That's what this is all about. Her past hadn't existed, but then all of a sudden it does exist. It comes to her. It becomes part of what later transpires. It precipitates." He breathed in deeply.

Ringmar was still.

"She comes to this city and her life comes to an end. Her life as an adult. First her understanding of life ended, and then life itself."

56

A FEW MINUTES AFTER MIDNIGHT, BREMER DROVE HIS CAR
off into the night. He said nothing, and Winter didn't accompany him
to the garage. Beier came down to homicide in person. He'd remained
at the station the whole time.

"There was a lot of junk in the car," he said.

"So it's impossible?"

"I didn't say that. I just said there was a lot of junk in the car. In the
trunk, on the floor, in the glove compartment, et cetera, et cetera."

"Uh-huh."

"There were cigarette butts in the ashtrays, and there was also a butt
wedged deep underneath the seat struts, and I wonder what it was doing
there."

"Say that again?"

"A small cigarette butt was stuck between the carpeting on the floor
and the base of the seat strut, and it took some time to find it. You need
professionals to find stuff like that."

"You mean it was hidden there?"

"Maybe. It's mostly filter. You don't know which brand Helene
Andersén smoked, do you?"

"No. So it could be hers?"

"I'm just trying to be optimistic here," Beier said. Anyway, we
found it and now it's on its way over to the National Center for Forensic
Science."

"Jesus Christ," Winter said. "It'll take months for them to do a DNA
analysis."

"You want to do it yourself?"

"We have to get top priority on this one. You're well respected down
in Linköping, Göran."

"I'll do what I can," Beier said. "I am susceptible to flattery. But as you know, you normally have to wait in line."

"We have something to compare it to, for Christ's sake," Winter said. "Tell them that. This isn't a blind analysis. We don't need to sit and wait for a prosecutor to issue a warrant for a DNA sample."

We've got a body, he thought. We've had it for a long time now.

Winter went back to his room, sat down. Another thought in his head had grown apace with his fatigue that evening. Lately he hadn't had much time to wonder why Helene had been left where they'd found her. Why in the ditch next to the lake? The dump site was far away from Helene's apartment. It also lay far away from Bremer's house. And now Bremer was a suspect. Winter closed his eyes and thought about the dump site, far away from Helene's house and far from Brem—

He opened his eyes, got up, and left the room. Down the corridor in the situation room, he stood in front of the big map of Greater Gothenburg on the wall. He used a sticker to mark the approximate location of Helene's apartment in North Biskopsgården. Then he looked eastward on the map and found Ödegård—Bremer's house. He marked it.

He tagged the dump site by Big Delsjö Lake.

He measured the distance from Biskopsgården to the dump site. He then measured the distance from Ödegård to the same place.

As the crow flies, the distances were exactly the same.

Winter yielded to the streetcar on Västergatan and walked south between buildings that obscured each other. It was nine o'clock. At the front entrance he punched in the code he'd been given yesterday. The heavy door clicked, and he walked into the stairwell and up to the second floor. The mail slot said "Greta Bremer." He rang the bell and waited. Steps sounded from inside, and the door was opened cautiously. All he saw was a shadow.

"Yes?"

"My name is Erik Winter. Inspector with the Gothenburg Police Department. Homicide squad. I called yesterday."

"It's him," a voice said inside. "The one who was supposed to be coming."

The door opened. The woman may have been fifty or somewhat younger. She was wearing an apron. Her hair was hidden beneath a scarf, and in her hand she was holding a little brush that might have been intended for clothes.

She backed up, and Winter stepped through the doorway. Three yards in sat a woman in a wheelchair. In the half darkness Winter couldn't make out the features of her face. Her hair seemed long. The apartment smelled of the street outside. They've just aired it out, Winter thought hastily.

"Well, come in, then," the voice in the wheelchair said. The woman gripped the wheels with an experienced hand and rolled backward.

Winter followed her into a living room, where the plant detritus on the floor attested to the fact that the room had indeed just been aired out. The windows opened inward. The woman who had opened the door for Winter excused herself.

"That's my home helper," Greta Bremer said. "When you can barely move, you can't manage without a home helper."

Winter could see her face now, or parts of it. She wore dark glasses that were more brown than black. He could just make out her eyes, but that was it. Her hair was gray and a little tousled. Her skin was thin and delicate, as if made up of cracks that had healed irregularly over a long period of time. Winter guessed that she was seventy, maybe older, but the illness she suffered from may have added many extra years to her face. He still didn't know her age.

"So you're here about my brother," she said without looking at Winter. "Have a seat first." She hadn't yet turned her face toward him. She behaved as if she were blind, and Winter wondered if maybe she was. He didn't want to ask. She would tell him. "You want to ask me questions about my brother. I doubt I can answer a single one of them."

"I would like—"

"We haven't seen each other in many years."

"Why not?"

"Why not?" She turned her face toward Winter, but he still couldn't see her eyes. "How should I put it? We have nothing to say to each other. It's best not to meet up when you have nothing to say."

Her voice was impassive, which made it even more awful, Winter thought. There was no bitterness, only a voice that could just as well have come from the wall as from a living person.

"What happened?"

"Do I have to tell you that? It has nothing to do with what you've come here for." Her profile was lit up by the window. "Why are you here, Inspector?"

"I mentioned a bit about it on the telephone."

He explained a little more now—told her about the few leads they had and felt how tenuous it all sounded.

"I have nothing to say about all that," she said. "I know nothing about him."

"When did you last see each other?"

She was silent, but Winter couldn't tell whether she was considering his question.

He repeated it.

"I don't know," she answered.

"Is it more than ten years ago?"

"I don't know."

Winter glanced toward the entrance hall, where the home helper wasn't quick enough pulling her head back into the shadows. She's curious, thought Winter. I would likely have done the same.

"He's been in prison," Greta Bremer said. "But of course you know that."

Winter nodded.

"Must you come here asking questions I can't answer? Aren't there any computer lists you can ask today? Don't you have files?"

"We have files," Winter said. This conversation is becoming increasingly bizarre, he thought to himself. She doesn't want to say anything more, or else she can't.

"I haven't seen him in many years and I thank God for that," she now said. She hadn't moved.

"Have you visited his house?" Winter asked.

"Yes. But, like I said, that was a very long time ago."

"When was it?"

"There's no point in your asking. Ask the archives."

Winter got up and walked closer, but Greta Bremer remained in the same position. He touched the wheelchair cautiously. "Is this one of the newer models?"

"What difference does it make?"

"I noticed that you had no trouble maneuvering it on your own."

"It's easier than having someone else push it. Try it out yourself and you'll see how heavy it is to walk behind."

Winter stood behind the chair and released a brake. Her hair moved below him. There were strands of it on the fabric and on the thin, broad pillow she had to support her back.

"Try pushing it around a little," she said.

Winter rolled it back and then two yards forward into the room.

"Heavy, isn't it?"

"Very," he said.

"You can put me in the hall," she said. "I assume you're going to leave now."

When he left, he saw the woman from the home-help service standing in the kitchen with her back to him, bent over the sink.

Busy on the phone, Ringmar waved to the chair in front of his desk. Winter waited, and the conversation came to a close.

"As far as we've been able to determine, they are brother and sister," Ringmar said. "The documentation checks out. She's sixty-six years old. Too old to be a suspect."

"Sibling love," Winter said.

"What? Yeah, well. There are many fates," Ringmar said. "Must have been an odd conversation you had."

"She seemed very distant." Winter held up the copy of the slip of paper they'd found in the dress in Helene's basement storage room. "But this is what I came in for. If I've read correctly, this was found on Helene when she was brought into Sahlgrenska Hospital?"

"Yes. Meticulous beyond the call of duty, they took it and put it in an envelope with her other possessions, which consisted of little more than a pair of pants, a shirt, and a dress."

"And she's had it with her throughout her life."

"What are you getting at?"

"I don't know. But I can't let go of it, as you can see. I have it with me, here in my hand. And there's something else."

"Yes?"

"I've been thinking about this code—but let's leave that for a moment. I've also looked at these lines that might just be some kind of map." Winter leaned forward and showed Ringmar.

"After we drove out to Bremer's, I studied the big map in the situation room and compared it to the lines here on this one. You see? If you turn off at Landvetter township and drive parallel to the highway—on the old road—and turn left where we turned left, and assuming that the crossroads in the forest looked the same back then as they do now, then I'll be damned if it doesn't match up with Bremer's house. It's even marked, there in the upper-left corner, after the last cross."

"And you've compared it to the map?"

"Carefully. I'll show you later so you can see for yourself."

"Well. I don't know what to say."

"You'd like to say that I have an active imagination. But that comes in handy sometimes."

Winter considered the slip of paper again. "I don't know what to say either. But it all tallies up. The *L* would stand for Landvetter and the *H* for Härryda."

"And the *C* for *cabin*," Ringmar said.

"Maybe."

"A place to meet up again? Wouldn't verbal instructions have sufficed?"

"If you speak the same language," Winter said. "This was probably meant to be destroyed afterward."

"But it didn't turn out that way."

"No. Helene's fingerprints as a child are on it. That's conclusive."

"Jesus Christ." Ringmar looked at the letters and the numbers.

"But what about the rest?"

"I don't know. It could be the number of people, sums, dep—"

"What is it?" Ringmar asked.

"I was thinking—that 23 followed by a question mark. Could that be a departure time? The departure time for a ferry, for example?"

"They couldn't have been stupid enough to think they could just drive onto the ferry after committing one of Denmark's biggest bank heists ever?"

"No. But maybe someone else was going to take it. Someone who wasn't along for the robbery or who wasn't counting on being recognized. Can you check with the Stena Line to see if there were ferries leaving from Frederikshavn at around 2300 back then?"

A new enlargement arrived from Denmark later that afternoon. The figure in the window was a man who looked like he could have been a young Georg Bremer. It would never be enough to convince a prosecutor, much less to stand up in a court of law. But a court had nevertheless given the go-ahead. Winter got the news when Michaela Poulsen called.

"It was the enlargements that did it," she said. "We're going in this afternoon. There's a guy here from the National Center of Forensic Services at the moment, so we won't need to send things over there for analysis. If we find something, that is."

"There could be several layers of wallpaper," Winter said.

"The NCFS guy just shook his head. Stuff like that only makes you more determined as an investigator, right?"

Halders came running in, out of breath. It was like a confirmation. It was a confirmation.

"Let's bring him in again," Winter said.

51

GEORG BREMER SAT BENEATH THE INTERROGATION LAMP WITH his head bowed over the table. He didn't want to have a lawyer present. He hadn't said a word since he'd been taken back into custody. Winter had decided to conduct the interrogation himself. Cohen had agreed. Gabriel Cohen wasn't territorial like that.

EW: We've asked you to come back here to answer some more questions.

GB: Yeah, that's obvious.

EW: We're really trying here. We're doing all we can to understand what happened.

GB: Good luck, that's all I can say.

EW: That's all you can say?

GB: That's it. What else can I say? I'm someone who minds his own business.

EW: I see. But you must have some acquaintances, some people who know you. That's where we need your help. If you could ask one of your acquaintances to speak to us.

GB: I have . . .

EW: I didn't catch your answer.

GB: There was no answer. I didn't answer anything.

EW: If one of your acquaintances could tell us what you were doing on the evening in question, it would be a big help to all of us.

GB: I told you, I was alone.

EW: Were you at home the whole evening?

GB: Yes.

EW: Do you ever lend your car to anyone?

GB: What?

EW: Do you ever lend your car to anyone?

GB: Never. How would I be able to leave the house?

EW: You own a motorbike.

GB: It doesn't run. It's always taken apart. If I'm going to drive anywhere, I have to put it together and that takes weeks.

EW: Are you a good mechanic?

GB: I can take apart a motorcycle and put it back together again.

EW: How long have you had a motorcycle?

GB: Long time. Since I was young, and that's a long time ago.

EW: When you were doing break-ins, did you drive a motorbike then?

GB: I may have. But I paid my debt.

EW: You weren't alone then. There were more of you driving around on motorbikes doing break-ins.

GB: I don't know anything about that. I got my punishment. I've lived on my own ever since and before that too.

EW: But you still have friends from that time.

GB: No.

EW: You left your car with a friend, Jonas Svensk.

GB: He's not a friend.

EW: What is he, then?

GB: He's a mechanic. A Ford mechanic. He fixes cars.

EW: We spoke about your car before. It was seen in the early hours of the morning on the eighteenth.

GB: Like hell it was. Where?

EW: You deny that your car was seen on the morning of the eighteenth?

GB: I was at home, asleep in bed. If my car was seen, then somebody stole it and put it back again before I woke up.

EW: Witnesses saw your car out on the road on the night in question.

GB: What witnesses? Must be you guys in that case. The police become witnesses whenever necessary.

EW: What do you mean by that?

GB: I mean that you're trying to frame me.

EW: Have you had any visitors to your home in the past three months?

GB: Three months? Maybe I have.

EW: Who's visited you?

GB: Some neighbor passing by. That happens on occasion.

EW: The closest farm is a mile and a half away.

GB: Well, it doesn't happen often.

EW: So who have you invited inside?

GB: No one. I haven't invited anyone inside.

EW: Witnesses say they saw you driving home with a woman and a child in the car with you.

GB: That's a lie. That never happened.

EW: We have people who claim that it did.

GB: Would that be neighbors claiming that? What did you say yourself just now? That the closest neighbor is a mile and a half away? They must have very good eyesight in that case.

EW: There are houses close to the road.

GB: None that anybody lives in.

EW: There are people living in houses close to the road.

GB: Oh yeah? Well, I've never seen any.

EW: You were seen.

Bremer had been seen. Halders and Djanali had started by tracking down everyone who had a house or a vacation home around Bremer's. Mostly, the houses lay south and west of there.

"I've seen the old guy drive past a few times. A couple of times with people in the car." The man was recently divorced and had been allowed to rent the shed for a cheap price, and he had sat there and thought about how grief affects you. He'd had a bit to drink and staggered around in wide circles through the forest in a nervous and hungover state of mind that sharpened his powers of perception. "You can't see the road from my place, but it's no more than a few hundred yards away. Once I was up at his house. It must have been his, because I recognized the car parked outside."

"Did you see anyone else there?"

"No, not then. But a few times I saw the car pass by with people in it. I know that one of the passengers was a child and maybe a woman. Could have been a guy. The hair was pretty long and fair."

"Do you remember approximately when this was?"

"Last summer, but I don't know exactly. I'm divorced—bah, fuck it. It was warm anyway. July, August. A ways into August. Before the rains came."

"Are you still living in the cabin?"

"Sometimes, but not often."

"Have you seen this man since the summer? Say, after August."

"Sure."

"Has he had any people there with him? Any visitors?"

"There have been people in there. Not often, but people have driven there. Cars, motorbikes."

"Motorbikes too?"

"Well, he owns a motorbike. Right? Seen him driving on one at some point anyway. A couple of times. There have been people up there on motorcycles."

"Would you recognize any of the riders if you saw them again?"

"Not a chance. I ran off as soon as I saw the gang."

"How about this child you saw and that person who may have been a woman—when did you last see them?"

"It was a long time ago. Last summer, like I said."

"When it was hot?"

"When it was hot as hell."

Winter met Vennerhag at a nondescript location. They could see ships and hear the sounds from the bridge above the car they were sitting in.

"Don't come to my house anymore," Vennerhag said. "It doesn't look good."

"Yeah, what will the neighbors say?"

"The mood out there right now is very tense, and I don't want to be fingered as a fucking snitch."

"You are an informant, Benny. And my brother-in-law, almost."

"Is that how it is now?"

"What do you want?" Winter asked.

"There are rumors floating around that Jakobsson got whacked. He was small fry, so everybody's surprised. His brother's been kicking up a real stink about it. He must have been to see you at the station."

"Yes."

"Well, that's what I wanted to say. Jakobsson. But it's a rumor."

"Where from?"

"Don't know. You know how it is with rumors."

Winter didn't answer. He wondered briefly if the BMW they were sitting in was stolen, maybe even from another country. The chorus from the bridge overhead rose higher when the streetcar drove over it, toward Hisingen. There were parked cars all around them, and Winter guessed that 10 percent of them were stolen and had been dumped here when the gas had run out or when the junkies had stolen new ones to drive the stretch between the Femman Mall, right next door, and the projects in the northeast. Halders knew.

"The Hells Angels have split again and a new brotherhood has emerged," Winter said, after a minute's silence. "Do you know anything about it?"

"I don't know anything about those psychopaths." Vennerhag squirmed uncomfortably in his seat and looked at Winter. "Absolutely nothing. You know better than that."

"No rumors from that quarter? Or about them?"

"I would cover my ears if I heard anything. It's dangerous. Believe me. The less you know the better, and all that."

"There aren't many who do know," Winter said.

"That's part of the business plan."

"Just like they're part of society, huh?"

"Well, you're part of society," Vennerhag said. "Law enforcement is part of society just like the alternate power is part of society."

"You're quite the philosopher, Benny."

"And yet your sister still didn't want me."

"You too are part of society, after all."

"Gee thanks."

"What for? I wasn't talking about a very nice society."

"No. If it was a nice society, there would only be room for cops. But I'll tell you something, Erik. We're both just as replaceable. Just as pathetic."

"You can go to hell."

"Too close to home for you?"

Winter didn't want to listen. He saw a radio car drive past, over by the Shell station. Maybe they'd already taken down the plate number of the car he was sitting in.

"If you don't know anything about the Angels, you have to help me with Georg Bremer."

"I told you—he's nothing. If he says he's been clean since he got out of prison, then that's the truth. I haven't heard anything anyway. I hadn't even heard of him before you mentioned his name."

"I'm talking about your business contacts. Someone might know something. He doesn't need to have done anything—petty stuff or whatever it might be. I just want to know where he's been. If anyone's seen him. Anywhere. And if he knew Jakobsson."

58

PROSECUTOR WÄLLDE DECIDED TO ARREST BREMER IN THE
morning. He could be held in custody at police headquarters for up to
four days before charges had to be filed.

"Do your best," Winter said. What he meant was that Wällde should
give the clock a chance to run out, ignore the directive stating that he
should "expeditiously determine whether charges shall be filed."

"It doesn't feel like there's probable cause even for an arrest," Wällde
said.

"And yet you did it."

"That was for your sake, Inspector. And maybe some good will come
of it."

"Hand on your heart, Erik. Do you think the girl is still alive?"

Winter looked around, as if someone had snuck into his office and
was waiting for his answer.

"No. I think that's out of the question." He saw that Ringmar was also
convinced. Ringmar's fifty-year-old face was pale and looked decayed in
the dim light that had settled over the cityscape like a prelude to winter.
"We can find her body if we get Bremer to talk. Or someone else."

"Or someone else."

Winter ran his left palm over his face. He squeezed his eyelids
together and turned to Ringmar. "She hid that butt there on purpose,"
he said.

"What?"

"I think it's Helene's cigarette butt. She knew that something was
going to happen. She stuffed it in there as far as it would go—where
nobody could find it unless they really went looking for it like Beier and
his team."

"We'll know if it's her saliva on it when the NLFS people are done."

———

Before Winter pushed through the decision to issue a search warrant, he spoke to Beier. The head of forensics was under pressure and tired of shouting at the lab in Linköping.

"Well, I'll be damned," Beier said. "Prints after twenty-five years. So you want us to tear off wallpaper and expose God knows how many layers—three maybe, or five—to see if there are any prints left underneath or in between?"

"Yes. There may only be one layer. The top one. Then there's no problem."

"Don't forget that we have to go through the entire house."

"Yeah, sure. But if. I'm saying *if*. Could there be anything still there? Traces of fingerprints?"

"The wallpaper glue will have destroyed everything, I think. Especially after such a long time. It's damp and it penetrates the paper."

"But you can't swear that that's the case?"

"I seldom swear."

"Then I'd like to give it a try. Would you give it a try, Göran?"

"Okay. We'll give it a try."

"The Danes are doing the same."

"What?"

"Haven't they been in touch with you yet? If not, then they will be at any moment. They're removing the layers of wallpaper at that summerhouse in Blokhus."

"What do they want to find exactly?"

"Evidence from back then," Winter said. "We know Helene was there. What if our Georg Bremer was also? What if we can prove it? What if we can prove that Helene Andersén was in Bremer's house as a child? Or as an adult?"

"Then we'll get invited to the FBI in Washington and lecture on it," Beier said. "That is, I will."

The winds swept in a circle around Ödegård, howling along its walls, which shuddered inside. The sky was black in the middle of the day. Night in the middle of the day, Winter thought, standing in front of the windmill. The vanes were spinning in all directions, aimlessly. The forest had moved in closer since they were last here; it loomed over him and everyone else who had come looking for clues. One of those who stood looking on was Birgersson. He'd come out here together with Wellman, and that was a sensation.

"How did you manage to stop the press from stomping around out here among the technicians?" Wellman asked.

"I thought that was your doing," Winter said.

Wellman let Winter's answer fly off with the wind around the lot and glade. He looked around. "One hell of a disturbing place, Ödegård."

There was the loud crack of snapping floorboards coming from inside the house. A saw was being used. Perhaps shovels.

"Someone's been digging in the basement," Birgersson said.

"What did you say?" Wellman asked.

"The dirt in the basement has been dug up recently." Birgersson looked up at the sky as a plane swooped down over them on its way to landing. "Jesus Christ. Am I dreaming or am I still awake?"

"I'll ride in with you," Birgersson said, when Winter headed toward the car. Wellman had already returned to the office.

They drove through the forest. Winter could only see it depicted in crayon, naturalistically, as it really was.

"You know we can't hold this bastard if we don't find something new," Birgersson said. Winter kept to the right on the dirt road when they met a radio car on its way out to Ödegård.

"Part of the job of an investigator is also to rule out suspects," Winter said. "I learned that one from you, Sture."

"Are you trying to prepare yourself mentally for a failure?"

"That's a big part of the job."

"You're in the process of putting together a very sleek chain of circumstantial evidence, but it's still thin."

"That was nicely put."

"Come on, Erik. For Christ's sake."

Winter merged onto the highway, and Birgersson rolled up his window when they reached high speed. As the fog thickened across the fields in toward town, the cars were visible only by their low beams. Winter was overtaken by the airport bus. It careened along past them as if it were straining to take to the skies itself.

"I questioned Bolander yesterday," Winter said. "The member of the brotherhood who is set to go on trial for the shoot-out at Hising—"

"I know who he is. I am your boss, you know."

"Of course he didn't give away anything, but there's still a connection to the gangs. I've tried to focus on that as I've read through everything. Several of the names that have come up in this case have had some kind of connection."

"To what?"

"To those organizations. I say 'those' because there are several of them."

"Yeah?"

"That's it. We can't get any further. You'll get all that in writing later, so you can file it away, Sture. We can see a possible connection but that's about it. We've sent all the files back and forth and searched back in time—well, you know with Brigitta Dellmar and Denmark and the threats against me. The possible threats."

Birgersson seemed to sink deeper into his seat. As they approached the Delsjö junction, he looked down at the lake and the parking lot beneath them. "The press is starting to lose interest in the girl," he said. "It's disturbing. Although it's always disturbing where the press is concerned. When an investigation begins, it's like going around with a boil on your ass, having them breathing down your neck all the time, and when the investigation plateaus and they start to lose interest, you realize you may never solve the case."

"We will solve this case," Winter said. "And the media interest has picked up again. After Bremer."

"I'm counting on your being right, Erik."

Winter rang Bremer's sister's doorbell unannounced. A streetcar passed by with the sound of water being flung by a powerful force. The fall had rained its way into November. He felt the dampness on his forehead and hands.

He pushed the bell again. No sound came from inside the apartment, so he rang it a third time and something shuffled inside. The lock cylinder turned. The door opened and he saw her face. She looked him over for a few seconds.

"You again?"

"I'd just like to ask a few more questions," Winter said.

It sounded as if the old woman was sighing deeply. She hadn't moved in her wheelchair.

"I was asleep," she said. "I usually take a nap in my chair when the home helper is off looking after other worthless old geriatrics."

"May I come in?"

"No." She didn't move. "If all you have is a few more questions, then you can ask them now."

"There are some things regarding your brother—about his past."

"It's pointless."

"It's important," Winter said. "I'll come back later. I'll call and we can set up a time."

A day and a half passed. Winter questioned Georg Bremer again, but it felt pointless—lifeless words passed back and forth. He read the transcripts from the past few months. He waited.

Then Beier called, from Ödegård.

"There's a second layer, and I don't know how old it is, but it's got prints. They could be from Bremer, if he put up the wallpaper, in which case we're, well, back to square one. But they could also be from somebody else. It's not much. And they're small."

"Small?"

"Small. That's all I can tell you right now. Could be because of how much time has passed, the glue, moisture. But now you know, so stay off our backs for a bit. We'll work quickly, I promise. But don't get your hopes up."

"This could take you to Washington," Winter said. "Think about it."

59

WINTER WAS ON HIS WAY TO THE DAY'S QUESTIONING SESSION with Bremer when Michaela Poulsen got in touch. Her voice was neutral.

"The layer of wallpaper underneath may have had prints, but the technicians say that time and wallpaper glue have destroyed everything."

"Our glue isn't as high quality as the kind you use in Denmark. They've found something here."

"Really?" Now he detected a hint of excitement in her voice. "What have they found?"

"I don't know yet."

"I should add that they're not quite done here yet. Now they've brought in the heavy guns, and by that I mean heavy. Heavy metals. White lead. Its powers of adhesion on greasy surfaces, for example, are truly awesome."

Winter sat a bit away from the table and listened while Cohen handled the questioning. Bremer seemed to be in another world—his own, which perhaps he created a long time ago.

GC: Yesterday you told us you worked with others when you carried out those burglaries.

GB: Was that yesterday?

GC: It was yesterday. You confirmed that you were a member of an organization.

GB: Not a member. I've never been a member of anything.

GC: That's what you said yesterday.

GB: Then I used the wrong word. I didn't mean member.

GC: Are you in the habit of driving around town in your car?

GB: What kind of a question is that?

GC: Are you in the habit of driving around town in your car for no reason?

GB: I still don't understand.

GC: Some people just go driving around in their cars. As a form of relaxation. I've done that myself.

GB: I may have done that on occasion.

GC: Are there any particular places you drive to?

GB: No.

GC: You can't name any places?

GB: I don't know what the point of this is. A few times I guess I may have driven out to the shore. Looked at the sea. I don't know, when you live in a forest maybe you want to see the sea sometimes."

Winter saw how Bremer gazed at the wall to his right, as if there were a window there through which he could see the sea. His face was stiff and featureless.

GC: Do you remember that we said people had seen you driving in your car with passengers?

GB: Yes.

GC: Do you admit that you've had passengers in your car?

GB: Who are these people? It's not true.

Winter knew Cohen would start to turn up the heat now; that is, if it was possible to do that in the world where Bremer currently found himself.

GC: Why don't you admit it?

GB: What?

GC: Why don't you admit that you drove Helene Andersén and her daughter, Jennie, in your car?

GB: I didn't.

GC: It's not a crime to give someone a ride.

GB: I know.

GC: Then say it.

GB: What am I supposed to say?

GC: That those two individuals rode in your car. That they were at your house.

GB: They weren't at my house. I'm the only one at my house.

Winter tried to study Bremer's bowed face. There was something in his eyes that he'd also seen in his sister's. A dull sheen, but something else besides. A sadness or knowledge—or was it simply fear?

The home helper waited in the hall for the conversation to begin. There was no door, and Winter couldn't exactly lock the woman in the kitchen if there were one.

Greta Bremer looked even more frail this afternoon, the day gone and her face lit by a dim floor lamp. "What is it you want, now that you've forced your way in here?"

"Just to ask you a couple of questions. About your brother."

"He always gets by," she said. "You know all about his past, I assume?"

"Excuse me?"

"You've checked in your files, haven't you?"

She looked at him or at the home helper that Winter knew was listening in the gloom of the hallway.

"We're searching," Winter said. He waited as the streetcar rattled past outside. "Do you know if Georg ever used to travel to Denmark?"

"Denmark? What would he travel to Denmark for?"

"I'm talking about way back. Twenty-five, thirty years ago."

"I don't know what he was doing back then. Break-ins, that's what he was doing. And other things."

"What do you mean by other things?"

"I don't know. Maybe you know."

"I'm asking you, Miss Bremer."

"He broke into people's houses."

"In Denmark?"

"You know better than I do."

"How do you mean?"

"You're a policeman, aren't you? You know."

The courts couldn't find sufficient grounds to bring charges against Bremer. "A free man. Fucking courts," Halders had said during the investigation briefing that afternoon. "They ought to go out there and see for themselves—then they'd understand." His eyes were bigger than Winter had ever seen them before.

"It was the judge himself who made the decision," Ringmar said. Winter said nothing.

He seems to be in his own world, thought Aneta Djanali.

Another day passed and Winter called Spain, ready for his father to answer. He didn't. It was his mother's voice.

"How are things now?"

"Much better, Erik. It's nice of you to call. We're back home, as you already know."

"Was it an inflammation?"

"Mostly overexertion, like I thought. Your father's not a young man anymore."

"I'm glad it's better."

"You sound a little tired, Erik."

"I am a little tired. Not very."

"When all this is over, you must come down here and rest up a little. Your father would be so happy."

Winter mumbled an answer and said good-bye. He put down the receiver and stood up. It was definitely November outside. The cars' headlights swept light across the field. Soon Christmas would be here. Angela had night duty. And I may not have Angela anymore, he thought. Should I start preparing myself properly for that?

He walked up to Beier's laboratories and found Bengt Sundlöf hunched over a microscope. The fingerprint expert was so focused on his patterns of loops, arches, and whorls that he didn't hear Winter enter. It was only when Sundlöf looked up to peer into another microscope that he saw that he had company.

"How's it going?"

"Well, there are similarities, but I can't say as yet if we can make it up to twelve points. Or even ten."

"How many do you have now?"

"I'd rather not answer that yet. But I've got a special feeling, sitting here working with this one."

"How do you mean?"

"Well, the fact that it's even possible. I have to admit that I never thought it would be."

"Is it really from a child?"

"Looks like it. I have the two different sets here and I'm comparing them to the woman's prints—and those of her as a girl."

Winter turned around.

"Makes you think, doesn't it?" Sundlöf said.

Winter gave a jolt in bed. The phone was ringing. His reading lamp was on and he was still holding the file in his hand. The alarm clock said it was three in the morning. The phone rang and rang.

"Yes, hello?"

"It's Göran. Time to get up."

"What is it?"

"Two things. The NLFS is done with the DNA analysis. Mogren owed me a favor and called me half an hour ago. It's hers. Helene's. She's had that cigarette butt in her mouth."

"We knew that, didn't we?"

"We never know anything until it's been proven," Beier said. "Now it's been proven. And there's something else that's also been proven. Sundlöf is standing right here, so it's better he tells you himself."

Sundlöf's voice came through the receiver. "I have a definite match. We made it to twelve points."

Winter's face felt like it had been dipped in fire. It was as if his hair was no longer there.

"You're sure?"

"I'm damn sure, Winter. We have fingerprints here that show conclusively that she—Christ, I'm getting them mixed up—Helene, that is, that she was in that cabin as a child." Sundlöf went silent in order to breathe. "The old coot wiped everything clean that was on the top layer of wallpaper, but he couldn't get rid of what was underneath."

"No." Winter's head was still on fire. "He couldn't get rid of everything."

"I'm handing you back to Göran."

"I've got the whole team together up here," Beier said. "Are you going out there right away?"

"You better believe it." Winter now started to feel the coolness in the room from the wind slipping in through the half-open balcony door and on down the hallway into his bedroom.

"I'll come with you," Beier said.

Halders drove. Winter had called him immediately, and Halders had called Aneta, who was now sitting next to him in the front seat. Winter and Ringmar were in back. Beier rode in the radio car behind them.

The forest was without color at four thirty in the morning. No planes slicing through the air above them. No lights as far as the eye could see. A starless void. The glow from the city didn't make it out here.

A dim lamp was burning above the porch, and Bremer's Ford was parked as if the driver had been in a hurry. The car shone mutedly in the light from the porch that was shrouded in fog.

"What was that?" Djanali said, when they had climbed out of the car.

"It's the horses beyond the trees," Winter said. "They're nervous."

"That's nothing compared to what I am," she said.

The radio car pulled up behind them, and Beier and the uniformed officers climbed out. A proper police state, thought Winter. Pick them up in the dead of night.

The police prepared themselves. Winter banged on the door, and the sound resonated through the house with a hollow echo. He banged again with his knuckles, but no one came to the door in their nightshirt. He felt for the handle and pressed down. The door opened inward. Winter called out Georg Bremer's name but nobody answered.

"Stay down, for Christ's sake," he heard Halders hiss behind him to Aneta or someone else. Ringmar stood next to him.

"Let's go," he said to Ringmar and the others behind. "Bertil and I will go inside. Two men go round the back, and Fredrik and Aneta wait down here."

They stepped into the hall. The rooms smelled of earth, maybe of horse.

"Christ it's cold," Ringmar said in a low voice.

It was cold. Not as cold as out there, but cold like a house that hasn't been heated for days.

In the kitchen Winter touched the wood-burning stove, which felt ice cold. Through the window he could see the field behind the house. The sky was bigger there and tinged with light. Morning was on its way.

"He's not down here."

"Maybe he's not here at all," Winter said.

Ringmar didn't answer.

"Let's go upstairs," Winter said, and went back to inform the others.

"I'll go with you," Halders said.

They climbed the steps. Every third one creaked. "Georg Bremer," Winter called out. He held his gun in his hand. Steel glinted in Halders's hand too, as they stood in the hallway at the top of the stairs, and suddenly a moonbeam shot between them and lit up their weapons. Winter followed the beam with his eyes, from right to left. It shone a few feet down the hall and in through a door a bit farther on and came to rest on two bare feet that floated in the air above the floor.

"Damn it!" Ringmar shouted, and set off down the hallway and in through the door ahead of the others. Winter ran and saw him lift the feet and legs and body in the darkness of the room.

"Where's the light switch?" Halders yelled, fumbling at the door.

The room exploded in light from a bulb dangling from the ceiling. Winter blinked and forced his eyes to see. Ringmar held up the body hanging by a rope from a thick iron eyebolt that had been drilled into the ceiling next to the light fixture.

Halders tried to lift the rope over Georg Bremer's blackened face, but he couldn't. He took out his knife and cut it through, and together Winter and Ringmar laid the body down on the floor. Only now did Winter register the smells in the room. He saw that Halders sensed it too, his face set as if in plaster, his stubbled head a skull in the harsh light. Ringmar's face was invisible, bent over the body, until he glanced up at Winter and pointed. Winter looked and saw the A4 sheet of paper that Bremer had fastened with pins through his shirt and into the skin of his chest. One of the pins had come off when they'd lowered the corpse, and the sheet of paper rested loosely against the body. Winter had to tilt his head in order to read what was written in capital letters with black marker: "I KILLED THE CHILD. GOD HAVE MERCY ON MY SOUL." He read it twice without really understanding. Then he heard Ringmar's high-pitched wheezing. He heard Halders's stomach revolt onto the threshold of the room. He read it again and closed his eyes. Voices sounded from the ground floor below. He saw figures in the darkness outside the room. He saw Aneta Djanali lean over Halders, who was sprawled across the threshold with his head out in the hallway. He heard Ringmar speak to someone about something. He heard the words a second time: "Send down more units and machines. We have to dig. We have to dig up this place."

60

THE MACHINES ROARED AT ÖDEGÅRD. THEY FOUND THE CLOTHES
beneath the concrete floor in the basement. Everyone tried to prepare
themselves, mentally and otherwise.

When he drove between the cabin and the city, it was as if the world
had lost all depth and become a shallow shroud of fog between life and
death. Ödegård was death and the other was life. You could just make
out the lights of the city, ten miles off through the drizzle of the gray
morning, like urine on dirty snow.

He went upstairs to Beier once he'd read the message on his desk. It
was the last time.

Winter drove home and parked the car in the garage. He walked over
the hill and rang the doorbell. Nobody opened. It was like last time. He
pressed it again, and the door clicked and he saw her eyes glimmering
inside, down low. He hadn't heard the wheelchair.

"You again," she said.

"You'll have to let me in this time."

"Why should I do that?"

"It's over now, Brigitta."

"That makes it a bit less conclusive," Beier had said.

"But it's enough, isn't it?" Winter had asked.

"Yes. Otherwise the test wouldn't be so expensive and take so much
time."

"How many have they done?"

"Don't ask me. Come back when they've set up a database. That
could happen this year, by the way."

———

She rolled ahead of him into the room that shook from the streetcars outside. It wasn't a room to live in. Maybe she doesn't, Winter thought. Live. She lives, but hardly a life.

"What was it you called me?"

"Your real name. Brigitta."

"Never heard of it."

"I said it's over now. You don't need to feel afraid anymore."

She didn't answer. Her face bore a faint shadow from the day.

"Do you hear me, Brigitta?"

"Why are you calling me that?"

"That's your name."

"I mean, why are you suddenly calling me Brigitta? What makes you think that—"

"I don't just think it," Winter said. "I know."

"How?"

"It's not the falsified documents identifying you as Greta Bremer," he said. "They're excellent forgeries."

She nodded. He thought it looked as if she nodded.

"And your appearance. You couldn't possibly be the fifty-five-year-old Brigitta Dellmar."

"There, you see? I can barely move, after all."

"I wanted to believe that you were Brigitta," Winter said. "But it felt impossible. And I found nothing to support that theory."

She now turned her face toward him for the first time.

"Well? How do you know then?"

Winter took a step closer and came up next to her in the wheelchair. He slowly reached out and plucked something from the pillow behind her back.

"This," he said, and held up a strand of hair that may have been visible in the light of the window.

"What is that? My hair?"

"A strand of your hair," Winter said. "Ever heard of DNA?"

"No."

"You've never heard of DNA?"

"Sure."

Winter let the strand of hair drop from his hand and sat down in one of the armchairs.

"You took a strand of hair the first time you were here," she said. "You stood behind me while I was sitting here."

"Yes. I saw an opportunity."

"This damned wheelchair."

"You are Brigitta Dellmar?"

"You already said I am."

"I'd like to hear it from you."

"Does it make any difference?"

"Yes."

She rubbed her deformed legs.

"I am Brigitta Dellmar," she said. "I am Brigitta Dellmar, but that doesn't do anyone any good."

"And Georg Bremer isn't your brother."

"He isn't my brother."

"Why did he tell us that you were his sister?"

"He thought that he could scare me. And I've passed for his sister all these years, without actually being it. I've had to play that role. It was their decision." She looked straight at Winter. "But he couldn't scare me."

The telephone rang, and she lifted the receiver on the third ring and said yes and listened. She said, "Wait," and turned to Winter. "Is this going to take long?"

Winter didn't answer that insane question.

"I'll call you back," she said, and hung up.

"You called Bremer's house two days ago," Winter said.

"How do you know it was me?"

"Wasn't it?"

"Yes, it was me. I called him after he'd returned from the police, the last time."

"Didn't you realize that we'd see who had called him?"

"Maybe."

"Why did you call him?"

"It was time for him to die. He had lived for too long. He killed my baby," she said, and her face cracked in front of him. She slumped to the side in her wheelchair and lay as if dead, with her ruined visage facing downward. She turned a hundred years old in front of Winter. She said something, but it was muffled by the fabric and stuffing.

She sat up again, and Winter saw the tears smeared across her face.

"I told him that he had killed my child. That I knew. He didn't know I knew," she said, and now she cried out, a soft wail that came from deep within and intensified. "He didn't know *that it was all my fault.*" She fell silent and looked at Winter.

I can only wait, he thought.

She sat with her chin against her chest, then raised her head again.

"I told him that he had killed his own child. *I said that!*"

Winter was silent. A streetcar passed by outside without sound. The clock on the wall had stopped.

"I told him that he had killed his own child, that Helene was his child." She looked straight at Winter. "There is nothing more heinous than killing another human being. What does it mean, then, to kill your own child?"

"You told him that Helene was his daughter?"

"Yes."

"Was she? Was it true?"

"No."

"But you said it to him?"

"I wanted him to suffer for what he had done. He hadn't suffered. He doesn't know what suffering is. He doesn't know. He didn't know."

"What do you mean when you say that it's all your fault?"

"She was my girl," Brigitta Dellmar said now, lost in another time. "Helene was my girl. She wasn't like anyone else. We were never like anyone else."

"She is your girl," Winter said.

"She's had it so tough." Brigitta Dellmar suddenly reached out and grabbed hold of Winter's hands with hers. "She's suffered, and it's been all my fault, and in the end I couldn't stop myself from telling her. I told her."

"What did you tell her? That you were her mother?"

"What? That I . . . ? She knew I was her mother. She knew that I was her mother."

Winter felt her fingers grasp at his. Her grip was hot and cold, and he could feel her pulse.

"When did she find out?" Winter leaned forward. "When did she find out?"

"She's always known. She's always . . . Ever since she was a little girl."

"But she was a foster child for many years," Winter said. "She was alone when she came back here."

"She knew," Brigitta Dellmar said. "Inside she knew. When she came back here and was a big girl she found out again."

Winter asked, and she told him everything. She had been wounded. They had kept her hidden, and then she had kept herself hidden away from the world for such a long time that she had ceased to exist. She didn't know how many years. They had let her keep some of the money and created a new identity for her and she had returned to Sweden, to her so-called brother. Ha-ha!

When the girl tried to make a life of her own, and bore a child, she was there. Suddenly she was there.

"Who is Jennie's father?" Winter asked.

"Nobody knows."

"Not even you?"

"It was as if she wanted me to be the last to know."

"Why?"

She shrugged her shoulders. Winter's breathing now started to return. The hairs on the back of his neck were damp with sweat.

"It was all my fault. I contacted her again. She had been having a difficult time connecting with other people, and now it became impossible. She turned in on herself more and more."

"How often did you see each other?"

"Just occasionally. I helped her to get her memory back, and that was the death of her."

"Excuse me?"

"Her memory. It caused her death."

"How do you mean?"

"I told her things she didn't know anymore. And things she never knew and yet thought a lot about. What happened."

Winter nodded.

"Bremer murdered her father. He carried it out."

"Her father?"

"Kim. My Kim."

"Kim Andersen? You mean Kim Andersen? The one who was also known as Kim Møller?"

"Bremer murdered him."

"You told Helene that?"

"I told her everything. I told her everything. And she went to see him. I knew where he was. She made several trips down there. In the end she knew enough that she told him. But he thought she was lying. He was sure that he was her father. I was afraid, terribly afraid. Helene seemed to be beside herself with fear when she found out what had happened to her father, Kim. That Bremer had murdered him. What had happened to her . . ." Brigitta Dellmar dropped her head forward. She seemed exhausted from having spoken for so long. "I wanted my money too, and it scared me, but I needed . . . Helene needed . . . We had a right to our money. And Jennie too."

Winter breathed harder, steeled himself.

"Where's Jennie?"

She looked at him, past him. Her gaze had melted away. "He could murder again. He did it."

"He did it? He murdered Jennie?" Winter's mouth was so damn dry he couldn't hear whether he had uttered the words.

"He could do it again," Brigitta Dellmar said. "He was crazy. He killed Oskar. Poor Oskar. That was also my fault. He must have done it."

"Oskar? Oskar Jakobsson? Bremer killed Jakobsson?"

Winter couldn't tell how much of her was actually there in the room with him. She had started to move her head back and forth.

"Did Bremer kill Jakobsson?" Winter repeated.

"He must have. Oskar was still a threat. Just like Helene. Helene got in touch with Bremer, but I'm not sure exactly when. He must have regretted that he hadn't—"

"Regretted what? What did he want to do? What did he regret?"

"She wanted to know. That was it. She just wanted to know. She wanted what she had a right to. She told me, but not much. Then it was too late."

"What was too late?"

"I don't know what happened," Brigitta Dellmar said.

"Where is Jennie?" Winter asked again. "You've got to answer me."

"Poor Oskar," Brigitta Dellmar said. "He knew nothing. He was nice. They knew each other. Didn't you know that? They were old acquaintances."

"There were a lot of old acquaintances," Winter said.

Bremer gave Jakobsson the money to pay the rent. Perhaps to make us think that it was Jakobsson. No. For some other reason. Maybe so that we would eventually find him and punish him for what he had done to the child he thought he was the father of.

"I didn't have the courage myself," she said. She was suddenly *here* again; her eyes had regained their sharpness. "I didn't have the courage. I don't have the courage. I have my own guilt. They know. *They* see."

"Who are they?"

"You know."

"We know and we don't know. We can't prove anything."

"That's how it's always been," she said. "No one is ever free."

"Bremer is dead," Winter said.

"He's finally dead? Is it true?"

Winter realized that she didn't know.

"We haven't made it public yet," he said. "But he's gone. He hanged himself."

"He listened to me," she said.

"Where's Jennie?" Winter asked yet again.

"I tried to protect her," Brigitta Dellmar said. "I tried to protect her when I knew that Helene wanted to know everything."

"Protect her? From whom?"

"From him. From everyone. I tried to protect her." She looked at Winter. "She was also alone. She needed protecting."

"Why didn't you report that she was missing? You could have done it anonymously."

"I didn't know."

"You didn't know that she was gone?"

"Not at first. Not then. We had broken off contact then. I hadn't seen her for a long time. It was like that with her. Suddenly she didn't want anything to do with me. And of course I can understand that." She looked at Winter, right into his eyes. "Maybe it's all a dream," she said. "A fairy tale." She moved her damaged body. "Maybe it never happened. None of it." She sat up. The telephone rang. "Let it ring," she said. "Do you have a car? Can you carry me?"

She directed him south, down onto the Säröleden highway. They could see the sea. She didn't say a word. Winter drove two miles, past Billdal. She gestured for him to take the next exit on the right.

The paved road soon gave way to dirt. Winter thought about Öde-gård again, but the road here ran across coastal land. Seabirds took off in long lines. Feeling as if his breath was being thrust out of his lungs, he rolled down the car window. The smell of damp salt grew stronger in the air the closer they got to the sea.

She pointed to the left. The road narrowed. She made a call from his cell phone. The road turned into a glade. The clouds were suddenly gone, the sun distant yet still there. The house lay in a depression with a fence around it, and a man came up to the car when it pulled up in front of a robust gate. The man was armed. Brigitta Dellmar nodded. They drove into the yard, and Winter parked in front of the house. The sea's presence was even stronger now, a murmuring in the mind, and the sun had begun to sink into it. Brigitta Dellmar sat still next to Winter in the car. She pointed to the west. Winter got out and took a few steps from the car, and she gestured again with her hand. She's insane, he thought. I'm insane. The man stayed by the gate with his weapon, a machine gun, as Winter approached the gable end of the house. He walked up the slope and saw the fields open up toward the water. The sun was right in his eyes. He heard voices and cupped the palm of his hand over his eyes to see. The girl was on her way toward him from the sea. The woman was walking next to her. The girl was holding something. They came closer. The woman was blonde. They were twenty-five yards away. They drew closer. Winter saw only the contours of the woman's face, outlined against the sun.

They stood before one another. Jennie was holding pebbles in her hand, and long strips that might be seaweed. Winter was blinded by the sun and the wetness in his eyes, by the salt that ran down his face. He squatted down in front of the girl. The woman remained standing there. She didn't move. He closed his eyes, and when he opened them again she was gone, as if dissolved into the haze. Winter cautiously reached out with his hand and touched the girl's shoulder. It was like brushing against a little bird. She wasn't afraid.

"Who are you?" she asked.

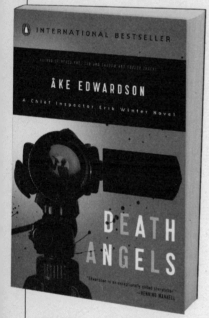

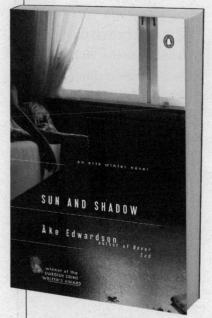

AVAILABLE FROM PENGUIN

Never End

A Chief Inspector Erik Winter Novel

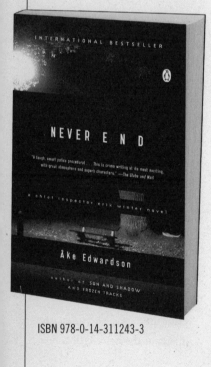

It's summer in Sweden. As the coastal city of Gothenburg suffers through a heat wave, Chief Inspector Erik Winter broods over a series of unsolved rape-murders. The crimes bear an eerie resemblance to a five-year-old case that the mercurial detective has refused to let go cold. Has the same rapist reemerged to taunt him, or is a copycat at work?

ISBN 978-0-14-311243-3

PENGUIN
BOOKS

AVAILABLE FROM PENGUIN

Frozen Tracks
A Chief Inspector Erik Winter Novel

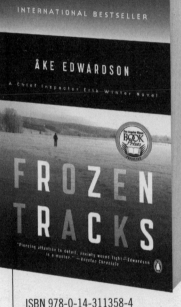

ISBN 978-0-14-311358-4

The autumn gloom comes quickly on the Swedish city of Gothenburg, and for Chief Inspector Erik Winter the days seem even shorter, the nights bleaker, when he is faced with two seemingly unrelated sets of perplexing crimes. The investigation of a series of mysterious assaults and a string of child abductions takes Winter to "the flats," the barren prairies of rural Sweden, whose wastelands conceal crimes as sinister as the land itself.

PENGUIN
BOOKS